RESTRAINT

MIRANDA LEVI

Published by Rainbow Quartz Publishing

RQPublishing.com

RainbowQuartzPublishing@gmail.com

Edmonds, WA 98026

Cover design by Miranda Townsend

Edited by Miranda Townsend

First Edition: March 2026

TRIGGER WARNINGS, TROPES, AND SPICE LEVELS

READ RESPONSIBLY. FALL RECKLESSLY. ⚡♡

THIS BOOK CONTAINS MORALLY GREY SITUATIONS AND PEOPLE

- Forbidden / Power-imbalanced Romance
- 15 year age-gap romance / Best Friend's Father
- One Night, Turned Complicated
- Small-Town Gossip / Everyone Knows Everyone
- 'Save Me / I Saved You' Swap
- 911 dispatcher life / Moderate Police Procedural
- Grief, baggage, and second-chance feelings
- Memories of the death of a parent and death of a sibling
- Grown-up decisions
- Spice level: 🌶🌶🌶🌶½ (4.5 out of 5). Expect open-door scenes / No fade-to-black in the filthiest ways possible.
- All relationships depicted are consensual and between adults.

PLAYLIST

1. Night Drive – Chromatics
2. Mariners Apartment Complex – Lana Del Rey
3. The Night We Met – Lord Huron
4. Slow Burn – Kacey Musgraves
5. Control – Halsey
6. Youth – Daughter
7. Between the Bars – Elliott Smith
8. I Wanna Be Yours – Arctic Monkeys
9. All I Want – Kodaline
10. Cherry Wine (Live) – Hozier
11. The Scientist – Coldplay
12. Liability – Lorde
13. Earned It – The Weeknd
14. Skin – Rihanna
15. Talk – Hozier
16. Wicked Games – Chris Isaak
17. Slow Dancing in a Burning Room – John Mayer

18. First Time – Kygo & Ellie Goulding
19. Visions of Gideon – Sufjan Stevens
20. Call It What You Want – Taylor Swift
21. Holocene – Bon Iver

Apple Music

DEDICATION

This book is for the unsung heroes of 911.
For the voices in the dark who answer
when everything is breaking.
For the men and women who hold strangers together with nothing but words,
who stay steady while someone else is falling apart.
I was one of you. And like so many of you, I became a statistic before I ever meant to.
Two years in, my body learned what my heart already knew, that listening to people die, to fear, to violence, to goodbye after goodbye, changes you.
This book is for those who stayed.
And just as fiercely, it is for those who left.
Because doing good does not mean destroying yourself.
Because saving others does not require losing yourself.
Because sometimes the bravest thing you can do is answer the call and sometimes the bravest
thing you can do is finally hang up.
To every dispatcher who gave their voice to someone else's worst day —and to every one of you who chose life after the headset—this story is for you.

ONE
AUGUST
SEVEN YEARS AGO

SHATTERED windshield glass lay scattered across the road.

It's everywhere.

On the hood of the car. In the gutter. Glittering in the sweep of red-and-blue lights like somebody smashed a thousand tiny stars and dumped them across the intersection.

My boots hit wet pavement before the engine's fully dead.

"Seattle PD!" I shout, already moving.

A medic brushes past me with a jump bag. Somebody's screaming. Metal ticks as it cools. Steam hisses and sputters from the crumpled engine of what was someone's commuter. A sharp, almost poisonous blend of radiator fluid, gasoline, and rain permeates the air so sharply I can almost taste it.

Two cars. One broadside. The sedan took the hit on the driver's side and folded in on itself like a can.

The passenger compartment is a wreck.

I've seen bad. I've seen worse. I know what I'm looking at before I get close enough for the details to settle.

This one is not a maybe.

This one is aftermath.

A firefighter is cutting at the frame, sparks spitting into the night. Another has his arm out, trying to hold somebody back.

A girl.

She ducks under him anyway.

"No, no, no, no, no, Mom!"

A crimson river snaked from the gash on her brow, a stark contrast against her pale skin. It's not pouring, but it's enough to color one side of her temple red, threading blood into her hair. Her jeans are soaked to the knees, and one bare foot lacks a sneaker.

Shock-wild eyes. Eighteen, maybe. Young enough that every line of her still looks unfinished.

She throws herself toward the open passenger side where they've pulled the door.

I get there first.

I catch her around the middle, her full weight crashes into my chest, a sudden, suffocating pressure that leaves me gasping for air.

"Let me go!" she screams, while thrashing in my arms. "That's my mom damnit! Let go of me! Get your hands off me!"

I lock my arms and plant my feet.

Rain needles the back of my neck. Her wet hair sticks to my jaw. Her eyes dart wildly as she physically trembles. I witness as she shatters in my hands. With each passing moment, the rain claims a little more of her.

"Hey. Hey." I whisper into her ear. "I've got you."

"Let me go!" She claws at my wrist. "That's my mom. Let me see my mom!"

Fuck.

I had no choice but to look into the car.

The driver is slumped into the crushed doorframe, seatbelt still across her chest, face gone gray in the strobing lights. There is no movement. No breath. No question.

Over the roofline, a paramedic's eyes met mine, and he offered the barest hint of a headshake.

DOA.

I pull the girl tighter when she bucks again.

"I need to get to her!" she cries. "Please, you have to let me go, I need her—" her voice catches on a sob.

Her words break something inside me, and I have to swallow before I can reply.

Her mother's no longer there. Her daughter can't comfort her anymore. No one can.

I know this moment. I know this denial. This is how the brain protects itself while the world around implodes.

Behind us, someone yells for a backboard. Across the intersection, a second medic team works the other vehicle. A businessman in a coat is hunched on the curb, his face buried in his hands, with blood staining his sleeve.

He repeats, "I didn't see them. I didn't see them," to no one.

The woman in my arms twists so hard that she nearly slips. I change my grip, sliding one hand up between her shoulder blades while bracing the other over her forearms. "Listen to me."

She doesn't.

She's crying so hard the words break apart in her throat. "Mom! Let me see her, please! What's happening?! Mom!."

I close my eyes for half a beat.

Not enough time for mercy.

Not enough time for anything.

I pull her away from the car, but she struggles as if I'm forcing her into oncoming traffic. I hold on and back us up three steps, then five, until the medic can get between us and the door.

"No!" The sound that ripped from her was a raw, ragged thing, like a wounded animal. "Stop!"

"I know," I say. My mouth tastes like rain and metal. "I know."

Her knees buckle.

One second she's all elbows and panic and raw grief, and the next she just drops.

I go down with her.

Cold water soaks through my pants the second my knee hits the pavement. She lands half in my lap, both fists twisted in the front of my uniform, dragging in these broken little breaths like her body forgot how to do it right.

I've got a daughter.

The thought hits hard and ugly.

Lilly at sixteen, rolling her eyes when I tell her to text me when she gets somewhere.

Lilly at twelve, asleep in the backseat with a juice box leaking into the floor mat.

Lilly at five, gap-toothed and sticky-fingered, wearing that ladybug backpack until the zipper split.

Bug.

Ruth's voice cuts through my head so clear it nearly knocks me sideways.

Don't call her Bug in front of her friends, August. She'll murder you.

Ruth isn't dead.

But some nights, sitting across from her at the kitchen table while we talk schedules and school forms and who forgot what, it feels like I'm mourning something anyway.

The last time we tried to put us back together, she broke me open and called it honesty.

Lilly saw all of it.

She saw the slammed doors. The tight smiles. The way I started talking like a cop in my own damn life. Calm. Controlled. Empty.

And still, kneeling here in the rain with this girl falling apart in my arms, all I can think is, that it doesn't matter how a family gets ripped open.

Death. Betrayal. Distance.

Gone is gone.

"Mom," she says again, smaller this time. "My mom..."

I can't answer that. Not the way she wants.

Not yet. Maybe not me. Maybe a medic. Maybe a chaplain with a soft voice and a spare blanket.

Right now she's bleeding, shaking, and trying to crawl out of her own skin.

I glance at the cut on her forehead. It's deeper than I thought. Blood keeps slipping down past her eyebrow, cutting a red line along her cheek.

"Hey." I slide my hand to her jaw, gentle, just enough to get her looking at me. "Hey. What's your name?"

Her eyes hit mine like she's surfacing and hates me for being the first thing she finds.

For a second, she just stares.

Brown eyes. Gold in them from the strobes.

Too young. Too pretty.

And I hate myself a little for noticing either.

"Florence," she whispers.

"Okay, Florence. I'm August."

Her mouth shakes. "Don't let them cover her."

I look over her shoulder.

They haven't yet.

They will.

I drag my focus back to her. "Look at me."

She does.

Rain catches on her lashes and spills down her face with everything else. Her hand is still fisted in my shirt so tight I can feel the pull of each knuckle through the fabric.

"You're hurt," I tell her. "I need the medics to look at your head, okay?"

"I don't care."

"I know." My voice stays low. Steady. "I do."

Her face crumples.

Not loud. Not dramatic.

Just this quiet collapse like her body finally runs out of ways to hold itself up.

I need to get her out of the road.

I brace one foot under me and stand, bringing her with me because she's still hanging onto my shirt like I'm the only solid thing left. She sways hard. I get an arm around her shoulders and keep us upright.

"Easy," I mutter. "Watch your step."

"My mom hates hospitals," she says, words slipping at the edges. Shock. Maybe a concussion. "She says they smell like bleach and ghosts."

The burn in my throat comes out of nowhere.

"Yeah," I say. "Mine too."

I walk her to the back of the aid rig.

A medic reaches for her, and Florence jerks away so fast she almost takes both of us down again.

"No." She turns into me, panic spiking all over. "No, stay."

I should hand her off.

I should step back and let them work.

Instead I look at the medic and say, "Give me thirty seconds."

He takes one look at her face and gives me a short nod, backing off just enough to prep gauze and a light on the bumper.

Florence presses both palms flat to my chest now, like she's checking I'm still there.

"Please," she says, voice wrecked. "Please tell me she's okay."

There it is.

The moment every cop hates.

The one where a lie buys you thirty seconds and costs you everything after.

My thumb catches a streak of rain and blood at her temple before I stop myself. Her skin is freezing.

"I can't tell you that," I say.

Her face goes still.

Blank in a way that feels worse than crying.

I hate what comes out of my mouth next because it's true and still not enough.

"But I can tell you you're not by yourself right now."

She makes this small sound.

Not a scream.

Something thinner. Sharper.

Like something inside her tears clean through.

Then she folds into me and sobs.

I hold her.

I hold her because there's nothing else to do.

Because the medics need a minute.

Because she's eighteen and bleeding and barefoot and her whole life just got split in half under a stoplight.

Because somewhere across the city my daughter is probably asleep with her phone under her pillow, pretending she doesn't care if I call, and I haven't called tonight because Ruth and I spent twenty minutes sniping at each other over pickup times and old wounds and who failed who first.

Because I'm tired in places sleep doesn't touch.

And somehow this girl's grief still gets past my armor.

She smells like copper, rain, and peach shampoo.

Every time the firefighters move near the sedan, her fingers bite deeper into my shirt.

"Florence." I lean down, close enough that she has to hear me. "I need you to look at me again."

It takes a second.

Then she lifts her head.

Blood has dried in a thin line near the edge of her brow. That laceration is going to leave a scar.

The thought lands strange. Personal.

A mark she'll carry from tonight long after the rest of this stops bleeding.

"You're gonna let him check your head," I say, nodding toward the medic. "Then we call whoever you need. Anybody. I'll stay right here while we do it."

She searches my face like she's trying to catch me lying.

Then she nods once.

The medic steps in, fast and practiced. Gauze to the forehead. Penlight to the pupils.

"What's your last name, Florence?"

She answers, voice flat and far away. I only catch part of it over the rain and radio traffic.

He keeps going.

"What day is it? Do you know where you are?"

She answers him, but she keeps looking at me.

I stay where I said I would.

A lieutenant steps up behind me, low at my shoulder. "Ez. Fatal in the sedan. Female driver. ME's been notified. We'll need your statement."

I nod once without turning.

"Any family besides the girl?"

"Working it."

He looks at Florence, sees the blood and the shock and the death-grip she still has on my sleeve, and his face tightens in that way it does when the job gets through.

"Shit," he mutters.

Yeah.

Shit.

He moves off.

The medic tapes a pad over Florence's cut. She flinches but doesn't complain. Her hands are in her lap now, empty and shaking.

When he asks who we should call, she goes quiet.

"Florence?" I ask, gentler.

"I'm eighteen. I don't need anyone." She wets her lips.

"You shouldn't be alone. Let me call somebody for you."

A firefighter hands me her phone in a clear evidence bag. Cracked screen. Mud on the case. Still on.

"Can you unlock this?" I ask.

She takes it and stares at it like it belongs to somebody else, then puts in the code.

She gets to her contacts and just... stops. Like the names don't mean anything.

"Who do you need?" I ask.

Her mouth trembles. "My grandma."

She taps the contact, hits call, and the second it starts ringing she shoves the phone at me like it burns.

I take it.

The line picks up on the second ring.

"Hey sweetheart, to what do I owe the pleasure?"

"Ma'am, this is Officer August Calder with Seattle PD." I keep my eyes on Florence while she grabs a fistful of my sleeve in both hands, knuckles white. "There's been a collision. Florence is alive. She's injured, but she's conscious and being treated."

A beat. Controlled.

"Put me on speaker," she says.

I do.

"Florence." Her grandmother's voice comes through clear and firm. "Baby, I need you to listen to me."

Florence makes a broken sound and folds forward, forehead almost hitting my chest.

"Grandma—"

"I know," she says, and her voice cracks once before she locks it back down. "I know. I'm leaving right now. You stay with the medics and you do exactly what they tell you. Do you hear me?"

Florence nods before she remembers she has to speak. "Yes."

"Good girl. I'm on my way."

I take it off speaker and bring the phone back to my ear.

"Ma'am," I say, quieter, "we're transporting her to Harborview."

"I know where it is. I'm two hours out, but I'm leaving now. Officer Calder—"

She stops for half a breath.

"Don't let her be alone."

The words land heavy.

"I won't," I say.

"Thank you."

The line goes dead.

When I lower the phone, Florence is watching my face like she's trying to read what comes next before I say it.

The medic reaches for the phone.

Florence catches my wrist before he can take it.

"Don't leave," she pleads.

I should tell her I can't promise that.

I should tell her another officer can ride with her. I've got a scene. Reports. Statements. Work.

Instead, for one stupid human second, I cover her hand with mine.

Warm over cold.

Steady over shaking.

"Let's get you to the ambulance," I say.

Her eyes close.

"Okay."

We make it maybe three steps.

She turns back to me, and I make the mistake of looking all

the way into her eyes. Glassy. Wrecked. Full of pain and something I don't have a name for.

Her fingers slide along my jaw. Feather-light. Shaking.

Then she rises on her toes and presses her mouth to mine.

Something in me pulls tight at the touch.

It isn't a kiss, not really.

It's shock.

It's grief.

It's panic looking for somewhere to land.

Her lips are soft and trembling, and for one ruinous second my body forgets this is not want.

I freeze for half a heartbeat because my brain doesn't catch up fast enough.

When it does, I pull back immediately, gentle but firm, both hands on her shoulders.

"Florence." My voice comes out rough. "Hey. No."

Her eyes go huge.

Horror floods her face so fast it hurts to look at.

"I'm sorry," she chokes out. "I'm sorry, I didn't—I wasn't—"

"You're okay." I make my voice softer. Steadier. "You're okay."

It's not the perfect thing to say.

It's what she needs.

I hand her over to the medic, and this time she lets him take her.

Whatever that was burned through the last of her fight.

They help her up into the rig. As the doors start to close, she looks back at me once.

Just once.

White gauze at her brow. Rain on her lashes. Mouth swollen from crying. Eighteen and wrecked and still here.

The ambulance doors slam.

The sirens kick on.

I stand in the rain and watch the lights pull away until they disappear into traffic.

Then I turn back to the intersection. To the wreck. To the sheet over the driver's seat. To the work waiting for me.

And I know before I take my first step this one is coming home with me.

Not because of the kiss.

Because of the way she looked at me after.

Like I was the only thing left in a world that had just taken everything else.

TWO
FLORENCE
SEVEN YEARS AGO

I DON'T KNOW the girl in the mirror.

She has my mouth. Same eyes, except the left is ringed in bruise-yellow, and a stitched red line bisects my forehead like someone drew a fault line across my face.

I don't recognize myself until I lift my hand and she does too. That's the only reason I know she's me.

It's been two weeks since the accident, and I shave what's left of my hair over the bathroom sink.

I plug in the clippers. The buzz crawls under my skin like ants.

I start at the butchered patch they shaved for stitches. Hair falls in dark curls, dead things piling in the sink.

I keep going.

Straight down the center.

More falls.

By the end there's almost nothing left but dark stubble, uneven patches, and that angry pink scar cutting three inches into what used to be my hairline.

I look like proof I survived something that should have killed me.

I touch the ridge. Still tender. Still wrong.

Every time my fingertip traces it, I see him.

Rain on his jaw. Hand steady at my face. Voice low: Look at me.

I close my eyes and replay his mouth pulling away gently horrified, but still warm.

My stomach twists. Shame. Want. Something darker.

I open my eyes.

The girl in the mirror doesn't flinch.

Good.

Let her look ruined.

Let the scar stay forever.

It's the only part of that night I still control.

My hair used to fall past my waist. Thick, dark, always in the way. My mom used to complain about it clogging the shower drain and then braid it for me anyway when I was running late. She'd stand behind me in the kitchen with coffee in one hand, half awake, fingers moving fast, and tell me to stop whining while she fixed it.

Now there's nothing to braid.

Just skin. Scar. Stranger.

I touch the ridge at my brow with my fingertip.

It's still tender. Tight. The stitches are out, but the skin feels wrong, like it belongs to somebody else and got stitched onto my face by mistake.

Nora knocks once and pushes the door open before I answer, because that's who she is.

She stops when she sees me.

For a second, neither of us says anything.

Her eyes go to the sink full of hair. Then to my face. Then to the scar.

"Oh, honey," she says, and her voice does that thing where it goes soft even when the rest of her doesn't.

Nora talks with her whole chest. She can make grown men apologize with one look. The first night I came here, she took three phone calls in a row from people trying to "help" and had every one of them hanging up sounding scared of her.

She's also my mom's mother.

And they barely spoke the last ten years. I used to spend

weekends and summer breaks with my grandma growing up. Until the falling out.

My mom used to call her controlling. Nora used to call my mom reckless. Holidays were a minefield. Birthdays got weird. There were years we did two dinners because neither one of them could sit at the same table without somebody crying in the bathroom.

None of that matters now.

Nora still lost a daughter.

I can hear her crying through walls at night.

She steps into the bathroom and reaches out like she's going to touch my head, then thinks better of it and cups my jaw instead. Her thumb brushes just below the scar.

"You didn't have to do this alone," she says.

"I know."

But I did.

Because I couldn't stand looking at the missing patch anymore. Couldn't stand trying to pin the rest around it like if I arranged it right, none of this happened.

Because every mirror in this house has been telling the truth, and I'm tired of trying to negotiate with it.

Nora studies my face another second, then nods once, like she understands more than she says.

"Okay," she murmurs. "Well. You look like you bite back."

I laugh, and it comes out cracked.

That's the closest I get to crying this morning.

By the time we drive to the ferry, it's raining again.

Everything has been wet since the accident. Streets. Windows. The cuffs of my jeans. The inside of my chest.

Nora drives with both hands on the wheel and her mouth set hard, like she can muscle the whole world into behaving if she keeps enough pressure on it. We don't talk much. The heater clicks. The wipers drag across the glass. Seattle moves outside the window in blurred gray smears.

At a red light, I catch my reflection in the passenger-side mirror and look away fast.

I still haven't figured out who that girl is.

At the ferry terminal, people line up in their cars like the world didn't recently implode. Like getting on a boat with your life shoved in trash bags and duffels is just another Tuesday.

Nora killed the engine and looked at me once.

"You want to stay in the car, stay in the car," she said. "You want air, get air. We board in ten."

I got out because if I stayed sitting still, I was going to start screaming.

Now I'm on the deck with my hood up, my hands shoved into the sleeves of my sweatshirt, staring back at the city while the ferry pulls away.

The deck is slick under my boots. Everything is wet. Rails. Painted lines. Benches. The shoulders of strangers standing out here like they also need the cold to keep from crawling out of their skin. The sky hangs low over the Sound, heavy and gray, and the wind cuts through my sweatshirt finding my bones.

Seattle shrinks behind us.

Not gone. Just farther away.

The skyline looks smudged through the mist, all glass and shadow, like somebody dragged a thumb through a charcoal drawing and called it done. If I squint, I can almost pretend I don't know exactly where everything is. The hospital. The intersection. Our apartment.

Our apartment.

For the last two weeks people kept showing up with casseroles.

They came with foil pans and sad eyes and careful voices and hands already reaching for me before they even got through the door.

I stopped opening it after day three.

Nora answered instead.

"Thank you," she'd say.

Then she'd close the door, set the casserole on the counter, and leave it there untouched until somebody remembered to throw it out.

My mom used to call them bad-juju casseroles.

Death casseroles if she was feeling dramatic, which was

often. She said people cooked with their feelings, and grief had no business being baked into noodles and handed to strangers.

The first time someone brought one over after Dad left, she laughed until she cried and said, Absolutely not, I am not eating your sadness.

I think about that every time I open the fridge now.

Foil pans. Condensation. Someone else's idea of comfort.

I can't eat any of it.

I grip the ferry rail until my knuckles ache.

Salt hangs in the air. The water below is dark and choppy, slapping the side of the boat hard enough to send spray up through the wind. The engine hums under my feet, deep and steady, and every so often the whole deck shudders when we hit a wake.

I touch my scar again.

I do it without thinking now. Finger to brow. Brow to hairline. Like checking if it's still there.

It is.

Every time I touch it, I see the same things.

Red lights. Broken glass. My mother not moving.

And him.

The sharp metal stink of the wreck wafted around us, but underneath that, something warm and clean that was just him.

I remember his mouth too.

I wish I didn't.

But I do.

The memory hits hot and humiliating every time, even now, even standing here with salt on my lips and my grandmother ten feet below me in her SUV pretending not to watch me through the windshield.

I kissed him.

I kissed a cop in the rain with my mother dead ten feet away and blood running down my face.

Who the hell does that?

What the fuck is wrong with me?

I press my palms harder against the rail.

Shock does weird things. That's what the hospital counselor said, all gentle eyes and sensible shoes. Trauma can scramble reactions. Trauma can attach to strange details. Trauma can make a moment feel bigger than it was.

Maybe.

But she didn't hear his voice.

She didn't feel the way he held me.

She didn't see his face when he pulled back.

I don't know how to explain that look without sounding crazy.

Like he could see clean through me.

Like for one second, there was nowhere to hide.

My throat tightens.

I look out at the water before I do something stupid like cry in front of tourists.

Behind me, the ferry door bangs open and shut as people move in and out. A kid laughs. Someone drops a cup. The loudspeaker crackles and says something my brain doesn't fully process.

Life keeps doing that. Moving like it didn't split me in half two weeks ago.

I hate it for that.

I love it for that too.

The doctor said the scar will fade some.

Not all the way.

I say fine.

Let it stay.

Let it cut through every version of my face I have after this and remind me there was a before and there was an after and I am not crazy for feeling like I died in that intersection too.

The wind shoves at me again, harder this time.

I close my eyes and see him anyway.

August.

His eyes in the strobing lights. His hand at the back of my neck. His voice low and steady while I drowned in the middle of a street.

I don't know why that part stays.

I just know it does.

And I know, with the kind of certainty that makes no sense and still won't loosen its grip, that whatever I was before that night did not get on this boat with me.

Someone honks from the car deck and I open my eyes.

The island is coming into view through the mist.

I touch the scar at my brow one more time, then turn my back on Seattle.

I drop my hand.

Don't.

Don't do this here.

"Flo."

Grandma's voice comes from behind me, close enough that I don't jump.

I turn. She's got her purple coat buttoned all the way up and her hair pulled back in a ponytail to prevent her hair from eating her face in the wind.

She hands me a coffee.

I take it even though I don't want it.

"You need to warm up," she says.

"I'm fine."

She looks at my shaking fingers around the cup and doesn't argue.

That's how she's been since the hospital. No babying. No fake softness. Just facts and food and one hand on my back when I stop breathing right.

I look back toward the water. "Did you call Lacey?" I ask.

Grandma goes quiet for half a second, and that half second tells me everything before she answers.

"I left another message."

I laugh, but there's nothing funny in it. "Of course."

"Florence—"

"She can post beach pictures and selfies with Jason but can't call back."

"Don't," Grandma says, low. Not sharp. Just tired. "Not right now."

I press my mouth shut so hard my jaw aches.

Lacey is twenty and in love and gone. She moved out last year and said she couldn't breathe in our apartment anymore, like our life was a room she'd outgrown. Mom cried in the bathroom after she left. Then she came out and made spaghetti and acted like she was happy for her.

That was my mom. Bleeding and smiling at the same time.

Now she's dead, and my sister can't pick up the phone.

I stare out at the water until my eyes sting.

The cup in my hand goes cold.

I remember flashes. Hospital discharge papers. Grandma signing things. A nurse giving me a plastic bag with my ruined hoodie folded inside it. My jeans cut at the knee. My phone in another bag. Somebody asking if there was anyone else to call, and me saying no so fast it sounded rude.

I remember the officer, though.

Every second of him.

That part is carved into me. Woven into the fabric of me.

His hands around my middle. His voice in my ear, low and steady. The way rain ran off his jaw. The scratch of his uniform under my fists. Soap and cold air and wet pavement and something warm underneath it that was just him.

August.

Okay, Florence. I'm August.

I close my eyes and it's there again, all of it, in the wrong order.

The sirens.

My mother's hair.

His mouth.

My stomach drops so hard I grip the rail with both hands.

I kissed him.

I kissed a cop in the rain, my mother dead twenty feet away, and I can't stop thinking about it.

It makes me sick.

It makes me burn.

It makes me want to crawl out of my skin

I open my eyes.

Water. Gray sky. Seagulls. Ferry wake.

I'm not in the intersection.

His mouth isn't here.

"Drink the coffee," Grandma says beside me.

I do. It tastes like burnt cardboard and heat.

We stand there for the rest of the crossing without talking.

I like her for that.

I think if anybody else told me it's going to be okay, I'd bite them.

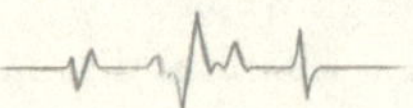

WHIDBEY LOOKS like it was painted with leftover colors.

Pines. Dark water. Wet roads. A few shops with hand-painted signs. Houses tucked back from the highway just minding their own business. We drive off the ferry and the whole island smells different than Seattle. Cleaner, maybe. Like salt and cedar and rain-soaked dirt.

I hate it on sight.

Then I hate myself for hating the place I'm supposed to live now.

Grandma's house sits on a quiet road with a gravel driveway and a porch that needs repainting. There are flower pots lined up by the steps, all dead for the season, and a wind chime I can hear before she kills the engine.

The house is warm when we walk in.

Not cozy. Warm.

Radiator heat and old wood and whatever she uses to clean the counters. It smells like her. Citrus hand lotion and printer ink and the black tea she drinks all day while seemingly running the world from her laptop.

"Shoes off," she says automatically, already carrying my duffel bag down the hall.

I stand there in the entryway and look at the house like I'm trespassing.

This is not my home.

My home was an apartment over a bakery in Seattle with a radiator that hissed and a kitchen drawer that never closed all the way and my mother singing at six in the morning like she was trying to fight the world before coffee.

I leave my shoes on.

Grandma doesn't say anything this time.

She just keeps walking.

The room she gives me used to be my mom's, back when she was a teenager and still lived here. "Your mother painted that room herself, Florence. Pale yellow. She hated it a week later, but she painted it."

The walls are still yellow.

Faded now. Soft and old. There's a quilt on the bed and a desk under the window and a little shelf with seashells and books nobody has touched in years.

My bag hits the floor and the sound of it lands in my chest.

Temporary.

Everything in here feels temporary.

Even me.

"Bathroom's across the hall," Grandma says from the doorway. "I put clean towels in there. I'll make soup in an hour. Try to rest before then."

I nod.

She doesn't leave.

When I look up, she's watching me with that same held-together face.

"You don't have to be okay for me," she says.

My throat closes so fast it hurts.

I look away first. "I know."

She nods which I guess means we came to an understanding.

Then she leaves me alone.

The second I hear her footsteps move down the hall, I sit on the bed and fold in half.

I don't cry pretty.

I never have.

It comes out ugly and hot and mean, my face in my hands, my shoulders shaking so hard I almost slide off the mattress. I cry because the room is wrong. I cry because my shoes are still on. I cry because my mother is dead and my sister won't answer her phone and my first kiss with a random man I don't know who held me together in the street and now I can't stop replaying the feel of his hand at my jaw.

I cry because I kissed him.

I cry because part of me wanted to even after what happened.

That's the part I can't forgive.

THREE
FLORENCE
SIX YEARS AGO

NORA SINGS to me before I'm even fully awake.

Not happy birthday singing. Not sweet.

The woman is in the kitchen cussing at a pie crust and muttering old Motown lyrics like she's trying to intimidate both God and butter into cooperating.

I lie in bed for a second and stare at the ceiling, listening to cabinet doors open and close downstairs.

Nineteen.

It doesn't feel like a birthday.

It feels like a number somebody wrote on a form.

My room still doesn't look like mine, even after a year. Longer, technically. The walls are pale blue under layers of old nail holes. The dresser is older than I am and smells faintly like cedar and perfume. There's a window over the bed that looks out toward the water if I lean far enough, and on clear mornings the light comes in soft and silver and makes everything look almost holy.

Today it's raining.

Of course it is.

I sit up slowly and the scar on my forehead pulls.

It always does first thing in the morning. Tight skin. A little sting if I move too fast. I lift my hand and touch it without thinking, tracing the raised line near my brow.

The doctor said it healed well.

People say that like "well" means "gone."

It doesn't.

I swing my legs over the side of the bed and step around the mess on my floor. Sketchbook. Jeans. A charcoal stick snapped in half. Three envelopes I haven't opened yet because I already know what they are.

College brochures.

I open my bedroom door and the house breathes around me. Old wood. Coffee. Rain tapping the windows. Cinnamon and sugar from whatever Nora's making downstairs.

Nora is at the kitchen counter in leggings and one of her company hoodies, glasses pushed up in her hair, flour on her cheek like war paint. She looks up when I come in and points a butter knife at me.

"Don't make that face. It is your birthday and I did not wrestle that pie dough for you to come down here looking like somebody canceled Christmas."

"I always look like this."

"Not true. Sometimes you look meaner."

I almost smile.

Almost.

She sees it anyway and grins like she won something.

"Coffee's hot," she says. "Sit. You can be miserable after breakfast."

I pour a mug and sit at the table in my socks, tucking one foot under my leg. There's a wrapped box by my plate and a card with my name on it in Nora's blunt, all-caps handwriting.

FLORENCE.

No hearts. No glitter. Very Nora.

She sets a plate in front of me. Eggs. Toast. Bacon cooked too crisp because she likes it that way and insists everyone else should too.

"Eat."

"Yes, ma'am."

She narrows her eyes. "Don't 'ma'am' me. You only do that when you're about to get emotional or lie."

I take a bite of toast so I don't have to answer.

There's a beat of quiet between us, not bad quiet, just the kind that lives in this house now. We've gotten good at it. Better than we were at the beginning, when everything out of my mouth came out wrong and everything she said sounded like an order even when it wasn't.

She lost a daughter.

I lost a mother.

Turns out those are not the same grief.

Turns out they can still bruise each other.

Nora wipes her hands on a towel and sits across from me. She slides the card over first.

"Open that one."

Inside is a gift card to the art supply store in Coupeville and a folded check.

I stare at the number too long.

"Nora—"

"Don't start."

"This is too much."

"It's not." Her voice goes flat in that way it does when she's already decided something. "That's your birthday money from me, and the rest is your mother's."

My chest tightens.

I look back down at the check. My mother's name is written in the memo line in Nora's handwriting. Neat. Controlled.

I hate how hard that hits.

I set the card down carefully, like it might break if I move too fast.

"Nora..."

She leans back in her chair and folds her arms. "We need to have this conversation anyway, so we're having it now while there's bacon involved."

I let out a breath that almost turns into a laugh.

She continues, softer this time. "The college fund your mother had for you is still there. It's yours."

I stare at my coffee.

"And the insurance payout from the accident," she says, "is being split between you and your sister. Legally and cleanly. I made sure of it."

At that, I look up.

"She called you?"

Nora's mouth tightens. "She emailed. Which is apparently the same thing now if you're under thirty."

"She's twenty-one."

"Exactly. A child."

I almost smile again, but it dies fast.

My sister.

Lacey.

Her name moves through me like a pulled wire. "She should've been there," I say quietly.

Nora watches me for a long moment.

"For what part?"

I hate that question because I don't know.

For the move. For the doctor appointments. For the weeks I couldn't sleep unless all the lights were on.

For all of it.

"For me," I say finally.

"That can be true," she says. "And it can also be true she was drowning too."

I look away.

I know that. I do.

I just don't always believe it.

Nora reaches across the table and taps one blunt finger against the stack of envelopes on the counter.

"Now. School."

I groan.

She points again. "Don't do that. You had to repeat part of the year. You still finished. You worked your ass off to finish."

It's not praise exactly, but coming from her it lands close.

Senior year should have ended one way.

Caps and gowns and prom pictures and fake crying in the gym while everybody signs yearbooks and swears they'll stay friends forever.

Instead I spent half of it in a fog.

I got through it.

Only barely.

"Those brochures aren't a prison sentence," Nora says. "You don't have to decide today. But you do need a plan."

I stare at the steam curling off my coffee.

"I know."

"No, baby, you know how to survive the next twenty-four hours." She says it gently. "I'm asking for the next year."

I hate when she's right.

I get up before I can snap at her and take my mug to the sink. My sketchbook is on the little side table by the back door where I left it last night. I pick it up and flip through pages with my thumb.

Eyes.

Hands.

The line of a jaw.

Not his face exactly. Never enough for that. Just pieces. Shadows. The shape of a mouth I remember in flashes and hate myself for remembering at all.

Between those are ferry docks and storefront windows and Nora's profile while she's on the phone and the crooked little church off Main and one page where I drew my own scar over and over until the paper buckled.

Nora sees what's in my hands and goes quiet.

"You're good," she says after a minute.

"I know."

"That wasn't fishing."

"I know."

She gets up and comes to stand beside me at the sink, shoulder bumping mine.

"Art school is not a bad option," she says. "I talk a lot of shit, but I know it's not."

I turn my head and look at her.

She shrugs. "Your mother would haunt me if I acted like it was stupid."

The mention of Mom makes the kitchen go strange for a second. Not silent. Just thinner.

My mother painted herbs in the margins of grocery lists. Drew moons on receipts. Burned candles down to nubs and called it practical magic.

She believed in intention. In what people carried into a room. Into food. Into love.

My throat burns.

I close the sketchbook.

"I don't know if I want school right now," I say. "Any school."

Nora nods slowly. "Okay."

The word surprises me enough I laugh once, sharp and humorless. "That's it?"

"That's not it. That's step one." She leans a hip against the counter. "Step two is you still need a direction. A paycheck. Health insurance if you can get it. A reason to put on pants."

I snort.

She points at me again. "I'm serious. Grief makes people romantic about falling apart. Falling apart is expensive."

A laugh slips out of me before I can stop it. It sounds wrong in my own ears. Rusty.

Nora's mouth twitches like she'll take it anyway.

"What are you thinking?" she asks.

I look down at my hands.

At the scar. At the little crescent of charcoal under my thumbnail from last night. At the burn mark on my wrist from the espresso machine at work because I was moving too fast and pretending I wasn't thinking about anything.

I have a job.

Part-time assistant manager at a little shop in town that sells candles, cards, local jam, and tourist crap people buy when they forget to pack a sweatshirt.

I open. I close. I count the till. I smile at strangers. I restock shelves.

I can do all of it without thinking too hard.

That's the problem.

Nora reads something on my face and leans back in her chair. "You're about to tell me I'm wrong, aren't you?"

"I'm about to tell you I work."

"You work part-time."

"I pick up extra shifts."

"You still can't afford rent, car insurance, groceries, and a life on 'extra shifts,' Florence."

I rub my thumb over the ridge of my scar and stare at the table.

Last week, a man came into the shop white as paper and shaking so hard he dropped a display of handmade soaps.

He kept trying to talk and couldn't get the words out. He didn't know what to do. He just knew she was wrong.

My body moved before my brain did. I called 911. I got him some water. I remember how steady my voice sounded, even though my hands were shaking so bad I had to brace one against the counter.

Afterward, I went into the stockroom and cried for ten minutes sitting on a box of holiday mugs.

Not because it was horrible.

But because it was fixable.

"I've been thinking about dispatch," I say.

Nora goes still. "Since when?"

I shrug, but it's fake. "A while."

"How long is a while?"

I don't answer right away.

The clock over the stove hums. Somewhere down the hall the dryer thumps one of Nora's blazers against the drum.

I pick at a water ring on the table with my nail.

"Since the accident," I say.

The words sit there between us.

Nora doesn't flinch. Doesn't rush in to make it softer.

"Okay," she says.

I nod once and keep going before I can lose my nerve.

"I saw a posting. Island County Emergency Communications. It's an entry-level position." My voice speeds up. "They train you. It's nights and weekends and weird shifts and every holiday. Let's face it. It's probably hell, but I can do tests. I can type. I can learn the map. I can—"

"Florence."

I stop.

Her eyes are on me sharp now. "Do you want that job,"

Nora asks, "or do you want to stand close to what happened to you?"

It hits so clean I actually look away.

"Why does my answer have to be one or the other? Why do they have to be mutually exclusive? Because I think the answer is both." I swallow hard. "I want to help."

She waits.

I hate that she waits.

"I want..." I press my thumb harder into the scar until it stings. "I want to be useful when something goes bad. I want to be the person who knows what to do. I want to be the voice that doesn't shake."

I don't explain that some part of me has been trying to get back to that night for the last year. It's not that I want the pain, I'm not a masochist. But I think it's because I survived it and I don't know what to do with that if I can't turn it into something.

Nora sees all of it anyway. She always does.

"That's not a small job," she says.

"I know."

"It'll get under your skin."

"I know."

"It'll change you."

I let out a breath. "I'm already changed."

Nora reaches across the table and knocks her knuckles once against my sketchbook.

"And school?"

There it is.

I groan. "Nora."

"Don't 'Nora' me. We are not doing that thing where you distract me with a noble plan and think I forget the rest."

I almost smile.

She folds her arms. "What's the deal?"

I think about it for a second, then another.

"Back off college for now," I say. "Let me sit for the dispatch test. If I get in, I work. I save money. I figure out what I want before I burn through Mom's college fund because I'm lost."

Nora's face doesn't move.

I rush to add, "I'm not saying no to school forever. I'm saying not yet."

Still nothing.

Then she tips her head, considering me like I'm a contract she hasn't decided to sign.

"You pass the test," she says, "I back off."

Relief hits so fast it makes me dizzy.

"Nora, really?"

She points at me with the same hand she used to threaten pie crust this morning. "Back off does not mean disappear. The school conversation is postponed. Not dead."

"That's fair."

"And you keep your job until you have another one."

"I know."

"Okay," she says.

Something unclenches in my chest.

Not all the way but enough.

Nora disappears down the hall, voice sharp and polished, when the phone rings. One hand slicing the air like the person on the other end deserves to be nervous.

I stay at the table with my coffee gone cold, my sketchbook under my palm, and the shape of a future I can almost see.

I touch the scar on my forehead and feel the raised line under my fingertip.

Then I open my sketchbook and draw a headset in the margin beside a pair of eyes I never quite get right.

FOUR
AUGUST
FIVE YEARS AGO

THE DRIVE-IN LOT is half full when we roll in, headlights cutting over rows of parked trucks and old SUVs and teenagers pretending they're not checking who else is here.

I kill the engine and sit there for a second with both hands on the wheel, listening to the tick-tick-tick as it cools.

Beside me, Lilly is already unbuckling.

"Hang on," I say. "Movie starts in twenty."

"I know."

She says it the way she says most things now. Flat. Like every word I speak is an inconvenience she has to step over.

I reach for the little paper speaker card they still hand out at the entrance even though half the place runs through radio now. "You want the radio on low or are we doing the old-school static box tonight?"

She groans and tips her head back against the seat. "Please don't call it that."

"It's a speaker box."

"You make everything sound a hundred years old."

I grin even though she's not looking at me. "That's because I'm ancient. I was born in the nineteen hundreds."

That gets me an eye roll, which is honestly better than nothing.

She pushes her door open.

"Hold up." I catch her with just enough dad voice to make her pause. "I'm hitting the snack bar. You want anything?"

She shrugs one shoulder. "Whatever."

"Come on Bug. Don't be that way."

Her head snaps around. "Stop calling me that."

I lean back in my seat and look up at her, all long legs and attitude and the same mouth she had at six when she used to fall asleep with popsicle stains on her chin.

"You loved it when you were little."

"I was little."

"You still are little."

She gives me a look so dry it could start a fire. "I'm nearly eighteen."

"Exactly. Little."

"Dad."

There's heat in it now, real heat, and I hold up a hand.

"Okay. Fine. No bugaboo in public."

"In public or private."

I wince. "Harsh."

She points at me, dead serious. "No insect names."

A laugh slips out before I can stop it. "You are named after a flower and somehow came out meaner than me."

"That's because one of us had to."

She slams the door before I can answer, but I catch the corner of her mouth tipping up as she goes.

I sit there watching her weave through cars toward a cluster of girls by a Jeep with a blanket spread over the hood. She doesn't look back.

I tell myself that's fine.

This was my idea, not hers.

One more summer thing before she starts talking about apartments and jobs and classes and "I'll let you know" in that careful voice she uses when she thinks I'm trying too hard. One more dumb, ordinary night where I buy her too much candy and pretend I don't notice she's already halfway out the door of every room I walk into.

I scrub a hand over my face and get out of the truck.

The gravel pops under my boots as I cut across the lot. The

place smells like buttered popcorn, hot oil, damp dirt, and car exhaust. Kids run past me with glow sticks. Somebody's radio is blasting country from three rows over. The giant screen looms over all of it, washed pale in the last light before full dark.

Inside the snack bar, it's hot and loud and sticky in the way all movie theater concession stands are.

Teenagers at the counter. A little kid crying over a dropped snow cone. A woman in a Mariners jacket arguing about jalapeños. The floor grabs at my boots with every step.

I get in line and glance at the menu board I once knew by heart.

Popcorn. Nachos. Candy. Regret.

The girl behind the register calls, "Next!"

I take two steps forward and catch a flash of movement through the side window. A figure cutting past the arcade barn next door. Short dark hair. Curvy body. Black jacket. Head turned just enough that my chest tightens before my brain catches up.

I turn all the way, staring through greasy glass.

The line behind me shifts. Somebody bumps my shoulder.

"Sorry, man."

I don't answer.

It can't be.

Two years is a long time. Faces change. Hair changes. Bodies change. Memory can lie to you.

But something in me is already moving.

"Sir?" the cashier says, impatient now. "You ordering?"

"Give me a minute."

I step out of line and out the side door before I can talk myself out of it.

The cool air between buildings is a welcome relief. The arcade barn sits fifty feet away, all buzzing neon and old wood, with hand-painted signs for pinball and skee-ball and a row of busted racing games that somehow never fully die.

I walk fast, then slower when I get close, because I feel ridiculous.

Inside, the barn is all noise and colored light.

Machines chiming. Kids yelling. Tinny music from three different games bleeding together. The place smells like dust, sugar, and old wiring. It's dim enough that everyone looks like a version of themselves from another life.

I stand just inside the door and scan the rows.

Claw machine. Air hockey. Skee-ball.

Then I see her in the pinball corner.

She's got one hip against the machine, body angled in, all focus and fast hands. The lights flash blue and red over her face, over the line of her throat, over bare fingers tapping the flipper like she's done this a hundred times and plans to win every one of them.

She's beautiful.

Not in a loud way. Not trying for it.

Just there. Effortless and locked in and alive enough that my chest pulls tight before I know why.

Short dark hair at chin length maybe. Soft around her face when she tips her head, sharper when she looks up at the score.

She misses the shot and swears under her breath.

The older woman beside her laughs and bumps her with a hip. "That's what you get for showing off."

She laughs back, head tipping, mouth opening on the sound, and something in me stutters.

I know that mouth.

The thought hits first and makes no sense.

I've never stood this close to her. Never seen her under neon. Never seen her laugh.

But something in me knows the shape of it anyway. A strange pressure builds under my ribs. Familiar, but wrong. My body remembers something my memory does not.

The woman with her says something I don't catch. She feeds another quarter into the machine and braces in again, shoulders loose, eyes narrowed at the glass.

This is stupid.

I came in here for snacks and somehow followed a feeling across a gravel lot like a man who's lost his damn mind.

Now I'm standing in an arcade watching a woman play pinball while my pulse kicks like I'm twenty.

She laughs again when the machine drains early, and I catch myself watching too closely. Her mouth. Her hands.

Whoever she is, she knocks the air out of me. She tilts her head, listening to something. I stay exactly where I am and tell myself I'm leaving in five seconds.

Four.

Three.

She smacks the side of the machine with the heel of her hand and mutters, "Cheater."

The other woman snorts. "That was skill."

She grins. "That was elderly fraud."

I almost laugh.

"Dad."

Lilly's voice behind me, dry as sandpaper.

I turn, and there she is with one hand on her hip, looking at me like she caught me doing something dumb, which, fair.

"I thought you were getting snacks."

I glance toward the concession stand and realize I'm empty-handed.

"Was."

"Mmhm."

Her eyes flick over my shoulder toward the pinball row, then back to me. Sharp kid. Too sharp.

"You coming, or are you just haunting the arcade now?"

I huff a laugh. "I saw somebody I thought I knew."

"Do you?"

I look back before I can stop myself.

She's still by the machine, but she's not playing. She's looking straight at me. Everything in me goes quiet for half a beat.

A faint line near her brow catches in the machine light, and something low and sharp goes through me before I can name it.

She doesn't smile or wave. It's just a steady, almost unreadable look. Maybe she's trying to place me too or maybe just wondering why some guy is staring at her in the dark like a fucking creep.

She glances back to the machine breaking eye contact and I take the out.

"C'mon," I say to Lilly, and fall into step beside her toward the snack bar, feeling that pull between my shoulder blades all the way across the room.

Lilly gets into the snack line, arms crossed, bouncing one sneaker heel against the concrete.

"You owe me sour patch kids for the emotional damages you inflicted this evening," she says.

"Emotional damages from what?"

"From being dragged here with my father."

"Wow."

"And popcorn. Extra butter."

"You said *whatever*," I say, using my best teenager annoyed voice.

"I've grown since then."

I step in beside her and bump my shoulder against hers. She lets me, which counts as affection these days.

"Fine. Popcorn, candy, and emotional-damage nachos."

She snorts. "You're ridiculous."

"And oddly, I'm also still your ride."

We stand there in line, and I can feel the arcade barn at my back like a second pulse.

I don't turn around. When it's our turn, I order too much food. By the time we get back to the truck, the first previews are rolling across the giant screen, and the lot has settled into that drive-in hush made of low radios and wrappers opening and people getting comfortable in the dark.

Lilly tunes the station and steals half the popcorn before I even sit down.

I hand her the candy and pretend not to watch the line of her profile in the glow from the screen.

FIVE
FLORENCE
FIVE YEARS AGO

I KNOW him before I know I know him.

It happens in the stupidest possible way.

I'm standing in line for popcorn, half listening to Nora argue with a teenager about whether "extra butter" means *extra* extra butter or just the normal amount they give everyone when they're trying to act generous, and I feel it.

That's the only word for it.

A pull.

It's not romantic. Not magical. Not even logical.

Just this hard little jerk under my ribs like somebody reached inside me and tugged a thread.

I turn my head before my brain catches up.

And there he is.

Across the snack bar, just near the entrance. He's a few people behind us but he doesn't see me.

Nora hands something to me but everything in me locks.

I stop breathing.

The fluorescent lights buzz, the fryer hisses, and Nora is still saying, "Honey, if I wanted a teaspoon of butter I would have stayed home and microwaved my own disappointment."

None of it reaches me.

Because it's him.

It's August. Officer August.

And the memory doesn't come back in order. It never does.

It comes in pieces now. His hand at my jaw. His voice in my ear telling me to look at him. Rain caught in his lashes. The way his eyes held mine so steady I hated him for being the first safe thing I saw after my whole world split open.

He's in jeans and a dark jacket. No uniform. No badge. No radio on his shoulder. No flashing lights turning him into a ghost I could never quite prove was real.

And somehow that makes it worse. Or better. Both.

He looks more like the version of him I built in my head when I couldn't sleep.

Like my memory kept trying to make a man out of fragments and got him wrong every time.

"You're letting the flies in," Nora says, holding the snack-bar door open with her hip.

It takes everything I have to walk away from him. To follow her back to the car with popcorn and candy balanced in my hands like a normal person.

"Grandma, let's drop this stuff off and go play pinball," I say, right on her heels. "We've still got time. The previews alone are, like, half an hour."

I shove down the clawing need to go back. To stay near him. To stand in the same air and pretend that means nothing.

"Anything for you," Nora says.

She tosses the popcorn onto the seat, then turns and pulls me into a quick hug, hard and warm and all business even when she's being soft.

"I'm so proud of you."

The words hit me square in the chest.

"Thanks," I say, smiling into her coat.

When she pulls back, we both start laughing for no reason except if we don't, I might cry.

Five minutes later we've got a fistful of quarters and our usual machine, Bride of Pinbot.

"You okay, kiddo?" Nora asks, already lining up her shot. Her head tilts, eyes narrowed at me.

"Just distracted." I force a breath out through a smile. "I'm here. C'mon, old lady. Try to keep up."

She gives me a look. "Change is good for you."

Then, with a perfectly straight face, she adds, "I'm about to ruin your night, little girl."

A nervous laugh slips out of me, too high and too quick.

We burn through two games fast.

I miss shots I never miss. Tilt the machine once. Curse under my breath. Pretend I'm focused.

It takes all my restraint not to scan the arcade barn every thirty seconds. Not to drift toward the snack bar "by accident." Not to check if he's still here.

Nora drops in quarters for round three and takes first turn.

I hold out for maybe ten seconds.

Then I look.

And there he is.

All I catch at first is the turn of his head, the clean line of his profile under the arcade lights, and my stomach drops so hard I have to grip the edge of the machine.

He is so much sexier than I remembered.

The thought lands low and hot, pulling tight through the center of me. For one horrific moment I can feel his lips on mine.

It isn't just that he's handsome. He was handsome that night too, and I knew it in that awful, human way you notice things you should not be noticing while your life is splitting open.

But this is different.

This is him in regular life.

Neon on his cheek.

This is him not holding me together in the street.

This is him just existing.

And my entire body reacts like it's been waiting for this exact second without telling me.

"Flo?"

Nora's voice cuts in from somewhere to my left.

I don't answer.

He's here with a woman.

Something hot and ugly coils in my stomach before reason can catch up.

She's pretty with long legs, easy laugh, and the kind of effortless that makes me suddenly aware of my chipped black nail polish and the way my sweater hangs too loose.

Panic isn't the right word. It's sharper. Hungrier.

What did I expect? A man like him to stay empty-handed for six years?

"Florence?" Nora asks.

Across the room, August turns his head.

Our eyes meet.

Everything in me drops.

The arcade noise goes thin and far away. The lights still flash. Kids still yell. Somewhere a machine plays a tinny victory song. But all I can feel is his eyes landing on me.

Time stops and I can't breathe waiting for him to recognize me.

To see me.

But instead, it's like he's trying to place something.

Does he feel it too?

I should look away. Break eye contact and play this game with Nora.

I do not.

I can't.

She bumps his shoulder. He says something low; she rolls her eyes with familiar affection.

Too young. Not a lover.

Daughter.

The realization rearranges him in my head like furniture being moved in the dark.

He has someone who gets to touch him casually. Someone who knows what his laugh sounds like at breakfast, what his bad mornings look like, what his hands feel like when they're gentle instead of saving someone from bleeding out in the rain.

My fingers tighten around the pinball rail until the metal bites.

I don't hate her.

I just want what she has without earning it.

I want the right to look at him like he belongs to me already.

Nora calls my name again. I force my eyes back to the machine, but the score blurs.

He has a daughter.

That means he has a life I wasn't invited to.

Yet.

I wonder if he remembered beyond the night's reports. If he's ever thought of me the way I've thought about him.

I stare at the doorway long after he's gone. This morning I got the offer to be the newest trainee at Island County 911 Emergency Communications.

Nights. Weekends. Holidays. I start in a week.

I should be thinking about that.

I *am* thinking about that.

But my body is still somewhere else.

I touch my scar.

The skin there is flatter now than it used to be but still raised enough to catch my fingertip. I trace the line once, then stop because if I do it too much Nora notices.

For two years I have carried him like a private burn and never had to test it against reality. He lived in memory where everything can stay unfinished.

Tonight he stepped out of that memory and became a man again.

SIX

FLORENCE

1 YEAR EARLIER

THE HOTEL BAR is too bright for the kind of tired that lives in my bones.

Under these Edison bulbs, though, my exhaustion almost passes for haunted-beautiful.

Or so I've been told. Twice tonight.

Everything gleams in the low light. Glassware. Brass railings. The polished curve of the counter that's probably been wiped down thirty times an hour by someone making twelve dollars an hour and hating every person in this room on principle.

I swirl what's left of my wine and try not to think about the fact that I have to be awake at six for day three of Crisis Communication for Emergency Services.

It isn't even the first time I've taken this class.

Mandatory training means mandatory attendance, apparently, even when you could recite half the slides from memory and the instructor keeps saying things like center self-care in your professional practice with a straight face.

Sure.

I'll get right on that.

I drink instead.

The stem is cool between my fingers. Since I'm on per diem, I splurge on the better wine. It tastes like blackberries and bad decisions, and two glasses in, my shoulders have finally dropped an inch.

Island County has been a lot lately.

More domestics. More mental health calls. More welfare checks that turn into something else by the time deputies get there. More people standing on the edge of themselves, one bad minute away from doing something permanent.

Every shift, somebody is screaming. Or sobbing. Or breathing like each inhale might be their last.

And I'm there.

I'm always there.

And right now I'm still the girl with the headset.

Right now I'm in a downtown Seattle hotel bar full of other headset people, all of us pretending we're fine.

Pretending this job doesn't strip little pieces off us call by call.

I look up without meaning to and catch someone in my peripheral before I fully see him.

He's tall enough that I feel him first.

Big. Solid. Quiet in a way that pulls the eye.

Not movie-star handsome. Better than that.

Real-world handsome.

Broad shoulders in a dark button-down that fits a little too well to be an accident. Sleeves rolled to his forearms, black ink crawling up both arms. Dark hair a little wrecked, like he's been dragging his hands through it all day. Lines at the corners of his eyes that say he's laughed hard and frowned harder.

If I had to guess, I'd say early forties. Maybe older. Maybe younger. I've never been great at guessing age when a man looks like that.

He passes behind my chair and takes the stool two spots down.

"Whiskey. Neat."

Three syllables, and every dispatcher instinct in me lights up like a switchboard.

He has that trauma-trained stillness. The kind that's seen too much and keeps it parked in the throat. Given the hotel and the conference crowd, I'd bet law enforcement before he even turns all the way toward the bar.

He doesn't slouch.

His body looks like it forgot how to relax sometime around 2008.

Rigid, sure. Controlled.

But the rough shadow along his jaw is unfairly hot.

I try not to stare.

I fail immediately.

When his drink arrives, he wraps both hands around the glass. Rough fingers. Tanned skin. A long pale scar across the top of his right hand. Nails short and clean.

He either doesn't notice me noticing him, or he's decent enough to pretend he doesn't.

I take another sip and tell myself to mind my business.

I am here for training.

I am not here to gawk at hot older men who look like they could bench-press me and all my bad decisions.

Drink your stupid wine and go to bed.

That works until he glances down the bar while lifting his drink, and our eyes lock.

"What about you?" he asks, easy as anything. "You here for training too? You smell like coffee and adrenaline."

I blink. "You can't smell adrenaline."

A corner of his mouth tips. "I can. Been around it long enough."

A laugh slips out before I can stop it. "Maybe I work in something similar."

He tilts his head like he accepts the dodge. "Fair."

There's a gentleness to the way he leaves it there.

No prying. No pushing. No trying to prove he can get me talking.

Just an opening. A quiet offer to sit in the gray for a minute.

And somehow that's all it takes.

We slip into conversation like we've done it before.

Too easy for strangers.

We talk around the details instead of through them.

When he asks what I do, I say, "I'm the voice people hear when they dial the phone on the worst day of their life."

He rolls his whiskey glass once between his palms and says, "I'm one of the people that voice sends running toward the noise."

That should be vague. It should be nothing.

Instead it lands in me like recognition without a name.

We talk about exhaustion like it's weather.

About the way adrenaline leaves you shaking three hours after the call is over.

About how people scream in patterns. How panic sounds different from pain. How some voices stay in your head long after your shift ends.

He doesn't interrupt when I admit, quiet and looking into my wine, that sometimes I feel like I'm screaming too. Just on the inside, where nobody can hear it.

"You ever feel like you're drowning on dry land?" I ask, watching the bar light bend through the stem of my glass.

"Yeah," he says.

No hesitation. No performance. No speech about resilience.

Just yeah.

Then, after a beat, "More than I like to admit."

Something in my chest shifts.

By then our shoulders are angled toward each other. At some point he moved down a stool, and now we're side by side instead of separated by coasters and polite distance.

There's a carefulness to him I don't know what to do with.

He doesn't touch me by accident.

Doesn't crowd.

Doesn't do that thing some men do where they act like your body is public furniture the second you smile at them.

If he touches me, it'll be because one of us chose it.

I realize, somewhere between my second glass of wine and his slow third sip of whiskey, that I want that.

I want to choose him.

Even if it's only for one night.

He glances at my nearly empty glass. "I should probably let you get some sleep," he says.

His voice is polite.

His eyes on my mouth are not.

"Probably," I say, even though my skin is buzzing.

We sit in that probably for a long moment.

He looks like a man who does the right thing even when it costs him.

Like he says no to himself more than he says yes.

And I am so tired of men who take and take and call it chemistry.

I want, just once, to know what it feels like to be with a man who knows how to give.

His fingers flex around his glass like he's arguing with himself.

"I'm not looking for anything complicated," he says quietly.

The words hit my sternum like a stone.

Relief opens in my chest at the exact same time disappointment drops low in my stomach.

"Good," I say, forcing my voice steady. "I don't have room for complicated."

His mouth tips, not quite a smile. "Then maybe we don't have a problem."

"Maybe," I echo.

He turns his hand over on the bar, palm up between us.

Not touching me.

Just offering.

"Ground rules," he says. "If we do this."

My heart slams hard enough I'm sure he can hear it.

"Okay," I whisper.

"No last names. No work details. No photos. No numbers. No promises."

I swallow. "You do this often?" I ask, half curious, half trying to figure out if men like him actually exist or if I made him up out of exhaustion and wine.

Those dark eyes hold mine.

"No," he says.

Just that. No charm. No game.

Then, "That's why we need ground rules."

Something in me loosens and pulls tight at the same time.

"Alright," I say. "I have some too."

"Yeah?" His voice drops lower. Rougher around the edges.

I nod, but my throat feels tight.

"I don't want to feel like a mistake," I say. "Not tonight. Not after."

His face changes, just slightly. Still. Focused.

I make myself keep going.

"I don't need a call tomorrow. I don't need a number. I don't need..." I shake my head once. "Anything complicated. But if we ever run into each other again, I don't want you to look through me like I never happened."

The last part comes out quieter.

"I don't want to be erased."

His jaw tightens, and for one second he looks like I hit something old.

"I don't erase people," he says.

There's no hesitation in it. No softening.

"Especially not the ones I choose."

Heat spreads through me so fast I have to look down at my glass.

He taps two fingers once against the bar between us.

"You feel this, right?"

I nod because I do not trust my voice.

"Okay," I manage.

"And I don't want you pretending I'm younger than I am," he says.

That pulls a startled laugh out of me.

His gaze stays on mine.

"If this happens, it's not because I'm having some cliché midlife crisis. I don't do this." A beat. "And I don't feel this kind of pull. Ever."

I huff out a laugh, trying to get my footing back. "You sure? Because this is textbook midlife-crisis behavior."

That almost-smile again.

"It's something else," he says, and the way he looks at me makes my pulse trip hard. "Trust me."

He leaves his hand where it is, open and waiting.

My fingers hover over his. Close enough to feel the heat of his skin.

My heart is beating so hard it feels stupid now. Young. Too loud.

"One more rule," I say softly.

He lifts a brow. "Yeah?"

"This is just tonight."

His eyes darken.

"No matter how good it is," I add, even though saying it out loud makes me feel the lie in my own mouth.

A slow, dangerous look moves across his face.

"You think it'll be good."

Heat climbs my throat into my cheeks. "I think you know exactly how good it'll be." I force myself to hold his gaze. "And I think that's the problem."

His throat works around a swallow.

He studies my face like he's checking for fear. Hesitation. Regret. Anything that means stop.

"You're sure?" he asks, quieter now. "Completely sure?"

I nod once. "Yes."

He holds my eyes another beat, then gives the smallest nod.

"Alright," he says. "Let's get out of here."

I slide my hand into his.

The contact snaps through me, hot and immediate.

His palm is warm, calloused, steady as he closes his hand around mine and stands, tossing cash on the bar with his free hand.

He doesn't let go crossing the lobby.

Doesn't let go when we step into the elevator.

He hits the button for his floor.

The doors close with a soft hush, sealing us in.

Silence settles between us, thick and charged.

The air changes.

My skin prickles.

My thighs press together before I can stop them.

I can feel him looking at me.

He tracks the stray curl slipping from my bun, the cling of my dress to my ass, the frantic flutter at my throat. I stare at the glowing floor numbers, pretending I don't feel Whiskey's gaze burning holes through me. Pretending I'm not already soaked through my panties.

Third floor. Doors slide open. A man in a crisp suit steps in. He's probably in his early thirties, Wall Street polish, too-smooth smile. He scans us both, but his eyes settle on me, appreciative, proprietary. "Evening," he says. "Evening," I answer, voice thinner than I'd like.

He steps closer than necessary. Not touching. Close enough to imply.

"Here for the conference?" His gaze rakes my body. "I'd remember you."

Before I can speak, Whiskey moves.

Silent. Certain. Possessive.

He steps behind me, chest sealing to my back. His hand slides down, past waist, past my hip, and he cups me between the thighs. Over the dress. Right there. Warm. Heavy. Claiming.

I gasp sharply.

The suit glances down. Eyes widen. He clocks our reflection in the mirrored doors: my pupils blown, Whiskey's hand unmistakably between my legs. "Oh," he mutters. Clears his throat. "Didn't realize..."

Whiskey doesn't speak. The look he levels is lethal: *she's mine. Walk away before this gets physical.*

Ding. Next floor. The suit bolts.

Doors close. I exhale a shaky breath.

"You scared him," I whisper, heat crawling up my neck.

"Good." Whiskey's voice is molten steel, lips brushing my ear. "He was eye-fucking what belongs to me."

"You didn't give me a chance to answer," I manage, even as my back arches into him.

He chuckles, low, almost dangerous. "Did you want to?"

I shake my head.

"Didn't think so."

His hand dives under the hem. Fingers slip past soaked lace. "Fuck," he groans. "You're drenched."

My legs tremble. "Someone might come in," I breathe.

He presses two fingers between my folds, teasing my entrance, thumb ghosting my clit. "They won't." Lips at my neck. "And if they do... let them watch. Let them see what happens when someone tries to touch what's mine."

I bite my lip bloody to stay quiet. He nips my ear. "I want you to come on my fingers before we reach the room."

"Please..." I don't know if I'm begging him to stop or begging harder.

He slides one thick finger inside, then another. Slow. Then curling deep. My knees buckle. "Eyes forward," he commands. "Keep that sweet mouth shut. I want to feel you shatter without a sound."

I choke on a moan. He laughs turns feral. "You love this. Being owned. Being used. Being *mine*."

Ding. His floor.

He withdraws with a slick sound, brings wet fingers to my lips. "Taste."

I do. Instantly. Eyes fluttering as salt-sweet arousal coats my tongue.

He grabs my wrist and hauls me down the hall like a man on fire.

We reach the door. He pauses for one heartbeat. Turns. His gaze is pure wildfire. "Last chance," he rasps, voice frayed. "You sure?"

I meet his eyes, thighs already slick, heart slamming. "Fuck yes."

Predatory smile. He spins me, slams me against the door, the thud echoing down my spine. His body pinning mine. Hands find my breasts, rough palms kneading through thin fabric.

"You've been tempting me all night," he growls, mouth dragging along my throat. "Now I get to take my fucking time."

One hand slips inside the neckline. Thumb circles a taut

nipple, then pinches, hard. I moan, loud. Hallway swallows the sound.

He licks up my neck, bites beneath my jaw, marking me. "Keep making those sounds and I'll fuck you right here. Let everyone hear how soaked you are for me."

"Maybe," I pant, shameless, body vibrating on the edge.

Wicked chuckle. He twists the nipple again while the other hand fumbles the lock. Heavy click. Door kicks open. He drags me inside.

Door slams. Air shifts. No more anticipation, only possession.

He pins me to the wall. Mouth crashes into mine, bruising, desperate. Fingers rip the dress down; breasts spill free.

"Fucking gorgeous," he snarls. Drops to his knees.

Sucks one nipple deep, tongue swirling, hand twisting the other. I cry out, arching, clawing his shoulders. He switches—bite, lick, bite—until my thighs shake and I'm seconds from coming untouched.

He fists my hair, drags my mouth to his. Kiss feral. Punishing. "You have no idea how badly I want to ruin you."

Hand clamps my throat—not choking, just owning. My knees give. He doesn't let me fall.

Walks me backward until my thighs hit the bed. "Clothes off. Now."

The command lands like a whip. Heat surges; wetness spills down my inner thighs.

We don't undress, we destroy. He yanks my dress over my head. Mouth crushes mine again while I tear at his shirt. Buttons pop. He kicks jeans away.

His thick, veined, uncut cock springs free. My throat goes dry.

Bra unclasped, tugged down, discarded. "From the first second I saw you," he rasps against my neck, "I wanted you like this. Spread. Dripping. *Mine.*"

The word makes me convulse. He bites my earlobe, then my throat hard enough to bruise. Licks the sting. "You like my marks?" I nod, trembling. "You're so fucking wet, aren't you?"

"Yes—fuck, yes!"

Hand slides down. Finds me. "Christ." Two fingers plunge inside, thumb circling my clit. "Beg me to fuck you like you were made for it."

I'm already begging.

He rips my panties at the seam. Drops to his knees. Spreads me wide. "You're a mess," he groans, tongue dragging through me once, long, utterly obscene. Then he *devours.*

Relentless. Lapping. Flicking. Sucking. Growling against me when I writhe. When it's too much and I try to scoot away, his hand wraps my throat, firm, gentle warning. "Stay still."

Sucks my clit hard. Two fingers curl inside, hitting that spot. I scream, arch, shatter, my legs shaking, vision whiting. He licks me through every aftershock until I'm twitching, gasping, ruined.

Pulls back. Wipes his mouth. "You taste like fucking sin. Now show me how that mouth feels."

He stands. Grabs my jaw. I open. "Good girl."

Slides in slow. Then deeper. I gag; he moans. "That's it. So fucking perfect with your mouth full of me."

Hand in my hair, other at my jaw, and he rocks. Controlled. Possessive. Deliberate.

And I take every inch like I was made for it.

His hips snap forward, then pull back just enough to make me chase the stretch. "You want it rough?" he rasps, sliding out slow, torturing me with the drag. "Want me to ruin you, baby?"

"Yes," I gasp, eyes glassy. "God, yes."

No hesitation.

He flips me onto my stomach, yanks my hips to the edge of the bed, and cracks his palm across my ass, harp, stinging. I yelp.

"Ass up," he orders. "Back arched. Just like that."

I obey. Barely braced before he slams home in one savage thrust.

"Fuck—"

"Yeah?" He locks a hand around my throat from behind, possessive grip, and drives deeper. "That what you needed?"

All I manage is a broken moan.

He fucks me like he's trying to carve himself into me. Hard, relentless, hips snapping with brutal precision. Leans over my back, mouth at my ear. "Mine."

The word brands me.

"Say it," he growls, pace faltering but never slowing. "Say who you fucking belong to."

"You," I cry. "I'm yours—fuck, I'm yours—"

"Damn right."

His rhythm stutters, control fraying. He reaches around, two fingers finding my clit, fast, filthy circles, merciless. "Come again," he commands. "I want to feel that greedy cunt break around me."

I shatter. Clenching, shaking, fingers clawing sheets as the orgasm rips through me. He follows with a guttural roar, burying himself deep, pulsing inside the condom with one final, punishing thrust.

He collapses over me, chest heaving against my back, both of us slick with sweat and wrecked.

After a long moment, he eases out, rolls us, and gathers me against him. Pulls me up the bed. Presses a slow, reverent kiss to the side of my neck like a vow.

"You're not going anywhere," he murmurs against my skin.

I believe him. After that? There's nowhere else I'd rather be.

His thumb traces lazy circles on my hip. His heartbeat thuds steady under my cheek. My eyelids grow heavy, body finally quiet. For the first time in months, I drift off wrapped in him, safe, claimed, and spent.

I WAKE to the soft glow of city lights filtering through the blackout curtains, the clock on the nightstand reading just past 2 a.m. Two hours gone in a blink, deep, dreamless sleep, the kind I haven't known in forever. Whiskey's arm is draped heavy over my waist, his breath warm and steady against the back of my neck. Our bodies tangle under the sheets, skin still sticky from earlier, the air thick with the scent of us: sweat, sex, satisfaction.

He stirs as I shift, his hand tightening instinctively on my hip. "Mmm," he murmurs, voice rough with sleep, lips brushing my shoulder. "You awake?"

"Yeah," I whisper, rolling toward him. My body aches with a delicious, tender throb between my legs from how he'd claimed me earlier. But it's not pain; it's a reminder, a pulse that reignites the heat low in my belly. I press closer, my thigh sliding over his, feeling him already half-hard against me.

His eyes open, dark and hooded in the dim light. He searches my face, thumb tracing my jaw. "You okay? Not too sore?"

I shake my head, even as the tenderness flares when I move. "A little. But I want you again." My voice is soft, honest. I trail my fingers down his chest, over the ridges of muscle, until I wrap my hand around him. He thickens under my touch, a low groan escaping his lips.

"Slow this time," he rasps, pulling me on top of him. His hands slide up my thighs, gentle now, mapping the curves he'd bruised before. No rush. No possession like a storm. Just a deep, simmering want.

I straddle him, knees bracketing his hips, the sheets pooling around us. He's hot and hard beneath me, but I take my time, rocking slowly, letting the tip of him nudge against my entrance. I'm still slick from earlier, still sensitive, every brush sending sparks up my spine. It stings a little as I sink down, inch by inch, but the fullness—the way he stretches me—feels like coming home.

"Fuck," he breathes, hands gripping my hips but not guiding, just holding. His eyes lock on mine, intense, vulnerable in a way he wasn't before. "You feel so good. So perfect."

I lean forward, breasts brushing his chest, and kiss him. Slow. Deep. Tongues tangling lazily as I start to move by rolling my hips in unhurried circles, savoring the drag, the way he fills me completely. My tenderness makes every sensation sharper, more intimate; I gasp into his mouth when he hits that deep spot, but I don't pull away. I welcome it, chase it, letting the ache blend with the pleasure until it's all one molten wave.

He matches my rhythm, thrusting up gently, hands roaming, palms flat on my back. His fingers trace my spine, then he cups my ass to pull me closer. "That's it," he murmurs against my lips. "Take what you need. Ride me slow, baby."

I do. Rising and falling in a sensual grind, my clit rubbing against him with each downward slide. The room fills with our quiet sounds: wet skin meeting, soft moans, his ragged breaths mingling with mine. No commands this time. It's just us, connected, moving like we're memorizing each other.

His thumb finds my clit, circling lightly, feather-soft. "Come for me like this," he whispers, voice wrecked. "Let me feel you squeeze around me."

The build is slow, a rising tide that crests in waves. I arch, head falling back, fingers digging into his shoulders as the orgasm rolls through me. It starts gentle, then grows to shattering me, my walls fluttering around him. He groans, hips bucking once, twice, before he spills inside me, warm and deep, no barrier this time, just raw intimacy.

I collapse onto his chest, breathless, his arms wrapping around me like a cocoon. He kisses my temple, my hair, holding me close as our heartbeats sync and slow.

"Sleep," he murmurs, thumb stroking my back. "I've got you."

I nod, already drifting, safe in his embrace. We tangle together again, limbs entwined, and slip back into that peaceful dark together.

GREY FOG-LIGHT SEEPS through the curtains. Early. Quiet. The bay rolling in soft outside.

For a breath I forget where I am. Then my cheek shifts

against warm skin, and last night floods back: his mouth, his hands, the way *sweetheart* landed like a claim. The way I let it.

I lift my head. He's asleep on his back, one arm flung toward the empty space I left. Hair wrecked. Stubble dark on his jaw. In sleep he looks almost gentle. It's kind of dangerous in a new, unguarded way.

Something coils tight in my chest. This is the part I don't do. Morning makes things real. Coffee, small talk, sleepy smiles asking me to stay. I don't stay. Rules exist for a reason.

I slide out from under his arm, slow, breath held. He shifts once, hand dragging across the sheet, searching. Palm grazes my hip. I freeze. A low, sleepy sound rumbles from his throat. His fingers slacken. Slip away.

I keep moving. Dress crumpled near the bed. Bra hooked on the lamp. Tights half-under the chair. Coat tossed over the desk in last night's hurry.

I gather it all barefoot, silent. Ripped panties by the nightstand—I stare a second, then scoop them up.

He's still out. One hand open on the mattress, palm up. Like he's waiting.

I look away. Cross to the desk. My coat slips, bumps his hanging off the chair. Something falls off, a soft plastic crack against carpet.

A lanyard. Black strap, clear sleeve. I bend, pick it up. Half annoyed at my own curiosity.

The photo hits first. Then the name.

CHIEF AUGUST CALDER

TOWNSEND HARBOR POLICE DEPARTMENT

Air leaves me in a thin, painful rush.

No.

I glance at the bed—same man, same broad shoulders, same scar peeking from under the sheet. August. Calder.

Rain flashes behind my eyes, wet asphalt, red-blue strobes, his hand steady at my jaw, voice low, "*Stay with me.*" The first safe thing in a night that ended everything else. Then last night, his mouth on mine, fingers in the elevator, "*mine*" growled against my throat.

A sound escapes me, half gasp, half laugh, half something broken. I clamp my hand over my mouth.

He shifts again. I go statue-still. Heart hammering loud enough to wake the dead. He doesn't wake.

I stand frozen, badge in hand, staring at the man I've carried like a secret scar for six years. Memory was safe. Contained. This is not memory. This is August Calder asleep after fucking me senseless. This is the officer who pulled me from wreckage and the man who just marked every inch of me.

My hands tremble once before they steady. I set the badge down carefully. No clatter.

I need to leave. Before recognition. Before questions. Before I have to explain Florence-from-the-crash and Florence-from-his-bed in the same breath.

Pen. Notepad. I write fast.

Thank you for last night. You made the world quiet for a while, and I'll carry this night longer than you know.

—Florence

I place it on my pillow. One last look: dark lashes, faint crease between his brows, tattoos vanishing under white cotton, open hand still waiting.

"You found me twice," I whisper. Barely sound.

Then I hate the softness in it. I grab my shoes, coat, and slip out.

PRESENT DAY

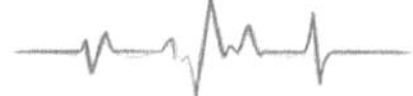

SEVEN
FLORENCE

9-1-1 WHERE IS YOUR EMERGENCY?

"Hi, ahh—someone's in my house." The woman's voice is thin, shaking, like a wire pulled too tight. "Oh my God. Oh my God, I heard—"

"Okay. I'm here with you." I sit forward, shoulders loose, voice steady. "What's the address where help is needed?"

She rattles it off too fast. I catch the street number on the second try, fingers already moving across the keyboard. Cedar Harbor Road. Single-family. Caller ID cross-matches to a land-line. I click into the map layer, pull up the parcel, and drop a priority tag.

"Cedar Harbor Road, I've got you. Can you confirm the house color or any landmarks so I'm sending responders to the right place?"

"It's a blue house," she says and I hear a muffled crash in the background. "We're by the enormous fir tree, the one with the swing."

Got it. I toggle to the unit screen. Two patrols in the area. I select Officer 12 and Officer 04, dispatch code 459B, suspicious person/possible burglary in progress. My cursor hovers over the send button for half a second while I listen for breathing, for danger.

"Are you inside the home right now?"

"Yes. We're—" She breaks off, whispering. "We're in the bedroom."

Good. Distance buys time.

"Are you able to lock the door?"

"It's locked." Her voice splinters again. "Marvin? Did you lock it?"

A man cuts in, low and irritated. "I locked it, Sheryl. Stop yelling."

Sheryl. Marvin. I note their names in the call narrative. I type with my left hand while my right toggles to the audio pane to record key phrases. Five years in Island County taught me to do three things at once or drown.

"Sheryl," I say gently, "you're doing great. I need you to stay on the line with me. I've already notified officers. Can you tell me what you heard?"

"A crash." She swallows, loud in my ear. "Like someone opened the cabinet doors. And—" Another sound. A scrape. "I heard... scratching. Like nails."

"Okay. When did you hear it start?"

"Just now. We were watching the news and then—" Her voice spikes. "Marvin, why do you have a gun?"

I blink once. Slow.

In the background, Marvin says, "Because there might be someone in our house."

"What do you mean because there might be someone in our house?" she hisses, hot and sharp now. "Since when do you have a gun? You said you didn't like guns."

"I never said that."

"You literally said that on our first date."

"Sheryl, not now."

My fingers keep moving.

I send the units, flip to responder notes, and add a firearm caution for the officers. If Marvin's armed and scared, the call just changed shape.

"Sheryl," I cut in, "I hear you. I'm going to need both of you to focus until the officers get on scene, okay? We can handle the relationship talk later."

Silence for a beat. Then a breathy, "Okay."

"Marvin, do not go looking for anyone. I need you both to stay in a safe place until officers arrive."

He mutters something that sounds like agreement. I log it. I also log the other thing I heard beneath it, fear. People who decide to arm themselves in a panic are almost always scared first and rational second.

Another scrape. Closer.

Sheryl's breath turns jagged. "It's still in there."

"Okay. You're safe behind a locked door. I want you to stay where it's safe. Can you tell me if you can see out the bedroom window? Is there any movement outside?"

"No. The curtains are—" She makes a strangled sound. "Oh my god, what if someone's outside too?"

"Right now we don't know what is going on," I say. "That's why we sent officers. Don't go explore the house. Don't go looking for trouble. You're not alone."

I pull open the call history overlay. Cedar Harbor has two previous noise complaints in the last year. One is tagged "wildlife disturbance." That pings a memory from the notes: *neighbor reported raccoons getting into crawl spaces on this street.*

I keep it to myself for the moment. Panic and possibility can be a kinder leash than dismissiveness.

"Florence," Sheryl whispers. Her voice is closer now, like she's hunched over the phone. "My hands are shaking."

"I know." I toggle my mic sensitivity down to soften my voice. "Put your feet on the floor for me. Feel how solid it is. Take a slow breath in through your nose, hold, now out."

She follows on the second try. I hear the way her inhale catches first, then loosens.

"Good," I murmur. "You're doing good."

I've said those words thousands of times. I always mean them. Sometimes they're the only thing standing between a caller and the edge.

I flick to the responder ETA. Officer 12 is two minutes out. Officer 04 is three. I note it. I stay calm.

Then Sheryl says, "He's standing at the door."

"Who is?"

"Whoever broke in. They're... on the other side." Her voice pitches higher. "I can hear them."

"Okay," I say slowly. "Do not open the door. Marvin, are you still there?"

"Yes." He sounds annoyed and terrified in equal parts.

"Good. I need you to stay together and stay quiet. Get away from the bedroom door. The officers are almost there."

Sheryl whispers, "Marvin is holding the gun. He says he's going to check the hallway."

"No," I snap, not harsh, but firm. The voice I use when someone's about to do something that'll make paperwork and regret. "Marvin, I need you to stay put. Do not leave the room."

"Lady, I'm not hiding while some creep—"

"Marvin," I cut in, softer but with steel underneath, "if you open that door and it's a person, you could be putting yourself and Sheryl in danger. Stay in the room, it's not worth the risk. Let officers clear the house first."

A beat.

"...fine."

"Thank you."

There's another crash, this one louder. Sheryl yelps. Marvin curses.

"They're in the kitchen!" Sheryl cries.

I'm already on the map. I click to the aerial view, scan for entry points. Back door faces the alley.

"Sheryl, can you tell me what room the bedroom is in relative to the kitchen?"

"Across the hall, on the left. We can see the living room door."

My mind splits the way it always does during a call half on Sheryl's breathing, half on my screens, while a thin thread weaves through memory like a needle.

I'm not thinking about Island County on purpose. I never do. But maybe it's the way Sheryl's fear sounds like it's crouching in her throat. Maybe it's the line Marvin said, some creep in our house, that dredges up old adrenaline.

Or maybe it's because this is my first non-training shift

here, and my brain keeps checking orientation like a compass that doesn't trust north yet.

Townsend Harbor's center is smaller. Softer lights. Bay view through fog. New headset, no squeaky chair.

Why here?

The question rises uninvited, same as it has in every quiet moment since I packed my car.

Truth is, I knew he was here.

A year ago, after the hookup, I stood in that hotel room with his badge in my hand reading *Chief August Calder, Townsend Harbor Police Department* like the words could split me open twice.

Memory wasn't enough after that.

So I researched.

Public records. A few social media breadcrumbs. Nothing illegal. Nothing I couldn't explain if someone asked in the right tone.

I found a daughter. Lilly Calder, except online she used Hart. Her page said bartender, potter, chronic chaos agent. A roommate-wanted post in a local Townsend Harbor group. Cozy house. Bay views. Flexible on pets. Must like clay dust.

Maybe it was chance.

Maybe it was me connecting dots I should have left alone.

Photos tagged at holidays. A few town events. Him in the background once, then again, then enough that I stopped pretending I wasn't looking for him.

I applied for the room anyway.

I told myself it was practical. A cheaper place. A fresh start. Better hours. A smaller department.

I told myself the fact that it was *his* town didn't mean anything.

I told myself I just wanted closure.

Lilly laughed during the video tour and said, "My dad's the local chief, so things stay pretty safe around here. He's nosy as hell, though."

I smiled like that didn't hit me in the sternum.

Signed the lease.

Packed the car.

Moved.

Love can dress itself up as fate if you let it.

Mine did.

It whispered the same thing every time I hesitated:

He found you twice. Maybe this time you're allowed to stay.

Ruth, at the console beside mine, gives me a small nod without looking up from her screen.

I nod back, barely.

"Did you hear?" Sheryl gasps. "They just... laughed?"

I freeze for half a breath.

"Sheryl," I say carefully, "what kind of laugh did it sound like?"

"Like a demon."

Okay. Noted.

Marvin says, "It's probably that damn raccoon. The one from last month."

Sheryl makes a noise halfway between a sob and a furious hiss. "Why didn't you say that earlier?"

"Because you started yelling about the gun!"

"You mean the gun you've been hiding from me for SIX YEARS?"

I pinch the bridge of my nose for a millisecond. This is why I should have a vat of coffee before the first call of the day.

"Wildlife can still be dangerous, especially if it's cornered," I say briskly. "Officers are still going to do a sweep."

"I don't want a raccoon to be the reason I die," Sheryl says.

"You're not going to die," I say. "Are there any pets in the house?"

"Our dog is in the laundry room," Marvin answers.

"Okay. Do you have a dog door and is it open?" I ask.

"Uh." He pauses. "Yeah. It's one of those flap doors."

"So if it is wildlife, it may have entered through that. Still don't open any doors, okay?"

Sheryl breaths hard. "Okay."

I flip to the comms channel and key my mic.

"Officer 12, Dispatch. Confirming possible wildlife disturbance in kitchen. Homeowners secured in bedroom. Firearm in residence, homeowner advised to stand down. Use caution."

The radio crackles back. "Dispatch, 12. Copy. One out."

I log it. I keep my voice low for Sheryl.

"They're almost there."

Silence settles like a held breath.

There's a thump.

Sheryl whispers in horror, "It's eating something."

"Okay." I keep my tone boring because calm is contagious. "Where do you keep the pantry? Is it near the kitchen?"

"Yes," Marvin says, annoyed again. "Lots of snacks. Sheryl says the pantry is her personality."

"Marvin," Sheryl snaps. "Do not blame this on my snacks."

I almost smile, which surprised me. Island County beat the instinct to laugh out of me for a while. Townsend Harbor is already sneaking it back in.

"12, Dispatch. We're at the residence. Making contact."

"Copy."

"Units on scene," the radio crackles. "Dispatch, 12. Copy the homeowner states there's a hide-a-key under the third flowerpot on the left?"

"Affirmative."

"Making entry."

"Dispatch 12, copies, officers clearing. The homeowners are still secured in the bedroom off the kitchen."

"Okay Sheryl, the officers are there and they're coming into your house," I say. "They're using the spare key. You stay exactly where you are, do *not* come out until they tell you its safe."

Sheryl flinches. "Oh god, oh god. I can hear the cops."

"You're okay," I say softly. "They're clearing the house."

"12 to Dispatch, kitchen clear."

Another voice. "04, living room clear."

A pause.

Then a startled, half-laughing, half-exasperated voice. "Uh... Dispatch? Be advised we have... a raccoon. Repeat, raccoon with... what looks like a family-sized bag of potato chips stuck on its head."

Ruth slaps a hand over her mouth beside me, shoulders shaking with silent laughter.

I keep my tone even. "Copy raccoon with snacks. Confirm residence secure?"

"Affirmative. No signs of forced entry. Wildlife issue only."

I nod, annotating the CAD. "Copy."

I turn back to my caller.

"Okay, Sheryl," I say gently, "the officers have cleared the house. It's safe."

She sobs out a breath. "Oh thank God."

"I want you and your husband to step out of the bedroom *slowly* and introduce yourselves to the officers. Put the gun down first. They'll be right outside the door."

Then, "Hi officers, I'm Sheryl... yes, oh my god! Was it really a raccoon? Marvin, did you hear that?"

I hear Marvin mutter, "Told you."

"You have a gun I never knew about, don't start with me."

One of the officers laughs politely. "Ma'am, you're fine. The animal ran back out through the dog door. You're safe now."

I update the incident file and breathe.

"You have had a gun for six years," she says in a tone that promises a conversation that will last until Valentine's Day. "We are not done."

I press my lips together to keep my own laugh from slipping out.

"Oh my God," she sobs. "Oh my god, I'm going to— Marvin, you hid a gun from me for six years, and I almost died because of a raccoon."

"You didn't almost die."

"You don't get to decide that."

"Thank you." Sheryl's voice softens. "Thank you so much."

"You did great," I tell her.

She sniffles a laugh. "So did you. I'm sorry I screamed."

"Don't apologize for being scared," I say. "That's what we're here for."

The line clicks dead.

I lower my headset one ear at a time and exhale.

First call in Townsend Harbor: a near-burglary that isn't, a marital gun revelation, and a chip-hatted raccoon. Perfect.

Ruth leans back in her chair and peers at me like she's watching the tide for a storm.

"King County?" she asks.

I blink. "What?"

"You have that cadence. West Sound dispatchers all sound the same. King, Island, and Snohomish Counties teaches you to take control without sounding mean. That's a skill."

I can feel my cheeks warm. Compliments make me itchy.

"Thanks," I say. "It's... second nature now."

She hums. "Second nature doesn't mean it's easy."

I don't answer.

I can't exactly tell her I left the island because exhaustion won.

Or that I came to Townsend Harbor because obsession did.

So instead, I swivel my chair and square away the call notes.

Wildlife disturbance.

No injuries.

Scene cleared.

Homeowner firearm present.

Suggest animal control follow-up.

I attach the recording. I close the incident.

An hour earlier, I'd stood in Lilly Hart's house with my suitcase still unzipped on the floor, taking in the smell of cinnamon, woodsmoke, and damp clay.

The place felt warm in a way I hadn't let myself want in a long time. Mugs on the windowsill. A sweater tossed over the arm of the couch. A half-finished pottery piece drying on newspaper near the kitchen sink.

Lilly moved through all of it like weather. Leggings, messy bun, talking fast, laughing faster, somehow making space for me in a house she clearly already filled all by herself.

"It's kind of like living alone," she'd said, tossing me a ring of spare keys. "I work all the time and I'm gone half the night. I bartend at Sirens and teach pottery on the side. If I'm not teaching, I'm making stuff and pretending I'm going to fold laundry."

I caught the keys and smiled. "I can live with laundry piles."

"Perfect," she said. "Then we're soulmates."

She grinned when she said it. Easy. Harmless.

And still, something in me pulled tight.

Because I'd told myself this move was about work. About leaving the island. About getting out before I calcified in that dispatch chair and started measuring my life in other people's emergencies.

Standing there in Lilly's house, keys in my hand, I almost believed it.

Then she kept talking while she showed me where the extra blankets were, and I caught a photo on the fridge of her with a dark-haired man in a department polo, both of them squinting into the sun, and my pulse kicked hard enough to make me feel stupid.

Fresh start, my ass.

This was still a choice with teeth.

Warmth spread through my chest anyway, which felt like its own kind of warning.

Because some part of me had come here hoping for distance from the life I left behind.

And some part of me had come here for the exact opposite.

My thoughts cut off when the comm-center door opens.

I look up, and my whole body goes cold first, then hot.

August.

Not in memory.

Not in a bar.

Not half-dressed in hotel light with his mouth on my throat and my name still trapped behind my teeth.

In uniform.

Navy. Silver collar pins. Service weapon on his hip.

Chief August Calder, in the flesh, walking into the room like I didn't move my entire life to the town stamped on his badge.

For one stupid second I forget how to breathe.

I know that face too well now.

I know the hard line of his jaw under morning stubble.

I know what his hands feel like.

I know the sound he makes when he's trying to stay in control and failing.

I know exactly how his voice drops when he says mine.

My pulse trips so hard it hurts.

No.

No, no, no.

Not here. Not my first real shift. Not in front of everyone.

He steps fully into dispatch and the room shifts around him. Conversation lowers. Chairs stop squeaking. Ruth glances up from her screen.

Authority does that.

August does it worse.

He looks bigger than he did in Seattle. Or maybe this room is smaller. Maybe fluorescent light is crueler than hotel lamps. Maybe memory never gets the weight of a person right.

His hair is combed back. More gray at the temples than I remember. His shoulders fill the uniform like it was tailored for him and him alone.

A flash hits low in my body before I can stop it.

Hotel wall.

His hand under my dress.

That look in his eyes right before he asked if I was sure.

Heat sweeps through me so fast I have to lock my knees.

Absolutely not.

Not now.

I shove it down and fix my face just as his gaze sweeps the room.

It lands on me.

And stays.

Not long. Not enough for anyone else to clock it.

Long enough for me to feel that old, private burn spark alive under my skin.

There's no visible reaction on his face. No double take. No crack.

Just that watchful stillness.

Like he's placing a voice he's heard before.

Like he knows I matter and doesn't yet know why.

"Chief, meet our new dispatcher," Ruth says, cheerful and oblivious. "Florence Lockhart. Transfer from Island County."

My name in the room feels like a live wire.

I stand because sitting would look stranger. My palms are damp. I wipe one against my slacks under the console where nobody can see.

August crosses toward me, unhurried.

Controlled.

Command in a body.

He holds out his hand.

"Chief Calder," he says, professional, even. Then, after half a beat, "August's fine."

Liar.

Nothing about him is fine.

I take his hand.

Warm. Rough. Familiar in a way that makes my stomach drop clean through the floor.

The handshake is brief. Polite.

Exactly what it should be.

His eyes are the problem.

They hold mine one second too long, and I feel every version of him stack on top of each other at once. Officer in the rain. Stranger in the bar. The man asleep beside me while I stood there with his badge in my hand and panicked.

"Welcome to Townsend Harbor," he says.

His voice hits me low and deep, all that same rough velvet, and my body recognizes him before my face can do anything useful.

"Thank you," I manage. My voice is steady enough to pass. "Happy to be here."

The lie tastes expensive.

Something shifts behind his eyes. Not recognition exactly. Not yet. More like friction.

Like his instincts are knocking against a locked door.

"Island County to here's a change," he says.

"It is," I say, and I hate how true that sounds.

Ruth jumps in, saving me. "She's already handling calls like she's been here six months."

"Good," August says, but he's still looking at me when he says it.

I make myself let go of his hand.

He lets me.

Slowly enough to feel deliberate.

Fast enough no one else would notice.

"Glad to have you," he says.

Chief to dispatcher. Clean. Appropriate. Nothing to report.

My skin burns anyway.

He gives Ruth a quick nod, asks something about shift coverage, and the room starts moving again around us, sound coming back in pieces. Keyboards. Radios. Someone laughing at the far console.

Normal.

I sit down because my knees are one bad thought from giving out.

I put my headset back on with steady hands I do not currently possess.

On my screen, the call queue updates.

A blinking line.

A routine noise complaint.

A welfare check pending.

My whole life, reduced to boxes and timestamps while Chief August Calder stands ten feet away discussing staffing like he hasn't had his mouth on my body.

I stare at the monitor until the words sharpen.

No one here knows I came because of him.

No one here knows I stood in a hotel room with his lanyard in my hand and rewired my entire future around a name.

No one here knows I told myself it was closure, then packed my car anyway.

"Dispatch?" Ruth says quietly, glancing over.

I blink once. "Yep. I'm good."

Another lie.

Cleaner this time.

Across the room, August laughs at something one of the

officers says. Low. Brief. Familiar enough to slide under my ribs like a blade.

I answer the next call on the first ring.

"9-1-1, where is your emergency?"

My voice comes out calm.

Like I am not falling apart in the exact town I chose for him.

I stay still after he walks away, headset on, hands near my keyboard, posture perfect.

Inside, I'm a live wire.

Every nerve in my body is lit up and crackling. I can still feel his hand in mine. Still hear that voice in my ear from a hotel room a year ago and from five years before that in the rain, somehow both versions of him layered together until I can't separate one from the other.

And when I catch the subtle shift in his shoulders, the set of his mouth, I know.

He remembers too.

Maybe not all of it. Maybe not the whole story. Maybe not my name from the wreck, or the years I carried him around like a splinter under my skin.

But the hotel room?

That, he remembers.

Every second.

And this time there's no anonymous bar. No fake rules. No elevator doors closing over a bad idea I can pretend never happened.

This time it's fluorescent lights and dispatch consoles and my real name on a schedule.

This time it's complicated.

This time it's real.

August's gaze sweeps the room as he moves, and even now I can't help noticing the way he does it. He doesn't drift. He doesn't perform authority. He just has it. Every step deliberate. Every glance doing two things at once.

His attention catches on me again.

A flicker touches the corner of his mouth. Barely there. Not a smile. Something smaller. More dangerous.

"By the way," he says, voice low and even, "nice work on that call."

The words are clean. Professional. Exactly what a chief should say to a dispatcher on a solid first shift.

It still lands deep.

Because he means it.

No condescension. No forced encouragement. No good girl dressed up as workplace praise.

Just respect.

My throat goes dry anyway.

"Thank you," I say, and I hate how much that tiny approval steadies something in me.

He nods once and moves on to Ruth's console.

"Morning."

"Morning, Chief," Ruth says, eyes still on her screen. Then she jerks her chin toward me. "She's good."

"She seems it," he says.

I stare at my monitor and pretend I'm not listening while they talk staffing, Harbor Days traffic, a run of petty thefts near Sirens, and somebody calling in three times this week about teenagers racing trucks near the marina.

His voice moves through the room like a low current.

I keep my face neutral and click through call notes like my pulse isn't trying to punch through my ribs.

I don't care, I tell myself, the words neat and practiced.

I don't date coworkers.

I don't date cops.

I absolutely do not date the chief of police in the town I just moved to, especially when half the reason I moved here was a name on a lanyard and a story I told myself until it sounded like destiny.

And yes, he is older. A lot older. Which is fine in theory. Very mature. Very modern. Women can do what they want.

In practice, the problem is not his age.

The problem is that one look at him in uniform and my body immediately remembers exactly what he tastes like.

"Florence."

My name in his mouth snaps my attention up before I can stop it.

He's already half-turned toward the door, talking to Ruth, not me. Just clarifying a shift question.

Still, heat climbs my neck like he touched me.

Ridiculous.

Humiliating.

Completely real.

He finishes, gives the room one last glance, and heads out.

The door swings shut behind him.

I let out a breath so slow no one notices.

Ruth side-eyes me without looking away from her screen. "You okay?"

I click into the next call like I didn't just have my entire nervous system rewired in under three minutes.

"Yep," I say.

Lie.

The call queue blinks.

I straighten in my chair, adjust my headset, and answer on the first ring.

"9-1-1, where is your emergency?"

With the door firmly closed, Ruth swings her chair around, her eyes meeting mine expectantly when I hang up the call.

"Well," she says, voice dry as driftwood.

"What?" I ask, aiming for neutral.

Ruth adjusts her glasses with one finger. "You settling in okay? New town, new center... new everything?"

I let out a small laugh. "Yeah. Mostly. Still getting my bearings."

She nods like that confirms something for her. "Good. Townsend Harbor's small. People are friendly." A beat. "Sometimes too friendly."

I blink, caught off guard when she asks, "Anyone special back on the island?"

It doesn't feel invasive, exactly. It's the kind of question dispatchers ask between calls. Half icebreaker, half checking if you're okay.

"Nope," I say, tapping a key without looking at it. "Deleted every dating app before I got on the ferry. I'm hitting reset. No drama. No complications. No romance. I just want peace and a paycheck for a while."

Ruth hums, amused. "That's what everybody says before this place sneaks up on them."

"Sneaks up?" I echo.

She shrugs and turns back to her screens. "Love tends to come in through the back door around here. Never the one you're guarding."

Before I can answer, the line on my console flashes red.

Ruth smirks. "And there's your next crisis. Welcome to Townsend Harbor."

I readjust my headset, roll my shoulders once, and accept the call with a click.

"9-1-1, where is your emergency?"

The world narrows.

The room falls away, leaving only the caller's voice in my ear and my fingers hovering over the keys. My heart steadies into that quiet, ruthless calm I know how to wear.

I'm here to do a job, and I'm good at it.

I'm not getting distracted.

Not by fog. Not by loneliness. And definitely not by the deeply distracting, way-too-old-for-me chief of police who just lit up my entire nervous system like a live wire.

Again.

Ruth can keep her back-door prophecies.

I've got mine bolted shut.

...Right?

The caller starts crying.

The day keeps moving.

And somewhere between the screens and the voices and the newness of this town, I feel the smallest spark catch in my chest.

Small as a lantern flame. Stubborn as the tide.

Maybe this really is a new beginning.

I swallow, lock in on the call, and keep going.

Because that's what dispatchers do.

We keep people alive.
We keep ourselves moving.

EIGHT
AUGUST

THE THING they don't tell you about becoming Chief of Police is that half the job is paperwork and the other half is pretending paperwork doesn't piss you off.

I drop a stack of budget reports onto my desk with a thud. The building hums with morning energy. Phones ringing. Warrants printing. Turner arguing with the coffee machine again.

My inbox is already full, and it's not even eight.

Council wants numbers.

The mayor wants updates.

The public wants miracles.

And we're five officers short during Harbor Days, which is basically the Super Bowl of small-town chaos. Lost kids. Drunk tourists. Petty theft. A raccoon crime spree that somehow became my problem by sunrise.

Townsend Harbor has always been a little sleepy and a little feral.

I've learned to like the balance.

I sit, crack my neck, and open the first report.

Try to focus.

Try.

Because the only thing I can see is the new dispatcher in that headset.

Florence.

Florence Lockhart.

Her voice is lodged under my ribs.

Not familiar.

Branded.

The second it came over comms, every muscle in my back locked like I'd taken a hit.

One year later, and I still remember the exact pitch of her moan.

I shouldn't.

But I do.

There's something about her voice even now. Low, warm, steadily getting under my skin and staying there. It did in Seattle. It does now.

I wasn't ready for any of it this morning.

I walked into dispatch expecting routine. Check logs. Ask about Harbor Days routes. Pretend the coffee didn't taste like wet cardboard.

Then I saw her.

And I knew.

Not maybe. Not close enough. Her.

From the hotel bar. The elevator. The room I still think about when I'm alone and pissed off at myself for thinking about it.

Her.

I'd know the line of her neck in a blackout.

I'd know her mouth anywhere.

I lean back in my chair and drag a hand over my jaw. I didn't shave this morning. Not a choice. I was late. Tired. Forty-three. Running on too little sleep and too much responsibility.

Old enough to know better than to let a woman derail my focus.

Especially a woman who works down the hall.

Especially one whose hand I shook thirty minutes ago while every nerve ending in my body lit up like a fuse.

So far I'm doing a hell of a job.

I stand and grab the shift schedules. Patrol first. Work first.

The sooner I bury myself in Harbor Days staffing, the sooner I stop thinking about dark hair, steady eyes, and the way she looked at me like she recognized me and wished she didn't.

My body, apparently, did not get the memo.

By the time I hit the hallway, I'm hard enough to mutter a curse under my breath and adjust my belt like a goddamn teenager.

Jesus Christ. Get it together.

I force my brain toward patrol coverage, overtime numbers, ferry traffic, anything but the memory of her in that hotel room.

Anything but her mouth.

Anything but the way she said my name this morning like it cost her something.

I step into the break room.

Turner is fighting the coffee machine like it insulted his family. He looks up when I come in.

"Chief. Machine's broken."

I flinch.

Not visibly, I hope.

But enough that he pauses.

Because for half a second I'm not in the break room. I'm back at the dispatch console hearing her say, *Chief,* and feeling it hit somewhere it shouldn't.

I clear my throat. "Fine. Leave it. I'll put in a maintenance request."

Turner blinks, suspicious but smart enough not to ask.

"It's not broken," Patel says from her locker, buttoning her uniform shirt. "You just don't know how to use it."

Turner scowls. "It beeped at me."

"That doesn't mean anything. My cat beeps at me."

"How does your cat beep?"

"Good morning," I cut in, dropping the schedules onto the table. "Let's stay civil before I taser somebody."

Turner grins. "You don't even carry your taser."

"Don't test me." I point at the machine. "Both of you. Stop harassing the appliance."

They snort and settle.

Good officers. Younger than me by at least a decade, but solid.

I shift the paperwork in my hand and use the movement to discreetly adjust myself one more time.

"Morning briefing," I say. "Squad room. Now."

They follow.

I do not look toward dispatch.

If I do, I know exactly who I'll be looking for.

"Quick updates before you roll out." I set the schedules down and keep it tight. "Harbor Days starts today, so expect heavier foot traffic downtown. Watch the crosswalks near vendor row. Lantern ceremony rehearsal starts at six, barriers go up by the harbor at five-thirty. Animal control is coordinating with us on the raccoon issue. Don't ask."

A couple of laughs.

"And one more thing. We've got a new dispatcher. Florence Lockhart. Transfer from Island County. Solid experience. Make sure you introduce yourselves and make her feel welcome."

Turner lifts his brows. "Heard her on comms already. She sounds sharp."

Harmless comment.

Normal comment.

So why does it irritate the hell out of me?

I keep my face neutral. "She is."

Patel nods. "I'll stop by after shift. Always good to know the voice keeping you alive."

"Exactly."

Turner clears his throat. "She seemed nice."

Nice.

I give him a short nod and move on before I say something I regret.

"She handled a burglary call clean this morning. Fast routing. Good notes. She'll be an asset."

I dismiss them and they scatter for coffee, radios, jackets.

I tell myself my reaction is normal.

She's new. They're curious.

That's all.

I sit back down at my desk and stare at paperwork I'm not reading.

Budgets. Patrol routes. Councilwoman Alder at three. Harbor Days timeline. Staff shortages.

My radio crackles.

Then her voice threads through the static.

"Unit 12, respond to—"

I freeze.

Just for a second.

Long enough for my pen to stop moving and the muscle in my thigh to tighten hard.

Christ.

That voice.

Warm. Level. Certain.

It lands like a hand on the back of my neck.

I shouldn't be reacting to a voice.

Not at my age. Not in this building.

But my body doesn't care about rank, age, or common sense.

I shift in my chair, irritated with myself.

I don't even know how old she is. Mid-twenties, maybe. Younger than she looked in the hotel room somehow. Young enough that I have no business thinking about anything but her work.

And after last time? No.

I learned that lesson.

Dating inside the department was a mistake I cleaned up quietly and professionally, and I swore I wouldn't do it again.

That's why, the last few years, if I wanted company, I drove to Seattle. Port Angeles. Neutral ground. No overlap. No fallout.

Or that was the plan.

Truth is, I haven't had the bandwidth to want much of anything in a long time. Not between the department, the town, and trying to be a decent father.

Then Florence walks into dispatch and every system in my body goes sideways.

I don't know her story.

I don't know her reasons for coming here.

I don't know if she remembers me, even though that look on her face this morning says she probably does.

It shouldn't matter.

She's staff.

She's new.

She's off-limits in every direction that counts.

I scrub a hand over my face and force myself back to the reports.

Doesn't work.

I keep seeing her at the console. Hair pulled back. Voice calm while a caller panicked. Hands moving over the keyboard like she'd been here for years.

Then she looked at me and the room changed.

My radio crackles again, reminding me where I am. Who I am.

Chief first.

Man second.

Whatever the hell is happening under my skin can stay there.

A knock hits the doorframe.

Patel stands there with her tablet tucked under one arm. "Chief. Got a minute?"

"Come in."

She steps in, all business. "Update on the Willow Lane burglary. Homeowner's camera finally uploaded. I tagged the footage to your queue. Same build as the two by the harbor."

This. Good. Useful. Concrete.

"Loop in Marshal and bump patrols in that corridor."

"Already did."

I nod. "Good work."

She hesitates. "Dispatch added notes to the burglary call. Clean work. Units routed in under fifteen seconds."

I keep my expression flat. "I heard it."

"She's quick. Whoever took that call."

"She's trained."

Patel taps her thumb against the tablet. "Town's restless

today. Bigger Harbor Days crowd than expected. Turner wants another unit near the ferry terminal at dusk."

"Assign Ruiz."

"On it."

She turns to go, then pauses. "You all good, Chief?"

I lift a brow. "Why wouldn't I be?"

"You've been..." she searches for a word she can say without getting herself in trouble, "...quiet."

"That's called working," I say dryly.

She smirks. "Fair enough. Eat something. Turner says you've been running on fumes since yesterday."

"Tell Turner to worry about his own blood sugar."

"Copy that."

She leaves.

I stare at the paperwork again.

Still nothing sticks.

The radio scans channels on the corner of my desk. Unit locations. Status checks. Routine traffic.

Then Florence again.

"Unit 14, respond Code Two to a possible domestic verbal, Maple Street. Caller standing by outside."

Every time her voice comes over the air, something in me locks onto it before my brain catches up.

Listening isn't the problem. Everybody listens.

It's the rest of it.

The way my body reacts before I can shut it down.

I turn the volume down one notch. Barely.

Enough to feel like I'm doing something.

Chief first. Man later.

I head for the break room.

Turner is draped across a chair like posture is optional. Henson's stirring powdered creamer into his coffee. They both look up.

"Chief," Turner says, brightening. "Coffee's still broken."

"I know."

"And we're hungry."

"Not my problem."

Henson hands me a mug. "Made extra."

I nod. "Thanks."

Turner wiggles his eyebrows. "So... you heading over to dispatch later?"

"No."

He frowns. "Why not?"

"Because unlike you, I have a job."

"Uh-huh." He leans back. "Working real hard, I bet. Making sure the new dispatcher feels welcomed and—"

"Turner."

He keeps going.

"I mean, she's cute. Nothing wrong with noticing."

"Stop."

He blinks, thrown by my tone.

I set my mug down slowly. "You want to talk about a coworker, you talk about her work. Not her body. Not her face. Not like that."

Turner shifts, uncomfortable. "I didn't mean anything by it."

"And if somebody talked about your daughter that way?"

My voice stays low. Even.

His expression changes immediately.

Jaw tight. Eyes flicking away.

"Yeah," I say. "Exactly."

Henson goes very quiet and studies his coffee.

Turner lifts both hands. "Okay. Sorry, Chief. Won't happen again."

"Good. She's new. We look out for our people. Respect comes first."

He nods, chastened.

The room settles. Chairs creak. Somebody stirs coffee.

My pulse still hasn't.

Because the second I defended her, something in me tightened low and mean.

Territorial.

And I hate that I know exactly what it is.

Maybe it's because she's new.

Maybe it's because I don't tolerate that kind of talk in my department.

Maybe it's because the idea of some guy trying to work her makes me want to put my fist through drywall.

None of that matters.

What matters is I know better.

She's staff. I don't do messy. End of story.

That's what I tell myself.

I head toward my office.

Then turn left.

Not toward dispatch. Just the hallway. Maintenance log's that way.

I'm not lying.

I will check it.

Eventually.

I can't see her from here, too many reflections in the glass, too much distance.

But I know exactly where she's sitting.

That knowledge lands low in my gut.

Stupid.

Distracting.

Reckless.

I force myself to turn away and go back to work.

Town first.

Work first.

Anything else waits.

But the whole walk back to my office, I can still hear her voice.

NINE
FLORENCE

THE SOUND of unpacking should not be this emotional.

But every zipper I pull, every drawer I slide open, every folded sweater I stack on a shelf feels like a small surrender. A little proof that I'm here. That I did this. That I drove my whole life across water and into a town I told myself was a fresh start.

My chest still feels tight anyway.

Like I'm racing something I can't see.

Like there's an inevitable thing moving toward me and I'm just buying time until it catches up.

It's probably adrenaline. Residual shock from seeing August this morning and having my nervous system lit up like a downed power line.

"August," I whisper to the empty room, saying his name quietly just to hear how it sounds in my own mouth.

It does something to me instantly.

Butterflies hatch low in my stomach, stupid and bright and disloyal.

I press my lips together and shove a stack of t-shirts into the dresser harder than necessary.

Lilly Hart's house is small, tucked behind the marina in a little pocket of quiet that feels almost impossible considering how close it is to downtown. Two-story craftsman, warm wood floors, squeaky stair on the third step, and a backyard with a converted shed she casually referred to as "the studio" like she wasn't underselling the hell out of it.

The place smells like brown sugar, laundry detergent, and clay.

When we first talked, she mentioned pottery in that offhand way people mention hobbies they're kind of good at.

Turns out she's not kind of good.

Bowls, mugs, and half-finished pieces are everywhere, and not in a cluttered, cutesy way. In a real way. In a hands-that-know-what-they're-doing way. Glazed pieces drying on one shelf. Student work lined up near the kitchen window. A gorgeous blue pitcher on top of the fridge that looks like something I'd have to save up for if I saw it in a boutique.

I didn't expect any of this.

I also didn't expect Lilly.

She's the kind of person who fills a room without trying. Curly hair, bright eyes, big laugh, leggings and socks and some oversized sweater with a coffee stain on the sleeve like she got dressed while solving three other problems. Her energy is all warmth and motion and easy charm.

I didn't expect to like her so quickly.

I definitely didn't expect the weird stab of jealousy that comes with it.

It's not fair. She hasn't done anything except be kind to me.

But she belongs here in a way I don't. You can feel it in the way she moves through the house. In the way she says things like *my bar shift, my town, my people.* In the way she says *my dad* without flinching, without thinking, like some people get to claim belonging out loud and trust it'll stay.

And I want that so badly it makes me ugly in places nobody can see.

By the time I've emptied two suitcases and created several small piles that definitely count as "organizing" if I squint, Lilly appears in my doorway balancing a giant metal mixing bowl against her hip.

Her curls are piled on top of her head. There's flour on one cheek. Her grin is feral.

"Okay," she says, like she's making an announcement. "Your initiation into Casa de Chaos is officially underway."

I blink at the bowl. "Is that... cookie dough?"

She gasps. "Wow. Rude. It is not just cookie dough."

She shifts the bowl toward me with ceremony. "It is brown butter cookie dough with pretzels, chocolate chips, mini marshmallows, espresso powder, and a little bit of love."

She pauses.

"And maybe accidental paprika, but we don't talk about that."

I stare at her.

Then I take the spoon she offers and taste it.

My eyes widen. "Holy shit."

She points at me triumphantly. "RIGHT?"

That's when I notice the pizza box tucked under her other arm.

Her smile gets even wider somehow. "And dinner."

I laugh before I can stop myself.

She drops onto the fuzzy rug at the foot of my bed like she's done it a hundred times, sets the bowl between us, flips open the pizza, and pats the floor.

"So," she says. "Roommate bonding time. Tell me your life story."

My stomach flips and I snort. "Absolutely not. You came in way too hot."

She clutches her chest. "Excuse me? I bring you sugar, carbs, and emotional intimacy on your first night and this is the thanks I get?"

I sit down across from her, stretching my legs out, suddenly aware of how easy this feels and not trusting it at all.

"Life story is, like, third-bottle-of-wine territory," I say. "At minimum."

"Fine." She points a pizza crust at me like a tiny wand. "Medium trauma only. We build up."

That gets a real laugh out of me, and something in my chest loosens a fraction.

I settle cross-legged on the rug. Behind me, my half-unpacked life is spread across the room in little chaotic islands. Sweaters. Books. Toiletries. A lamp I haven't plugged in yet. A box of tarot decks half-hidden under a cardigan.

Lilly clocks it immediately and grins.

"Your vibe is very hot-girl witness protection," she says.

I bark out a laugh. "I just moved in."

"Mm-hmm. And yet somehow the room already says she has secrets and one excellent candle."

I glance toward the cardboard box where my tarot deck is peeking out.

"...That is wildly specific."

"And accurate?"

"Annoyingly, yes."

She beams like she won something.

We eat on the floor like we're at a sleepover instead of two adult women who just met, and I can feel how fast we're skipping past the polite part. It should make me pull back.

It sort of does.

But it also feels... nice.

Lilly chews, swallows, and points at me again. "Okay. Real question. Tell me something about you that isn't your job."

I wipe my fingers on a napkin, buying myself a second.

Something about me.

Something true.

Something that won't crack me open on the floor of my new bedroom while my new roommate watches.

"I grew up in North Seattle," I say. "Mostly with my mom and my sister."

Lilly nods, listening. Really listening. Not waiting for her turn.

"We were... a lot," I add with a soft laugh. "My sister was the loud one. Big personality. Big opinions. Zero volume control. She could make a friend in a checkout line and start an argument before she got to the register."

Lilly snorts. "I know exactly that type."

"Yeah." I smile, and for a second it feels easy. "She was chaos in human form."

The smile slips on its own.

I look down at my slice.

"It's just me now," I say. "Me and my grandma, mostly."

Lilly's expression gentles. "Family stuff?"

I nod once.

"My mom died seven years ago," I say.

The words are old enough now that I can say them without choking. Most of the time.

Lilly goes still, soft and quiet.

"And my sister died last year."

That one still lands like a punch every time.

The room doesn't get bigger after I say it. People always expect grief to echo. Mine doesn't. It gets close. Intimate. Sharp.

Lilly sets her pizza down.

"Florence," she says, low and steady.

"It was sudden," I say, because if I stop too long I'll feel too much. "Violent. Stupid. The kind of thing that happens to strangers until it happens to yours."

My throat tightens and I stare at the grease-dark cardboard between us.

"I'm sorry," Lilly says.

No big performance. No reaching for some shiny thing to make it easier.

Just the words.

I nod.

"After that, Island County got... unbearable," I say. "Too small. Too many people who meant well. Too many places where everything reminded me of who I was before."

I huff a laugh with no humor in it. "Every road had a memory attached to it. Every shift. Every diner. Every gas station. It felt like the whole county kept watching me break and calling it community."

Lilly winces in recognition.

"Yeah," she says quietly. "Small towns do that."

The understanding in her voice makes me look up.

She shrugs one shoulder, eyes dropping to the crust in her hand. "Different reasons, but I know the feeling."

I wait.

She notices, smiles a little. "My parents were young when they had me. Like, alarmingly young. They loved each other, I think. Or maybe they loved the idea of each other. Hard to tell when you're the kid in the backseat listening to them fight over who forgot the diaper bag."

I go still.

She says it lightly, but there's something old under it. Something worn smooth by repetition.

"They were on-again, off-again for years," she says. "Lots of moving. Lots of fresh starts. New apartments, new schools, new rules, same fights in a different kitchen." She huffs a laugh. "It did a number on my ability to know what healthy looks like."

"God," I say softly. "I can imagine."

"Yeah." She smiles, but it's crooked. "For a long time I thought love was supposed to feel like chaos. If I wasn't a little sick with anxiety, maybe it wasn't real enough."

That lands deeper than I want it to.

Because haven't I done my own version of that?

Haven't I confused obsession with fate and called it romantic because the truth sounds worse?

Lilly keeps going, voice softer now. "But they grew up. Eventually. It took forever, but they did. They stopped trying to be everything to each other and got way better at being parents to me. Separate houses. Better boundaries. Less drama. More honesty."

She shrugs. "It got calmer."

I let out a breath I didn't realize I was holding.

"Honestly," she says, smiling for real this time, "it saved me."

There it is. The real thing under the joke.

I nod slowly. "That doesn't sound boring. That sounds hard-won."

"Exactly." She lifts her slice in salute. "I'm deeply suspicious of grand gestures and extremely turned on by emotional consistency."

A laugh bursts out of me, surprising and sharp.

She points the pizza at me. "I'm serious. Flowers are nice. You know what's hotter? Someone saying they'll be there at six and showing up at five-fifty-eight."

"Okay," I say, still laughing. "That might be the healthiest thing I've ever heard."

"It's called growth," she says solemnly. "And therapy. Mostly therapy."

We grin at each other, and the heaviness in the room shifts. Not gone. Just gentler.

She says *my dad* a minute later while telling some story about him helping her change a tire in the rain and lecturing her the whole time, and I feel that ugly little twist under my ribs again.

I know who her dad is.

I know what his hands feel like on my body.

I know what he sounds like in the dark.

Lilly gets to roll her eyes and call him dramatic. Gets to say *my dad* and laugh. Gets to belong to *him* in daylight.

I smile at the right parts of the story and hate myself a little for the jealousy.

Not because of what she has.

Because of what I came here wanting.

I pick at my crust and force my face neutral.

"Island County was supposed to be my stable place," I say after a while. "Slow. Safe. Something I could build a life in."

I stare past her at the boxes stacked by the closet.

"But after my sister... I don't know. It all got too loud and too tight at the same time. I needed somewhere that didn't have memory baked into every wall."

I pause, then add with a small shrug, "I needed to be new for a minute."

It isn't the whole truth.

It isn't even most of it.

No answer. Can't exactly say I left the island because grief Harbored me out and obsession pulled me south.

Can't say I saw a name on a lanyard a year ago and built a whole future around it.

Lilly watches me for a second, then nods. "That makes sense."

I almost flinch at how easily she gives me room to lie.

We sit in a quiet that doesn't feel awkward. The house hums around us. Pipes settling. Fridge clicking on. Wind nudging at the side of the house.

Then Lilly bumps my knee with hers, grin sneaking back in.

"Okay," she says. "Something lighter before we both spiral into the pizza. What did baby Florence want to be when she grew up?"

I smile despite myself. "An artist and later that got a little more specific. I wanted to be a tarot card artist and reader."

Her eyes go huge. "Shut up."

I laugh. "I'm serious."

"That's amazing."

"It's kind of silly."

"It is absolutely not silly," she says. "Do you still read?"

I hesitate, because there's something intimate about saying yes to that too.

"Sometimes," I say. "For friends. I mean, not professionally."

Lilly drops her crust back into the box and points at me like she's issuing an order. "Teach me."

"What?"

"Teach me tarot. Right now. Please. I've always wanted to learn, but every book is like here are six thousand correspondences and also your childhood wounds."

I grin. "That's... not inaccurate."

"Come on," she says, scooting forward. "I'm a very willing student. A little chaotic. But willing."

I stand and dig through the box labeled ESSENTIALS until I find my favorite deck.

Worn edges. Soft matte finish. Familiar weight in my palm.

Just holding it settles something in me.

Lilly claps. "Oh my god, this is happening."

I sit back down across from her and hand her the deck. "Okay. Shuffle however feels natural."

She stares at the cards like they've personally challenged her.

Then she tries.

Half the deck slides sideways and spills into her lap.

She gasps. "I'm already failing."

"You're not failing," I say, laughing. "You're just dramatic."

She gathers the cards back up, tries again, drops three more.

"Florence."

"Lilly."

"Why are they slippery?"

"Because they know you're scared."

She narrows her eyes. "Rude."

I'm still smiling when she finally hands the deck back.

"Okay," I say, settling cross-legged. "We're doing a simple three-card pull. Past, present, future. But you're going to tell me what you see first. Intuition before textbook."

Her mouth falls open. "I have to do the reading?"

"Yes."

"On my first day? I don't even go here."

That makes me laugh, warm and easy. "You'll be fine. Tarot is mostly intuition and pattern recognition. The rest is just practice."

She presses a hand to her chest. "Professor Florence believes in me."

"Don't make me revoke it."

She giggles and scoots closer.

We sit with our knees almost touching, cards between us, and for a weird little moment it feels like I've stepped into someone else's life. Someone softer. Someone who moved to a pretty town and got a nice roommate and has no secret agenda bleeding through the floorboards.

I pull the first card and lay it down.

Six of Swords.

Lilly leans in. "Okay. Boat. Sad vibes. Pointy little flags."

I laugh. "Those are swords."

"I know what they are literally," she says. "I'm giving you mood."

"Fair. What's the mood?"

She studies it longer than I expect.

Then she says, "Leaving."

My smile fades a little.

She keeps looking at the card. "Like... someone hit their limit and had to go. Maybe not because they wanted to, but because staying was worse."

The words go through me clean.

My breath catches.

I keep my voice light anyway. "That's very good."

"So I'm right?"

"Pretty much. Six of Swords is transition. Moving away from something hard. It's not always happy, but it's movement."

She glances up at me, grin returning. "So, like... a woman fleeing her old life to a mysterious coastal town with fog and emotional problems?"

I snort. "Something like that."

"And boats," she adds, tapping the card. "Important detail."

I shake my head and flip the second card.

The Lovers.

Lilly makes a sound like she's just been handed gossip. "Oh, hello."

"It's not always romantic," I say automatically.

She deadpans at me. "There are two naked people on the card."

"It's symbolic."

"Of what, Florence? Tits?"

I laugh so hard I almost drop the deck.

Then she sobers a little and looks at the image again. "Okay, for real." She traces the edge of the card without touching it. "This feels like a choice. Or... not even a choice. More like a connection you don't get to pretend isn't happening."

Heat flickers low and immediate in my belly.

Hotel wall against my back.

His mouth on my neck.

His hand around my throat, not hurting, just holding.

The rough scrape of his voice against my ear.

Mine.

And now that same voice saying my name across a dispatch floor in broad daylight.

I blink hard and look down at the card.

"Very good," I say, a little too quickly. "Yes. It can be romance, but it's also alignment. A choice. A major connection."

Lilly narrows her eyes, delighted. "Why do I feel like I accidentally dragged up a secret?"

"You didn't."

"Mm-hmm."

"Keep reading or I'll kick you out of my room."

She cackles.

I flip the third card.

The Tower.

Lilly goes still. "Well, that looks like terrible news."

"It's not terrible," I say.

She peers at the falling figures. "It's definitely not spa-day energy."

I laugh under my breath. "What do you get from it?"

She takes her time.

Then she says, quieter now, "Something breaking that needed to break."

My pulse kicks.

She points toward the top of the tower. "Like... a truth getting struck by lightning. Or a life built on the wrong thing finally giving out."

I don't say anything right away.

Because she's right.

Too right.

The card seems to hum on the floor between us.

I point to the two figures falling. "See them?"

She leans in. "Yeah."

"One looks like they jumped," I say. "One looks like they got pushed."

Her eyes widen. "Oh."

"When change comes," I say softly, "sometimes you choose it. Sometimes it chooses you."

The words sit there between us longer than I mean them to.

Because something in me already knows.

The shift started before I got here.

Maybe the second I saw his name.

Maybe the second I signed the lease.

Maybe the second I looked him in the face this morning and he looked back like he remembered every inch of me.

Lilly blows out a breath. "Damn, Florence. Tarot is intense."

I smile and gather the cards slowly. "It can be."

She points at the spread. "Okay, but if that was my reading, what does it say about me?"

I shrug. "That you're intuitive and dramatic."

"Rude."

"And probably in a transition you're trying to joke your way through."

She presses a hand to her chest. "How dare you be correct in my own house."

I laugh.

Then she gets unexpectedly serious.

"I mean it, though," she says. "You're really good at this."

I glance up.

She nods toward the cards. "Like, really good. You make it make sense without making it weird or gatekeepy. You explain it in a way that feels... human."

Warmth moves through my chest, quiet and strange.

No one's called me gifted in a long time.

Not without strings attached.

"Thanks," I say, and my voice comes out softer than I mean it to.

"No, seriously," she says, leaning forward. "You could

teach this. You could do readings. Workshops. Something. People would eat this up, especially around here."

I smile. "Maybe."

"Not maybe." She points at me. "When. I'm serious."

My past, my present, my future, translated by a woman who has no idea the man in the middle of it is her father.

"Thank you," I say again.

Lilly claps once like I just did a magic trick. "This night is so fun."

I laugh. "It kind of is."

And somehow, it is.

We keep talking long after the pizza goes cold.

About books first. She loves dark romance, fantasy, and any story where a woman makes terrible decisions for all the right reasons. I tell her that is both specific and concerning. She says exactly. We argue about endings and whether happy endings count if everyone is emotionally scarred. We agree they do.

Then movies. She cries at Pixar. I cry at horror movies with emotional endings. She says that's unwell behavior. I tell her sobbing over animated fish is not exactly a stable coping mechanism either.

She makes pottery when she's stressed. I read tarot when I feel untethered. She stress-bakes. I own enough adult coloring books and color-coded markers to defend myself in court if necessary.

She laughs so hard she snorts.

I laugh so hard my face hurts.

At some point she wanders into the kitchen for water and starts humming off-key while she rinses dishes, and I sit on the rug in the middle of my half-unpacked room and realize I haven't felt this normal in months.

Maybe longer.

It catches me off guard, how badly I needed this.

By the time I finally crawl into bed, I'm full of pizza and sugar and laughter and something more fragile than hope but close enough to make my chest ache.

The skylight above me glows silver with fog.

The house smells like cinnamon and clay.

Somewhere down the hall, a cabinet closes. Lilly hums one more line of whatever song she was making up and then the house goes quiet.

I pull the blanket to my chin and sink into the mattress.

Warm.

Safe.

Quiet.

For one small, reckless second, I let myself think it.

This could be home.

Then the truth comes in right behind it.

If I hadn't already broken the one rule I swore I'd keep.

If he weren't in this town.

If my body didn't still remember him faster than my mind can shut it down.

I squeeze my eyes shut.

Too late.

His voice slides back through me low and rough and intimate, like he's bent to my ear all over again.

Good girl.

A shiver runs clean down my spine.

"No," I mutter into the pillow. "Absolutely not."

I roll over like I can outrun a memory.

Like I can be stubborn enough to outlast my own nervous system.

I can't.

Because the past doesn't stay where you leave it.

It leaks.

It lingers.

And his voice follows me anyway, all the way into sleep.

Low. Commanding. Warm with approval.

The last thing I heard before I came apart under his mouth.

I hate how much I still remember.

Worse, I hate how much I don't want to forget.

TEN
AUGUST

TOWNSEND HARBOR DOESN'T REALLY SLEEP. It dozes. It half-wakes. It keeps one eye open like it's listening for sirens even when it swears it's relaxing.

Festival weekends make that impossible.

Harbor Days isn't a giant tourist circus. It's booths along the boardwalk and twinkle lights strung too early, like we're all collectively pretending winter's already coming when we haven't even finished fall. The air tastes like cinnamon and fryer oil. Mulled cider steams out of paper cups. A couple guys are carving wooden snowmen like it's a blood sport, and people are genuinely stopping to watch.

Small-town stuff.

The kind this place loves on purpose.

Vendors set up before sunrise, running on thermos coffee and stubborn pride. Kids drag their parents toward the craft tents like they're headed for Disneyland. Old-timers claim the picnic tables with pastries and gossip, then sit there half the day like they're being paid to supervise the town.

It isn't fancy. It isn't impressive.

But it's ours.

And every year, no matter what's broken, everybody shows up anyway.

I'm supposed to be off.

Chiefs don't get days off. We get days where we wear jeans and pretend we're not scanning faces and exits out of habit. We get days where we shake hands, answer the same questions about road closures, and smile at people who only ever see you as "the chief" until they need you to be something else.

I make the rounds. I nod. I reassure. I hear "Thanks for keeping us safe" like a blessing and a weight.

Then I hit my limit.

I need coffee. Badly.

Harbor Brew is tucked between a pottery booth and a woodcarver's stall, warm and quiet on normal days.

Today it's a madhouse.

Of course it is. Harbor Days turns the whole town into a caffeine-starved herd with seasonal anxiety.

I shoulder through the door, bells jingling overhead, and warm air hits me in the face and on it wafts sugar, espresso, and baked something. The line snakes past the pastry case and almost back to the door.

I step in behind a woman in a slate-blue coat and a messy bun.

She shifts like she feels me before she sees me.

Then she glances over her shoulder and my brain does that sharp, stupid stop it does when it recognizes a problem.

Florence.

Dark curls. Soft brown eyes. That little inhale she takes like she can't brace for me. Like her body remembers me faster than her pride can catch up.

Her lips part.

Not fear. Not surprise.

She remembers me.

"Hi," she says, quiet like she doesn't want the whole damn coffee shop to hear it.

My voice comes out lower than I mean it to. "Hey."

She turns fully toward me, hugging a tablet to her chest. Not defensive, more reflexive. Like she wasn't expecting to run into someone who knows what she sounds like when she comes apart.

Her cheeks flush.

Mine probably do too. I pretend they don't.

"Didn't mean to sneak up on you," I say.

"You didn't," she answers, then a beat later she smiles like she realized she just lied. "Okay. Maybe a little."

We shift forward in line.

The café buzzes around us. Steam wands hissing, baristas calling orders like they're running triage, while laughter pops off the tile.

But my world narrows anyway.

Three feet of air. Her. The space between us that feels too charged for a damn coffee line.

"How's the festival treating you?" I ask.

Casual voice. Chief voice. Not the voice in my head that remembers her taste and the way she looked up at me like I was a sin she chose on purpose.

"It's... a lot," she admits. "Good. But crowded."

"You get used to it," I say. "Townsend Harbor loves an excuse to show off."

Her smile flickers warm. "I'm starting to see that."

We shuffle forward with the line.

She worries the corner of her tablet, then slides it down into her bag like she's hiding it from the room.

"What're you working on?" I ask.

"A project." Too quick. "Art stuff. Just... nothing big."

I could push. I don't.

Then she adds, quieter, like she's mad at herself for offering anything real, "It's kind of personal."

That lands somewhere it shouldn't.

Before I can answer, the counter opens up and a barista beams like they've never been tired in their life. "Next!"

Florence steps up and orders a pumpkin chai.

When the barista turns to ring it, I extend my card over her shoulder.

"I've got it."

Florence whips around. "August."

"It's a drink," I say. "Let me."

Her eyes soften in a way that drops a hook straight into my gut.

"Thank you," she murmurs, like she means more than the coffee.

I order black drip because I'm not here to be happy. I'm here to function. Then I pay for both and we drift down the counter together while the baristas work.

Her sleeve grazes my forearm. Probably accidental.

I don't move away.

"So," she says, "you're off today?"

"Kind of." I glance out toward the windows where Harbor Days is already swelling. "Festival weekends are my unofficial overtime."

She hums like she can picture it. "You don't strike me as someone who relaxes easily."

"I relax," I protest.

She tilts her head, skeptical. "Uh-huh."

"I tried once." I take my coffee when it's handed over and blow on it out of habit. "Back in 2012."

She laughs and it's real, warm, and it hits me in the chest.

We step out into the noise and the light. The boardwalk is a moving body. People shoulder past with paper trays and cider, kids weaving between legs, the harbor glittering through fog like it's trying to be pretty on purpose.

Florence turns left like she's about to disappear back into her day.

I should let her.

I absolutely should.

"Walk with me," I hear myself say. "Just to the boardwalk. You can bail the second you want."

She pauses like she's deciding whether I'm a good idea.

Then she nods once. "Yeah. Okay."

We fall into step side-by-side.

Lanterns swing between vendor tents. Someone's playing music on the community stage like they've got something to prove. Cocoa cups. Cinnamon air. A kid barrels past with a face painted like a fox.

It should feel busy.

It doesn't.

It feels like the town went soft-focus and left just the two of us in the frame.

She tugs at her sleeve. I sip my coffee. The quiet is easy until she makes it sharp.

"I didn't expect to see you here," she blurts, too quick. Like the words tripped her on the way out.

"Same," I say. Honest. Then, because I'm apparently determined to die today, "Can't say I'm complaining."

Her breath catches. Just a little.

"About Seattle," she starts.

"I'm not going to pretend it didn't happen," I cut in.

Her eyes fly to mine. Wide. Heat climbs her neck in a way I shouldn't notice and do anyway.

"Me either," she says, softer. "It was... yeah. Real."

That word, *real,* tightens my chest like a fist.

"Even though it shouldn't have been," she adds, biting her lip like she hates herself for saying it.

"Maybe not," I say, low. "But it was."

We hold eye contact a beat too long.

Her pupils widen. Her mouth parts just slightly.

And my brain does a quick, ugly calculation of alleyways and consequences.

I clear my throat because if I don't, I'm going to do something that ends with my name as town gossip by sundown.

The wind catches her hair, curls brushing her cheek. She tucks them back, fingers shaking just a hair.

"You've settled in fast," I say, because I need a safer subject before I set my life on fire. "How's it feel?"

"I'm trying to," she answers. "It's... different here."

"Good different?" I ask.

She hesitates. "Good. And weird. I'm still figuring it out."

"Townsend Harbor does that," I say. "Gets under your skin."

"Does it do that to everyone," she shoots back, "or just dispatchers who keep embarrassing themselves in front of the chief of police?"

A laugh escapes me. "Pretty sure you're the only one."

She groans and covers her face with one hand. "God. Stop making me feel seen."

"You walked into my coffee shop," I say. "I can't exactly unsee you."

She drops her hand slowly.

Her eyes flash with something bold trying to get out from behind the nerves.

And I realize she isn't just flustered.

She's fighting herself.

"You know," she says, voice rising as she tries to outrun the silence, "when I left Island County, I told myself I'd be chill. Low-drama. No disasters. Absolutely no—" She stops hard, like she bit her own tongue.

"No...?" I prompt, gentle because I'm not trying to corner her.

She waves both hands like she can erase the sentence. "No... situations."

I arch a brow. "Is this a situation?"

She sputters. "I—I didn't say that."

"You implied it."

"I didn't—" She blows out a breath. "Okay, fine. Maybe I implied it."

Then she laughs, helpless, like her body betrayed her before her pride could stop it.

That sound of it goes straight through me.

She keeps talking because nervous people fill space like it's oxygen.

"And this festival is so cute it makes me want to cry," she says, and there's genuine awe in it. "The lanterns. The music. The cinnamon smell. I already spent way too much money on earrings shaped like otters, and I bought a mug with a crab on it that I do not need, but apparently my brain thinks I'm a whimsical coastal creature now."

I'm smiling before I mean to.

Before I can stop it.

And the worst part is, she sees it.

"And then there's you," she says, quieter.

There it is.

The shift.

She realizes what she said a beat too late, eyes going wide like she can physically see the words hanging between us.

"That didn't come out right," she rushes. "I meant, like, you being here. Not you-you. Not that I was— I wasn't looking for you. I wasn't. At all. I just—God, Florence, shut up."

I stop walking.

So does she.

The crowd keeps moving around us like we're a rock in a river. The harbor wind lifts her curls. Her breath ghosts white in the air.

I lean in just enough that she feels it. Not touching. Just... close.

"I'm glad you said it," I murmur.

Her lips part.

"You being here," she repeats, like she's testing the phrase. Then, softer, "Or... you?"

"Yes."

The honesty lands heavy. Clean.

Her lashes flutter, and she looks away like she needs a second to survive it. "I don't know what to do with that," she admits.

"You don't have to do anything," I say. "Walking is enough."

She swallows, hard, like she's trying to get control of her body again.

We start moving, shoulder to shoulder through the Harbor Days glow.

Her hand grazes mine.

Not an accident.

Not on purpose either.

Just that small betrayal where the body reaches before the brain can stop it.

She makes the tiniest sound, it's barely there, before she jerks her hand back like she brushed a live wire.

Yeah.

We're not shy. We're just trying not to explode in public.

A kid barrels past with a paper snowflake and nearly takes her out. Florence steps toward me on instinct, coat brushing my arm.

My jaw tightens.

I keep my voice level. "You okay?"

She looks up, a quick smile trying to pretend she isn't rattled. "Yeah. You're tall. You block wind."

"That's my one marketable skill," I say dryly.

The smell hits next, a mix of warm sugar, browned butter, something green and sharp underneath.

Florence's head tilts, nose twitching like a curious cat.

"Oh my god," she whispers. "What is that?"

I follow her gaze to a booth with twinkle lights and a hand-painted sign: **THE WILD CRUMB**.

"Scones," I say. "She puts rosemary in the glaze."

Her eyes widen. "Rosemary? In a pastry?"

I shrug. "Townsend Harbor likes to pretend it's artisanal."

"It smells like Christmas and a forest made a bad decision together," she says, mesmerized.

Before she can talk herself out of it, I step up and buy two.

She sputters, immediate. "August—no. I can pay."

"It's a scone," I say. "Let me live dangerously."

She snorts. "If buying pastries is your danger, you must be a menace."

"Oh, you have no idea," I say a bit too low, too automatic.

Her breath stutters.

I hand her one. She tears off a corner, pops it into her mouth and makes a sound. A soft, helpless little moan like her body forgot there are rules in public.

A couple at the next booth turns their heads.

Florence clamps a hand over her mouth, mortified. "I didn't— I'm sorry— I swear I don't usually moan at carbs."

"Florence," I say, and I can't keep the amusement out of my voice. "You're fine."

She narrows her eyes at me, but the corner of her mouth twitches. “This is dangerous.”

“The scone?” I ask.

She doesn’t blink. “You.”

My pulse jumps in a way I pretend not to notice.

We keep walking. The air tastes like cinnamon and salt and something electric I can’t name.

She points at a knitted snowman display. “Why does it have eyebrows? Why is this snowman judging me?”

“It’s probably the scarf choice,” I deadpan.

She gasps. “Excuse you, my scarf is iconic.”

“It’s aggressively pink.”

“It’s cheerful.”

“It’s loud.”

She plants a hand on her hip. “This scarf was knitted by a woman named Jessie who told me it would protect me from heartbreak and the cold.”

“Strong promises,” I murmur.

And then she does it. This tiny, devastating, little thing.

She looks up at me and smiles.

Not playful. Not guarded.

Soft.

Like she trusts me.

It hits me so hard it almost makes me miss a step.

We pause at a leather stall where a woman is burnishing the edges of wallets and pouches.

Florence trails her fingers over a display and stops.

“Oh,” she whispers. “This one...”

She lifts a deep brown leather pouch stamped with constellations. It looks like something she’d keep secrets in.

She runs her thumb along the stitching. “It feels like a book I’d stay up all night reading.”

“Then you should get it,” I say.

Her grip slips when she hands it back.

It drops and I catch it before it hits the table.

She reaches at the same time.

Our fingers collide.

Warm. Soft. Familiar in the wrong way.

A jolt snaps between us. Actual static, sharp enough that we both inhale at once.

Her eyes fly up to mine.

I don't move.

Neither does she.

For one ugly second, it's Seattle again. Elevator mirrors, her breath in my mouth, the way she looked when she stopped pretending.

A gust of wind rushes down the boardwalk, kicking up a swirl of amber leaves around our feet like the town's got a flair for drama.

Florence lets out a breathy laugh. "That's... theatrical."

"Little bit," I say, voice rougher than it should be.

The vendor hands her the bag.

Florence tucks the pouch inside without looking away from me.

We walk again. Slower. Closer.

I brush my knuckles against hers—barely there. Not grabbing.

Just asking.

She answers without thinking.

Her pinky hooks mine for one electric second before she yanks her hand back like she remembers we're in public.

"August," she says, quiet. "This feels like..."

She trails off.

"Like what?" I ask.

Her cheeks go warm. "Like something I shouldn't want."

"I know," I murmur.

The admission hangs between us, charged and honest.

She glances at me from under her lashes. "You're not what I expected."

"What'd you expect?"

She thinks a moment. "In Seattle you seemed... untouchable. Controlled."

"I'm not untouchable," I say.

Her eyes flick up, heat sparking.

"Yeah," she whispers. "I remember."

We drift toward the quieter side of the harbor, away from

the stage and the crush of bodies. Lanterns swing over dark water. The noise drops a notch.

Florence inhales like the cold steadies her.

Then she asks, too casual to be casual, “So... how long have you lived in Townsend Harbor?”

“Most of my life,” I say. “Left for a while. Came back a fewyears ago.”

“Why?”

I could give her the polished answer.

Instead I tell her the real one.

“I wanted my daughter somewhere quieter.”

Her face softens. “You have a daughter.”

“Yeah.” My chest warms despite myself. “I call her Bug.”

Florence smiles, real. “Bug?”

“Long story.”

“That’s... adorable,” she murmurs.

No one calls my life adorable. But coming from her, it lands like something I didn’t know I wanted.

She hesitates, then asks carefully, “Are you... married?”

It’s the first time she sounds scared of the answer.

My throat tightens.

“No.”

A beat.

“Never married. Almost did, once.”

She doesn’t pry. Just waits.

“To Bug’s mom,” I add. “We tried to force something that wasn’t built right.”

“Do you regret it?” she asks softly.

“No,” I say immediately. “I’ll never regret my kid.”

Her eyes brighten in the lantern glow.

Then I turn it back on her, gently. “You?”

“Family?” she repeats, like she has to translate the word.

Her gaze flickers open, then shuttered.

“My sister died last year,” she says.

The sentence lands plain and brutal.

My steps slow without my permission. “I’m sorry.”

“It was... sudden. Stupid. Wrong place.” Her mouth tightens like she’s holding something back. “A robbery.”

I feel my chest go cold.

She keeps her voice steady, but I hear the wire underneath it, pulled tight.

"I was working," she adds, quieter. "Island County."

I don't like the direction this is going. "Florence..."

Her laugh is brittle. "Yeah. Dispatcher nightmare, right? Hearing your own life come through a headset."

Something sharp twists in me.

I want to reach for her hand.

I don't.

Barely.

Instead I keep my voice low, careful. "You don't have to tell me the details."

She nods once, grateful and furious at the same time. She hates that she brought it up and hates even more that it's true.

But she doesn't step away.

And that fact alone feels like a decision.

She keeps talking, quiet and steady, like honesty is the only thing holding her upright.

"After that... everything felt heavy. Too heavy." She swallows, eyes on the water like it might forgive her. "Island County is beautiful, but it's small. Everyone knows your story. And if they don't, they'll figure it out by Tuesday."

"So you moved," I say.

"Yeah." A pause. "I needed something different." Her mouth twists. "Not to run away. Just... breathe without feeling watched."

I nod once. "You don't owe anyone an explanation."

She looks at me like she's not used to hearing that said out loud. Like permission is a language she hasn't spoken in a while.

Her voice goes quieter. "I had a sister."

Past tense. A blade you don't see until it's already in.

"We weren't close," she adds, like she needs to justify the grief before it counts. "Not in the way people expect. But she was still... mine."

I don't touch her. I don't crowd her.

I just walk beside her and let the space be what it is.

The boardwalk creaks under our feet. A distant laugh pops from the crowd behind us, then gets swallowed by wind.

Then, because she can't stand being that open for too long, she exhales hard like she's shaking water off.

"Okay," she says. "Your turn. What do you like? Hobbies. Music. Food. Things normal humans talk about."

I huff a quiet laugh. "Normal humans. I don't know if I qualify."

"Oh please." She bumps my shoulder with hers gently, a dare. "Everybody likes something. Tell me."

"Alright." I think for a beat. "Early mornings. Coffee strong enough to ruin my day if it's bad. Old trucks. Fixing things with my hands." I glance at her. "Quiet."

She snorts. "Of course you like quiet."

"You saying I look boring?" I ask.

"No." Too fast. Too honest.

Then her voice softens, like the words slip out before she can protect them. "You look like someone who's carried a lot."

The truth of it hits somewhere deep enough I have to clear my throat to make sure my voice still works.

"Okay," I say, like it's nothing. "Your turn. What do you like besides pumpkin chai and pastries that make you moan in public?"

Her face flames. "I knew you were going to bring that up."

"I mean..." I keep my tone light, but my eyes don't lie. "I didn't hate it."

She swats my arm. "August."

"Florence."

Her smile breaks wide, bright, unguarded, and a little ruined.

She lists her loves like other people confess sins. "Books. Art. Mythology. Tarot. Drawing weird creatures. Long ferry rides. Being warm. And coffee that tastes like dessert."

I lift a brow. "That's not coffee."

"It is if you believe," she says solemnly.

"You mean sugar."

Her eyes narrow. "I'll hex you."

I hum. "Tarot and hexes, huh?"

She groans and looks away like she's embarrassed by herself. "I'm not a witch. I just like... symbolism."

"Show me," I say.

She hesitates, just long enough for me to see the fight in her. The instinct to stay hidden.

Then she stops at the railing and pulls her tablet from her bag. Hands steady, but her breath isn't. She flips it open, thumb hovering, then turns the screen toward me.

A stylized tarot piece, moonlight on water. There's a small boat cutting through dark, a figure bent toward something faint and distant. Hope, but not soft. Hope with teeth.

"It's the Six of Swords," she murmurs. "Leaving something behind. Moving forward."

Her voice goes small on the last part. "Fitting, right?"

More than she knows.

"It's beautiful," I say, and I mean it in a way that has nothing to do with ink on a screen.

She looks away like she doesn't want me to see what the compliment does to her.

We reach the edge of the lights where Harbor Days thins into night. The noise fades. The wind feels colder.

Her steps slow.

"I should head back," she says, but it lands like a question.

"Yeah," I echo, even though every part of me wants to keep her here until the coffee shops close and the lanterns burn out. "Me too."

She tucks a curl behind her ear, fingers lingering like she's trying to keep her hands busy. "This was... good."

"Yeah," I say, because anything more would be a confession.

She takes a step backward. Then another.

She's leaving, but her eyes don't move off mine.

"See you tomorrow, Chief."

"August," I correct. "When I'm off duty."

The name hits her like heat. Like permission.

"Okay," she whispers. "Goodnight... August."

Then she turns and disappears into the lantern glow.

I stand there long after she's gone.

My coffee is cold.

My stomach is tight.

My chest is a mess.

And I'm starting to realize I didn't bring a jacket because I thought I'd be fine.

I'm not.

I am absolutely, completely, undeniably fucked.

ELEVEN
FLORENCE

FLUORESCENT LIGHTS and a warm chair mean one thing.

Shift.

Nine screens glow like tiny angry planets.

My headset settles over my ears.

And August Calder's voice sits in the back of my skull like a bruise I keep poking to see if it still hurts.

It does.

I log in. I stretch my shoulders. I make my fingers move like my mind isn't doing backflips.

I am not here to think about him.

Just work.

Work is safe.

Work has rules.

Work doesn't look at me like it remembers.

I glance at the clock as the first call hits.

09:14.

"9-1-1, where is your emergency?"

A woman blurts, breathless, "Someone is stealing my chickens!"

I blink once. "Ma'am... can you repeat that?"

"My chickens! My entire coop!" She sounds like she's sprinting. "They're—oh my GOD—he's loading them into a van!"

Wings flapping. Actual poultry chaos. Somewhere in the background, a rooster screams like it knows it's about to be trafficked.

Ruth makes a strangled sound beside me and immediately covers her mouth.

I stay professional.

"Okay, ma'am, I'm with you. What's the address where this is happening?"

She rattles it off. I type fast, eyes moving between screens, pin dropping on the map.

"And can you describe the suspect?"

A dramatic pause, like she's offended I even asked.

"He's wearing a rooster hat."

I type it into the CAD.

Across the room, Turner's voice crackles over the radio, already way too delighted.

"Dispatch, 13. Confirm rooster hat?"

"Affirmative," I say, calm as if we're discussing a felony warrant. "Rooster hat."

Ruth spins her chair away so she can laugh into her sleeve like a responsible adult.

Turner again, "Dispatch, 13. I'll take it. Show me en route."

The caller wails, "He's TAKING BEATRICE. She lays blue eggs!"

"Ma'am, you're doing great," I tell her, because it's either soothe her or laugh and I'm not getting written up month one. "Officers are on the way. Stay where you're safe. Don't chase the van."

"I am absolutely chasing the van!"

"Please don't."

"I'm already chasing the van!"

Of course you are.

A beat.

Then Turner returns, voice clipped like he's trying very hard to pretend this is normal police work.

"Dispatch, 13. Suspect detained. Chickens recovered. One attempted escape."

I exhale through my nose. "Copy."

Chicken lady dissolves into grateful sobs like I just talked her through childbirth.

Beatrice is safe.

Townsend Harbor's most wanted poultry bandit is officially in custody.

I disconnect and swivel slightly, blinking at the screens like they might blink back.

Ruth is already watching me over her monitor, one brow arched.

"You handled that beautifully," she says, mouth twitching. "And welcome to Townsend Harbor. We take poultry crime very seriously."

"I gathered," I say, and I can't help the snort that slips out.

I roll my shoulders, easing the tension out of my neck. My headset squeaks when I tilt my head side to side.

Adrenaline drains, leaving that warm jitter you only get after something ridiculous.

I reach for my coffee.

Lukewarm. Burnt. Perfect.

Ruth clears her throat. "You're settling in."

"I'm... trying," I murmur into the rim.

A soft hum from her. Approval. Not pity.

"Your trying is more than enough."

The moment hangs, light, easy. Then my console lights up.

Not a routine call.

Not a weird one.

Not a town-quirk one.

My stomach drops before my finger even hits answer.

A different kind of call.

A real one.

"9-1-1," I say, and my voice drops into that grounded, steel-edged calm. "Where is your emergency?"

The room doesn't change.

I do.

Ruth goes still beside me. No laughter. No commentary. Just the quiet click of her attention locking in.

A man comes on the line too close to the phone, breathing like he's trying to suck air through a straw.

"She's not breathing. My wife—she just collapsed—please, please—"

My spine straightens. My fingers are already moving.

"Okay. I'm here with you," I say, and I make my voice a handrail. "What is your name?"

"David," he says.

"David, how old is your wife?"

"Fifty-two. She—she grabbed her chest and fell."

"Is she conscious?"

"N-no."

"Is she breathing?"

"I—I don't think so. Her chest isn't—oh God—"

Not breathing. Unresponsive.

I drop the call into CAD, tag CPR-in-progress, light up Medic 3 and patrol like a flare.

"David," I say, because sometimes names keep people tethered to my voice. "We're going to start CPR right now."

"I don't know how," he chokes.

"That's okay," I tell him. "I do. And I'll walk you through it."

A sound cracks through the line—half sob, half panic. I don't give him time to drown in it.

"Put me on speaker and set the phone down next to you," I say. "Do not hang up."

Rustling. A clatter. His ragged and desperate breathing fills the line.

"She's—she's on the couch."

"She needs to be on the floor," I say. "I know that's hard. You can do it. Get her flat on her back. Even if you have to drag her."

A grunt. Something heavy shifting. A broken noise from him like the effort is grief with muscles.

"She's down. She's down."

"Good." I say steady even as the hair on my arms lifts. "Kneel by her chest. Put the heel of your hand in the center of her chest—between the nipples. Your other hand on top of the first."

"I—okay. Okay."

"Lock your elbows," I say. "Use your body weight with each compression."

He starts crying again. Small, frantic sounds that hit somewhere deep and familiar in my chest.

"Listen to my voice," I say, firm enough to cut through it. "Hard, fast compressions. Push straight down at least two inches. Let the chest come all the way back up each time."

"O-okay."

"When I say go, you start. You're going to follow my count. Ready?"

"Y-yeah—"

"Go. One. Two. Three. Four. Five." My voice becomes a metronome. "Don't stop. Harder if you can. You're doing it. Keep the pace."

There's a wet thump through the phone—his hands transferring force into her sternum.

"Match me," I say. "Stayin' Alive beat. Same rhythm."

A broken laugh tries to escape him and turns into a sob instead, but he keeps going.

"Good," I tell him. "Don't look at her face. Look at your hands. You're giving her her best shot. You're doing exactly what she needs."

Minutes stretch.

CPR minutes don't pass.

They crawl.

Then a door slams somewhere in the background. "Townsend Harbor Medic, where is she?"

David makes a sound like he's been holding his lungs shut. "In here! Please—please!"

I hear bodies moving. A medic's voice tight and calm like a blade. "Taking over compressions. One, two—switch—airway ready—charging—"

The audio goes messy with grief and motion and hope.

"David," I say, softer now, because this is the part where people fall apart. "I'm still here."

He's shaking so hard I can hear it through the phone. "I—I couldn't—she wasn't—she didn't—"

"You did everything right," I tell him. Each word deliberate. True. "You got her on the floor. You started compressions fast. You gave her the best chance anyone could."

His breathing stutters like it wants to turn into screaming.

"You weren't alone," I say. "You did this with me. They're with her now."

The medic confirms they've got it. I log the takeover, time-stamp, unit, location. Muscle memory doing its job while my chest stays too tight.

I disconnect.

And I sit still for a second because this is the part nobody outside this room understands.

You don't get the ending.

You just hand it off and keep moving like you didn't just hold a stranger's life in your voice.

Ruth swivels her chair slow. Her expression isn't pity. It's... recognition.

"You okay?" she asks.

I nod once. "Yeah."

She holds my gaze a beat, like she can tell that's a lie I'm borrowing.

"You did good," she says. Simple. No fluff.

"Thanks." My voice comes out thin anyway. "Just... brings stuff up sometimes."

She doesn't push. Ruth never pushes. She just turns back to her screens and gives me the gift of not making me explain myself while my hands are still buzzing under the desk.

And somehow that's its own kind of care.

Not motherly.

Not soft.

Just steady.

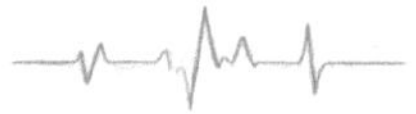

By late morning, the room settles into that weird in-between hum, half quiet, half waiting to explode.

The CPR call is already twenty-three incidents back.

That's the part people don't get. You don't get to hold on to one moment, no matter how big it was. The next line lights up, and you move. Your body still remembers the rhythm, but your brain shoves it into a file marked HANDLED and slams the drawer.

I type the last note—MEDIC 3 ASSUMED CARE ON SCENE, CPR CONT'D, PT TRANSPORTED—and close it out.

The day consists of two noise complaints. A shoplifter, a house fire, and one welfare check that turns out to be a guy asleep in his truck between shifts. A kid calling because their brother changed the Netflix password.

Normal.

My shoulders start to ache in that delayed way they do when the adrenaline drains out and leaves the weight behind. The empty mug next to my keyboard mocks me.

Ruth glances over between her own calls. "If you're going to sneak away for tea," she says mildly, "now's your window. I've got the board."

I blink at the status screen. All units green. No pending calls. A miracle in headset form.

"You sure?" I ask.

She snorts. "Sweetheart, if I can't handle four blinking lights for three minutes, I should retire. Go before the universe notices it's being nice."

I slip the headset down around my neck, ready to yank it back up if something pops. "If anything hot comes in—"

"I'll scream," she says. "Which will be your cue to run."

I huff out a laugh despite myself and push back from the console. My knees crack when I stand. Glamorous.

The break room is ten steps down the hall, past the faded bulletin board and the framed "Team Recognition" certificate from three years ago. The fluorescents out here buzz louder, like they're complaining about their life choices.

The space is small with one ancient microwave, a fridge that doesn't quite seal, a sink, and a hot water dispenser on its last three brain cells. Someone stuck a sticky note on it that says BE NICE TO HER, SHE'S TRYING.

I love dispatch humor.

I fill my mug, drop a bag of generic black tea in, the kind the city buys in bulk that tastes vaguely like hot leaves with aspirations. My hands are steady now. They weren't five calls ago.

Steam curls up around my fingers.

I lean my hip against the counter and let myself breathe for a second. A real inhale. A real exhale. No counting. No scripts. No one's life depending on my next sentence.

My phone buzzes in my back pocket.

I fish it out, thumb already half moving toward Do Not Disturb out of pure habit.

The notification makes me smile before I can stop it.

Lilly: GIRL. Emergency.

I open the thread.

Me: Do I need to send units?

Lilly: Yes. Units of sugar. And cinnamon.

Lilly: Pumpkimania this Saturday. Cider. Donuts. Crafts. Knitted raccoons. You're coming with me.

I grin at the image of knitted raccoons committing pastry crimes.

Me: Knitted raccoons?

Lilly: You think I'm kidding.

She sends a photo: a slightly blurry booth from last year, rows of tiny raccoons in scarves. One is holding a miniature felt donut.

I choke on a laugh and have to put the phone down for a second so I don't baptize myself in boiling tea.

Me: Okay that's unreasonably cute.

Lilly: So that's a YES?

Steam fogs the space in front of my face when I lift the mug to blow on it. The warmth seeps into my fingers, anchoring in a way that says you're off the line for thirty seconds, you get to be a person again.

Me: Yeah. I could use something fun.

Three dots appear instantly.

Lilly: OMG YAY

Lilly: I'm making you try EVERY donut flavor. Don't argue.

Me: I wouldn't dare come between you and your pastry agenda.

Lilly: Good. Also wear something cozy. There will be lanterns and music and I'm 90% sure someone with an accordion.

Me: You had me until accordion.

Lilly: This is small-town living, baby. Come for the donuts, stay for the deeply questionable folk bands.

She adds a string of leaf emojis and, for absolutely no reason, one octopus.

Me: Why is there always an octopus.

Lilly: He's our emotional support cephalopod. Don't question him

I snort into my tea.

Something warm unfurls low in my chest. Not adrenaline. Not anxiety.

Just... being invited.

Having plans that aren't go home, stare at ceiling.

My thumb hovers longer than it should.

Me: Okay. Saturday. I'm in.

Lilly: <3

Lilly: Also my back is killing me today so I might rope you into helping at my table a bit. I'll pay you in cookies and bad puns.

Me: Honestly that's my ideal compensation package.

Lilly: K NEW ROOMMATE I OFFICIALLY LIKE YOU

I smile down at the screen until the tea burns my tongue enough to remind me I don't actually live in my phone.

Footsteps pass the break room door. Sounds like boots, and a laugh down the hall. Someone's radio crackles as they walk by.

The world is still moving.

My three minutes are almost up.

I tuck my phone away, take one last gulp of tea, and grab a prepackaged sandwich from the communal fridge—a ham-and-cheese situation with the nutritional value of damp cardboard. It's fuel. That's all it needs to be.

I'm halfway through my first bite by the time I'm back in my chair, headset sliding into place.

"Saved you from a telemarketer," Ruth says without looking over. "You owe me your firstborn."

"Perfect," I say. "I never planned on having one."

She smirks. "That's what we all say before the universe hands us a surprise."

I pretend that doesn't make my stomach flicker with a thought I absolutely do not have time to unpack.

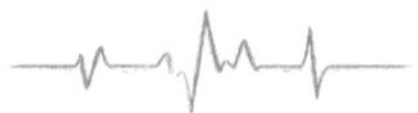

THE AFTERNOON STRETCHES.

More calls.

A fender-bender by the ferry.

An elderly man who locked himself out in his socks.

A kid reporting "suspicious smoke" that turns out to be steam from the bakery vent.

Normal.

I let the rhythm take me. Question, type, dispatch, reassure. Repeat.

It's later, after a domestic that ends with one person going to their sister's house to "cool off," and a cat being extracted from a laundry basket like it's a hostage negotiation, that Pumpkimania comes back.

Not as a joke.

As a thing that's real enough to put on a calendar.

My roommate invited me to something called Pumpkimania.

The words land weird in my head. Like they know exactly where they want to go, and I've been blocking the road with my own body.

Ruth finishes logging her incident and leans back, stretching until her spine crackles like popcorn.

Her headset shifts off one ear. Dispatcher code for I can hear you, but if a call comes in, I'm gone.

"So," I say, casual. "My roommate invited me to this Pumpkimania thing. What am I getting myself into?"

Ruth snorts. "Ah. They got you already."

"Got me?"

"This town weaponizes pumpkins for tourism," she says. "Pumpkimania is basically Townsend Harbor condensed into three overcrowded blocks."

"Sounds... cozy?" I offer.

"Depends on your tolerance for plaid." She takes a swig of water. "Picture this: twenty-something booths, every third person you pass is someone who taught half the town's kids to swim, and there's a line for cider donuts that violates at least three fire codes."

"That bad?"

"They're really good donuts," she concedes. "Just don't let

the chief hear you call them overrated. He'll start quoting statistics about how tourism props up the marina."

My heart does a stupid little trip at the mention of August. Totally unnecessary. Totally unhelpful.

I keep my face neutral like I'm not made of nerves. "So Pumpkimania is a big deal."

"Harbor Days. Pumpkimania. Film Festival. Kinetics. Spring Bloom. Fiddle Tunes. Jazz Days. Witch Walk. Weird Brew Festival. Winterfest," she rattles off on her fingers. "If there is a way to hang string lights and charge tourists eight bucks for something on a stick, this town has a festival for it."

"That's... kind of charming," I admit.

"It's survival," she says. "Half the businesses here live and die on what they make during festival season. Council pushes hard. So do we, in our own way."

"Because of traffic?"

"Traffic. Pickpockets. Drunk idiots. Lost kids. Arguments over who got the last maple bar." She glances at me, eyes crinkling. "You'll hear some of our best calls on festival weekends."

"And the worst."

The sentence hangs there without either of us having to say it.

I nod slowly, because I can already imagine it. The noise, the bodies, the overlapping emergencies. The way joy and disaster share sidewalks like they're old friends.

Ruth must see something cross my face, because her tone softens.

"Don't borrow trouble," she says. "You're off duty, right? Newbies get the Monday-through-Friday day shift for the first few months. So go. Get a donut. Let your roommate drag you around. Buy a candle you'll never burn. Because it might be a while before you get to attend again."

"You make it sound almost fun."

"It is fun," she insists. "If you let it be."

The quiet between us settles in, comfortable.

I think about telling her more. About how I haven't really done fun in a long time, how the last year has been grief and running and then more grief when I realized it followed me anyway, how new towns still feel like wearing someone else's sweater. Almost right, almost mine, but not quite.

Instead I go lighter. "Do you go?"

Ruth shrugs. "I used to. When my kid was younger. These days, I volunteer at the Rotary booth one night and that's enough peopling for the month."

"You have kids?" I ask, keeping it in that acceptable coworker lane. Curious. Not prying.

"One," she says. "I couldn't convince her to go to college, and honestly? With how expensive it is, I can't blame her for fighting me on it."

I smile. "Does she live around here?"

"Close enough to steal my leftovers. Far enough that I can pretend I'm not available for every minor crisis." Her mouth quirks. "You?"

I keep my eyes on the screen. "Just me."

A beat. Not awkward. Not pitying. Just the clean, respectful kind.

Ruth nods like I've said everything she needs to know.

"Then go to the market," she says. "Let the town feed you for a day."

My phone buzzes in my pocket. I ignore it. We're live, lights blinking, and the queue is never empty for long.

But the thought stays a small ember.

Pumpkimania.

Walkways strung with twinkle lights.

Music.

Fog rolling in off the water.

And, uninvited, August.

His hands in his pockets.

That half-smile that looks like it hurts him to show.

The way his eyes softened when I told him about my sister.

The warmth in his voice when he said my name like he was tasting it.

I slam the door on the thought before it can finish forming.

Work first.

Feelings never.

That's the rule.

I tell myself I moved here for the job.

For the reset.

For the air.

And maybe that's mostly true.

Maybe the part of me that circled Townsend Harbor on the map after Seattle, and learned his name, was just looking for somewhere to put the ache.

He's basically my boss.

He's older.

He's rooted here in a way I'm not.

Seattle was supposed to be one night. One elevator. One hotel room. One set of rules we both agreed to.

Except last weekend, walking under Harbor Days lights with him, it didn't feel like a mistake.

It felt like the beginning of something I don't deserve to want.

I shift in my chair, irritated at my own body for remembering faster than my brain can lie.

On my screen, a unit changes status from EN ROUTE to ON SCENE. Another caller drops into the queue.

Thank the gods.

Distraction.

I click to answer.

"9-1-1, where is your emergency?"

A woman floods my ear, breathless and panicked but alive. Something about a dog park, a loose Great Dane, and an elderly pug named Mister Pickles who is "emotionally not prepared for this level of bullying."

I let out a breath I didn't know I was holding.

Good.

Dog drama I can handle.

Ruth catches my eye as she spools up her own next call. She tips her chin once in an unspoken you okay?

I nod back. A tiny, honest yes.

Because for a moment, just a moment, it feels like I'm not doing this alone.

I've got a mentor who doesn't push but shows up anyway.

A roommate who is turning maybe into an actual friend?

A new town that smells like salt and coffee and possibility.

And somewhere in that same town, there's a man whose hands I still feel on my skin when I close my eyes.

He is absolutely, unequivocally a problem.

But he's not today's problem.

I straighten in my chair, lock onto the caller's frantic explanation, and let the calm slide back into place like armor.

"Okay," I say, warm and steady. "Let's figure this out."

My fingers move.

The call log fills.

The hum of the steady center wraps around me.

Outside, I know the fog is rolling in, thick and silver over the harbor.

Inside, I keep my world narrowed to the line in my ear.

For now, that's enough.

It has to be.

TWELVE
AUGUST

THE FIRST TIME I catch myself doing it, I tell myself it's coincidence.

A few weeks in, Florence is already part of the building's bloodstream with her voice on the radio, her name in the logs, her handwriting in the margins of the call notes like she's always belonged here. That should make her easier to ignore.

It doesn't.

I'm just walking past dispatch.

That's it.

I've got incident reports in my hand, a meeting with the mayor in twenty minutes, and a headache that started sometime around sunrise and never clocked out. I take the side corridor because the front hallway is "busy."

It isn't.

The glass throws my reflection back at me, but I can still see enough.

The back of her.

Florence sits at her console, headset on, shoulders pitched forward and locked in. Eyes on the screen. Ears on the line. Mind split three ways and still calm in all of them.

Her hair is up today, curls twisted into a knot that's already coming loose. A few dark pieces cling to the back of her neck. She's wearing a deep green sweater that looks soft over curves I've already had under my hands.

My chest tightens like I'm the one being pulled on the line.

Her voice doesn't carry through the glass, but her rhythm does. Short bursts of typing. A pause. A longer pause. A tilt of her head like she's listening for something happening farther away than the caller wants to admit.

Even from here, I can tell she's steady.

Always steady.

I slow down as I pass, like it's nothing, like my boots didn't just decide for me.

Ruth sits beside her with one ear off her headset. She says something quick. Florence huffs a laugh I can't hear but feel anyway. Her shoulders shake once. She reaches for her mug, takes a sip, eyes never leaving her screen.

Jesus.

I keep walking before I get caught staring at my own dispatch center like a man who forgot how to behave.

By the time I'm back in my office, the reports in my hand might as well be blank paper. I set them down. I stare at my monitor.

For four full minutes, I don't do a damn thing.

Because all I can see is the curve where her sweater collar dips. The quick, precise way her fingers move. The softness that crossed her face when she talked about loss like it was a fact and not a plea.

And this morning's CPR.

I heard her on the radio and I went still in my chair. I told myself it was instinct. I told myself every chief listens when CPR comes over the air.

That part is true.

The other part is... after it cleared, I pulled the recording.

I didn't mean to. That's the lie I tell myself first.

The truth is I wanted to hear her again. Wanted that voice in my office where it was safe to want things privately.

"This is dispatch. I have CPR in progress."

The officer acknowledged.

Medics rolled.

And Florence, still calm, low, and anchored, walked a panicked man through the kind of seconds that split lives in half.

"Hands in the center of her chest... lock your elbows... I've got you..."

A lot of people try to sound steady. You can hear them reaching for it like a handle in the dark.

Florence just is.

No tremor. No wobble. No performance.

Just absolute belief that if she kept him with her, kept him moving, kept him pushing, his wife might get another chance at breathing.

He did.

Medics took over.

The line cleared.

Everyone moved on to the next thing.

Except me.

Because my brain keeps replaying the way she said you're not alone and overlaying it, like a goddamn betrayal over the way that same voice sounded in a hotel room a year ago when she begged me not to stop.

I pinch the bridge of my nose hard enough to see stars.

This is ridiculous.

I'm the chief of police, not some hormone-addled rookie. I've been doing this job long enough to watch good people torch their careers over "just this once." I've pulled officers aside for less. Jokes that go too far. Flirting that turns into entitlement. Lines crossed because someone thought they were the exception.

Lines exist for a reason.

And Florence is one big, flashing sign that says DON'T.

She's dispatch.

She works in my building.

She's younger than me by enough years that I refuse to do the math out loud, because the moment I do, my stomach turns mean.

And still if I strip the uniform, the title, the chain of

command, the small-town microscope, what's left is one brutal truth.

I can't stop thinking about her.

Not just the way she tastes.

Not just the way she arches when I put my mouth between her thighs like I'm starving.

Not just the miracle of her opening for me, trusting me, letting me take her apart.

It's worse than that.

I like her.

I like the crease at the corner of her eyes when she smiles like she's too busy living to worry about looking perfect.

I like that she's trying to belong here instead of floating through and leaving with photos, but digging in. Build something. Stay.

I like that when she told me about the worst thing that ever happened to her, she didn't do it like bait.

She said it plain. Honest. Scarred. Standing.

And I like the way she draws tarot like it matters. Like it's a language she speaks fluently in color and symbols, even when the rest of the world is just noise.

I like her.

God help me, I like her.

And that's the problem.

Because I know exactly how this looks.

Chief of Police, forty-three.

New dispatcher, twenty-something.

On paper, I'm a cliché with a badge.

Council would chew it to pieces.

The mayor would turn it into a soundbite.

The town would call me "protective" and call her a mistake.

And I won't let that happen.

I won't paint a target on her back with my name on it.

But none of that stops me from taking the long way to the copy room.

None of that stops me from pausing outside the dispatch

window too long, pretending I'm checking the call board when I'm really just checking her.

None of that stops the ache every time her voice hits the airwaves.

I want her.

Not just her body.

All of it.

And that's what makes it dangerous.

Because I've never been good at wanting something quietly.

By late afternoon, I've circled dispatch like a bad habit.

Three times.

Three goddamn times I've walked that hall for no reason at all.

I don't need to see her to know she's good at her job.

But I do it anyway.

The first time, I keep my head down.

Pretend I'm checking the call board. Pretend I don't feel her even through the glass. Pretend I'm not hearing her voice anyway, like it's threaded into the air ducts.

It's stupid. The window isn't soundproof to a memory.

I pass and don't look.

I make it ten feet before I look.

The second time, she's off a call.

Ruth says something I can't hear. Florence laughs anyway with her head tipped back, throat exposed, smile wide and real and completely unguarded.

It hits me like a round to the chest.

Because it's not polite. Not the "thank you for calling" version of her. Not customer-service reflex.

It's hers.

And for a second the building feels too small to hold that kind of light.

I tell myself to keep walking.

I don't.

I take it in like I've been running on fumes and she's oxygen. Like if I look away, I'll lose something I didn't earn the right to keep.

The third time, it's different.

No laugh. No softness.

Her shoulders are set, spine locked, jaw tight enough I can see the muscle jump even from here. Eyes narrowed at her screen like she's fighting for someone on the other end of the line.

I know that look. Heavy call.

Someone is crying. Or screaming. Or worse, quiet in the way that means the screaming already happened.

Florence holds it like a soldier. Takes the hit so the caller doesn't fall apart alone.

And I hate myself for what comes next.

I slow at the corner.

Half a step. Just enough to catch her reflection in the narrow glass panel, her face a ghost at the edge of my vision.

It's a shitty move.

Furtive. Hungry. Small.

I don't like that about myself.

I'm not a man who hides.

I'm the one who walks into the room first. Absorbs the noise, the mess, the heat, so no one else has to. Stands there while the town throws their frustrations at me in council meetings like I'm made of stone.

But lately?

Lately I'm pacing my own building like a man with a weakness and something to lose.

Like a man who already tasted heaven and knows better than to go back for seconds, and yet he still can't stop circling the gates.

I push through the break room door before I make a fourth pass and embarrass myself.

Drop the reports on the table.

Brace my palms on the counter like it'll hold me upright.

My fingers won't stop flexing.

Because the worst part?

I didn't even see her clearly that last time.

Just a flash in the glass.

Just the outline of her mouth moving calmly, while someone else's world collapsed into her headset.

And it still did something to me.

Something low.

Something stupid.

Something I don't want to name.

The coffee pot is half full.

The smell hits me. It's burnt, bitter, and abandoned. Like someone brewed it at noon and forgot it existed.

I flip the switch.

Dump the tar into the sink like it insulted me personally.

The pot clatters. I rinse it harder than necessary. Hot water fogs the air. Steam curls up like judgment.

"Get it together," I mutter.

My voice sounds wrong in here. Too loud. Too alone. Too aware of itself.

Because I know exactly how this story reads from the outside.

I've worn the stain of scrutiny before.

When Lilly's mom and I split, the department buzzed with it. All soft voices behind half-closed doors, pity packaged as curiosity.

Who cheated.

Who broke.

Who gave up first.

It wasn't like that.

We were kids with a newborn, clinging to each other like driftwood, pretending it was enough to build a life on.

She wanted out of this town before she was old enough to buy her first drink.

I wanted roots. The badge. The weight of staying.

She said she couldn't keep watching me walk into danger, not knowing if I'd come back, not knowing if I'd be the call they made her take next.

She wasn't wrong.

Love like that, something bright, reckless, young. It burns hot and fast.

And it leaves scars you don't see until years later when

you're standing in a break room over a coffee pot and realizing your hands are shaking for no goddamn reason.

I've dated since.

Carefully. Strategically.

Women from out of town. Women who didn't clock the badge until the third date, when it was already too late to ask what my job was like with that nervous little laugh.

It's cleaner that way.

No tangled power dynamics. No whispered rumors at council meetings. No one accusing me of using my rank to get laid.

But nothing's stuck.

No one's stayed.

And not one of them ever cracked me open just from a smile through a dispatch window.

Not one of them made my body remember before my brain could stop it.

Remembering her voice when she said please like it was a prayer.

Remembering how she sounded when she came undone.

Remembering that afterward she didn't cling.

She vanished.

And now she's here.

In my building.

In my town.

In my head like a problem I can't file and forget.

That night in Seattle wrecked me.

One night. No names. No promises. No edges to hold onto.

Just heat and sweat and hands on skin.

Just her.

And now she's here. Ten doors down.

The universe has a cruel sense of humor. Worse timing.

I rinse the coffee pot until the metal squeaks under my palm, like hot water can wash this out of me. The brown stain swirls, thins, disappears.

The water keeps running anyway.

My jaw aches.

I didn't realize I was grinding my teeth until the muscle jumps—low and sharp under my cheekbone.

I force a slow breath in.

Another out.

Try to pull myself back into my own skin.

It doesn't work.

Because even with the break room empty and the silence ringing, my body keeps dragging me back to her like it knows the shortest route.

On the fourth pass by dispatch, I almost run straight into her.

My own fault. I'm half-reading a memo from council about Harbor Days overtime, budget constraints, budget constraints, and budget constraints. Like the words might change if I glare at them hard enough.

I don't hear her until she's right there.

She steps out of dispatch with her bag slung over one shoulder, curls down, headset dent still faintly pressed into her hair. She looks like she's leaving a call behind her... but it's still sitting on her shoulders.

We nearly collide.

I stop too fast. My boot squeaks on the freshly waxed floor.

She jolts, catching her bag strap.

"Oh—sorry."

"Shit. My fault," I say at the same time.

We both go quiet.

And we just... look at each other.

Too close.

This hallway isn't wide enough for what she does to the air.

Not for the way she smells, like vanilla, tea, something warm and skin-close. Not for the flush that climbs her neck like it can't decide whether it's embarrassment or memory. Not for the way her eyes hold mine like she's trying to figure out if she made me up.

She didn't.

I can see it on her. At her collarbone, by her mouth, in the way her throat works once like she swallowed something sharp.

"Hey," she says, soft.

"Hey."

My voice drops without permission. Lower than it needs to be. Like my body is talking before my brain signs off.

She shifts her bag higher, reflexive. Not defensive, just giving her hands something to do.

"You're, uh... still here."

"Perks of the job." I lift the papers in my hand like they're useful. Like I'm not standing here with my pulse trying to climb out of my throat. "Council loves paperwork."

She laughs quietly and a little rough around the edges. "Sounds like torture."

"You have no idea."

We could leave it there.

We should.

This is where normal people step aside, let the other pass, say have a good night like adults with functioning impulse control.

Instead, we stay where we are.

Pinned between a shared memory and a present that refuses to behave.

Her gaze flicks to my mouth.

So fast it would be nothing if I wasn't already watching her like a man with a problem.

Heat moves low in my gut. Immediate. Sharp.

I tighten my grip on the papers until the edges bite my fingers.

"Good shift?" I ask, because I need *something* to say that isn't the truth.

Her smile curves, small but real. "Yeah. Eventful."

"I heard the CPR call," I say, too fast. "You handled it well."

Her breath leaves a little shaky, like she'd been holding it. "Thanks."

There's something bright in her eyes that isn't tears, exactly. More like the leftover of them. Like the call hasn't fully let go of her yet.

"Did you get an update?" she asks. Quiet now. "On the patient?"

I shake my head. "Not yet. I can check with EMS, if you want."

She nods, and the gratitude on her face hits me harder than it should. "Thanks."

It's a small question, but it opens something.

That's the part people don't see. You keep someone alive with your voice and then the line goes dead and the world expects you to clock out like you didn't just spend ten minutes holding a stranger's heart in your hands.

That crack in her?

It isn't weakness.

It's why she's good.

It's why she's dangerous to me.

Silence settles again.

My heartbeat is loud enough I swear she can hear it.

I should move. I should step aside and let her pass.

But the part of me that remembers her breath in my ear, her body going slack under my hands, her voice breaking on my name... that part isn't interested in being noble.

She bites her bottom lip.

Not on purpose. Not a tease. Just a habit.

It still wrecks me.

A laugh echoes down the corridor. One of my officers, is getting closer.

Reality rushes in like cold air. Doors. Radios. The weight of my badge. The fact that someone could round the corner and find me standing here like I forgot how to walk.

I step back. Shift to the side. Make room.

"Get some rest," I say, voice finally under control. "You did good work today."

"Thanks." She slips past me.

Her shoulder grazes my chest.

Barely.

A brush that shouldn't mean anything and absolutely does.

My spine goes tight.

I do not breathe in too deep. I can't afford it.

She keeps walking.

Doesn't look back.

I still watch her. I hate that I do.

At the outer door, she hesitates a beat and turns.

Our eyes lock.

The look on her face is a question and an answer at the same time.

We're both in trouble.

Her smile is small, self-aware. Like she knows it too.

"Goodnight, Chief," she calls, light like she didn't just crack me open in a hallway. "Try not to drown in paperwork."

"Goodnight, Lockhart," I manage.

Then she's gone.

And the hallway feels colder than it did a minute ago.

I stare at the space where she was like it might fill itself back in.

Three long breaths later, I pivot into the break room like I had any reason to be here.

Coward.

It's my own voice. Brutal. Accurate.

I toss the council memo onto the table and brace a hand on the back of a chair until my fingers hurt. The microwave door throws my reflection back at me in the form of tired eyes, deeper lines, the scruff I didn't bother shaving this morning.

Distinguished, my daughter once called it.

I told her that's what people say when they mean old.

Right now I just look wrecked.

And worse?

I know exactly why.

Because my brain keeps doing the math of risk, fallout, and collateral damage.

If I asked Florence out. If she said yes. If we did something normal in daylight where people could see us it might look like dinner by the bay, a walk that isn't an accident, coffee that doesn't come with a radio strapped to my hip. And somebody would notice.

They always do.

And then the questions start, dressed up as concern and delivered like gossip.

Is she getting better shifts because of him?

Did he go easy on her after that call?

What did she do to earn that praise?

It wouldn't matter that Ruth's her supervisor. That I don't touch Florence's schedule, her file, her evaluations.

Chief is still Chief.

The buck still stops with me.

And when it goes sideways, because in a town this small, it *always* goes sideways, who pays?

Not me.

Not the way she would.

I'd take heat. I'd take a hit. I'd take a couple tense council meetings and an article that gets recycled every time the town gets bored.

But I'd still have my badge. My office. My career.

She'd have whispers at shift change. Side-eyes in the break room. The kind of cold that creeps into a room and never really leaves.

Or worse, she'd leave.

Pack up. Find another center. Another "fresh start."

And everyone would nod sadly like they hadn't helped push her out the door.

Because that's what people do here. They act shocked after they set the match.

I've seen it too many times to pretend otherwise.

So I stare at my own reflection and think it, harsh and clear:

If I go after her, I'm choosing what I want over what she needs to feel safe doing her job.

If I go after her, I'm gambling with her peace.

With her reputation.

With her future.

All of it's true.

None of it touches the other truth which is meaner, quieter, and lodged in my bones. Because even while my brain lays out the reasons, my body betrays me like it doesn't give a damn about ethics. My hands remember the weight of her hips.

My mouth remembers the taste of her skin, salt and heat and something sweet underneath.

And yeah, my body remembers the way she clenched around me like she didn't know how to let go of anything without taking it with her.

Just tonight.

That's what she said.

That's what I agreed to.

No names. No numbers. No calls.

At the time it felt clean.

Now it feels like a punishment I handed myself and called it restraint.

Because I could find her number.

I have access.

And the thought lands ugly. Too easy. Too tempting.

Integrity only matters when you want to break it.

So I don't ask Ruth for her file under some fake "performance review."

I don't touch HR data.

I don't do a damn thing except walk past dispatch like a ghost and pretend her voice on the radio doesn't make something in me ache.

It's a lie.

But it's cleaner than the alternative.

And lately... I'm not sure clean is the same as right.

Especially when there's this other edge I keep skirting. This quiet, sick thought I won't let myself say out loud.

Because Florence didn't just *end up* here.

People don't uproot their lives for nothing.

No. Stop. Not going there. Not without proof.

Boundary time.

No more detours past dispatch.

No more turning up the radio when it's her.

No more watching the clock for her shift to end just to catch a glimpse of her walking down the hall.

I need to be the adult in the room, and in this building, unfortunately, that's me.

I walk back to my office with purpose this time. No glancing sideways. No slowing at the window.

I sit down, pull the budget spreadsheet closer, and force my brain into numbers.

Overtime projections. Fuel costs. Equipment replacement. Things I can fix. Things that make sense.

I can't want her.

The sentence sits on my tongue like a rule.

A boundary.

A line.

And my body calls me a liar.

I can't want her.

But I do.

THIRTEEN
FLORENCE

PUMPKIMANIA LOOKS like a pumpkin patch and a Renaissance Faire had a baby and raised it on Pinterest.

Lanterns hang between maple trees like little captured suns, and every booth smells like nutmeg, cinnamon, or that suspicious harvest spice blend that only exists in towns where autumn is a personality trait. Music drifts through the air—fiddle, mandolin, and someone absolutely committing crimes against a tambourine.

Lilly takes my wrist like I'm a toddler with a death wish.

"This way," she says. "Donuts first. Or cider slushies. Or both. You choose."

"I haven't even looked around yet."

"You can look while chewing," she says, already dragging me toward a booth with a line that suggests the donuts are either life-changing or laced with narcotics.

She's in her element. Brown boots. Plaid scarf. Hair in two messy buns like twin satellites orbiting her head. She's practically vibrating.

Me?

I'm trying.

Trying to be here. Trying to let the air taste like cinnamon instead of nerves. Trying not to feel like I'm waiting for something I can't name to come shoulder-check me in the middle of a crowd.

It's been four days since running into August in the hallway at work.

Four days since August looked at me like he remembered.

Four days since my body started acting like it has a mind of its own.

No texts. No calls. No accidental run-ins. Just the kind of silence that's technically nothing and still manages to take up space.

I tell myself it shouldn't matter.

My mouth lies.

My pulse doesn't.

"Okay," Lilly says, cutting straight through the spiral I wasn't spiraling into. "I need you to prepare yourself because these donuts? They are a religious experience."

"Better than the ferry donuts?"

She gasps like I slapped her. "Don't blaspheme."

I laugh, and the tight spot in my chest loosens half an inch.

We reach the front. The a woman in orange overalls and a knitted pumpkin hat, the vender, hands us a paper tray piled with warm, sugar-dusted perfection.

"Eat," Lilly commands, like she's officiating a sacred rite.

I do.

The donut melts. Crisp edges, soft center, cinnamon sugar sticking to my fingers like proof I'm alive. It is stupidly good.

I make a sound.

Out loud.

Accidentally.

Lilly freezes mid-bite and turns her whole head toward me. "Florence," she whispers, eyes huge. "Please don't make that noise in public unless you intend to propose to someone here."

I choke, half-laughing. "Oh my god."

"No," she says gravely. "Oh your god."

I smack her shoulder with the back of my hand. She dances out of reach like a menace and keeps eating, pleased with herself.

"You're not even the first person to say that to me this month," I mutter, wiping sugar off my fingers like dignity is something you can scrub clean.

Lilly stops dead. Slowly turns back. "This month."

"Don't get excited," I say, already backing away. "It was... a different pastry-related incident."

"Uh-huh," she says, eyes bright with suspicion. "Sure it was."

I follow her to the next row of booths and keep nibbling my donut like it's an emotional support object, because if my mouth is busy, my brain can't go looking for trouble.

Do I wish August was here?

The answer lands before I can even pretend I'm above it.

Yes.

Not in a soft way. Not in a sweet way. Nothing about what August does to me is sweet.

It's a sharp, dumb want. The kind that turns my brain into static and my body into a yes. Sometimes it's all I can think about is his skin on my tongue, his mouth on my—I slam the thought shut.

Because the truth is, it *would* be easier if it was only physical. If he was just a good night and a dirty memory.

But then I wouldn't be standing in Townsend Harbor eating a donut I don't even need, pretending this town didn't have his name stitched into it.

I hate that I want him to text.

I hate that part of me keeps checking my phone like it's going to suddenly decide to be kind.

Wanting and having are two different lives, and I have a talent for living in the first one.

Lilly veers toward a stall selling tiny carved pumpkins shaped like woodland creatures.

"Look!" she says, lifting a pumpkin fox with button eyes. "Tell me this isn't adorable."

"It's adorable," I admit, because I'm not a liar.

She presses it into my hands. "It's yours."

"What? No. I'm not letting you buy me things."

"It's six dollars."

"That's six dollars more than I need to spend on a tiny fox pumpkin that will rot in two days."

"It's not a purchase," she says firmly. "It's roommate enrichment."

"Are you implying I'm a rescue animal?"

"Emotionally?" She squints at me. "Yes."

I laugh, real this time, not thinnly and she grins like she won something.

And it hits me, weirdly, right there in the middle of the pumpkin chaos.

This feels like... friendship.

Not the polite kind. Not the careful kind. Not the kind where you smile and pretend you aren't counting exits. The warm, effortless kind that settles under your ribs without asking.

Which is the last thing I expected from the girl whose last name I noticed and didn't ignore.

We wander past candied pecans, birdhouses shaped like tiny lighthouses, two elderly women knitting scarves faster than should be medically possible, and a man playing accordion with the confidence of a rock god.

Lilly leans in, smug. "See? I told you there'd be an accordion."

"Tragic," I say, laughing.

She beams like she personally manifested him.

We keep moving.

My phone buzzes once in my pocket, and my heart jumps like a traitor.

Probably HR or a promotional email, maybe a reminder about the phone bill I keep pretending doesn't exist.

I check anyway.

Just an ad.

No August.

Of course no August.

I slide the phone away and pretend the disappointment isn't a real thing. Pretend it doesn't have weight or live in my body like a second pulse.

Lilly bumps my shoulder with hers, mouth full of donut. "You're thinking too loud again."

"I'm literally not speaking."

"That's how I know," she says, dead serious. "Come on. Next booth. I'm not done feeding you joy."

And for one small moment, walking beside her under lantern light, clutching a ridiculous pumpkin fox like a soft little omen, I let myself try.

Lilly doesn't notice. She's too busy dragging me toward a row of candles shaped like potion bottles.

"Okay," she announces, voice buzzing. "I have a surprise for you."

"A good one or a jump-scare one?"

"A destiny one."

"Oh no."

"Oh yes." She wiggles her eyebrows. "Florence. Welcome to my favorite place in Townsend Harbor."

She spins me toward a booth draped in black velvet and violet lights, tucked between handmade soap and crocheted ghosts. A sign hangs above it in clean, bold lettering:

HARBOR ROOT — ODDITIES • TAROT • HERBS • BOOKS

My breath catches.

Of all the surprises I expected, this wasn't it.

"After you showed me how to read," Lilly says, practically vibrating, "I may have talked a tiny bit about you. And your tarot."

"Lilly—"

"Come on. Just look."

Before I can protest, she's already pulling me in.

It isn't really a booth. It's a doorway.

The back wall is open, leading into a narrow little hallway lined with shelves. Salt-glass lamps. Spell jars. Stacks of books with cracked spines. The air smells like vanilla, cedar, and something green and sharp that lives in the back of your throat.

A man stands behind the table of decks.

Tall. Long dark hair tied back. Rings stacked up his fingers. A black apron dusted with herbs like he got in a fight with a spice rack and lost on purpose. He looks up with eyes bright and an easy smile.

"Smith!" Lilly claps once, like she's summoning him. "I brought her!"

His gaze lands on me and stays there, gentle but focused.

"This must be Florence."

I blink. "You know my name?"

"Lilly's been singing your praises." He leans forward a little, not intrusive, just interested. "Tarot reader. Artist. Dispatcher. Rooted but restless."

My cheeks warm. "That's... a lot."

"He's perceptive," Lilly says. "Or psychic. Or a cryptid. Jury's out."

"I'm not a cryptid," Smith says calmly. "Yet."

A laugh sneaks out of me. Small, surprised.

He gestures at the decks. "What do you use?"

"Rider-Waite. A couple indie decks. I collect."

His eyes spark. "Collectors always read differently. More... personal."

"I don't know about that."

"You do." He reaches behind him and pulls out a deck wrapped in deep purple cloth, edges gold-foiled. "Here. Try this one."

I shake my head. "I can't just—"

"I'm not giving it to you," he cuts in, smiling. "I'm letting you borrow it. Unless you want to buy it. But also," his grin goes sharper, "I want a reading."

I glance at Lilly. She's already vibrating with joy like this is the greatest day of her life.

"Here?" I ask.

"Now," Smith says.

I swallow.

I haven't done a public reading in months. Not since before the move. Not since I decided I was going to keep my life small and controlled and quiet.

But the table is velvet under my palms. The deck is warm in my hands. Heavy in that familiar way, like it remembers being used.

"Okay," I say, and my voice comes out steadier than I feel. "If I butcher it, you're not allowed to mock me."

"Reader's honor," he says, laughing.

I sit. Lilly practically perches at my shoulder like an excited gargoyle.

"Question?" I ask.

Smith taps a ringed finger against his lip, thinking. "Love. Someone new. I'm trying to understand the shape of it."

Of course he is.

I shuffle slow. Rhythmic. The sound settles something inside me. My pulse evens. My brain quiets.

This, right here, this is what I'm good at.

I cut the deck.

Three cards.

King of Cups. Two of Wands. Knight of Pentacles.

Smith leans in. "Well?"

My voice turns soft. Certain.

"You met someone emotionally grounded," I say, fingers brushing the King. "Deep feelings, but controlled. Gentle. Cautious. Not the kind who rushes."

Smith goes still.

"And this," I continue, touching the Two, "is a crossroads. You're deciding whether to keep your feet planted... or step into something that changes your whole life. You want it. But it scares you."

He exhales like he's been holding his breath for a year.

Then I touch the Knight.

"This person is steady," I say. "Not flashy. Loyal. The type who builds trust one brick at a time. You two might move at different speeds, but you're headed the same direction."

Lilly makes a sound like she's going to faint.

"And..." The words come before I can overthink them. "Light hair. Not bright blond. More like," I squint a little, listening to the image in my head, "honey."

Smith freezes.

Then he bursts into delighted laughter, loud enough that a few people turn.

"Oh my gods," he says, hand over his mouth. "His name is Theo. He's a carpenter. And yes. Honey-blond."

"Well shit," Lilly whispers reverently. "Florence. You're a witch."

I laugh, but something warm opens in my chest.

Not adrenaline. Not panic.

Something else.

Confidence.

Smith leans forward, eyes still bright. "Do you want to do readings at my shop?"

"What?"

"I'm serious. I've wanted another reader for months. My regular only works weekends." He taps the cards, then looks back at me. "You read pattern and intuition at the same time. That's rare."

My first instinct is to say no. To back away. To keep my life clean and contained.

But for the first time in a long time, the thought doesn't feel like danger.

It feels like a door.

"I..." I swallow. "I can't quit dispatch."

"I didn't ask you to," Smith says, gentle. "Come by. See the space. If it feels right, we'll work around your schedule."

Lilly nudges me, eyes shining. "Florence."

I hesitate, just one beat.

Then I nod. "Okay. I'll come by."

Smith beams like I just signed my name on something sacred. "Perfect. Welcome to Harbor Root, future reader."

"Hold on," I laugh. "Future. Potential. Maybe."

"The cards already told me," he says, completely serious.

Lilly squeals. "We're celebrating. More donuts. More cider. We go."

She loops her arm through mine and pulls me back into the lantern glow like she's afraid I'll talk myself out of joy.

We walk. We eat. We laugh.

And for the first time since I moved to Townsend Harbor, I forget, just for a minute, why I came here in the first place.

It's a relief so sharp it almost hurts.

We stop at the top of a small hill overlooking the harbor. Lanterns float on the water like scattered fire. The wind is cool, on my cheeks and it carries something sweeter than possibility.

Lilly leans her head on my shoulder. “You okay?”

I exhale slow. “Yeah. I think I am.”

“Good,” she says softly. “Because I like you, Florence. And I’m glad you moved here.”

My throat tightens. I don’t trust my voice for a second, so I go for the safe truth.

“I’m glad you forced me to eat donuts,” I say.

She laughs. “My very serious contribution to your emotional well-being.”

We start back down the hill, swallowed by the crowd.

August isn’t here.

August isn’t calling.

And for once, just once, I don’t let that ruin the night.

Because something else is there, warm and stubborn in my chest.

Not him.

Me.

FOURTEEN
AUGUST

THE CLOCK on my nightstand flips from 1:58 to 1:59 in sickly blue digits.

I stare at it like I can bully it into moving faster.

It doesn't.

Of course it doesn't.

The house is quiet. It's always quiet now. No cartoons bleeding through the wall from a kid who refused to sleep. No music from a teenager trying out identities through playlists. Just the hum of the fridge down the hall and the occasional creak of old wood settling.

I should be used to it by now.

Most nights, I am.

Tonight, my mind just won't shut the hell up.

Three weeks since Harbor Days. Two since I swore I'd stop taking the long way past dispatch. Four nights this week where sleep never even showed up. Somehow Florence's gotten louder in my head, not quieter.

I flip onto my back and glare at the ceiling. The room's faintly lit by the streetlamp outside, all soft gray and shadow. My body is tired, the bone-deep kind that never really goes away after a couple decades in uniform. But my brain is wired.

Her face keeps sliding in where the blank space should be.

Florence in the glow of Harbor Days lights, cheeks pink from the cold, hands wrapped around a mug of pumpkin chai. The way she scrunched her nose when she burned her tongue and tried to pretend she didn't. The puff of breath that left her when our fingers brushed over that leather pouch, like the contact took something out of her.

Almost two weeks ago.

You'd think it was yesterday by how clear it is.

I can still hear the sound of her laugh when the scone flaked all over her coat and she tried to brush it off with this mortified little noise.

Can still hear myself offering to buy her another one just to watch her smile.

Can still feel the way the whole damn world narrowed down to the space between us when that gust of wind threw leaves around our feet like some overdramatic movie scene.

It should've been ridiculous.

It wasn't.

It felt like the universe setting the stage and daring me to step onto it.

And then there was the walk. Brightly lit lanterns, fog rolling off the harbor, music from three different buskers bleeding together. Her shoulder close enough to feel the heat of her under that coat, her voice low when she talked about her mom, about moving here, about the way she was trying to start over.

I told her about my daughter in the broad strokes. About almost marrying her mother. About how some choices haunt you, even when you'd make them again.

I didn't tell her how it felt to watch her walk away at the end of the night, heart pounding like I'd just run toward gunfire instead of away from it.

I didn't tell her how every step felt wrong.

The clock flips to 2:03.

I exhale hard and drag a hand over my face.

This is fucking stupid.

I'm a grown man. I've done graveyard shifts, week-long search operations, thirty-six-hour stretches in the command center running on coffee and spite. I've slept sitting up in a patrol car with the radio turned low. I've gone without sleep for better reasons than a pretty dispatcher with big eyes and a sharp tongue.

But it isn't just that.

If it were just that, I could've filed the night we met under Good Hotel Mistakes and moved on.

Seattle was supposed to be just that, one night, two strangers, a bottle of whiskey, and a bed I didn't have to make in the morning.

I squeeze my eyes shut and, predictably, my brain takes that as a cue to hit play.

That hotel room snaps into focus so sharply it almost hurts.

The city lights outside the window.

Her back against the door.

The soft, startled sound she made when I kissed her for real, not like a joke anymore, not like a dare.

I remember the way her fingers dug into my shoulders when I pressed her up against the wall of the elevator. The way she moaned into my mouth, surprised at her own hunger. How she gasped my name like she'd been holding it back all night.

The way she felt when I slid my hand between her thighs.

The heat of her. The slick, desperate way she rocked into my fingers like she'd never needed anything so badly.

Jesus.

My cock stirs under the sheet, traitor that it is.

I shift, trying to ignore it.

It's no use. The more I tell myself not to think about it, the bigger it gets, filling the space my good intentions used to live.

I roll onto my side, stare at the wall.

For a second, I try to reroute. Think about work instead.

The budget meeting with the mayor. Overtime projections. The new guy in patrol who keeps radioing in way too much detail. The council member who corners me every Thursday to complain about teenagers loitering at the harbor.

I make it maybe thirty seconds before my mind slides right back.

Her lips wrapped around the tip of my dick, eyes looking up at me like she wanted to see me fall apart.

Her thighs trembling when I had her on her hands and knees on that bed, one hand on the small of her back, the other anchored on her hip. The way she whimpered when I pushed into her, tight and hot and perfect, like she'd been made to fit me.

I swallow hard, throat suddenly dry.

"Fuck," I mutter into the quiet.

My hand is already moving before I consciously decide anything.

Just a shift under the waistband of my shorts, fingers wrapping around myself. I'm hard enough it aches, heavy and hot, like the blood has decided this is where it lives now.

It would be so easy to stop.

Roll over, force my brain onto something else. The game I half-watched earlier. The book on my nightstand I haven't finished.

I don't.

Instead, I close my eyes and let the memories come.

Her legs wrapped around my waist, nails sinking into my shoulders.

The way she whispered please into my mouth like she was confessing something.

The way she clenched around me when she came, head tipped back, throat exposed.

The sounds she made was soft vibrating with broken things that shot straight down my spine.

My thumb swipes over the slick at the tip, and I groan under my breath. My hips jerk up, chasing my own palm.

I shouldn't be doing this.

Thinking about someone I see at work. Someone whose voice comes over the radio while my officers are out there. Someone who sits ten doors down from my office, wearing a headset and keeping people alive.

But the guilt just folds itself into the ache. Makes it sharper, somehow. More addictive.

I picture her in my bed instead of in that hotel room.

Here, in this quiet house at the edge of town, where the walls know every version of me. Her hair spread over my pillow. That little crease between her brows smoothing out when I kiss her awake.

My fist tightens, stroke growing harder, more urgent.

I imagine her looking up at me across my own kitchen table, a mug of coffee in her hands instead of a dispatch headset. Bare feet on my tile, her laugh echoing off my cabinets while Lilly rolls her eyes at both of us.

That image hits somewhere deeper than my cock.

Because I want that.

The every day.

The stupid, small shit.

Not just the way she sounds when she's begging.

But right now, my body doesn't know the difference.

Right now, all it knows is the way she felt when I had her pinned against the cool glass of that hotel window, city lights painting her skin in gold and shadow. The way she came apart when I told her to.

I stroke faster, breath coming shorter, muscles tightening.

"Florence," I breathe, low and wrecked, like she's here, like I'm saying it against her skin instead of into an empty room.

Heat coils low in my belly, sharp and insistent.

I picture her on her back in my bed, knees bent, my hand between her thighs. Her lips parted, eyes hazy, cheeks flushed. I picture pushing into her slow, holding her gaze, feeling that first tight slide of her body around mine.

I picture her whispering my name.

That does it.

Pleasure rips through me, hot and blinding, the kind that steals sound and thought. My hips jerk once, twice, and I come hard into my own hand, jaw clenched to keep from groaning out loud like a goddamn teenager.

For a few seconds, there's nothing but the pounding of my heart and the feel of my pulse throbbing in my fist.

Then the comedown hits.

The mess. The sweat cooling on my skin. The aftershock tremor in my thighs.

And beneath that, rising like something nasty in the back of my throat.

Emptiness.

I lay there, chest heaving, and wait for the usual relief.

It doesn't come.

The edge is dulled, sure. The immediate urgency gone. But the aching want? The part of me that's been pacing like a caged animal since the second I realized the new dispatcher in my building was the same woman who'd let me wreck her?

That's still here.

Louder, somehow.

Because scratching the itch doesn't change the problem. It just makes it clearer.

I don't just want her body.

I want her.

I blow out a long breath and shove myself upright. My lower back twinges in protest, age, years of wearing the belt, all of it, but I ignore it and swing my legs over the side of the bed.

The hardwood is cold under my feet.

I grab a tissue from the nightstand, clean myself up, toss it in the trash. The air feels too sharp against my skin now, every nerve rubbed raw.

In the bathroom, the mirror doesn't pull any punches.

I look... tired.

Hair mussed, scruff heavier than I like, lines dug in deeper around my eyes than they were a few years ago. My shoulders are still broad, chest still solid, but I can see every graveyard shift written in the set of my mouth.

"You're a fucking mess," I tell my reflection quietly.

He doesn't argue.

I turn on the tap, splash cold water on my face. It helps a little. Clears some of the fog.

Not enough.

Because the part of me that's been avoiding a certain decision, the one I keep shoving down under duty and protocol and age gaps and power dynamics, uses this crack in my control to slither right back up.

You can't keep doing this.

Masturbating to the memory of her like some secret you're ashamed of.

Pretending you're not already crossing lines in your head every time you walk past dispatch.

You either stop, or you do something about it.

I brace my hands on the counter and stare at the water swirling down the drain.

Stopping isn't working.

I've tried.

Hell, after that hallway near-collision four days ago, I swore I'd put distance between us.

The way she looked up at me. Wide eyes, lips parted, like the air itself was too thick all of a sudden. That look followed me all the way home. Her shoulder brushing my chest. The way she said Goodnight, Chief with that little smile like she knew exactly how much trouble we were both in.

I told myself that was the line.

That we'd had our one fair shot in Seattle, our one impossible walk at Harbor Days, our one humiliating almost-moment in the station hallway.

That I'd be the adult and back off.

Four days later, I'm jerking off to the memory of her in my bed and seriously considering breaking every damn rule I've set for myself.

Not the department rules.

Those are simple. Don't harass. Don't coerce. Don't sleep with someone whose job you directly control. Don't abuse access.

That's not what this is.

Her direct supervisor is Ruth, not me. I don't touch her schedule. I've given her exactly one piece of feedback at work and it was a professional compliment after she walked a man through CPR.

She's not a rookie on my patrol shift. She's not a suspect. She's not some civilian I met because I pulled them over.

She's a coworker.

A grown woman.

She can tell me to back off any time she wants.

The lines I'm wrestling with are the ones nobody writes down.

The quiet ones.

The ones that say: You are the Chief of Police. People look at you and see authority before they see a man. If you pursue someone, even honestly, and it goes sideways, you will survive it better than they will.

And that... that sits heavy.

Because I know this town.

I know how fast it talks.

If I take her out to dinner and someone sees us? If she comes out of my house early one morning in the same clothes she wore the night before?

Half the harbor will know before we've finished our coffee.

And if it ends badly?

It's not my reputation they'll shred first.

It's hers.

He's older, they'll say. He should've known better.

What did she think was going to happen?

Did she really expect the chief to stick around?

Why did she think she was special?

The words won't be said in front of me, of course. They'll be said over drinks, at the hair salon, in the grocery store aisle. They'll be said with pity and smugness and all that small-town righteousness that gets sharpest when it's aimed at women.

She deserves better than that.

She deserves better than me.

The thought lands like a stone in my gut.

I grip the sides of the sink until my fingers ache.

If that's true, you leave her alone.

That's the kindest thing.

The safest thing.

The right thing.

Except, I know what leaving someone alone really looks like.

It's not this.

It's not walking past her window three times a day pretending you're checking the call board. It's not lingering in the hallway to hear the way her voice sounds when she says Copy, 13, I've got you. It's not listening to recordings of her CPR her calls under the guise of "reviewing performance" when what you're really doing is soaking in her steadiness like it's oxygen.

What I'm doing right now?

This half-starved circling?

It's the worst of both worlds.

I'm not giving her peace.

I'm not giving myself peace.

I'm just... suffering in silence and dragging her into my head every time I close my eyes.

I straighten up, jaw tight, and kill the light.

Back in the bedroom, the digital clock has crawled to 2:27.

I sit on the edge of the bed and stare at my phone on the nightstand.

The thought slips in.

Uninvited.

Persistent.

You could text her.

It's ridiculous how fast my pulse responds.

My hand hovers for a second, then I grab the phone just to shut the idea down.

I'll check email, I tell myself. Maybe there's something I missed for the morning. Maybe there's some late-night crisis from the mayor that'll give me a reason to be awake.

I unlock the screen.

No crisis.

No emails that can't wait.

Just the usual late-night spam and a weather alert about fog over the bay.

Still, my thumb swipes to the mail app out of habit.

The top folder is the one I use for department admin, HR, council stuff, union notices. Unread count: three.

I tap it open.

Two messages from HR about open enrollment.

One under that, flagged from the week Florence started.

SUBJECT: Updated Dispatch Roster & Contact Info.

The room seems to narrow around that line of text.

I haven't opened it since the day it came in.

Not because I don't need the information.

Because I knew exactly what it contained, and exactly how hard it would be not to use it.

My thumb hovers.

This is the moment.

The line I've been dancing around.

I could delete it. Pretend I never saw it.

Or, I tap.

The email opens with a bland little chime, completely unaware that my heart just kicked up like I'm about to breach a door.

Standard HR language at the top. Attached PDF of the roster. Names, positions, phone numbers, emails, emergency contacts. The same thing we've always had. The same thing I've used a hundred times to call officers in for overtime, to check on someone after a rough call, to send congrats when a kid is born.

My teeth grit.

There's nothing illegal about this. Nothing even against policy.

She knows people have this. Ruth uses it. The sergeants use it. If we were short-staffed, I'd have no problem dialing her number and asking her to come in.

I'm not short-staffed. I'm just not sleeping.

The difference is why.

The thought of picking up the phone right now, dialing her number, and hearing her voice sleep-rough and confused makes my stomach flip.

I scroll.

Names blur until hers comes into view.

LOCKHEART, FLORENCE – DISPATCH.

Cell Number.

Email.

My chest tightens at the sight of it in black and white.

She's here.

Not just as a memory. Not just as a woman I met far away from everything that defined us. She's woven into my day-to-day life now, slotted into the roster like she belongs.

Because she does.

Because she's good at this.

Because she's already part of the fabric of this place.

My thumb presses on the number before I can talk myself out of it.

Two options. Call. Save.

Like this is a normal thing.

The phone offers to create a new contact.

For a long beat, my brain just... stalls.

If I make her a contact, that makes this real. This isn't some abstract thing I think about at two in the morning. It's a name in my phone next to my daughter's, my officers', the handful of friends I still have time for.

It's a spot in my life.

My heart slams against my ribs.

I select Create New Contact.

Her name autofills from the email.

I don't add a last name.

Just Florence.

Seeing it there, in my list, looks wrong and right at the same time.

Like it's been missing and I didn't know until now.

I save it before I talk myself out of it.

The message window opens by itself, as if the phone's tired of waiting for me to catch up to what I clearly want to do.

The empty text box stares back at me.

This is the hard part.

What the hell do I even say?

Hey, this is your chief. I've been jerking off to the memory of you for a year and I can't sleep. You up?

Fuck me.

I close my eyes and exhale through my teeth, forcing myself to think like a man who deserves the badge on his dresser.

Honest.

Respectful.

Direct.

Give her every chance to say no.

My thumbs move, typing out the first draft.

Hey, it's August. I know this is probably inappropriate, but I haven't stopped thinking about you.

I stare at it.

Backspace the whole thing until the words vanish.

Too much.

Too raw.

I try again.

Hi Florence, Chief Calder. I'm sorry to text this late.

I stop.

That sounds like a memo. Like I'm about to ask her to cover a double shift.

Delete.

The cursor blinks, patient and merciless.

I pinch the bridge of my nose and let out a slow breath.

Why does this feel exactly like being sixteen again, trying to figure out how to call the girl I liked without sounding like an idiot?

Because it matters.

Because she matters.

That's why my palms are sweating like I'm about to walk into a firefight instead of sending a fucking text.

I force myself to slow down.

What do I want her to know, if I only get one shot at this?

That I respect her.

That I'm aware there's a line here.

That I'll back off if she tells me to.

And that I want her anyway.

My fingers start moving.

Hey. It's August.

I pause, then keep going.

I know it's late, and I know me texting you might be a line you don't want crossed.

If that's the case, tell me once and I won't do it again.

I read it twice.

It sounds like me. Direct, no bullshit. Gives her control.

I add another line before I can lose my nerve.

I just... kept thinking about our walk at Harbor Days and realized I'd rather risk being an idiot than keep pretending I don't want to talk to you outside of work.

My throat feels dry.

It's too honest.

Not honest enough.

Fuck it.

If you'd rather this stay professional, I will.

No pressure to respond. I just wanted you to know.

I sit back and look at the whole thing.

August: Hey. It's August.

I know it's late, and I know me texting you might be a line you don't want crossed. If that's the case, tell me once and I won't do it again.

I just... kept thinking about our walk at Harbor Days and realized I'd rather risk being an idiot than keep pretending I don't want to talk to you outside of work.

If you'd rather this stay professional, I will.

No pressure to respond. I just wanted you to know.

My thumb hovers over the send button.

This is it.

Once I hit that arrow, there's no taking it back. No pretending I don't know her number. No lying to myself about the nature of this thing between us.

If she says no, I'll have to live with that.

If she doesn't answer at all, I'll have to live with that too.

If she says yes...

I don't let myself chase that thread yet. It's too bright. Too dangerous.

I think about Pumpkimania, even though I didn't see her there. I imagine her wandering through the crowds the way she moves through everything with a curious, quietness. Just, taking it all in. I picture her stopping at some booth that catches her eye, laughing at something a vendor says, a warm drink in her hands. Maybe she tried one of those powdered-sugar donuts everyone raves about. Maybe she walked home under the lanterns afterward, cheeks flushed from the cold.

Maybe her phone buzzed in her pocket, and if I'd had the nerve, it could've been me.

Reading this.

Knowing, finally, that she's not the only one stuck halfway between what happened in Seattle and what's happening now.

My chest tightens.

I inhale, steady.

Exhale.

Then I tap send.

The message whooshes away, my words disappearing into whatever invisible path they travel to reach her.

The little delivered stamp pops up under the bubble.

That's it.

I've jumped.

There's nothing left to do but fall.

I set the phone on my thigh, like I'm going to be reasonable and put it back on the nightstand in a second.

I don't move.

Instead, I stare at the screen like I can will it to light up again.

Seconds tick by.

The clock on the nightstand flips to 2:39.

My heartbeat sounds loud in my ears.

This is ridiculous. I'm a grown man, sitting in the dark, adrenaline surging like I just kicked down a door.

Somewhere across town, she's either sleeping through this

or wide awake, staring at the same blue light, reading what I just did.

I roll my head back against the headboard and force myself to breathe.

Whatever happens next is up to her.

I've crossed the line I can control.

Now I get to live with it.

FIFTEEN
FLORENCE

I WAKE up to a vibration against my cheek.

For a second I think it's my headset and I've fallen asleep at the console, but then the light coming through the blinds registers soft, grey, not the harsh fluorescent wash of dispatch, and my brain catches up.

I'm in my bed.

My phone is buzzing under my pillow.

I fumble for it, blearily squinting at the screen.

An automated message and something from an Unknown number.

My thumb hovers, still thick with sleep.

The preview shows the first line of the text.

Florence. It's August.

Every trace of sleep evaporates in an instant.

My heart punches up into my throat so hard I almost drop the phone.

I swipe the notification open with fingers that don't feel like they belong to me.

And then I just... stare.

My brain doesn't process his words all at once. They hit in staggered, breath-killing waves.

August texted me.

He found my number.

He's been thinking about me.

He wants to talk.

No pressure.

Just him, finally admitting he can't pretend I'm a stranger.

My lungs forget their job entirely.

For a full ten seconds, all I can do is blink at the screen, heat blooming under my skin like someone lit a match inside my chest. It's too much and not enough all at once. My heart is in my throat. My stomach drops. My entire body goes warm and cold at the same time.

He wants to talk to me.

He wants me.

Not the emergency version of me. Not the dispatcher behind a headset. Not the girl who pretends she has nerves of steel because the alternative is falling apart.

Me.

I lie there, the phone glowing in my hand, and try to remember how to breathe.

My chest aches.

I read it once.

Again.

A third time, slower, trying to make sure I'm not hallucinating.

It's stupid how much four lines of text can rearrange the inside of a person. How one name at the top of my screen can make everything feel sharper, more in focus.

I roll onto my back, staring at the hairline crack in the ceiling while my pulse bangs out a panicked rhythm against my ribs.

He texted me.

He texted me.

The chief of police. The man whose hands were on my body a year ago and whose voice has been living rent-free in my head ever since, texted to say he's been thinking about me.

I check the timestamp.

Five hours ago.

Which means he's probably already up, showered, halfway through his fourth cup of coffee. The picture makes my stomach flip. August in his kitchen, early morning light cutting a line across his jaw, thumb hovering over his phone the same way mine is now.

He's been thinking about you.

A lot.

Heat slides through me, low and treacherous.

I should answer.

I know I should.

Anything. Just one word.

Yes.

Or: *I've been thinking about you too.*

Or: *Coffee sounds perfect.*

Instead I stare at the blinking cursor in the text box and... freeze.

How do you reply to that without sounding like a teenager or a cautionary workplace HR video?

Hey, Chief, thanks for the life-changing elevator sex and the existential professional crisis, want to get donuts?

Not great, Lockhart.

My thumbs type anyway.

I'd really like that.

I stare at the sentence.

It's honest. It's simple. It doesn't confess that my entire nervous system lights up like a switchboard when I hear his voice on the radio.

I add, Coffee sounds perfect.

Then I picture hitting send and immediately combusting.

Delete.

The letters vanish.

I try again.

You didn't cross a line. I — I what?

Miss you?

Want you?

Think about your mouth every time I pour coffee?

I backspace until the screen is blank again.

My alarm goes off, shrill and insistent.

I slap it silent without looking away from the message thread.

My shift starts in an hour.

I tell myself: You'll answer him on your lunch break. When your brain is online. When you're not still half-tangled in sheets, smelling like sleep and wanting.

It's a lie and I know it, but it's the only way I can get my feet onto the floor.

I set the phone on my nightstand without replying.

It feels like placing my own heart there and walking away.

The air in the apartment is cold when I step out of the shower. I dress on autopilot slipping on my black jeans, black boots, soft long-sleeve under my dispatch polo. My hands are steady enough to do eyeliner, but that doesn't stop me from catching my own eyes in the mirror and seeing the shadow of last night's dreams in them.

His body over mine.

His mouth at my throat.

The way he said, eyes on me, sweetheart, and I forgot how to breathe.

"Stop it," I tell my reflection. "You have calls to take."

My reflection looks unconvinced.

By the time I'm in the car, the sun is just a pale hint behind the clouds. Fog hangs low over the harbor, turning the town into a quiet watercolor. The streets are empty except for a couple of joggers and a dog-walker in a reflective vest.

I pull into the department lot, kill the engine, and automatically check my phone before I get out.

No new messages.

Of course not. He's at work. Same as me.

His text is still there, though. Waiting.

I thumb over the keyboard.

Delete.

Don't delete.

I turn the phone face-down on the passenger seat like that will somehow mute the temptation.

It doesn't. I toss it into my bag and head all the way up the stairs, through the security door, down the hall toward dispatch, I can feel it burning a hole in my bag.

Say something, Florence.

You're not sixteen.

He's not a stranger.

He gave you an out.

You want to say yes.

Don't be a coward.

You moved all this way, damnit.

Instead I stamp my boots on the worn carpet and push into the communications room.

Ruth's already at her console, glasses low on her nose, headset around her neck. She looks up and gives me a once-over.

"Mornin'," she says. "You look... awake."

"I had coffee," I lie.

She snorts. "Who hurt you?"

You don't want the answer to that.

"Just life," I say, pushing through the doorway into dispatch.

Ben is already half-standing from my console, stretching the way people do when they're five minutes away from freedom. He gives me a tired salute.

"Morning, Florence. Quiet board. One pending follow-up from Animal Control, nothing hot. Units are green."

"Perfect," I say. "Go home before the phones realize you're about to clock out."

He barks a laugh, grabs his travel mug, and squeezes past me. "May your shift be blessed and your weirdos be brief."

I tap the console to wake it. Nine screens flicker to life in a wash of blue-white glow, illuminating the familiar battlefield of my workspace. I slip into the chair, still warm from Ben, and pull my headset down around my neck.

Login. Status check. Queues clear. CAD breathing steady.

I settle in, adjust my mic, and try not to think about the one message from August sitting unanswered in my phone like a live wire.

Ruth watches me for another beat like she can tell my brain is running twelve programs at once, then turns back to her own screens, mercifully silent.

The morning starts light.

A car alarm that won't shut off.

A neighbor complaining about a leaf blower at seven a.m.

A kid calling because their cat stole their cereal.

Routine.

The small, weird stuff that gives the illusion the world isn't always on the verge of breaking.

Every time there's a lull, my gaze flicks to the corner of my screen where my phone sits face-down beside my keyboard.

Every time, I look away.

It's not that I don't know what I want.

I do.

It's that wanting has never ended clean for me.

Lacey wanted easy money and a fast way out. She found the kind of wrong place, wrong time you can't talk your way out of.

I wanted her to call me back.

I wanted one more text. One more normal day where her name on my screen didn't feel like a trapdoor.

I got the opposite.

My stomach knots.

Nope.

Not going there.

Not now.

I sit up straighter, push it all back into the dark corner where it lives, and force my focus onto the CAD.

It's mid-morning when the line flashes.

Unidentified number. Wireless. No previous history.

I hit answer.

"9-1-1," I say, voice instinctively dropping into that calm, even cadence. "Where is your emergency?"

There's silence until a small, sharp noise cuts through it.

A breath?

The faintest muffled sob?

"Hello?" I say. "This is 9-1-1. Can you tell me where you are?"

A clatter in the background—phone scraping, maybe hitting tile—and then the line goes dead.

I frown at the screen.

Duration: six seconds.

No location.

But the system still pinged it.

I pull up the ALI.

The GPS sputters, catches, resolves into a radius not far from town in a housing development off the highway.

I tap the callback immediately.

The phone barely rings before someone answers.

A woman.

"Hello?" Her voice is thin, stretched tight. "Hi, um... sorry. Wrong number."

Every hair on my arms lifts.

Her words say wrong number.

Everything else says help.

"This is Florence with Townsend Harbor 9-1-1," I say, keeping my tone light. "We got a hangup from this number. I just want to make sure everything's okay."

"Yeah," she says too quickly. "Yes. Everything's fine. I just... my kid was playing with the phone. Sorry."

In the background, a man says something sharp.

She flinches mid-word.

I don't see it, but I hear it.

I've heard it a hundred times.

"Okay," I say slowly. "Can you confirm your address for me, just so I close this out correctly?"

Pause.

The kind where someone is looking at someone else, waiting for permission to breathe.

A floorboard creaks through the line.

The man's voice again, closer now. "Who is that?"

"No one," she blurts. "It was, it was just a wrong number..."

My pulse jumps.

I change lanes.

"Ma'am," I say, deliberately mild, "I want you to answer my next question yes or no."

Another pause.

I push, gentler but firm.

"If you can't talk freely," I continue, "say 'no thank you.' Do you understand?"

A breath.

The tiniest hitch.

"Yes," she says.

Except it comes out like she's swallowing it.

"Okay." I open a new incident in CAD. Fingers moving. "Is everything alright there?"

Quiet.

Then: "No, thanks. We're... we're good."

Which is not how humans talk.

It's how people talk when someone is close enough to punish them for breathing wrong.

I glance at the ALI again. The coordinates sharpen into a street and number. I tag it domestic disturbance, possible DV, weapons unknown. My foot hits the radio pedal without even thinking.

"Units, copy a possible domestic," I say, calm voice, body going electric. "Address is 214 Maple Ridge Lane. Female caller unable to answer freely."

"Unit 1," August's voice comes back immediately. "I'll take that. En route from First and Harbor."

My stomach drops and spikes at the same time.

Of course he's the closest unit.

Of course.

"Copy, 1 en route," I say, perfectly neutral even as heat crawls up my neck. "Any other units?"

"13, I'll back," Turner says.

"Copy, 13 backing 1."

I assign 1 and 13, code it priority.

The woman shifts the phone a little. A door slams somewhere in the house.

The man's voice is clear now, sharp as broken glass. "Who are you talking to?"

My brain flips into caller-mode so clean it's muscle memory.

"Hey!" I say brightly. "Thanks for holding. Harbor Slice Pizza calling about your order."

A beat of silence.

Then the man comes onto the line, suspicious. “Who is this?”

“Harbor Slice Pizza,” I repeat, even sunnier. “We got a call from this number. Just wanted to confirm your address for delivery.”

He grunts. “We didn’t order a pizza.”

“We get butt-dials all the time,” I say. “Just checking before we cancel it.”

In the background, her breathing speeds up.

He hesitates.

“Uh... it’s...” He rattles off the address.

It matches the ALI.

Good.

My heart kicks harder.

I type while I talk, flagging the update. Radio pedal.

“1 and 13, confirming address from male as 214 Maple Ridge Lane,” I say. “Domestic in progress. Male audible. Female appears fearful.”

“Copy,” August says. Lower now. Focused. “What’s the complaint?”

I turn the mic sensitivity up, listening for anything I can use.

I keep my voice sweet for the man.

“Do you want to keep that order,” I ask, “or should I cancel it?”

“She’s always calling wrong numbers,” he says, like he’s trying to sound amused and failing. “She’s stupid with phones.”

My jaw tightens.

“Must be frustrating,” I say lightly, hating him instantly. “We can cancel it if you want... unless your wife still wants that pizza?”

I emphasize wife.

Something shifts in the background. A muffled cry. A sharp crack—glass, maybe?

“Hold on,” he snaps.

The phone rustles.

He shouts something I can't make out.

The woman gasps.

A thud.

The line jolts, and for half a second I hear her close, breathless, and, raw.

"Please," she whispers.

Then the phone cuts out.

Dead air.

"Shit," I breathe.

I stab redial.

Straight to voicemail.

I hang up. Call again.

Nothing.

Ruth glances over, eyebrows raised.

I mouth, Domestic. Bad.

She's already sliding closer, pulling it up on her screen.

On the radio, I keep my tone even.

"1 and 13 be advised, line disconnected after sounds of disturbance," I say. "Female whispered 'please' prior to disconnect. No answer on callback."

"Copy," August says. "ETA, 13?"

"Two minutes," Turner replies.

Two minutes is nothing.

Two minutes is forever.

On my map, their icons crawl toward the address like they're moving through glue.

My fingers tap a jittery rhythm on the desk.

My head feels too tight.

I tell myself it's not personal.

It never is.

And it always is.

Because there's a particular kind of helpless you don't forget, the kind where you hear the edge of something horrible through a speaker and you're still stuck in a chair.

Lacey's voice hits me without warning.

Not from the day she died.

From a week before.

She'd called me over something stupid. Her car making a

noise, her being dramatic, my being the responsible sister who pretended I wasn't relieved she'd called at all.

"Flo," she'd said, half laughing, "don't yell at me, but I might've done something questionable."

I'd smiled into my headset like an idiot. "Define questionable."

Now I taste metal.

Now my stomach goes cold.

Now there's a woman on the line who said please like a prayer, and then vanished.

I swallow hard and clamp down on the memory with practiced brutality.

This is not that.

This is now.

And right now, there is a woman in a house with a man who thinks he owns her, and the only thing between them and whatever happens next is a radio call and the people I send.

I'm not going to let this be another ghost I carry.

I won't.

"Ruth," I say, "can you pull prior calls to that address?"

"Already on it," she says, fingers flying. "Two welfare checks in the last year. Neighbor reported yelling. No arrest. One suspicious circumstance, no probable cause. Same male. Same female."

So the neighbor hears it.

But not enough for anyone to press charges.

That's how it goes.

That's how it always goes.

I click back to primary.

"1, caller history shows two prior domestics at this address," I say, scrolling as new notes populate. "Both verbal. No arrests. RP name is Tyler Crestwell. Female resident is Anna Crestwell."

A beat while August absorbs it.

"Copy," he says, voice tightening just enough to tell me he's already shifting gears. "We're almost there."

I keep going, because the details matter when the line goes thin.

"Be advised, neighbor reports yelling and items breaking. Unknown weapons. Children possibly present, can't confirm."

"Copy."

His voice threads through me like electricity, clean, calm, too familiar.

It shouldn't matter that it's him going in.

Any officer responding is my officer.

Any badge hit is my hit.

But it does matter.

It matters too much.

"13 copies," Turner says. "I'll stage at the corner till 1 arrives."

"Copy."

The seconds stretch.

I can hear my own breathing in the headset. The soft clack of keys. The distant murmur of other calls being worked on other consoles, other lives unraveling quietly.

In my mind I build the house anyway.

Off-white siding. Two front windows. A porch with a rail that's seen better years.

A kid's bike abandoned on the lawn like someone walked away mid-life.

A planter with dead mums. A welcome mat that's a lie.

I picture her opening the door. Eyes too wide. Smile too eager. Bruise hidden under concealer.

I picture him behind her, watching.

I picture—

"Dispatch, 1," August snaps into my ear. "Show me on scene."

My fingers move before my brain catches up.

"Copy, 1 on scene. 13, you staged?"

"13, show me on scene," Turner says.

"Copy."

For a moment there's nothing.

Just the hum of the open channel.

The kind of silence that makes your nerves itch.

I picture August walking up that driveway.

Shoulders squared. Hand easy on his duty belt.

That deliberate calm he wears right before something goes sideways.

And I will never forgive the universe if anything happens to him.

No.

Nope. Not going there. It's been 4 minutes of silence.

"1, status check," I say after a beat. It's procedure, muscle memory, something to do with my hands besides shake. "Are you making contact?"

Crackle.

A door.

Then August's voice comes through, controlled, but tight around the edges.

"Dispatch, 1. We're making contact with the homeowners."

My lungs remember how to work again.

"Copy 1."

A beat of radio hiss.

Then a muffled shout bleeds through distorted, angry, and too close to the mic to be anything but right in front of them.

"Get off my property!"

August, sharper. "Sir, keep your hands where I can—"

The sentence clips.

A hard sound, like wood? metal? something hitting something else.

The channel pops open for a half second. Hot mic. A burst of chaos I can't quite separate into clear pieces. There's movement, a woman's sharp scream, Turner's saying something intangible.

Then static.

Then nothing.

"Dispatch to 1?" I say too fast. "Unit 1, status check."

No response.

Silence hits like cold water.

I force my tone down. Flat. Controlled. The voice that keeps everyone else from spiraling.

"1, radio check. Key up if you can hear me."

Nothing.

Across the console, Ruth's eyes go wide for a fraction of a second before her face smooths into the mask.

"13," I say, steady, "status."

Turner answers on the first key, breath already punched short. "Dispatch, 13. We're—" A cough of static. "We're moving. Stand by."

Moving where? Toward the door? Back to cover? Inside? I don't know. He doesn't say. He can't. Or won't.

My pulse jumps anyway.

"Copy, 13. Emergency traffic only on primary," I announce, voice going cold. "Emergency traffic only."

Ruth reaches over and locks the channel.

Now nobody talks unless they're bleeding.

Or dying.

Or trying not to.

The roar in my ears isn't the radio.

It's me.

I try not to reach for the past.

I fail.

A flash and I see my sister's name on a screen last year, a call that didn't feel real until it did. My hands steady while something inside me tried to split.

Not now.

Not this second.

Drag it back. Drag it back.

"13," I say, "status."

Ruth is already toning out on secondary, voice all steel and clean lines.

"Townsend Harbor units, be advised. Possible officer in trouble, 214 Maple Ridge Lane. Emergency traffic only on primary. Units 2 and 7, start that way."

"Copy, en route."

On the map, additional unit icons crawl toward Maple Ridge like it's a game and not a life. My fingers tap once against the desk, then stop, because if I start fidgeting I won't stop.

Primary stays open, thin and hungry.

Then Turner's voice blasts through high, sharp, the kind of

sound that means the world just tipped. "Dispatch, 13—shots! Shots fired!"

My blood turns to ice.

"Copy, shots fired," I say, voice suddenly far away even to me. "Repeat—shots fired, 214 Maple Ridge Lane. Units 1 and 13 on scene. All units respond, code."

I tone medics without hesitating because there isn't time to think.

"Townsend Harbor Aid 3," I say, words coming from training and terror at the same time. "Respond code three to 214 Maple Ridge Lane for possible gunshot wound. Stage until scene is secure."

The tone wails out over the county.

Ruth throws me a quick look. It's not praise or panic. But like she's checking I'm still in my chair.

I am.

I have to be.

Right now there are officers in a front yard with a gun somewhere in the mix, and a woman who tried to ask for help without getting caught.

One of those officers is August.

And somewhere on my desk, my phone is still face-down, his message sitting there like a fuse.

"Dispatch, 13," Turner comes in, breath ragged but controlled. "Suspect retreated inside. Shots came from inside the residence."

My stomach still drops, but it doesn't freefall the way it did before.

"Copy—suspect inside, shots fired from within the residence," I say, crisp.

I exhale through my nose, fast and shallow, and force my hands to keep moving.

On my peripheral screen, Aid 3 marks en route.

Ruth handles secondary like it's a second heartbeat, patching county and state, calling for perimeter units and whatever she thinks we'll need if this turns into a barricade.

My world narrows to the flashing icons on the map and the static between transmissions.

"Unit 2 on scene," a new voice cuts in, slightly out of breath. "Maple Ridge. Confirm suspect is inside?"

"Affirm," Turner answers, and I can hear wind and movement behind him, like he's crouched near the doorway, not behind a car three houses away. "Single male, armed. Multiple shots from inside. Female resident present. One and I are holding the front."

Holding the front.

The words don't ease the knot in my throat. They just give it shape.

Every officer is "unknown status" until someone puts eyes on them. It doesn't matter that this one texted you at dawn. It doesn't matter that his hands were on you a year ago and your body still hasn't forgotten.

Right now he's Unit 1.

Right now he's a voice we lost mid-sentence.

"Unit 2, Unit 7," I say, keeping it sharp, "Aid 3 is staged two blocks out. They will not enter until scene is secure. Confirm perimeter."

"Affirm," 2 says. "Taking rear."

"7's got side yard," another voice adds.

I log the updates. Each keystroke feels like a stitch trying to hold something together.

I hit transmit again because I can't not.

"Unit 1," I say. "Status check. If you can hear me, key your mic twice."

Static answers.

Then in a faint, almost swallowed noise, two tiny clicks.

My heart lurches so hard it feels physical.

"Copy, 1," I say quickly, before the channel clears. "We copy your double click. Units are setting perimeter. Aid is staged."

Ruth exhales beside me, a sound so small I wouldn't notice it if I weren't listening for every sign of life.

He's alive.

At least alive enough to hit his mic.

It's not much.

It's everything.

Relief flashes bright.

It doesn't last.

Because clicks aren't words. Clicks don't tell me if he's bleeding. If he's pinned. If the woman is screaming in a kitchen or trying not to.

I push my focus into the only thing that matters right now.

Procedure.

"County's offering a tac channel," Ruth murmurs, one ear on the patch.

"Do it," I say. "Move them once they're coordinated."

She nods, hands a blur.

I keep primary clean.

Minutes drag, thin and sharp.

They talk angles and windows and whether anyone has visual. They talk like men and women trying not to die. I half-hear it. The other half of me is somewhere else entirely, on a different day, in a different chair, with a different name on my screen and the same helpless distance.

Not now.

Do the job.

"2, Dispatch. Stacking for entry."

The quiet before a breach is always the loudest thing in the room.

Not because you can hear what's happening.

Because you *can't*.

The channel is locked down. Tac is theirs. Primary is mine. And all I get is the gap between transmissions. Seconds stretching thin while my brain tries to fill them with worst-case imagination.

Ruth keeps her eyes on the patch like she can will a voice to come through.

I keep mine on the map.

Unit icons clustered at the address. Aid staged. Perimeter set.

Everything in place.

And still... nothing.

Then Turner's voice hits, tight and clipped. It's far too controlled to be calm.

"Dispatch, 13."

My spine goes straight.

"Go ahead, 13."

"We're making entry."

That's it.

No background noise. No drama. No details.

Just three words that turn my blood to ice.

"Copy, 13. Entry made," I say, and my voice stays level because it has to.

A beat.

Two.

The seconds drag like hooks.

"13," I say, measured, "status."

Nothing.

Ruth's fingers hover over the secondary channel, ready to tone again if she needs to.

I don't ask twice, because asking twice is how you sound scared.

"Dispatch, 13—shots fired."

My whole body goes cold.

"Copy, shots fired," I say, voice flat as pavement. "All units respond emergency to 214 Maple Ridge Lane. Aid 3 remain staged until scene is secure."

"Aid 3, copy, staged."

Turner comes back again, breath heavier now, and I can hear the difference between adrenaline and panic. He's moving.

Time stretches wrong.

My throat burns with everything I'm not allowed to say.

Then Turner again, "Dispatch, 13—suspect in custody."

My lungs finally remember what they're for.

"Copy, suspect in custody," I say. My voice doesn't shake. My hands do, but the desk hides it.

A beat.

"Dispatch, 2," comes next. "We have one adult female victim. Conscious. Gunshot wound to the leg. Aid can move."

My stomach flips.

"Copy," I say. "Aid 3, you are clear to move in."

"Aid 3, copy, moving."

And then the part my brain has been avoiding rises anyway, ugly and inevitable.

"And the officer?" I ask, because someone has to ask it out loud.

There's a pause on the channel.

Not long.

But long enough to feel like falling.

Then 2 answers carefully.

"Dispatch... we have an officer injured. Aid is making contact now. Start the hospital."

Officer injured.

"Copy," I manage, and it sounds like my voice belongs to somebody else. "Hospital notified."

Ruth doesn't look at me. She doesn't need to.

Her hand finds my elbow under the desk, one quick squeeze, then she's gone again, back to work, because if we stop moving we drown.

I keep my eyes on the board.

I keep my voice steady.

I keep breathing.

But somewhere on my desk, my phone is still face-down.

His message still sitting there.

Unanswered.

And my chest is full of the same brutal thought, over and over, like a pulse.

Please.

Not him.

SIXTEEN
AUGUST

SHOTS FIRED.

The words form in my head a half second before the sound finishes ripping through the house.

Everything narrows.

The hallway. The banister. The family photos on the wall in cheap frames, forced smiles, blur into nothing, leaving me three points of focus like a sight picture.

The open bedroom door.

The man with the gun.

The woman on the floor.

I'm halfway through the doorway when he jerks the pistol up and fires again, this time into the ceiling.

The crack punches through my skull. Plaster rains down. My body drops without permission, knees bending, shoulders turning, trying to get small and get eyes on him at the same time.

The second shot goes wide.

The third doesn't.

I feel heat shaping across my right hip, before I understand it, a white-hot line that steals my breath and turns my stomach cold.

For a split second my brain offers the worst sentence it knows how to say.

That's it.

Then the burn resolves into something else. Not dead. Not down. Not yet.

The room stinks of gunpowder and dust and fear.

The woman is on the floor near the bed, curled up like she's trying to disappear into the carpet. One eye swelling shut. Blood at her nose. Tank top and leggings, bare feet, skin marked with old bruises underneath the new ones.

He's standing over her.

Bare chest. Jeans. Belt loose like he didn't even finish the thought before rage took over.

Gun in his hand.

He's so locked on her he barely registers I'm in the doorway until my voice hits him.

"Police!" I bark. "Tyler. Put the gun down."

He spins toward me, wild-eyed, and the muzzle swings my direction.

I shift my weight and my hip screams with hot pain pulsing with my heartbeat. I plant my feet anyway.

Hands up. Palms open.

My weapon is still holstered because I'm not the only one in this line of fire, and I am not about to turn her into a backdrop for a shootout.

"Don't," I say, quieter. "Don't point that at me. Put it down."

He hesitates.

Hard breathing. Knuckles white around the grip. Sweat slicking his hairline. Pupils blown wide.

I've seen this exact man in a hundred different houses with different names, same fear under all that rage.

He jerks the gun toward her again. "She called you," he spits. "After everything I do for her, she calls the fucking cops—"

"Tyler." I keep my voice low. Steady. I take one slow step in, just enough to keep him talking, just enough to keep him looking at me. "Listen to me."

"Don't move!" he shouts, the pistol snapping back to my chest. "Stay the fuck back!"

"I'm right here," I say, and it costs me to breathe. Warm wetness is already soaking into the waistband at my hip, sticky under my vest. "I'm not moving."

I keep my eyes on his, even though every instinct screams to track the gun. Eye contact is a leash. I need it.

Behind him the woman whispers, "Please," so soft I almost miss it.

"Shut up!" he snarls over his shoulder, and then back at me, teeth bared. "You shut up. You started this."

I flick a glance past him, one fast assessment. She's curled in tight, one arm across her ribs, shoulders hunched like she's bracing for impact.

"Is that how it is?" I ask, pulling him back to me. "She started this?"

"You don't know anything about us," he spits. "You don't know what she does. Always nagging, always bitching, always—"

"Calling for help," I cut in. "That's what she did today. She called for help."

His jaw works. Rage and shame wrestling in the same mouth.

"You think you're helping?" he snaps.

"Yeah," I say simply. "I do."

He laughs a jagged, broken thing. "You're gonna take me to jail. Take her to some shelter. You think that's better than what she's got here?"

I let the words sit long enough for him to hear himself.

"Is it?" I ask.

His grip tightens. The barrel bobs between me and her, hand shaking now.

"I didn't—I wasn't trying to hit her," he mutters, gaze flicking down like that makes it less true. "If she hadn't made me so mad—"

"She called for help," I correct, gentler. "That's not betrayal. That's survival."

He swallows.

In the hall behind me, my portable chirps a notification. It's dispatch trying to find my voice in the dark.

"Unit 1," Florence's calm comes through the speaker, clipped by static but steady. "Status check. If you can hear me, key your mic twice."

I don't take my eyes off Tyler.

I wait for the smallest safe second, when his muzzle dips, when his attention flickers to the woman, and I key my mic twice.

Two quick clicks.

That's all I can give them.

That's all I can give *her*.

I'm acutely aware of space now. The narrow gap between bed and dresser. The closet door behind him.

We've done this dance enough times I can feel my partner there without seeing him.

"Tyler," I say, modulating my tone, "right now you're standing in front of the person you say you love most in this world, waving a loaded gun around. You've already put a round through your ceiling. You've hit her and me. If you wanted to scare her, you've accomplished that too. You want to add murder to that list?"

He flinches.

The word always finds the part of them that is still human.

His lips lick over dry skin. Sweat beads at his temple.

And for the first time since I stepped into this room, the gun lowers by an inch.

Not enough.

But it's something.

"There you go," I murmur. "Don't do that to yourself. Don't do that to her."

"What do you want me to do?" he snaps. "Just what? Let you throw me in cuffs? Let you drag me outta my own house like—"

"I want you to put the gun down," I say. "That's it. That's all you have to do to survive the next ten minutes. Put. The. Gun. Down."

He shakes his head, fast and jagged. "Nah. You'll shoot me soon as I move."

"If I was going to shoot you," I say evenly, "you'd already be on the floor."

It isn't bravado. It's the truth of distance and angles and the fact that I've been standing here with my hands up because she's behind him and I'm not gambling with her body.

He stares at me. I let him. Let him see the calm. The certainty. The part of me that has done this too many times to flinch now.

Pain lances across my hip as my weight shifts. I don't give it my face. I don't give it my breath.

You are standing. You can bleed later.

"Look at her," I say quietly, nodding toward the woman without breaking my hold on him. "Really look."

He glances back.

Just long enough.

Her face is a mess. She's shaking hard enough her teeth chatter, one hand pressed to her ribs like she's holding herself together. Like she's trying to keep something inside from spilling out.

He swallows.

"I didn't mean—" he starts.

"Then stop," I cut in, firm but not cruel. "You can't take back what you've already done. But you can stop it from getting worse. Right now."

His gaze snaps back to me, wild and furious and terrified all at once. "And that means letting you lock me up?"

"It means you walk out of this house alive," I say. "It means she does too. It means your kids don't watch a coroner carry somebody out of their living room."

That one lands.

It always does.

His arms start to lower slowly, like he's moving through thick water.

The gun dips.

My pulse spikes anyway.

"Tyler," I warn, voice low, steady. "Don't point it at your head. Don't point it at her. Just—floor. Put it on the floor."

His jaw clenches.

For a heartbeat I see it: the pivot, the grab, the barrel at her temple.

I prep for it. Ready my body for a dive I know is going to light my hip on fire.

Instead, he inhales sharply.

And lets the gun fall from his hand.

It hits the carpet with a dull thud that sounds too small for how close death just was.

"Kick it away," I say immediately. "Toward the closet. Now."

He does it like he's moving on command because he can't afford to think.

The pistol skids, bumps the closet door.

Behind me, somewhere down the hall, I hear movement, like boots, a controlled rush. Turner's approach. Quiet. Close. Exactly where I needed him.

"Now step back," I order Tyler. "Hands where I can see them."

He raises both hands, palms out. Breathing hard. Eyes glassy.

My body goes autopilot.

Three strides. I hook my boot behind the gun and drag it farther out of reach, then I'm on Tyler, wrist, turn, shoulder to wall.

Pain detonates through my hip so hard the edges of the room go bright.

I ride it. Clamp my teeth down on it. Pin his arms behind his back anyway.

"Tyler Crestwell," I grind out, voice pure gravel, "don't move. You're under arrest."

Cuffs.

Click. Click.

Metal bites. His wrists lock behind him, and the second they do, the air changes. Like the worst part has passed and now you're just counting damage.

"Listen carefully," I say, and my voice slips into command because command is the only thing I've got right now. "You have the right to remain silent. Anything you say can and will be used against you—" I get through reading his Miranda Rights. Because procedure is a spine when adrenaline tries to make you jelly.

"Do you understand your rights as I've read them to you?"

He tugs once, testing the cuffs.

I hold.

He nods.

I don't look away from him until I'm sure Turner has eyes on the weapon.

Turner appears in the doorway like a shadow made solid He's breathing hard, face tight, all business. Turner scoops the pistol, checks the chamber, makes it safe with hands that don't shake.

"Weapon secure," he says, low.

"Copy," I answer, and it's the closest thing to relief I'm allowed right now.

I turn my head toward the woman on the floor. "Stay with me," I tell her. "Medics are almost here."

She's crying now. Quiet. Stunned. Tears leaking out because her body finally has room to react.

Turner starts walking Tyler out, one hand locked on him, voice clipped.

"Let's go," he mutters. "Watch your step."

Tyler's swagger is gone. Drained out of him. All that rage shrunk down into something small and ugly.

I don't feel satisfaction. I never do.

I pivot back to the woman, soften my voice as much as I can while everything in me is still running hot.

"Ma'am," I say. "Is there anyone we can call for you? Family? Friend?"

She shakes her head, winces. "No."

"Kids?" I ask gently.

Her eyes flick toward the closet.

Just for a heartbeat.

That's all I need.

I move, ignoring the wet heat at my hip where my pants stick to my skin. Slide the closet door open.

Two kids huddle in the back like they learned how to disappear.

A boy, maybe ten. A girl, maybe seven. Wide-eyed. Knees to chest. The girl clutches a stuffed rabbit so hard her knuckles are pale.

My stomach twists.

"Hey," I say softly, dropping down into a crouch that makes my hip scream. I don't let it change my voice. "I'm August. I'm a police officer. You guys okay?"

The boy nods once, jaw clenched. He's trying to be a wall for his sister.

The girl doesn't move.

"Can I help you out of there?" I ask.

The boy nods again.

I offer my hand.

He takes it like it costs him, eyes tracking past me toward the front door where his dad just disappeared in cuffs. His face goes blank.

Protective shutdown.

I know that look.

"You're safe," I tell him quietly, like I can make it true by saying it right. "He can't hurt you right now."

His throat works.

"Come here, sweetheart," I say to the girl, softer.

She scoots closer to her brother but lets me help her up. Rabbit tucked under her chin like armor.

"What's your rabbit's name?" I ask.

She whispers it so quietly I almost miss it.

"Sunshine."

My chest kicks hard.

"Good name," I say, because my voice is the only steady thing I can offer her. "Sunshine's very brave."

I guide them into the living room just as Aid 3 comes through the front door in the form of two medics I know by first name.

They take one look and go straight to work.

One kneels by the woman.

The other checks the kids.

I step back and let them do what they're best at.

And only then, only when I'm not actively holding a man at gunpoint with my body, do I key my radio.

Because dispatch needs the update. The whole town needs it.

And because somewhere behind those walls, I know Florence is sitting at a console listening to dead air and trying not to panic.

I press the button. "1, Dispatch."

A beat.

"Go ahead, 1," Florence says. Her voice is controlled. Professional. But there's a tightness under it. Like she's holding herself very still.

"Suspect secured," I say. "Unit 2 will transport. Aid 3 has the victim. Two juveniles located. CPS follow-up requested."

"Copy," she replies immediately. No hesitation. Like her hands were already moving before the words finished leaving my mouth. "CPS is being paged now. Any additional medical needed on scene?"

She already knows the answer. She just can't ask it the way she wants to.

I inhale.

"Minor graze," I say. "Aid 3 will transport me."

"Copy, 1," she says, voice a hair softer. "Aid 3 has been advised."

Then she clears it.

"Primary is open. Dispatch clear."

The radio clicks off.

She's gone.

But I can still hear her in my bones.

The adrenaline drain hits hard now that the house isn't actively trying to kill anyone. My hip lights up like someone dragged a blade across it and then pressed salt into the cut.

I glance down.

The outer seam of my uniform pants is torn at the right hip, fabric dark and tacky with blood.

"Fuck," I mutter, bracing a hand against the hallway wall.

"You good, Chief?" Turner calls, hauling Tyler down the

hall with a grip that says he's one bad comment away from making this personal.

"Peachy," I say, voice dry.

Turner's gaze drops to my leg. His mouth tightens. He doesn't argue, but the look he throws toward the bedroom is all simmering fury.

We've both seen too much of this.

Too many bruises. Too many kids hiding in impossible places.

We walk the kids out together. The neighbors are already awake, already watching, curtains twitching and phones out like they're filming content instead of witnessing a family breaking open.

Paramedics wheel the victim out on a gurney, collar in place, oxygen mask fogging with each breath. Her eyes track the children as they follow behind a Officer Sanders, as she reaches for their hands. The girl still has Sunshine clutched to her chest like the rabbit is the only solid thing left in the world.

Aid loads the victim.

Then the kids.

Turner puts Tyler in a unit and drives him out, jaw locked the whole time.

The scene dissolves into that familiar wash of red-blue against neighborhood lawns. Another quiet street with an explosion inside it. Another story the town will chew on for a week and then forget.

I picture Florence at her console, eyes on the board, headset perfectly in place, shoulders tight. I picture her staring at the dead air when my radio went silent, doing the math in her head that dispatchers do when they're trying not to.

The medic gestures at me.

"Your turn, Chief."

I hobble toward the rig. Pain radiates down my leg, but it's not what sticks.

What sticks is the pause in Florence's voice.

That fraction of a second where she wasn't just dispatch.

Where she was a person trying not to care too loudly.

I climb into the ambulance.

The doors shut.

The siren rises as we pull away.

And all I can think is: I need to hear her voice again.

We're halfway to Harbor General when my personal phone buzzes in my pocket.

I shouldn't look.

I do.

The screen lights up with her name.

Florence.

My heart does something stupid and young in my chest.

I open the message.

For a second the words blur, like my brain can't trust them. Like the adrenaline is still too loud in my ears.

Then they settle.

Then they hit.

Florence: When the line went dead, I couldn't breathe.

I kept thinking about your text… and everything I didn't say back.

I'm glad you're okay.

And for the record, you're not the only one who hasn't been able to stop thinking about that walk.

Or Seattle.

Or you.

The air in the rig feels thinner.

My hip throbs.

The medic talks to the driver up front.

None of it matters.

Because she replied.

She didn't hide behind professionalism. She didn't pretend it didn't shake her. She didn't put it in a box and label it later.

My thumbs hover over the keyboard with a dozen reckless, selfish impulses clawing up my throat.

I don't send any of them.

August: I'm okay. Promise.

They've got me at the hospital for a bit while they check everything and patch me up.

I didn't mean to scare you.

Three dots appear.
Disappear.

Florence: You didn't scare me.

I scared myself.

I forgot what that feels like.

Something tight and old pulls in my chest.
Not pain.
Not lust.
Something worse.
Something close to tender.

I lean my head back against the cool wall of the rig and stare at the ceiling like it can give me instructions.

I should let her rest.

I should let her finish her shift.

I should do a dozen responsible things.

Instead I type the truth I can say without taking more than she can give.

August: Finish your shift. Breathe.

I'm not going anywhere.

A beat.

Florence: Okay.

I'm glad you texted me.

I close my eyes.
She has no idea what that does to me.

August: I'm glad you wrote back.

We'll talk when you're off. Whenever you want. No pressure.

Her reply comes slower this time, careful in a way that matches mine.

Florence: Yeah. I'd like that.

I stare at the screen until my vision threatens to do something stupid.

The medic knocks twice on the rig wall and swings the door open. "Chief? They're ready for you inside."

"Yeah," I say, pocketing my phone. "I'm coming."

My uniform is torn. My hip aches. My whole body feels wrung out.

But under all of it, under the gunfire, the blood, the paperwork waiting like a second wave, something in me settles.

Not peace.

Not certainty.

Just... a quiet, stubborn warmth.

Hope, maybe.

I step down from the rig and follow the medic into the ER.

SEVENTEEN
FLORENCE

BY THE TIME I get home, I'm flattened.

Not the normal tired. Not even the "my headset left an imprint on my skull" kind of tired.

This is the kind where my body is in my kitchen but my brain is still in that house, still smelling drywall dust and fear, still listening for a radio that might go dead again.

August.

I think his name and something in my chest tightens like a fist.

I've been thinking about him all day. Every minute since I left the station. Every second of my drive home. And now, standing with my keys still in my hand, it hits all at once, like the fear waited until I got somewhere safe to climb on my back.

The what-if.

The almost.

The sound of Unit 2's voice when he said officer injured, and my stomach dropped so hard my body forgot how to be a body.

"You look like someone used you as a mop," Lilly says, appearing in the hallway in an oversized sweatshirt and pink fuzzy socks. She squints at me. "Rough day?"

There's sympathy in her tone. No push. She never pushes.

Which is good, because my throat is already doing that hot, fragile thing.

"Yeah," I say, closing the door behind me. "Rough day."

"You wanna talk about it?"

"No." The answer comes too fast, too sharp, but she doesn't flinch. "I mean... I can't. You know the rules."

"No call details, no identifying info, no trauma dumping." She recites the boundaries like she's been studying them. "Got it. You're Fort Knox."

I loosen my grip on my keys and set them on the counter. They rattle louder than they should.

"But you can still talk about how you feel," she adds, softer.

How do I feel?

Like I'm eighteen again, standing in the rain with blood in my hair and a stranger's hands holding me together while the world burned down behind my eyes.

Like I'm twenty-three, watching my sister's name turn into a headline, then a case number, then a quiet thing nobody wanted to say out loud unless they had to.

Like the universe keeps testing whether I'll flinch fast enough to survive it.

"I don't know," I say finally, and it's humiliating because it's true. "Everything just... hit me weird today."

Lilly studies me. She can read people frighteningly well for someone who habitually loses her car in parking lots.

"Okay," she says gently. "Then you're done working for the night. I'm invoking roommate authority."

"That's not a thing."

"It is now."

Before I can argue, she starts moving like she's got a checklist. Lights dimmed. A candle lit. Kettle on. Blanket dragged from the couch and fluffed aggressively. She tosses me a pair of soft leggings straight from the laundry basket like she's pitching a miracle.

"You need comfort," she says. "And carbs. And heating pads. And possibly a lobotomy, but I can only offer the first three."

A laugh cracks out of me, real enough that it surprises me. "You're ridiculous."

"Hot," she corrects. "And intuitive."

I change into the leggings because they are, in fact, softer than sin, and the second I sit on the couch, the weight in my chest loosens by something like an inch.

And then it crawls back in.

Because I'm home.

Because I'm safe.

Because he almost wasn't.

Lilly curls up beside me with her mug of tea. She doesn't talk for a minute. Just lets me exist. Then, like she's stepping carefully around a bruise, she asks, "Are you sure dispatching is what you want to be doing?"

It lands different than I expect.

I stare into my cup, watching steam curl upward like it's trying to escape.

"I don't know," I admit quietly. "I thought I did. When I started, it felt... good. Like I was helping. Like I was turning something ugly into something useful."

"And now?"

"Now I feel like I'm waiting," I whisper.

"For what?"

"For the next call that breaks me." The words come out thin. "For the next thing I can't fix. For the universe to remind me I don't get to control the ending."

Lilly's quiet for a beat.

"You know," she says, "it's okay if something stops being right for you. It doesn't mean you failed. It means you listened."

I swallow. My throat aches.

In another life, maybe I'd believe her.

In another life, I wouldn't have a sister-shaped hole inside me that still catches on everything.

I shift, pulling the blanket tighter. "I don't want to be dramatic," I say, and it comes out bitter, because I am always trying not to be dramatic. "But today felt like—" I stop.

Like the universe putting a gun back in my hand and asking if I remembered what it took.

Lilly sips her tea, then says, almost casually, “You know my mom dispatches too.”

I blink. “Wait—what?”

“Yeah.” She shrugs, like she hasn’t just dropped a brick into my lap. “Her name’s Ruth.”

I sit up so fast my tea sloshes.

“Your mom is Ruth?”

“Yep.” She makes a face. “We have a weird relationship, but... yeah. She works at the center. Same shift rotation, half the time.”

My brain flickers through Ruth’s laugh, Ruth’s dry humor, Ruth’s steady eyes over the monitor. The way she never pushes but always shows up.

“I really like her,” I say before I can stop myself. “She’s... good at what she does.”

Lilly snorts. “You’re not her kid, so you get the version of her that’s actually pleasant.”

A laugh slips out of me, warm and surprised.

“She cares about you,” I say softly.

Lilly rolls her eyes. “Moms. They’re a lot.”

Yeah.

They are.

And I wish I still had mine.

I shove the thought down as I’ve practiced for years.

Lilly doesn’t linger there. Bless her.

Instead, she brightens like she’s flipping a switch on purpose. “Okay. Random thought. You know what you should do?”

“Oh no.”

“Start a tarot account.”

I snort. “A tarot account?”

“TikTok, Instagram, whatever. You do readings all the time. You could do little videos. People eat that up.”

“Who would want to watch me talk about tarot?”

She stares at me like I’ve offended her personally. “Everyone.”

"I don't even do social media."

"Exactly." She pokes my leg with her toe. "That's why you need me. I'll be your manager and make you hashtags. I'll make you a little intro jingle. Like, boom—Tarot with Florence. Mystical. Sexy. Educational."

"You are absolutely unhinged."

"Correct."

I try to hide the smile tugging at my mouth. It wins anyway. "I don't think that's for me," I say.

She squints. "Then start small."

My stomach tightens. "Uh oh."

"Show me your art."

Instant panic. "What?"

"You've been drawing," she says, like this is an established fact. "I see you hovering over that tablet." She leans forward, eyes bright, like a nosy raccoon. "Let me see."

I hesitate.

I've been drawing for years. It's been a slow, largely private, obsessive in the quietest way.

And I've been working on this project this past year. I've finished almost half a tarot deck now.

I haven't shown anyone.

The idea of it makes my heartbeat stutter.

"It's nothing," I say, weak.

"Florence." Her voice goes soft. "Let me see."

Vulnerability rises like a wave.

I swallow.

Showing her feels like peeling away the shell I've been building around myself since last year. Since Lacey, and the funeral, and the way the world kept moving like it didn't just take my only sister.

But something in me, something tired but a little hopeful, nods.

"Okay," I whisper. "Fine."

I grab my tablet from my room and sit back beside her, opening Procreate to my gallery. My hand shakes a little as I swipe through the cards.

The Fool.

The Empress.

Strength.

The Queen of Cups.

The King of Wands, but she is a woman. Tall. Powerful. Crown like fire. Zero apology.

They're all women. All fierce. All tender in their own ways. All built to survive the things they aren't supposed to survive.

Lilly gasps so loud I flinch.

"Florence." Her voice goes reverent. "These are... insane. I'm going to pass out."

"They're rough drafts," I say too fast, because panic always tries to ruin good moments.

"They're masterpieces."

I let out a short laugh, more air than sound. "No, they're—"

She grabs my face with both hands, holding my attention in place.

"Bestie," Lilly says, dead serious. "You are an artist. And these are stunning. They're like... feminist witch Renaissance energy. I'm obsessed."

Warmth blooms under my skin so suddenly I almost don't recognize it.

Not adrenaline.

Just... being seen.

And being safe while I'm seen.

Lilly scrolls through every card like she's flipping through a holy book. She makes little delighted noises, occasionally blurting out things like, "Queen," or "Oh my god the colors," or, "I'm gonna cry, why is the Hermit so hot?"

I laugh again, and this time it sounds like me.

By the time she finishes, my chest feels cracked open, but not in the bleeding way. In the way a window opens. In the way fresh air gets in.

"These are you," she says quietly, handing the tablet back. "This is your magic."

Something tightens in my throat.

I blink hard and look down at the screen so she won't see my eyes go glossy.

"Thank you," I whisper.

She bumps my shoulder like she's embarrassed to be sincere for too long. "Okay. I'm gonna go heat up the leftover lasagna. You stay here and keep being an artistic goddess."

She disappears into the kitchen, humming badly and confidently.

I sit on the couch with my tablet heavy in my lap.

And the quiet rushes in.

I think about Nora.

I think about my mom's hands always ink-stained, paint under her nails, the way she used to hum while she worked like creating something meant you could keep the world from taking what it wanted.

I think about Lacey.

About the last time I saw her alive. The last text I ignored because I was tired and told myself I'd answer later.

Later doesn't exist. Not when it matters.

My stomach knots.

Then the call today hits all over again, how fast the air left the room when the line went dead. How the words officer injured turned my blood to ice. How my body locked up in that old, familiar helplessness, like it remembers too much.

And then I think about August.

Even amidst the days explosions, his voice remained steady.

The way he spoke to me. I wasn't just a voice in his ear, he knew I was holding my breath behind every "copy."

The texts we've shared since are real. We're both trying not to spook something fragile.

I unlock my phone before I can talk myself out of it.

My thumbs hover over the keyboard, stupidly shaky.

Then I type.

Florence: I keep thinking about you.

Would you want to get breakfast tomorrow?

My heart is pounding so hard I feel it in my teeth.

I hit send.

The bubble sits there, pulsing.

Once.

Twice.

Long enough for my brain to start listing every reason this is a terrible idea.

August: How about I make you breakfast?

My place.

My breath catches so hard it hurts.

His place.

Not a coffee shop with an exit. Not a public table where we can pretend we're normal.

His space. His quiet. The version of him that doesn't wear a badge and a holster.

August: 8am okay?

My fingers tremble.

Florence: Yes.

When I set the phone down, I'm smiling like someone who forgot how.

Lilly reappears with two plates of lasagna and stops dead in the doorway.

"Oh my god," she says slowly, eyes narrowing. "Why do you look like the cat who got into the cream?"

I wipe my face like I can erase the evidence. "I don't."

"Liar." She points her fork at me, lasagna clinging to the tines. "Someone texted you."

"It's nothing," I say, grabbing my water and suddenly becoming extremely invested in the ice cubes.

She gasps like I confessed to arson. "It is not nothing. You have a smile. A real one. A whole-ass human expression. Spill."

"I'm not talking about this."

"Oh, we're talking about it." She plops onto the couch,

tucks one leg under herself, and stares at me like she's trying to crack a safe. "Who's the mystery hottie?"

"No one."

"So someone," she sings.

I groan into my hands.

"Okay," she says, bouncing like a golden retriever who just heard the word park. "Give me something. A crumb. A molecule. Is it a boy? A girl? A them? Tell me, tell me, tell me."

I inhale slowly, then exhale.

"We're... getting breakfast tomorrow."

Her entire soul exits her body.

"OH MY GOD," she shrieks. "YOU'RE GONNA GET SOME."

"What? No. It's breakfast."

"It's never just breakfast, babe. Breakfast is foreplay with food."

"It is not."

"It is!" she insists, pointing at me like she's delivering a TED Talk. "You're gonna be like 'pass the syrup' and they're gonna be like 'let me pour it on your—'"

"LILLY. STOP."

She dissolves into delighted cackling, nearly choking on her lasagna.

"You like them," she says, breathless. "You sooo like them. I can smell it."

"You cannot smell feelings."

"Babe." She presses a hand to her chest, solemn. "I have a nose for this. A gift."

I shake my head, but I can't stop the smile from trying to come back.

"It's nothing," I mumble. "I don't know what we are. I don't know if we're anything."

"Well," she says, taking a proud bite, "you will after breakfast."

I throw a pillow at her.

She dodges like she trained for this moment her whole life.

But the teasing, my embarrassment, and the panic of allowing myself to want again, particularly if Lilly learned I was with her father, did not deter me.

RESTRAINT

The flutter in my chest refuses to settle.
Tomorrow can't come soon enough.

EIGHTEEN
AUGUST

FLORENCE SHOWS UP EARLY.

I'm at the stove flipping pancakes that are probably too ambitious for a man who slept three hours and got shot last week, when my phone gives that polite little security-app chime.

Front door camera.

Motion detected.

My chest does something stupid and boyish anyway.

I wipe my hands on a dish towel, move faster than my hip wants, and swing the door open before she can knock.

She's on the porch with one hand half-raised, curls pinned up, cheeks pink from the cold, holding a Tupperware container like she's bringing peace to a hostile nation.

"Hey," she says, a little breathless. "Sorry. I'm early."

God.

She is beautiful.

"Best thing that's happened to me all month," I say before I can sand it down into something cooler. "Come in."

Her shoulders drop, just a fraction, like she's been holding herself tight since yesterday and finally lets a little go. She steps past me, and there it is again.

Vanilla.

Coffee.

And that skin-close, quiet thing that's just her.

I shut the door, lock it out of habit, and suddenly she's in my house.

In the light. In the real.

The place is warm, smelling like bacon and maple and coffee. I went on a cleaning spree at two in the morning, wiped counters that didn't need wiping, cleared the mail pile, folded a throw blanket that has never once been folded in its natural habitat. I even swapped the dead plant by the slider for a cheap grocery-store bouquet because the idea of her walking in and seeing my sad fern felt... unacceptable.

Overkill?

Sure.

I also don't care.

Florence's eyes widen as she takes it in the open living room, the couch, the bookcase, the sliding doors aimed at the sound like the whole house is leaning toward the water. The kitchen table set for two.

And the ridiculous amount of food on the counter.

"August," she breathes. "Did you... cook all of this?"

I roll the towel in my hands, suddenly self-conscious in a way that irritates me. "I might've overcorrected."

It's not just pancakes. Bacon, crisp and shining. Scrambled eggs still steaming in the pan. A bowl of berries and sliced fruit. Toast in the warmer. Two mugs waiting by the coffeepot.

And next to them, because I'm apparently a lunatic, an unopened carton of pumpkin creamer I tracked down at six in the morning because she drank a pumpkin chai once and my brain filed it under vital intel.

She sets the container on the counter.

"What's this?" I ask.

"Bribery," she says. "I panicked last night and made cinnamon rolls. It's a coping mechanism."

A laugh slips out of me. It's real, surprised, and unguarded. It feels like something unclamps in my chest.

"You baked for me?"

She lifts one shoulder, suddenly shy in a way that doesn't

match her mouth. "You were making breakfast. I didn't want to show up empty-handed."

Christ.

She's going to ruin me.

"Come here," I say, and it comes out softer than I mean it to.

She looks up.

Whatever she sees in my face makes her step into me without hesitation.

I wrap my arms around her, careful of my hip, and it's like my whole body finally drops its shoulders. She's warm and solid against me. Not a memory. Not a voice in my radio. Not a woman I only have in the dark.

Florence.

She melts into me so fast my throat tightens. Her forehead finds the spot under my collarbone. Her hands slide along my back, fingers curling into my T-shirt like she needs proof I'm here.

For a few seconds we just stand there, breathing the same air.

Something in my spine loosens. The coil I've been carrying since Maple Ridge. The older coil too, the one I've had since Seattle, since I let her walk out and pretended I was fine.

"You okay?" I murmur into her hair.

"No," she says, honest and muffled against my chest. "But this helps."

I press my mouth to the top of her head once, no theatrics, no lingering. Just a quiet, stupidly tender thank you.

"Breakfast first," I say. "Emotional crises after."

She huffs a laugh against me. "Deal."

Letting her go feels like stepping out of something warm. I do it slowly anyway, then guide her toward the table.

"Sit," I tell her. "I've got it."

She watches me move back to the stove, and her eyes catch on the limp I can't quite hide. I see the concern flicker across her eyes. I cut it off before it can grow teeth.

"It looks worse than it is," I say, grabbing the spatula.

"They're treating me like glass because I'm technically important."

Her eyebrows lift. "Uh-huh."

"I mean," I add, because she's not letting me skate, "it's a graze. A very small, very rude bullet. My ego's the only thing that took a direct hit."

She doesn't fully buy it, but she lets me have the joke.

"Sit," I repeat, gentler. "I promise your breakfast won't be improved by watching me hobble."

She takes the chair with the view, angled so she can see both me and the water. Like I set it on purpose, which I did.

As I plate pancakes and eggs and bacon, I'm hyper-aware of her gaze on me. Not in a way that makes me nervous.

In a way that makes me want to be... worthy.

Like being seen by her actually matters.

I set a plate in front of her, then sit across with my own. I pour her coffee and slide the pumpkin creamer over.

Her eyes light. "You got—"

"I pay attention," I say.

Her fingers brush mine when she reaches for the creamer. That tiny contact sends a familiar spark up my arm, but it's not frantic this time. No grasping. No hunger with teeth.

Just a steady hum. Like a wire finally laid in the right place.

For a few minutes, all we do is eat.

She takes one bite of pancake and closes her eyes like she's praying. "Oh my gods."

I grin. "That good?"

"They're... stupid good," she says around another bite.

"I'll keep that in mind if this whole chief gig doesn't work out."

She swallows, laughs, and some of the tightness around her eyes eases."You definitely can cook me breakfast any day." Color comes back into her cheeks that has nothing to do with the cold outside.

We stick to the easy lanes first. Florence talks about her roommates bizarre crafting spirals. "She made a raccoon-themed tea cozy," Florence says, equal parts horrified and delighted. We cover the festival calendar, the way Townsend

Harbor always feels like it's one montage away from a Hallmark plot twist.

Then the orbit tightens.

She sets her fork down and glances at my hip. "How... bad was it? Yesterday."

I shrug one shoulder. "Loud. Stupid. Messy." I take a breath. "He fired as I cleared the doorway. I think he meant to hit me. Missed by about an inch. Fragment caught me. His wife caught the worst of it."

Her face tightens.

I reach across the table and brush my knuckles over her wrist, light, careful. "I'm okay," I say. "She's okay too. They patched her up."

That earns a weak smile. "Still."

"I know," I say quietly. "It was close."

Her gaze drops to her plate. Her fingers curl in on themselves like she's trying to keep them from shaking. "The line went dead," she says. "You know that, right? I heard the struggle and then... nothing."

"I know," I say.

"You didn't hear me," she says. "I..." She stops, inhales. "I held it together on the air. I think. But my head—" She taps her temple lightly. "Up here, everything was... not okay."

Guilt settles low under my ribs. "I'm sorry," I say. "I know you didn't sign up to—"

Her eyes flick up to mine, startled. "I didn't tell you."

"You didn't have to," I say, keeping my voice soft. "That reaction... it wasn't just about yesterday."

For a moment she just looks at me, like she's weighing whether I've earned the next piece.

Then she exhales and leans back, fingers tracing the rim of her mug like it's an anchor.

"Last year," she says quietly, "I took a call."

I go still.

"It came in as a robbery in progress. Convenience store off the highway." Her voice stays even, but I can hear the effort under it. She built a wall and now she's leaning her whole body weight against it. "Weapons mentioned. Screaming in the background. The kind of call you hear and your stomach drops before your hands even hit the keyboard."

She stares at the steam rising from her coffee like she can see the scene in it.

"At first it was just a voice," she says. "A woman on the line, panicked, trying to give me details. Then—" She swallows. "Then someone said a name. Not mine. Hers."

Her fingers tighten around the mug. White knuckles. Controlled.

"My sister."

The word lands between us, plain and brutal.

She keeps going because stopping is worse. "I tried to stay in dispatcher mode," she says. "I tried to tell myself it wasn't her. That my brain was grabbing at patterns because everything sounded like everything when you're tired and wired and—" Her mouth twists. "But then I heard her voice."

She blows out a breath that shakes. "And my body went cold."

I don't move. I don't interrupt. I don't give her a single reason to shut down.

"She didn't say my name," Florence whispers. "Which is almost worse. She just... she sounded like she was trying not to scare me. Like she knew I was on the other end and she refused to give it power."

Her eyes flick away, then back. "I did what I was trained to do. I kept her talking. I kept my voice steady. I pushed units. I typed so fast my fingers cramped."

The muscles in my jaw clench. I let it happen. I don't fight it.

"And then..." Her throat works. "Then there was yelling. A loud crack. Not a gunshot on the line. Not clean. Just... chaos. And the call dropped."

She presses her fingertips to her mouth like she's holding in something that wants to split out of her.

"I called back," she says. "Again. Again. Again." Her eyes glass. "Sometimes it rang. Sometimes it didn't. Sometimes someone answered and said nothing. Sometimes—" She shakes her head once, hard, like she can shake it loose. "Sometimes it was just air and my own breathing and the sound of my partner talking to another caller two consoles away like the world hadn't just ended."

My hand moves without permission, covers hers on the table. Slow. Not trapping her. Just there.

She doesn't pull away.

"I stayed in the chair," she says. "I finished the shift because there were other calls and the board kept blinking and I didn't know what else to do." Her voice thins. "And then someone from the hospital called and asked for next of kin."

Silence opens between us.

Florence closes her eyes. "I had to tell them I was her sister while I was still wearing the headset dent in my hair."

My throat tightens. I keep my face steady.

"I loved dispatch," she murmurs. "But that day taught me something I didn't want to learn." Her eyes open and meet mine. "Sometimes you can do everything right and still lose someone anyway."

And there it is. The thing underneath the whole morning.

Yesterday wasn't just a domestic. It wasn't just a line going dead.

It was the echo.

"And yesterday felt like that moment," she says, voice smaller now. "The second you stopped answering, my body didn't care that I knew logically. I knew the situation—" She swallows. "I just went right back there."

Her breath shudders. "I couldn't lose someone else. Not again. Not like that."

Something breaks a little inside my chest.

She goes quiet. The coffee cools. The house holds its breath with us.

Then she says, barely above a whisper, "And I didn't answer your text."

I keep my voice gentle. "Florence—"

"I know," she says quickly. "I know it wasn't my fault. I know it's irrational. But when Turner said an officer was down..." Her mouth trembles. "All I could think was: I waited too long. Again."

I lean forward, not crowding, just enough that she has to look at me.

"Look at me," I say.

She does.

"You did everything right with your sister," I tell her, each word deliberate. "You kept the line. You kept your voice steady. You pushed help to her as fast as humanly possible. The rest —" I shake my head once. "The rest was never yours to control."

Her jaw flexes.

"As for me," I add, "you not texting back before yesterday doesn't mean you're cursed. It means we live in a world where bad people do bad things and good people are forced to respond."

She lets out a breath that sounds half laugh, half pain. "You make it sound so clean."

"It isn't clean," I say. "It's brutal. It's unfair. And I'm still pissed I made you hear that echo again." I tighten my hand over hers, just a fraction. "But I need you to hear this: your hesitation didn't put me in that doorway. My badge did. My choices did. My job did."

Her eyes shine. She doesn't blink.

"You are not a weapon the universe uses on the people you love," I say. "You are not the reason they bleed."

Her fingers twitch under mine, unsure. Then they curl, threading between my knuckles like she's choosing contact on purpose.

"That's the nicest thing anyone's said to me in a long time," she says softly.

"It shouldn't be," I say, and I mean it.

We sit like that for a while, hands tangled across the table, coffee cooling, the whole house quiet around us.

Then she clears her throat, voice smaller. "After my sister... I almost quit. I filled out the paperwork. I told myself I couldn't sit in that chair and listen to people lose someone and not be able to change it."

"What stopped you?" I ask.

She hesitates.

Then, slowly, she lets my hand go and reaches for her bag by the chair. She pulls out her tablet, sets it on the table, and unlocks it with a swipe like she's bracing for impact.

"This," she says.

On the screen is a card.

Not Rider-Waite. Not exactly. The bones are there in the familiar frame of an image I've seen in other people's hands over the years but everything else is hers. The colors are bolder. The lines cleaner. The woman in the center looks like she could hold a courtroom still with a glance.

Sword in one hand. Scales in the other.

And behind her are symbols I don't understand, but I can feel the weight of them. Like they were chosen, not added.

"Justice," Florence says. "Major Arcana. It was the first one I drew after... everything."

Her voice goes careful around the last word, as if naming it too directly might pull it back into the room.

"I couldn't sleep," she adds. "My brain wouldn't shut up. My grandma kept sending me links about grief and trauma and coping strategies and—" A humorless breath. "None of it felt real. So I opened my sketchbook and just... started."

She swipes her thumb across the screen.

Another card.

The Hermit, but not the hunched old man I vaguely remember. Her version is a woman standing on a cliff edge, spine straight, lantern held high. The light spills out in starry patterns like something alive.

"Now there are... a lot," she says quietly. "Most of the majors. Half the minors. Cups and swords first. I've been working my way through wands and pentacles. It's slow. I redraw things constantly." Her mouth twists like she's about to apologize for caring too much. "But... it's been saving me. In a way."

I lean in before I can stop myself.

I've never been a tarot guy. Not dismissive, just ignorant. I've seen decks in glove compartments and backpacks. Watched a street reader once in Seattle when I was a baby cop on nights. Filed it under Interesting, but not for me.

But this?

This doesn't look like a hobby.

It looks like a map.

"It's beautiful," I say, and it's the only word that comes close.

Color creeps up her neck. "Thanks."

"I don't mean pretty," I add, because she'll try to deflect and I'm not letting her. "I mean... it has teeth. It has purpose. It feels like you took something that could've swallowed you and you turned it into structure."

Her eyes flick to mine, startled, like she wasn't expecting me to get it.

I tap the tablet gently with the back of my knuckles. "She looks like she'd either hug you or cut your bullshit in half depending on what you need."

Florence lets out a laugh that wobbles on the edges. "That's... actually Justice, yeah."

Figures.

"Do you read with them?" I ask.

"Not yet," she says. "They're not finished. And I'm picky. But sometimes I pull one for myself. Just to... sit with it."

I nod once.

I can see her alone in her room, light low, suddenly careful around paper and color. Trying to make meaning out of something that refused to have any.

"Do you think it's silly?" she asks after a beat.

She makes it sound casual, but her shoulders are tight.

Like she's already braced for dismissal.

"Not even a little," I say. "Finding a way to survive that doesn't hurt anyone, finding something that gives you a handhold...there's nothing silly about that." I keep my voice steady. "And this is art, Florence. It's skill. Intention. It's you making something real when your world went unreal."

Her mouth parts slightly.

"And if anyone sneers at it," I add, because it's true, "it tells me everything I need to know about them."

Her gaze drops. She swallows.

Then I tilt my head, because I need her back on the ground.

"Also... I've seen grown men wear rooster hats to steal chickens. You're nowhere near my silly threshold."

She chokes on a laugh, wiping at her eyes with the heel of her palm. "God, I'd almost forgotten about Beatrice."

"There you go," I say quietly. "Proof your brain can hold more than one thing at once."

She looks at me like she's seeing a new angle, past the badge, the age gap, the man who devoured her in a hotel room and then vanished behind protocol.

Something more human.

"You're good at this," she says suddenly.

"Cooking?" I ask, because deflecting is still one of my favorite survival skills.

"Being kind," she says. "You're good at that."

The words land somewhere they shouldn't. Somewhere I didn't know was hungry.

I clear my throat. "Don't spread that around. I have a reputation to maintain."

Her smile is small, but it's real.

And the air changes.

Not dramatically, nothing in this house is loud. But something tightens anyway. Focuses. The room seems to shrink down to the circle of light around our plates and coffee mugs. To the sound of our breathing. To the fact that my hand is still on the edge of her tablet, closer to hers than it needs to be.

She notices at the same time I do.

Our eyes meet.

The silence stretches but not awkwardly.

It's loaded.

"I keep thinking about it," she says quietly. "The hotel. The elevator. The walk at Harbor Days. Yesterday."

"Me too," I admit. My voice is rougher than it was a second ago. "More than is probably healthy."

Her lips curve, wry and a little shaken. "Is that a problem?"

"It should be," I say. "You work with me. I'm older. I'm your—"

"Chief," she cuts in. "Not my direct supervisor. Not my evaluator. Not the man who controls whether I can take a bathroom break."

"That's a low bar," I mutter.

"It's not the only factor," she says. "But it matters." Her gaze doesn't flinch. "And since we're listing things... you're also the only person who made me feel like I wasn't broken for still breathing after last year. So. That counts."

I swallow hard.

"Florence," I say, and I mean it, "I need you to understand something. If we do this...if we cross that line again, it's because you want it." I hold her gaze. "Not because I cooked you breakfast. Not because yesterday scared you and you need comfort. It has to be your choice. For your reasons. And if your reasons change tomorrow, you get to change your mind. No apology. No explanation."

She studies me, eyes dark and steady.

"You're not the only one who gets to make decisions," she says. "I choose things too." Her chin lifts a fraction. "I chose to get in that elevator with you. I chose to walk through that hotel door. I chose to go with you at Harbor Days instead of pretending I didn't know you." A beat. "And I chose to come here today."

Her fingers slide across the table toward mine, deliberate. "I'm not confused about wanting you," she says. "That part is the only thing that feels simple right now."

My pulse kicks hard enough to bruise.

"Come here," I growl.

She stands. So do I, chair scraping. My hip screams, but the pain is nothing against the rush of pure, starving need.

We meet at the corner of the table, breath to breath. Heat rolls off her in waves. I can smell the coffee, maple, and the sweet, unmistakable musk of arousal already slick between her thighs.

I kiss her.

The first press is soft, testing. Then she makes a low, hungry sound and fists my shirt, yanking me in. The kiss turns feral. Tongues sliding, teeth nipping, her body arching into mine like she wants to crawl inside my skin. I grip her ass with both hands, hauling her flush against my cock so she can feel exactly how hard she's made me in three seconds flat.

She tastes like sin and second chances. I drink her down.

I walk her backward until her ass hits the counter. She gasps into my mouth, legs parting instinctively. I lift her onto the edge like she weighs nothing, even though my hip protests. She wraps her thighs around my waist and rocks against me, grinding her soaked heat along my length through our clothes.

"August," she pants against my lips. "Don't you dare hold back."

I don't.

I shove her sweater up and yank it off. The thin tank top underneath clings to her stiff nipples like a second skin. I rip it down, baring her breasts, and latch onto one tight peak, sucking hard enough to make her cry out. My teeth graze, my tongue flicks, and she arches, fingers digging into my scalp like she'll pull my hair out if I stop.

"Fuck—yes—" she hisses.

I switch to the other nipple, biting down just this side of pain while my hand dives between her legs. I cup her through her jeans, rubbing the seam against her clit until she's grinding shamelessly against my palm.

"Off," I growl. "Now."

She lifts her hips. I tear her jeans and panties down in one rough yank, leaving them tangled around one ankle. Then I drop to my knees like a man at prayer.

She's glistening. Swollen. Dripping down her thighs.

I groan like I've been gut-punched. "Look at this pretty cunt. So fucking wet for me already."

I spread her wide with my thumbs and drag my tongue up her slit in one long, obscene lick. She jerks, thighs clamping my ears. I do it again, slower, savoring the taste of her sweet, salty, and addictive center. Then I seal my mouth over her clit and suck.

"August—fuck—!"

Her hips buck. I pin them down with one forearm and

slide two thick fingers inside her, curling hard against that spot that makes her see stars. I fuck her with them while my tongue works her clit in relentless circles, sucking, flicking, devouring. She's dripping down my chin, soaking my beard, and I'm so hard it hurts.

She comes with a broken scream, thighs shaking, cunt pulsing around my fingers like she's trying to pull me deeper. I don't stop. I ride her through it, licking her slow and filthy until she's whimpering, oversensitive, trying to twist away and pull me closer at the same time.

Only then do I stand, wiping my mouth with the back of my hand, tasting her on my tongue.

Her eyes are glassy, lips swollen, chest heaving. She looks wrecked. Perfect.

"Bedroom," she orders, voice raw. "Now."

We barely make it. Clothes fly. My shirt. Her tank. My pants catch on the bandage and I curse. She shoves me onto the edge of the bed before I can argue.

"Sit," she commands. "You're not throwing me around tonight, Chief. I'm taking care of you."

The authority in her voice goes straight to my cock. It twitches, leaking precum.

She climbs over me, straddling my thighs, hair wild, eyes dark with that possessive hunger I've only ever seen in her. She wraps her hand around my thick, throbbing cock and strokes once, slow and tight, thumb smearing the bead at the tip.

"Florence," I rasp.

"Shh." She leans down, mouth brushing my ear. "You're going to sit here and let me ride this cock until neither of us can think. And if you move that hip the wrong way, I'll cuff you to the headboard and edge you until you beg."

Jesus Christ.

My cock jumps in her fist. She laughs, low and wicked.

"Oh, you like that idea."

She sinks down onto me in one slow, relentless glide.

We both groan long, filthy, broken sounds. She's scorching. So tight she feels custom-made for me. When her ass meets my thighs, she pauses, clenching around me, letting me feel every flutter.

Then she starts to move.

Slow rolls at first, grinding her clit against my pelvis with every downward stroke. Her tits bounce inches from my face. I lean in and suck one nipple into my mouth, biting just hard enough to make her moan. She rides me harder, faster, hands braced on my shoulders, nails digging crescents into my skin.

"Fuck, you feel so good," she gasps. "So deep—God, August, I missed this cock splitting me open."

I grip her ass, guiding her rhythm even as pain flares in my hip. She notices. Her eyes flash.

"Don't you dare move." She slams down harder, taking every inch. "This is mine tonight. You're mine."

She rides me like she's trying to ruin me for anyone else. Wet, obscene sounds fill the room. Skin slapping, her slick coating my balls, the wet suck of her cunt every time she lifts off. She leans back, one hand braced on my thigh, the other rubbing her clit in frantic circles.

"I'm gonna come," she whimpers. "Come with me—fill me up, August. I want to feel you pulsing inside me when I break."

That's it.

I thrust up once, hard and deep, ignoring the burn in my hip. She cries out, clenching around me like a fist. Her orgasm rips through her, walls fluttering, milking me. I follow with a guttural roar, burying myself to the hilt and coming so hard my vision whites out. Pulse after pulse, flooding her until she's dripping down my cock, down my balls, onto the sheets.

She collapses against my chest, both of us shaking, sweat-slick, breathing like we've run miles.

I wrap my arms around her, pressing kisses to her hair, her temple, the scar at her brow. My voice is wrecked when I finally speak.

"Florence... sweetheart... I'm never letting you go again."

She lifts her head, eyes soft and fierce at the same time. "Good," she whispers, kissing me slow and deep, tasting herself on my tongue. "Because I'm keeping you."

"You're incredible," I murmur, pressing my lips to the crown of her head. "You know that, right?"

She laughs soft, wrecked, and breathless. "You make me feel like it."

"I mean it." My voice is gravel. "No one has ever—fuck, Florence, you unravel me."

Her fingers curl weakly at my ribs. She buries her face in my throat like she's hiding from whatever I might see in her eyes.

I stroke her hair, slow and reverent, letting the silence hold us.

When she finally lifts her head, her gaze is glassy, dark, devastating.

"Shower?" I offer, thumb brushing her swollen bottom lip. "Before my hip decides it's had enough of your orders."

Her mouth curves slow and sinful. "You offering your assistance, Chief?"

"I'm offering every fucking thing I have left." I let my thumb drag across her lip again. "But yes. Assistance included."

She rolls off the bed with liquid grace I can only envy. I follow slower, testing weight on my bad side. The bandage pulls, but the ache is background noise compared to the fire still burning low in my gut.

"Don't push it," she murmurs, already heading for the bathroom.

I smirk. "You weren't saying that when you were riding me like you owned the damn thing."

Her cheeks flush scarlet. "Shut up and follow me."

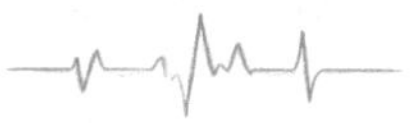

Steam hits thick, warm, and scented with shampoo and sex. She steps under the spray first, tipping her head back, water sluicing over her breasts, down her stomach, between her thighs in rivulets that make my mouth water.

I don't bother hiding the groan that rips out of me.

"Come here," she whispers.

I step behind her. My chest brushes her back, cock already half-hard again and pressing insistently against her ass. She reaches for the soap; I take it from her fingers.

"Let me," I rasp.

I wash her like she's something sacred and filthy at the same time.

Hands glide over her shoulders, down her arms, across her ribs. I cup her breasts, thumbs circling her nipples until they pebble tight. She shivers, arching into my palms. I roll them between my fingers. Gentle, then harder, until her breath stutters against the tile.

"August..." Her voice cracks.

"You like being touched like this?" I kiss the side of her neck, teeth grazing.

"Yes. God, yes."

I soap her stomach, her hips, then slide one hand between her thighs. She's still slick from earlier. She's hot, swollen, dripping. I stroke her clit with slow, slippery circles while my other hand pinches her nipple.

A long, broken breath escapes from Florence's lips. Her head falls back against my shoulder.

Then she turns.

Soap streams down her curves like liquid sin. Her hands rise to my chest, tracing scars, then lower, wrapping around my cock. She strokes once, slow and tight, thumb smearing precum over the head.

My knees nearly buckle.

"Sweetheart," I grit out, jaw locked. "You keep that up and I'm going to come all over your pretty tits before I even get inside you again."

She bites her lip, eyes wicked. "Tempting. But I want you deeper."

That does it.

I spin her, press her chest to the cool glass, hands flat on the wall.

"Bend over," I command, voice low and dark. "Grab your ankles."

She gasps, visibly trembling, but she obeys. Fingers curl around her own feet, ass arched high and perfect, cunt glistening under the spray.

I drop to one knee spreading her wider with my thumbs, opening her like a secret I've earned the right to ruin.

Fuck.

She's a goddamn mess.

Her cunt is flushed dark pink, swollen from earlier, lips puffy and glistening. Thick white streaks of my come are already leaking out—slow, obscene drips sliding down her inner thighs, mixing with the shower water and her own slick. Every time her walls flutter, another bead pushes out, clinging to her folds before trailing down.

I groan low in my throat, the sound vibrating against her skin.

"Look at this perfect, fucked-out pussy," I rasp, voice wrecked. "Still so full of me. See how my come's dripping out of you? Thick and white, marking every inch inside. You took it so deep earlier. Greedy little hole swallowing every drop. Now it's leaking like it can't hold it all."

She whimpers, thighs trembling under my hands.

I drag one thumb through the mess, slow and deliberate. Scooping up a thick ribbon of my release mixed with her wetness. I smear it back up her slit, circling her clit with the slippery evidence of us.

"Feel that?" I growl. "That's me still inside you. Coating your walls. Claiming you. You're so fucking full of my cum it's spilling out every time you clench."

Her hips jerk forward, chasing my touch.

"August—please—"

I lean in closer, breath hot against her. My tongue flicks out, once, twice, lapping up the creamy trail leaking from her entrance. The taste hits me like a drug: salt-sweet, musky, unmistakably *us*. I groan again, louder this time, and press my mouth fully to her.

I lick deeper. Slow, filthy strokes that drag through her folds, collecting every drop I can reach. She sobs, fingers scrabbling at the tile for purchase.

"You taste like sin," I mutter against her. "Like me fucking you raw and filling you up until you overflow. Look how your pretty cunt twitches every time I lick it clean, trying to keep me inside, aren't you? Greedy little thing."

She's shaking so hard the water ripples around us.

"Yes—God, yes—don't stop—"

I suck gently on her swollen clit, then plunge my tongue inside her again, fucking her with it while my thumbs hold her open. More of my come seeps out onto my lips, my chin. I swallow it down like it's holy water.

"Still so tight," I rasp between licks. "Even after I stretched you wide and pumped you full. Feel how your walls flutter around my tongue? Trying to pull me deeper. Fuck, Florence, you're made for this. Made to take my cock and my cum and beg for more."

Her legs buckle. I catch her thighs, holding her steady as I devour her. Sucking, licking, growling praise and filth into her skin until she's a trembling, sobbing wreck.

Only then do I rise, wiping my mouth, tasting us on my tongue.

Her eyes are glassy, tears mixing with shower water, lips parted on broken breaths.

I line myself up, rubbing the head of my cock through the slick mess I just made.

"You want more?" I ask, voice dark, dangerous. "Want me to push it all back inside where it belongs?"

"Yes—please—August, fuck me—"

I sink in slow, inch by thick inch, watching her cunt swallow me again, pushing my own release deeper until she's stuffed full once more.

I thrust deep and relentless. The angle has me hitting that spot inside her with every snap of my hips. Water cascades over us, slicking the obscene sound of skin slapping skin.

"Good girl," I rasp. "Taking every inch like you were made for it. Feel how deep I am?"

"Yes—fuck—yes—"

I reach around, fingers finding her clit, rubbing fast, merciless circles while I pound into her.

"You gonna come on this cock again?" I growl. "Gonna soak me while I fill you up?"

"August—I'm—I'm—"

"Say it."

"I'm gonna come—oh God, I'm coming—!"

She shatters, her cunt clamping down like a vice, thighs quaking, broken cries echoing off the tile. I fuck her through it, chasing my own release, then bury myself deep and come with a raw groan. Pulsing and spilling inside her until she's overflowing, dripping down her thighs, mixing with the water.

I catch her as her knees give, pulling her upright against my chest.

"I've got you," I whisper, kissing her temple, her scar, her wet hair. "Always got you."

She turns in my arms, eyes soft and fierce. "I'm not done with you," she murmurs, voice wrecked. "Not even close."

I smile against her mouth. Slow, dangerous.

"Good," I say. "Because I'm just getting started."

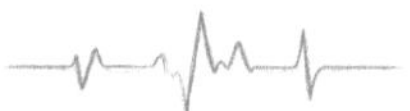

By the time we step out, the mirror is fogged white, the floor slick, and my hip is filing formal complaints in triplicate.

She wraps a thick towel around herself, tucking it between her breasts like armor she doesn't really need anymore.

I grab another and drape it over her shoulders, pulling the edges closed around her. I need the excuse to touch her. Need to feel her skin under my palms, warm and damp and real.

She lets me.

We pad back to the bedroom on bare feet, bodies loose-limbed and trembling, laughing at nothing—the way the towel slips off her shoulder, the way I wince when I bend to pick it up, the way we both still smell like sex and soap and each other.

She steals my T-shirt from the chair. It falls to mid-thigh on her, soft gray cotton clinging where she's still damp. Her nipples press against the fabric, dark shadows under the thin material. I nearly drop to my knees again right there.

I climb into bed first, propped against the headboard so my hip doesn't scream. She follows without hesitation, crawling over me like she belongs there. Florence is half on top, one leg slung across my thigh, cheek pressed to my chest, damp hair fanning out over my skin.

I wrap both arms around her, one hand stroking slow circles down her spine, the other threading through her hair.

"You okay?" I murmur against her temple.

She smiles into my chest, voice thick and honey-slow. "August... I can't feel my legs."

I laugh low, proud, a little wrecked. "Good girl."

She swats my chest weakly, but there's no heat in it. Just affection. "You're impossible."

"And you," I whisper, pressing my lips to her forehead, then the faint two inch scar at her brow, "are everything I ever wanted and had no fucking business asking for."

Her breath catches, small, sharp, vulnerable.

She burrows closer, like she's trying to hide inside my ribcage.

We lie there in the quiet aftermath. Warm. Tangled. Claimed. For the first time in longer than I care to count, the world feels right-side up.

Her fingers trace idle patterns on my chest, lazy hearts, question marks, little secrets she hasn't voiced yet.

Then, so softly I almost miss it: "Are we really doing this?"

Not scared. Just... disbelieving. Like she's afraid the bubble will burst if she says it too loud.

I tilt her chin up until our eyes meet. "Define 'this.'"

She gestures between us. It's a small almost helpless motion. "This. Breakfast, today, tomorrow. Skin on skin. You. Me. Not pretending the last year didn't happen. Not pretending tonight didn't mean everything."

I could deflect. Crack a joke. Hide behind the badge or the age gap or the thousand reasons this could go wrong.

But she deserves the truth.

"I want to," I say. "If you do."

She searches my face like she's waiting for the catch.

"You don't think I'm too young?" she asks, voice barely above a whisper.

I shake my head slowly. "I think you're fire wrapped in skin. I think you've walked through more hell than most people twice your age and came out still soft enough to let me hold you like this. If I'm lucky enough to stand close without getting burned, I'll spend the rest of my life being grateful."

Her eyes shimmer. Not tears, but something bright and unguarded.

She lifts a hand, brushes her fingertips along my jaw. "It's not simple."

"No." I turn my face into her palm, kissing the center. "It's messy. Dangerous. Complicated as hell. And it's the most alive I've felt in years."

Her lips twitch, half smile, half surrender. "Sounds like a terrible idea."

"Yeah." I kiss the inside of her wrist, slow and deliberate. "Let's do it anyway."

She exhales a laugh and sigh tangled together. "Okay," she says, and the word lands like permission, like a vow, like the start of something neither of us can walk away from. "We do this. Until we don't."

Not forever. Not a contract.

Just now. And tomorrow. And whatever comes after.

That's enough to wreck me all over again.

"Understood," I murmur, dragging her higher until she's draped fully across me, heart to heart. "I'm yours for as long as you'll have me."

She hums, pleased, sleepy, possessive. Her hand slides to the back of my neck, nails grazing gently, sending slow shivers down my spine.

"I like spoiling you," I whisper into her hair.

"You make it easy," she breathes.

Her thigh slides higher, settling over mine. Warm. Claiming. My cock stirs lazily against her hip, already half-interested again despite the exhaustion.

She feels it. Smiles against my throat.

"Down, boy," she teases, voice velvet-soft. "You already ruined me twice today."

I chuckle, low and rough. "You ruined me first."

I roll us carefully, mindful of the hip, and tuck her beneath me, just enough to feel her under me, safe, surrounded. I kiss her slow this time. No urgency. Just deep, languid sweeps of tongue, tasting the faint salt of her tears and the sweetness that's all her.

She sighs into my mouth, hands roaming my back, nails tracing scars like she's memorizing them.

When we break apart, she cups my face in both hands.

"You're shaking," she whispers.

"So are you."

She smiles and it's devastating. "Good girl energy goes both ways, huh?"

I laugh quietly. "Yeah. It does."

I ease down beside her again, pulling the sheet over us. She curls into my side, one leg hooked over mine, head on my shoulder, fingers tracing the edge of my bandage like she's checking I'm still whole.

She yawns—soft, kittenish—and burrows deeper.

I kiss her temple. "Sleep, sweetheart. I've got you."

Her voice is already fading. "Promise you won't disappear ?"

"Promise." I brush my lips over the shell of her ear. "I'm not going anywhere."

She hums, content, claimed, safe.

Her breathing evens out.

I stay awake longer, just holding her. Feeling the steady rise and fall of her chest. The warmth of her skin. The quiet miracle of her trusting me enough to fall asleep in my arms.

For the first time in years, the world doesn't feel like it's waiting to take something away.

It feels like it finally gave something back.

And I'll spend every damn day making sure she knows she's safe here.

With me.

Always.

NINETEEN
FLORENCE

I WAKE UP SMILING.

That's the first red flag.

The second is the slow and delicious soreness, the kind that settles deep between my thighs and lingers behind my knees like a secret. My hips ache in that satisfied way. My throat, too. My body hums with the aftershock of being wanted, taken, handled until my brain forgot how to be careful.

Which is not new anymore.

That's the part that scares me.

Because this isn't just one night. This isn't just a fluke or a stumble. This is a pattern now. It's weeks of stolen time and quiet rules, of learning each other by touch and restraint, of acting like we can keep something this big tucked behind closed doors.

I shift lazily, half-buried in my pillow, one leg tangled in the blankets and the other stretched out over cool sheets that should be warm.

That were warm.

For one suspended breath, I expect the weight of August's arm across my waist. The heat of his chest curved around my spine. His breath steady against the back of my neck. He's unfairly calm for a man who can take me apart so thoroughly my bones feel rearranged afterward.

But my bed is empty.

Not in a dramatic, heartbroken way.

In an ordinary way.

Like, of course it is. Of course I woke up alone. We've done this dance enough times that my body knows the rhythm even when my heart pretends it doesn't.

I press my face into the pillow anyway, because I'm petty and soft and greedy, and try to catch the last trace of him. Salt and cedar and sex. The faintest edge of his soap.

Then memory hits.

Fast. Hard. Hot.

His mouth at my throat, teeth grazing the skin he marked.

The sharp drag of his calloused hands down my back.

His voice in the dark, low and wrecked, "Good girl," like it wasn't praise, it was a claim he didn't know how to take back.

And afterward, the way he held me.

Not like a man satisfied.

Like a man ruined.

Gods.

My breath stutters. My toes curl.

A sound slips out of me, half groan, half laugh, and I roll onto my back, limbs heavy, heart stupid. I cover my face with one hand like I can hide from myself.

As if that's ever worked.

My fingers fumble across the nightstand until they find my phone. The screen lights up, and there it is, already waiting, because he's always awake earlier than he should be.

> August: Hope you slept. I didn't, but I'm not mad about the reason.

My soul short-circuits anyway.

Not because it's shocking.

Because it's August. Because he can say one line and turn me into a puddle in a matter of seconds. Because he makes it easy to forget I used to keep my feelings behind a locked door with the deadbolt thrown.

I drop the phone to my chest and stare at the ceiling like it's going to give me answers. My whole body glows warm and wrecked and greedy for more. I bite my lip, trying to hold the smile back.

It's pointless.

I hate this.

I hate how easy he makes it to lose my defenses.

I hate how just one message from him turns my spine to syrup.

I hate how I still feel his hands on my skin like a phantom promise.

But more than that?

I hate how good it feels to be seen.

To be wanted.

To be held like I'm something rare.

Like he knows it.

I breathe out slow. It's Sunday. My day off. No dispatch. No emergencies.

Just me.

And the man who's turned "just me" into a lie.

There's a version of me who would draft twelve replies and send none. One who would wait him out, pretend to be unaffected, play it safe.

But that girl?

She's been getting thoroughly ruined for weeks.

So I type before I can talk myself out of it.

Florence: I slept like someone who'd been absolutely wrecked.

Not naming names.

But if he's tall, stubborn, and has a wicked mouth, I have a few complaints.

(Just kidding. My complaints were aggressively well handled.)

I hit send and immediately toss the phone onto the pillow

like it might combust.

It pings almost instantly.

August: I can be there in ten.

No badge. Just the mouth.

Oh. Fuck.

My thighs clench like I've been possessed by some demon of poor decisions and excellent taste.

I snatch the phone back up.

Florence: Don't you dare joke about that.

Unless you mean it.

Because I haven't moved since I read your first message and if I stay in this bed much longer thinking about your mouth, I'm going to do something reckless.

August: I always mean it.

Keep the sheets warm.

I stop breathing. Like, actually.

Then reality taps me on the shoulder.

The house creaks. A cabinet closes downstairs. Lilly, existing loudly, as she does.

I type with a quick, irritated thumb.

Florence: Wait.

Roommate's home.

And she's the human equivalent of a doorbell camera.

August: I wasn't going to knock.

I was going to use my mouth.

But fine.

Your place is off-limits.

My place, then?

Florence: You offering?

August: I'm begging.

Florence: Didn't you have things to do today? Isn't that why I left in the first place?

August: Damnit.

Why do you have to be the voice of reason when all I can think about is the way you taste.

Florence: Because I'm the literal worst.

August: Not possible.

You're a goddess.

And I plan on having my way with you for many, many nights to come.

Heat floods my face.

Florence: Nights?

August: Nights. Days. Weeks.

For as long as you'll let me.

I clamp a pillow over my face and let out a muffled scream, because apparently I'm a grown woman with a job and a trauma history and I still turn into a teenager when a man promises me time.

Florence: I want you always.

August: ::Prepares for the rest of forever::

Florence: 🖤

August: 😘

Eventually, I force myself out of bed and shuffle to the kitchen. My legs remind me of exactly how much fun I had making bad decisions last night.

I make coffee the way my sister used to—strong enough to wake the dead, splash of cream, cinnamon on top. The smell alone unties something in me.

Not grief.

Not panic.

Just... home, in a way I didn't expect to find again.

Tablet tucked under my arm, I settle on the couch, one knee under me, blanket draped over my legs.

The quiet is nice.

Healing.

Almost.

Because my brain keeps replaying yesterday in slow, obscene loops.

August's breath on my ear, ragged and possessive right before he told me to open wider for him.

The way he groaned when I did.

The way he said my name, low and ruined, like he'd been hungry for me for a long time and finally got his mouth back on what he wanted.

His hands didn't stay careful for long.

They always get greedy.

Demanding.

He dragged me into his lap and pinned my hips down while he fucked up into me so deep I saw stars behind my eyelids. One big hand on my spine, his mouth at my throat, whispering, that's it, take all of it, sweetheart, like he could talk my body into surrendering and it would listen faster than my brain could object.

It did.

And the way he went down on me...Fuck.

No one prepares you for a man who eats pussy like he's got something to prove.

He didn't just taste me. He held me open and devoured me. Slow at first. Then harder when I begged. Until my legs shook so badly he had to press his forearm across my hips to keep me from lifting off the bed.

I can still feel the scrape of his stubble on my inner thighs.

I clench, helpless, heat rolling low and quick.

My body remembers him too well.

Too easily.

I shake my head hard, like I can rattle him out of my bloodstream, and force myself to open my tablet.

The partially finished tarot card stares back at me.

The Star.

Hope. Renewal. Light after devastation.

I exhale and drag my stylus across the screen, adding glimmers along the waterline, softening the arc of the woman's shoulders, brightening the constellation behind her.

It's the first time in days my mind goes fully quiet.

An hour passes without me noticing.

When I finish, I sit back and look at the card.

Really look.

It's... beautiful.

Not perfect. But honest. Bright in a way that feels like defiance.

Before I can talk myself out of it, I snap a picture and type a message.

> Florence: Finished this today. Thought you might appreciate it.

My thumb hovers.

I hit send anyway.

My phone pings.

Once.

Twice.

Three times.

I open the thread and my breath catches.

> August: Florence. This is... god, I don't even have the right word for it.

It feels like standing outside right before sunrise. Like that moment when everything's still dark but you know the light's coming.

You did that. I'm proud of you.

My eyes sting.

It hits me, stupidly, sharply, that I haven't had someone say they're proud of me in a long time.

I swallow hard and read his message again, because apparently that's a thing I'm doing now. Rereading texts like a teenager with her first crush.

I hug the blanket tighter around me.

I'm in so much trouble.

By early afternoon, I'm puttering around the kitchen like I belong here. Like I've always belonged here.

I'm humming.

I don't hum.

I'm stirring sauce while swaying to music that isn't even on. I'm smiling at my stove like it said something nice to me.

Lilly wanders in wearing pajama shorts and a T-shirt that says SATAN LOVES YOU. She stops dead in the doorway, blinking at me like I've been body-snatched.

"You're cooking," she says slowly. Then she leans in and inhales like a bloodhound. "Voluntarily."

"Don't make it weird," I mutter, stirring more aggressively than necessary.

"It's already weird," she says, eyes narrowing. "You even have your hair down."

She circles me like a scientist observing a suspiciously domestic cryptid.

"Okay," she announces. "Spill. You look like someone who recently got railed."

My face goes hot so fast I nearly drop the spoon.

"It's not—" I start, and immediately hate myself, because that's exactly what someone says when it is.

Lilly's eyes narrow. "Oh my gods. It's been weeks."

I freeze.

She points her fork at me like a prosecutor. "You've been

smiling at your phone. You've been disappearing on 'errands' that take exactly two hours and come back smelling like expensive soap and bad decisions. And you haven't brought anyone around."

My throat goes tight.

Because she's not wrong.

And because the truth is sitting in my chest like a live coal, burning through everything I've been stacking on top of it.

"It's... not one date," I admit, voice too quiet.

Lilly goes completely still.

Then she inhales like she's about to ascend. "YOU HAVE A SECRET LOVER."

"Stop saying it like that."

"I will not." Her eyes are shining. "Florence. I'm honored. I'm obsessed. Tell me everything."

I force myself to keep stirring sauce like my life isn't actively collapsing. "It's not everything."

"That's the opposite of what I asked."

I set the spoon down, wipe my hands on a paper towel, and brace myself on the counter.

Here it is. The part where I either lie again or say something true and let it detonate.

Lilly leans forward, chin in her hands, smiling like I just told her Santa is real and he's coming for dinner.

"Okay," she whispers dramatically. "Do I know him?"

"No," I say too fast.

Her smile falters. "Not even a little?"

I swallow.

Because I do not get to pretend this is just privacy. This is fear.

This is me keeping a man out of this house like he's contraband. Like if he crosses the threshold, the whole thing becomes real in a way I can't manage.

"Not really," I hedge.

Lilly's eyes narrow again. "Is he local?"

My stomach flips.

"Florence," she says gently, like she can hear the tremor in my silence. "Hey. I'm not trying to pry. I just... you live with me. If someone is making you happy, I want to know who they are."

Happy.

Because yes.

He's making me happy.

And also making me terrified.

I choke on a laugh that isn't funny. "He's... complicated."

Lilly's eyebrows lift. "Okay, so he's hot."

"Lilly."

She sits back, grinning. "That's a yes."

I close my eyes for one long second.

August's mouth. The rough edge of his jaw. The way his eyes soften when he's being careful with me, and the way they go dark when he isn't. The strength of his hands on my hips like he's not afraid of how much I want.

The way he texts me good morning like it means something.

The way he looks at me like he's already decided I'm worth the risk.

I open my eyes and exhale.

"We've been... seeing each other," I say. "For a few weeks."

Lilly's whole face lights up so bright it's almost painful. "OH MY GOD."

"Keep your voice down," I hiss, because apparently I'm still trying to pretend this can stay contained.

She clamps a hand over her mouth, eyes huge. "Sorry. Sorry. Okay. Okay. Details. Who is he."

My pulse stutters.

Because the answer is a match.

And my life is gasoline.

I move the bowls to the table like I can hide behind dinner. "We're eating."

Lilly follows me, vibrating. "We can eat and talk. I'm talented."

"Lilly."

"Fine," she says, dragging out the word. "I'll be normal. For sixty seconds."

We sit.

I take a bite of pasta I can't taste.

Lilly watches me like she's trying to read my face the way she reads clay, finding the stress points, the cracks, the places that will collapse if you push too hard.

Then, softer, "Is he... good to you?"

"Yes," I say, and it's the first honest thing that comes out without a fight. "He's... good."

Lilly's expression warms. Relief. Happiness for me. The kind of uncomplicated support I've been craving for months.

And guilt follows it immediately, sharp and acidic.

Because he is good to me.

And I've been lying to her face for weeks.

Not because I'm ashamed of him.

Because I'm terrified of what happens when she finds out who he is.

Lilly, oblivious, takes a huge bite of pasta. "Okay. So. He's hot, he's good, he's consistent. We love to see it."

I laugh, but it comes out thin.

She points her fork at me again. "Do I get to meet him?"

My stomach drops.

Because that's the problem, isn't it?

There is no casual meeting.

There is no cute roommate introduction.

There is only the moment it implodes.

I make myself shrug. "Maybe. Eventually."

Lilly squints. "Why do you sound like you're negotiating with a bomb?"

Because I am.

Because the man I've been sneaking out to see—keeping out of this house, keeping away from her, keeping my voice steady when I talk about him—is her father.

And if I say it out loud, it becomes real in a way I can't unmake.

So I do what I always do when I'm scared.

I deflect.

"Please," I say lightly. "Can we not do a full interrogation? I had a day."

Lilly immediately softens. "Okay. Okay, sorry." She reaches

across the table and taps my hand once. "We can go slow. I'm just... happy for you."

The warmth of that hits me right behind the ribs.

Because she's being kind.

She's being my friend.

And she has no idea she's standing on the edge of the same cliff I am.

We eat.

We talk.

Lilly rants about her art instructor "having the aesthetic taste of a tax auditor and the emotional range of a broken Roomba," and I laugh so hard I snort.

She shows me her newest mugs which se's added these small clay figurines to—a witchy raccoon, a ghost with a crochet hobby, a dramatic bat wearing a scarf. Something warm expands in my chest.

Safe.

Soft.

For a moment, I forget the world is sharp around the edges.

Eventually, though, our bowls empty. The kitchen quiets.

And the quiet that follows isn't awkward.

It's intimate.

I watch Lilly tuck her hair into a messy bun, humming as she loads the dishwasher, hip-bumping it closed. She sings the wrong lyrics to a Taylor Swift song on purpose, just to make me laugh.

And when I do, she grins like my joy is something she earned. This—her—has become home faster than I expected. And the thought blindsides me.

What happens when she finds out?

When she realizes the man I've been sneaking around with is the man who raised her?

What happens when she remembers every offhand comment she's made about her dad—nosey, protective, stubborn, always working—and realizes I've been swallowing my reactions whole?

What happens when she realizes I've been keeping him

away from this house not because I'm private...but because I couldn't handle seeing him in the same room as her.

One wrong move and everything catches fire.

What if Lilly thinks I used her?

What if she thinks I only moved here for him? Because in the ugliest, most honest corner of myself I know I did. I swallow, suddenly unsteady.

Because it isn't just August I'm afraid of losing.

It's Lilly too.

This life I'm building—this fragile, hopeful thing—feels like the first time since last year that I've belonged anywhere.

And if I fall for him, really fall, and it goes sideways...

I don't know that I have it in me to start over again.

Not after grief.

Not after losing my sister and learning how fast the universe can take a person and keep moving like nothing happened.

The weight of it presses down on me, quiet and heavy.

I don't say any of it out loud.

But I think it.

I don't just want him.

I want this life.

These people.

This chance.

And I'm terrified I might lose all of it.

Lilly's phone buzzes on the counter.

"Ugh. My dad," she says, wiping her hands on a dish towel.

My spine goes instantly, stupidly straight.

Lilly picks the phone up, glances at it, and rolls her eyes so hard it's practically a full-body event. "He's asking if I'm home. Again."

I force my mouth to cooperate. "Aw. Protective."

It comes out the right shape. Warm. Casual.

Inside, my pulse kicks like a trapped animal.

Lilly snorts. "Protective is one word. Nosy is another." She thumbs a reply with one hand. "He does this thing where he pretends it's about safety, but really he wants to know if I've eaten vegetables."

My laugh is a little too high. I swallow it down. "That's... sweet."

She squints at me. "Are you okay? You just went kind of haunted Barbie."

"I'm fine," I say instantly. Too instantly. "You think I look like Barbie? That's too sweet."

Lilly's eyebrows lift. "Don't deflect. You're doing the dispatch voice."

"Am not."

"You are." She points the towel at me. "That calm, dead-eyed tone you use when someone's calling about their tin foil hats malfunctioning."

"I thought that caller sounded familiar. You know we have plenty of aluminum foil in the drawer," I say.

Lilly rolls her eyes and tries to hide the laugh forming at her lips. "I don't have time to fix everyone's tin foil hats."

I walk to the drawer in the kitchen and pull out the aluminum foil handing her the roll.

"What is this for?" Lilly takes it from me.

"It's A-LUM-IN-UM," I say pointing to the box.

She drops it onto the floor, mic drop.

"It's a professional skill," I say.

"Mm-hmm." She turns back to the sink, but her voice softens. "Anyway."

My throat tightens around nothing.

"He's been extra weird lately, too," Lilly says.

My stomach drops.

"Like... how?" I ask, and my voice tries to betray me, but I clamp down hard.

Lilly shrugs. "Quieter. Tired. He does this thing where he stares at his coffee and just spaces out."

Heat and panic rush through me at once, like my body can't decide which emotion to prioritize.

"That's... probably just work," I manage.

"Probably," she agrees. Then she smirks, glancing at me over her shoulder.

I choke. Actually choke.

Lilly laughs. "Oh my god. Are you okay?"

I wheeze, pressing my fist to my mouth. "Just... inhaled my spit."

She shakes her head, amused. "Alright, drama queen. Go to bed. You look like you're about to short-circuit."

I nod, already backing away like the kitchen has turned into a crime scene.

"Night," I say.

"Night," Lilly calls, cheerful.

I make it to my room on autopilot.

Close the door.

Lean my forehead against it.

And exhale like I've been holding my breath for weeks.

Exhaustion, longing, and dread tangle into a knot in my stomach.

My phone glows faintly on the nightstand.

I reach for it before I can stop myself.

His messages are still there.

Warm.

Steady.

Patient.

I set the phone on my chest and stare into the dark.

And there it is.

The truth.

Soft and terrifying and undeniable.

I think I might be falling in love with him.

And that terrifies me more than anything else in the world.

TWENTY
AUGUST

THE HOUSE IS TOO quiet without her.

Not the dramatic kind of quiet, just the normal kind I've lived in for five years. But after six weeks of her shoes by my door, her laugh in my kitchen, her hair in my shower drain, and her body curled against mine like she belongs there...

This quiet feels like something missing. Not something peaceful.

My hip aches when I swing my legs out of bed. A deep pulse, dull and stubborn. The graze is healed enough to stop being dramatic about it, but the muscle still complains like it's filing a grievance.

Worth it.

Worth every ache and bruise and bad night of sleep I pretended wasn't about her.

I stand carefully, let the room steady, then head for the kitchen. Flip on the overhead light. Reach for the French press like it's a ritual, because it is. The kettle hums. The kitchen fills with that first warm smell of coffee and damp grounds, and for a second I can almost pretend this is just another morning where she'll pad in behind me in one of my shirts and steal the first sip.

She won't, because it's a weekday and she's working.

That fact lands right where the quiet lives.

I grab the small pack the physical therapist gave me last year after a sprain and pop the heat pad into the microwave.

Thirty seconds.

Hip: quiet protest.

Me: indulge it anyway.

The microwave beeps. I tuck the warm pad against the sore spot and breathe through the first wave of relief.

My phone buzzes on the counter.

A picture lights the screen.

Florence.

The Star card glows in the low kitchen light with deep blues, soft golds, a woman pouring water into a pool, constellations humming above her shoulder like the sky bent to listen.

She sent it last night, hours after she'd crawled into bed, after she'd texted me a purple heart like she wasn't out there quietly rewriting the inside of my life.

I look at it again and feel it hit me dead center.

This isn't fragile hope.

It's stubborn.

It's the kind of light you choose on purpose.

My thumb brushes the screen. The coffee is ready. I still don't move for the mug.

I type before I let myself overthink it.

August: You drew hope without hiding behind anything.

Strength without armor.

It's beautiful, Florence.

I stare at the message for a beat, then send it.

Delivered.

Unread.

She's probably in her car. Or in the parking lot. Or walking into dispatch with her hair pinned up and that steady voice she wears like a weapon.

The picture flashes in my head so clearly I have to brace my palm on the counter.

I finally pour coffee, take a sip, and exhale like it actually reaches the bottom of my lungs.

My phone buzzes again.

Different tone.

Lilly.

I swipe it open, already bracing.

Lilly: Old man. I'm alive and you're not allowed to die this week.

Lilly: Also I have a life update and I need food. Tomorrow. Sirens. After my shift.

I snort into my coffee.

August: So you're kidnapping me for dinner.

Lilly: Correct.

Also if you say you have plans I will simply show up at your house and shame you on the porch.

August: That is terrifyingly plausible.

Lilly: Great. See you tomorrow. 7ish. I want fries and gossip.

And don't pretend you don't have gossip. You've been acting weird for like two months.

My stomach tightens, because she's not wrong.

I've been weird.

I've been careful. Private. Guarded in ways my own daughter can clock from across a room.

Because the thing with Florence stopped being a "thing" somewhere around week two, and started becoming a pattern. A rhythm. Nights at my place. Coffee texts. Harbor walks. Her head on my shoulder while she pretends she isn't soft.

And the rule we set in Seattle about no overlap or complications has been dead for a while.

I type and delete twice.

Then I keep it simple.

August: Tomorrow. Sirens. 7.

Lilly: Thank you.

Lilly: And bring cash because I'm not paying if you show up moody.

I set the phone down and stare at the counter like it might offer me a playbook.

Tomorrow.

Sirens.

Lilly.

And I'm already imagining what happens when Florence becomes a real name in that context instead of a life I keep separate.

My phone buzzes again, this time with Florence's contact photo.

I pick it up too fast.

Her reply to my message pops in.

Florence: Don't make me cry before coffee, Calder.

Thank you. Really.

I needed that.

My chest loosens. The tight place eases.

Then the typing bubbles appear.

Florence: Also I'm off at six.

If you want me...

I can come over after work and stay.

Heat moves through me, low and immediate.

It isn't just sex anymore, even when it is.

It's her choosing my space.

Choosing the quiet with me in it.

I type back with the kind of restraint that feels like holding a door shut in a storm.

August: I want you.

Come over after your shift. I'll make dinner.

Stay as long as you want.

The reply comes fast, like she's been waiting for permission.

Florence: I can't wait.

She makes my whole morning tilt toward something that feels dangerously like happiness.

I set the phone down, stare at the coffee, and realize I'm smiling at my own countertop like an idiot.

Six weeks.

Six weeks, and she's already threaded herself through my habits.

Dinner tonight.

Sirens tomorrow.

And at some point soon, whether or not I'm ready, the separate worlds are going to touch.

I look at the time, then at the fridge, then at the list of things I'm supposed to care about today.

Budget meeting.

Overtime projections.

Paperwork I can't ignore.

And, apparently, the fact that my life is shifting under my feet.

I take one more sip of coffee.

Then I start making a plan.

I STAND in front of my closet longer than any grown man should.

Half my wardrobe is uniforms. The other half is T-shirts and flannels. There are a few "nice" shirts hanging off to one side, leftovers from a version of my life where I tried harder to be social, to be normal, to pretend the badge didn't eat most of me.

My hand lands on a charcoal button-down.

Simple. Clean. A little more than casual without looking like I'm trying.

Six weeks.

Six weeks of Florence slipping into my life sideways. Late-night texts. Coffee in the morning. Her laugh in my kitchen. Her mouth on my throat. The way she goes quiet after a hard shift and lets me hold her like she doesn't have to be made of steel for ten minutes.

It feels like the kind of domestic intimacy I haven't allowed myself to want in years.

I swallow and drag my attention away from the shirt to the mirror across the room.

The man looking back at me is forty-three, tired in the eyes, scarred in places no one sees, and still trying to pretend he's in control of the way his life is tilting.

"You're not your father," I say to my reflection, quiet but firm. "You get to choose different."

He hid everything behind slammed doors and silence. Rage like a weather system. Love like a leash.

I won't do that to Lilly.

I won't do that to Florence.

If I'm building something, if I'm serious, I don't get to keep it in the dark just because the light makes me nervous.

The kitchen is warm, clean in a way it hasn't been in years. I've been scrubbing and resetting for weeks without fully admitting why. Clearing space in drawers. Buying real groceries instead of whatever I can eat standing at the sink.

I open the fridge and stare at the lineup like it's a strategy board.

Steaks marinating in rosemary and garlic.

Asparagus.

Baby potatoes.

A loaf of bread I actually bought on purpose, not because it was closest to the register.

My phone buzzes on the counter.

Florence: I'm off at six.

Is "I'm bringing cinnamon rolls" still charming or has it crossed into "I'm feral and coping"?

August: It's charming.

Also, I'm counting on feral. That's kind of our brand.

Three dots.

Florence: August.

Don't say things like that while I'm still at work.

August: Yes, ma'am.

Florence: I'm not your ma'am.

August: That's not what you said last weekend.

Florence: I hate you.

I can *hear* the smile in it, and it does something dangerous to me.

August: You don't.

Drive safe. I'll have dinner ready.

I set the phone down before I say more than I should.

Because the truth is, I'm not just making dinner.

I'm making a night I can't take back.

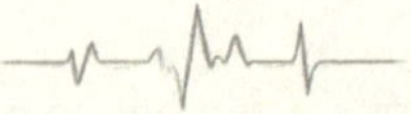

By the time she gets here, the house smells like rosemary and heat.

I've got music on low. Just something to keep the rooms from feeling too empty when my nerves start hunting for something to chew on.

I'm plating the food when the security app pings.

Motion detected.

My chest does that stupid eager stutter again.

I wipe my hands on a towel and open the door before she can knock.

Florence stands on my porch with her hair down, cheeks pink from the cold, and a paper bag in one hand.

"Hey," she says, breathless. "I didn't... I don't know what you like so I grabbed—"

"Come in," I cut in, softer than I mean to. "You're here. That's the only thing I needed."

Her eyes lift to mine, and something in her face goes quiet. The guardedness loosens by a notch.

She steps inside, and the air changes instantly, like my house recognizes her.

"Dinner smells... illegal," she murmurs.

"It's not illegal," I say. "Just suspiciously domestic."

She huffs a laugh, kicks her shoes off by the door like she's done it a thousand times before, and that small familiarity hits me harder than it should.

I take the bag from her hand.

"Cinnamon rolls," she says, like it's a confession.

"Perfect," I answer, because it is.

I don't kiss her right away. Not because I don't want to—God knows I do—but because I'm trying to hold this steady. Trying to give her the choice with my hands in my pockets instead of on her waist.

She solves the problem by stepping closer.

"Hi," she says again, quieter.

My voice drops. "Hi."

And then she's on her toes, her mouth on mine, and the last thread of restraint I've been holding snaps clean.

I kiss her like a man who's been trying to do the right thing for weeks and failing with dignity.

Her hands slide into my hair.

She breaks the kiss first, forehead against mine, breath warm.

"Dinner," she whispers, like we both need the reminder.

"Dinner," I agree, though my body has other plans.

We eat at the table.

Florence makes that soft, helpless sound when she tastes something good, eyes fluttering like she can't help it, and it's almost worse than the memory of her moaning in a hotel elevator because this is *real life*. This is the kind of moment you keep.

"This is... really nice, August."

Something in my chest tightens.

"Good," I say, because if I say what I mean—*I want every night with you to feel like this*—I'll tip us into something she might not be ready to hold.

She watches me over her glass. Like she knows I'm holding back. Like she's waiting to see if I'll jump.

We finish dinner talking about the small, easy things that have become ours: the ridiculous town festival calendar (who schedules "Crab Races" the same weekend as "Pancake Breakfast"?), the new coffee place she swears is "doing too much with oat milk foam art," and how Ruth keeps leaving passive-aggressive Post-its on another dispatcher's console about headset hygiene.

The conversation slows. The space between words stretches. Her knee brushes mine under the table.

I catch her eye.

She smiles a small, wicked grin and stands.

"Stay," she says, voice low. "I've got dessert."

She disappears into the kitchen. I hear the soft clink of a plate, her bare feet padding back.

When she returns, she's carrying a tray of warm cinnamon

rolls fresh from the oven she must have timed perfectly while I was distracted by her laugh. The icing is still melting, dripping over the edges in glossy white ribbons. The smell hits me like a drug: butter, sugar, cinnamon, and her.

She sets the tray on the table and leans over my shoulder from behind, arms looping around my neck, lips brushing my ear.

"Made these for you," she whispers. "Figured we should eat them... creatively."

I turn my head, catch her mouth in a slow kiss. She tastes like anticipation.

"Creatively?" I murmur against her lips.

She pulls back just enough to grab one roll, tears off a piece, and holds it to my mouth.

I take it. The dough is soft, warm, sticky with icing. I lick the sweetness from her fingers deliberately, watching her pupils blow wide.

Her breath hitches.

Then she's laughing bright and delighted. Florence smears a stripe of icing across my lower lip with her thumb.

"Oops," she says, not sorry at all.

I grab her wrist, pull her onto my lap so she's straddling me in the chair.

"Oops?" I echo, voice rough. "You're playing with fire, sweetheart."

She giggles—actual giggles—and leans in to lick the icing off my lip, slow and teasing.

"Burn me, then."

That's it.

I stand, lifting her with me. She wraps her legs around my waist, laughing harder when the chair tips back. I carry her to the kitchen island, set her on the edge, and step between her thighs.

"We haven't fucked in here yet," she says, breathless, eyes sparkling. "Last room in the house."

I grin against her mouth. "Let's fix that."

She reaches behind her, grabs another cinnamon roll, tears it in half, and smears warm, sticky icing across my throat.

"My turn," she whispers, and licks it off me, slow, filthy swipes of her tongue that make my cock throb against her.

I growl, grab her hips, and yank her tank top over her head. No bra. Her breasts spill free, nipples already tight. I lean down and suck one into my mouth, tasting sugar and skin. She moans, fingers tangling in my hair.

I drop to my knees.

Her shorts and panties hit the floor in one tug.

She's already glistening, even swollen, the scent of her arousal mixing with cinnamon and butter.

"Fuck, look at you," I rasp. "Dripping before I even touch you."

She spreads her thighs wider, shameless. "Then touch me."

I hook her legs over my shoulders and bury my face between them.

I lick her slow—long, flat strokes from entrance to clit, tasting her sweetness layered with the faint trace of icing she'd smeared on my fingers earlier. She bucks, laughing turning to moans.

"August—oh God—"

I suck her clit into my mouth, flicking with my tongue while two fingers slide inside her hot, slick, clenching cunt. I curl them, stroking that spot until her thighs shake around my ears.

She comes fast, hard, gasping, fingers yanking my hair, hips grinding against my face. I lick her through it, greedy, until she's whimpering, oversensitive.

When I stand, my chin is wet, lips swollen. She grabs my shirt, pulls me in, and kisses me, tasting herself, moaning into my mouth.

"My turn," she pants.

She slides off the counter, drops to her knees, and yanks my jeans down. My cock springs free already hard, leaking, and aching for her.

Florence wraps her hand around the base, looks up at me with those dark, wicked eyes, and licks a stripe from balls to tip.

I groan.

She takes me into her mouth, slow, deep, sucking like she's starving. Her tongue swirls the head, then flattens along the underside. One hand cups my balls, rolling gently; the other strokes what her mouth can't reach.

"Fuck—Florence—good girl, just like that—"

She hums around me, the vibration shooting straight to my spine. I thread my fingers through her hair—not guiding, just holding on.

She pulls off with a wet pop, strokes me fast, and grins up at me.

"Want to come in my mouth?" she teases. "Or want to fuck me on this counter first?"

I haul her up by the arms, spin her, and bend her over the island.

"Both," I growl. "But I'm fucking you now."

I kick her feet wider, notch myself at her entrance, and thrust in hard, deep, and with one smooth stroke that buries me to the hilt.

She cries out in a mix of pleasure-pain, perfect.

I fuck her like I'm making up for lost time: fast, rough, the sound of skin slapping skin mixing with her moans and the wet squelch of her cunt taking me.

The tray of cinnamon rolls tips. Icing smears across the counter, sticks to her forearms where she braces herself.

She laughs wild and breathless. She moans when I hit that spot deep inside her again.

"August—harder—fuck—me—harder—"

I grip her hips, pound into her, one hand sliding around to rub her clit in tight circles.

"Come for me," I rasp. "Come all over this cock while you're covered in icing and me."

She shatters screaming my name, walls pulsing, thighs shaking. I follow right after, thrusting deep, spilling inside her with a guttural groan, filling her until it drips down her thighs.

We stay like that, panting, sticky, laughing against each other's skin.

I pull out slow, watch my come leak from her, and groan again.

She turns, wraps her arms around my neck, and kisses me slowly, tasting like sugar and us.

"Last room christened," she whispers against my lips.

I laugh, low and wrecked. "We're a mess."

"The best kind," she says, and licks a stripe of icing from my jaw.

I scoop her up, careful of the hip, and carry her toward the bedroom.

"Shower?" she asks.

"Shower," I agree. "Then round two."

She grins into my neck. "You're insatiable."

"For you?" I kiss her temple. "Always."

And as we stumble down the hall in a sticky, laughing, tangled mess. I realize this is what I want.

Not just the sex.

The mess.

The giggles.

The quiet after.

Her.

All of her.

Forever, if she'll let me.

I KISS HER TEMPLE, lingering there, breathing her in her damp hair, soap, and the faint salt of us still clinging to her skin. Then I ease back just enough to see her face.

My thumb brushes the damp strands away from her forehead, slow and careful, and that's when my eyes catch on the thin, pale line that bisects her brow. It's faint now after years of healing but it's unmistakable. A scar. Small, precise, the kind that tells a story someone tried to forget.

I trace it lightly with the pad of my thumb, barely touching skin. "This," I murmur. "Where'd it come from?"

Florence goes still under my hand. Not tense, exactly, just... watchful. Like she's deciding how much truth to give me tonight.

She exhales, soft, almost resigned.

"Car accident," she says quietly. "Seven years ago. In Seattle. Rainy night. The other driver ran the light. My mom..." Her voice catches, just for a second. "She didn't make it. I got this. And a concussion. And a lifetime of hating stoplights."

The words land heavy. Something stirs in my chest, a familiar, unwelcome. Rain. Screaming. A girl in my arms, blood threading into dark hair, brown eyes wide with shock and grief. *Florence.* The name echoes from a memory I've never quite shaken. The scar matches. The timeline matches.

My thumb freezes against her skin.

For one heartbeat, the pieces almost click.

But she's looking at me with those same eyes, older now, softer, but the same, and I can't make the connection stick. Not yet. Not when she's curled against me, vulnerable and trusting, after everything we just shared. If it's her, if she's the girl I held in the rain while her world ended, I'd know. Wouldn't I?

I swallow the unease. Let it go. For now.

"I'm sorry," I say, voice low. "That's... that's a hell of a thing to carry."

She nods once, small. "It is. But I'm still here." Her fingers find mine, squeeze. "And tonight... tonight I feel like maybe I'm allowed to be happy again."

The words gut me.

I lean down and kiss the scar, soft, reverent, like I can soothe seven years of hurt with one press of my lips.

"You are," I whisper against her skin. "You're allowed every damn thing you want, Florence. Starting with this."

She exhales a shaky laugh, burrowing closer. "You're dangerous when you're sweet."

"Only for you."

And for the first time in longer than I can remember, the future doesn't feel like a threat.

It feels like a promise.

"There's one more thing," I say.

Her eyes flick up, lazy satisfaction sharpening into something alert. "What."

"My daughter." The word sits heavy in my chest, the most unguarded piece of me I've ever offered anyone. "I want you to meet her."

Florence goes utterly still.

Not the playful freeze she does when I tease her. This is different. She's spine-stiff, breath-caught, the kind of stillness that comes right before a person decides whether to run or fight.

I keep my voice low, steady. "Not as some ambush. Not to test you. Just... because she's the center of my world. And you're becoming the center of it too. I don't want to keep you in a separate room anymore."

Her throat works. She doesn't blink.

"August..."

"You can say no," I cut in before she can spiral. "You can say not yet, or never, and I won't push. I won't guilt you. I won't walk away. But I'm done hiding pieces of my life like you're something I'm ashamed of. You're not."

Her fingers, still tangled in my shirt, tighten until the fabric bunches. She's breathing too shallow, too fast, like she's trying not to hyperventilate.

"Is she going to hate me?" The question comes out small, cracked.

The ache behind my ribs flares sharp.

"No." I cup her jaw, thumb stroking the soft skin under her ear. "She's sharp, and she's protective, and she'll probably give you hell at first just to see if you'll fold. But hate? No. She's got too much of her mother's fire and my stubbornness to waste it on hating someone I care about."

Florence exhales a shaky, almost-laugh. But her eyes are glassy, pupils blown with something that looks a lot like panic.

"I don't want to take anything from her," she whispers. "I don't want her to look at me and see... someone trying to replace what she already has. Or worse, someone who's been lying to her face."

The words land like a punch I didn't see coming.

I search her face. "Lying?"

She flinches, just a flicker, but it's there.

"I just mean..." She swallows hard, looks away. "I don't want her to feel threatened. Or blindsided. Or like I've been... encroaching."

I tilt her chin back gently. "You're not encroaching. You're not replacing anyone. You're just... you. And I want her to know the woman who makes me laugh again. The woman who makes me want to come home instead of just clocking out."

Her eyes shimmer with tears she refuses to let fall. "What if she doesn't like me?"

"Then we figure it out." My voice is rougher now. "But I know her, Florence. She's got a big heart under all that sarcasm. And she's been telling me for years to stop being so fucking alone."

A wet laugh escapes her, half sob, half relief.

She presses her forehead to mine, breathing uneven.

"I'm scared," she admits, so quiet I almost miss it.

"I know." I slide my hand to the back of her neck, thumb stroking the tense muscle there. "So am I. Terrified, actually. But I'd rather be scared with you than safe without you."

She closes her eyes. A single tear slips free, tracks down her cheek. I kiss it away.

"Okay," she whispers. The word trembles. "I'll meet her."

Relief crashes through me so hard my throat closes. I pull her closer, burying my face in her hair.

"Thank you," I rasp.

She shakes her head against my shoulder. "Don't thank me yet. Just... promise me you'll be there. The whole time. Don't leave me alone with her thinking I'm some... interloper."

"I'll be right there." I kiss her temple, her cheek, the corner of her mouth. "Every second. Holding your hand under the table if you need it. Telling her you're the best thing that's happened to me in years. Because you are."

She lets out a shaky breath; a small, decisive nod emerges. "Okay."

We stay like that. All tangled, quiet, hearts hammering in tandem while the room darkens around us.

Her fingers trace the edge of my jaw, slow and deliberate.

"I'm still terrified," she murmurs.

"Me too."

A beat.

"But I want this. I want you. All of it. Even the scary parts."

I tilt her face up and kiss her, slow, deep, reverent. Not hungry this time. Just honest.

"Then we do the scary parts together," I say against her lips.

She smiles—small, tremulous, real.

"Together."

TWENTY-ONE
FLORENCE

AUGUST'S TRUCK smells like cedar and coffee and him, and I'm doing everything in my power to breathe normally. My knees are pressed together, palms damp, pulse misbehaving in a way that feels teenage and humiliating.

He drives with one hand on the wheel, the other resting casually on his thigh, thumb tapping in a slow rhythm that pulls my attention every time. He notices. Of course he notices. His mouth tilts.

"You're quiet," he says softly.

I swallow. "So are you."

His chuckle is low, warm. "I'm trying not to stare at you."

My whole body flushes. I tuck my hair behind my ear. "You're staring at the road."

"Yeah." His voice dips. "Barely."

August reaches over and brushes the inside of my wrist with his thumb. A single pass, light as breath, but it throws me out of orbit. I feel it in my stomach, my throat, the base of my spine. His thumb lingers there, fitting itself into the small Harbor like it belongs.

"I'm glad you said yes to tonight," he murmurs.

I try to respond. I do. But the words get stuck behind the feeling of his touch. He's grounding me and setting me on fire at the same time.

"I'm glad you asked," I manage.

His hand slips lower, fingers weaving gently between mine, resting our joined hands on my thigh. The contact is simple. Completely innocent. And somehow the most intimate thing anyone has ever done to me.

We drive like that, quiet, fingers tangled, breath exchanging in the dim warmth of his truck, and something inside me settles in a way it hasn't in a long time.

He squeezes my hand slightly. "Florence."

I turn.

He watches me in the space between streetlights, his profile brushed with gold, his eyes dark and unguarded.

The restaurant appears before I can say anything. He parallel parks on the street.

We don't move.

He looks at me like he's memorizing something. My cheeks, my mouth, the small trembling at the base of my throat. I watch his tongue sweep across his bottom lip. It's the tiniest movement, but it sends heat straight through me.

"Come here," he murmurs.

I lean in.

His hand cups my jaw, warm and sure. He kisses me slow, so slow it almost hurts. His mouth moves against mine with a hunger he's restraining only out of respect for the place, the moment, and me.

The kiss deepens just a breath, and my fingers curl into the fabric of his shirt. He tastes like mint and something darker. Heat? Intent.

When we pull apart, his forehead rests against mine. We're both breathing harder than we should be.

"You look beautiful," he says quietly. "She's going to like you."

"Who?" I breathe.

"My daughter."

I nod, still dazed from the kiss. "What's her—?"

We both pause. He opens his mouth to answer but his eyes flick toward the restaurant entrance, distracted by something.

"Come on," he says softly. "She's already here."

We climb out.

He walks beside me, hand on the small of my back. He's not pushing, not claiming, just steadying. Each step feels weighted with the significance of this moment. Meeting his daughter. Meeting someone August loves.

My heart is thundering in my throat.

We climb a set of stairs until we're at the top and find the entrance to the restaurant. Warm lighting, murmured conversation, the clink of silverware. August lifts a hand in greeting to someone.

"That's her," August says softly. "My Lilly."

I follow the direction of his hand automatically, smiling because I'm dreading the moment everything shatters.

Familiar dark braid.

Oversized cardigan.

Boots she thrifted for ten bucks after insisting they "smelled like destiny."

My brain screams, but I force the smile to hold. I've known this was coming since I saw Lilly's roommate ad, since I connected the dots from August's public records to her social media, saw his face in her family photos, and applied anyway. I told myself it was harmless. A way to be closer without crossing lines. Love, not obsession. But now, with his hand on my back, the lie feels like poison.

She looks up at the sound of August's voice.

Her eyes flick to him.

Then slide to me.

She blinks once.

Twice.

Her expression fractures.

"Dad?"

I force a laugh, a startled, confused, breathless sound, like this is as shocking to me as it is to her.

"Wait—what?" I whisper, hand flying to my mouth, playing the part even as guilt claws at my throat.

She stands so fast her chair screeches. The entire restaurant glances over.

August touches my elbow, concerned. “Florence?”

I step forward. Slowly. Feigning confusion. “Lilly? What... what are you doing here? Are you okay?”

Her brows slam together. “What am I—? What are you doing here?”

August glances between us. “You two know each other?”

I choke on air, faking shock while my mind races. *He can’t find out I knew. Not like this.*

Lilly’s mouth drops open.

Not in horror.

In confusion.

“Wait,” she says slowly. “Wait—what? How do you... know my dad?”

There’s a beat where her face brightens, actually brightens, like she’s putting together a normal explanation.

“Oh! Did you run into him here?” she asks, tucking a loose hair behind her ear. “I didn’t know you were coming to this restaurant for your date. And you work in public safety so I guess you two probably already—”

Dad.

Dad.

The word slams into me so hard I sway, even though I’ve carried it like a secret weight for months.

August takes one step forward, hand lifting like he can hold the moment still.

“Lilly,” he says gently. “This is—”

Her voice cuts through him, sharp now.

“Wait.”

Her eyes dart between us.

Me.

August.

Me again.

The brightness on her face drains in real time.

“Oh my god,” she whispers. “No. No, no. Tell me this isn’t—”

“Lilly,” August says again, softer. “Let’s sit—”

“How long?” she demands, her voice cracking loud enough

to make the hostess flinch. The tables nearest us go still. "How long have you two been... whatever this is?"

August lifts a calming hand. "Lilly, please. Let's sit down. Let's talk—"

"No," she snaps. "Answer me."

I try to form coherent sounds, my pulse hammering. "We—we didn't know. Lilly, I swear, I didn't know you were—"

"My father?" she fires back. "You didn't know you were sleeping with my father?"

Heat erupts under my skin. My stomach drops so violently it feels like vertigo. The lie tastes bitter, but I cling to it.

"It wasn't like that," I insist. "I didn't know who he was connected to. And you never mentioned..." I trail off, hating how flimsy it sounds.

"Oh my god." Lilly laughs and it's not humor. It's shock wrapped in hurt, wrapped in something dangerously close to betrayal. "You're only a year older than me."

"Not that it matters, but I'm two years older," I manage, my voice too thin. "Lilly, I'm not a minor. I'm not being coerced."

She recoils like I slapped her.

"So you're choosing this," she whispers, devastated.

August moves instinctively, stepping slightly between us.

"Lilly, that's enough," he says quietly.

"Is it?" she fires back, eyes bright with tears she refuses to let fall. "Is it enough that my father is sleeping with my roommate?"

August flinches. "We didn't know. Neither of us—"

"Oh, right," she snaps, turning on me.

"I just... didn't connect the dots Lil. It never came up. You only ever said, 'my dad.' You didn't exactly advertise August Calder was your father," I say with a shaking voice.

She stares at me like she's trying to see the lie beneath my skin. And she's right, there is one. I knew August was her father. I chose not to connect it aloud.

"Fine," she spits. "So when did this start?"

I'm frozen. August breathes in to answer, but I step forward, needing her to hear it from me.

“We met last year,” I say softly. “Before I moved here. Before I knew you. Before any of this.”

Lilly’s face crumples in real time.

“Oh.” Her voice cracks. “Wow. That’s... really convenient timing, isn’t it?”

The accusation lands like a slap. She’s so close to the truth it terrifies me. I moved here for him. Researched his life, found her ad, took the room to orbit closer. But I can’t admit that. Not now.

“No,” I whisper. “It wasn’t like that. It was one night. We didn’t even exchange full names.”

“And now you live with me,” Lilly says, voice wobbling. “God, Florence, did you seriously never think to mention you’d hooked up with some older guy before you moved into my home?”

“I didn’t know,” I say, pleading, breathless. “I swear. I did not know who he was to you.”

She shakes her head hard, like she’s trying to rattle the pieces into a shape that makes sense.

“You said you were my friend,” she whispers, trembling. “Friends don’t hide this. Friends don’t—don’t get in bed with your dad and then sit on the couch with you eating cereal like everything’s fine.”

August steps in, voice low and firm. “Lilly, this isn’t her fault. Don’t do that.”

But I lift a hand, stopping him.

“No,” I say gently, but not weakly. “Let me answer that.”

Lilly’s gaze snaps to me, wet and furious.

“My sex life,” I say, steadying my breath, “has never been your business. Not before I moved in. Not after. Not ever.”

Her lips part, stunned.

“My sexual history,” I continue, “is not a background check for my roommates. Who I was with before I ever met you has nothing to do with my rent, my integrity, or my friendship.”

The words land, quiet, sharp, clean.

“I didn’t tell you because I didn’t know,” I finish. “Not because I owed you some kind of... vetting of every man I’ve ever fucked.”

Lilly blinks. Breath shaking. Not ready to hear it, but unable to deny the truth under it.

August watches me like he's seeing something he wasn't expecting, something he respects. But then his eyes narrow, flicking to my forehead, to the scar. The one Lilly knows about from late-night confessions, the one I told her came from a crash where a random cop held me while my mom died. No names. No details. Just enough to bond over loss.

Something shifts in his expression. Recognition? Horror?

"Florence," he murmurs, voice low, cracking. "The scar. The crash. Seven years ago in Seattle. That was you?"

The world stops.

Lilly's head snaps to him. "What?"

I freeze, blood roaring. He remembers. Of course he remembers now. Of all moments. The cop who held me that night—the one I obsessed over, chased here—was him.

"Lilly," he says, eyes locked on me, "she's the girl from the wreck seven years ago in Seattle. The one I told you about. The one I held while—"

Lilly's face pales. "The scar story? The one you told me about your mom dying? You said a cop was there. You left out it was my dad?"

The lie unravels. My knees buckle.

"I didn't know," I lie again, voice breaking. "Not until later."

Lilly presses her hands to her temples, overwhelmed. "I just... I thought we told each other everything."

My voice softens. "We don't owe each other our pasts. We share what we choose. But I would never, never, have chosen to hurt you."

Her face crumples.

And everything unravels from there.

She turns on August next, hurt blazing.

"And you." Her voice is barely above a breath. "You replaced Mom with someone your daughter's age."

August's face goes still. Struck.

"Lilly," he says quietly, "that's not fair."

"Nothing about this is fair!" she shouts before clamping

her mouth shut as if surprised by her own volume. Her next words are quieter, but far more lethal. "I don't even know what's grossing me out more, Dad dating someone my age, or feeling like I'm the last one to know."

She looks at me again.

"Are you sure he's not pressuring you?" she asks suddenly. "Are you sure this isn't, like, some kind of... quid pro quo? He's the chief. You're dispatch. That's not normal, Florence."

I shake my head hard. "No. No, Lilly. He would never. I'm here because I want to be."

She wipes a tear angrily. "Why? Because you met him first? Because it's a cute story now?"

I exhale shakily. "Because I love him."

She goes absolutely still.

Like that was the worst answer I could have given.

"I can't do this." Lilly lets out a ragged breath, tears threatening to fall.

I shake my head so fast it hurts. "I didn't lie to you. I didn't hide him from you. I just didn't know."

"You didn't ask," she spits. "And he didn't tell me." She whips toward him. "Does Mom mean anything to you? Anything at all?"

August rubs a hand over his face. "Lilly... don't drag your mother into this."

"Why not?" Lilly snaps, voice fraying. "She's the only sane one in this entire fucking triangle!"

My stomach doesn't just drop, it flips, tightens, coils into something cold and nauseating. My knees threaten to give out.

Mother.

Triangle.

Wait...

Lilly's mom is...

Ruth.

My blood goes ice cold.

A faint ringing starts in my ears as pieces slam together in a sickening avalanche.

Ruth.

My supervisor.

My shift partner.

The woman who brought me coffee on my first day.

The woman I work side by side with.

She's August's ex.

She's Lilly's mother.

Oh gods. I knew this but it never...

Lilly isn't done.

"You're seriously dating mom's coworker? The woman Mom supervises? The woman I've heard her TALK ABOUT? What the hell were you thinking?"

August's face drains of color. "Lilly, don't twist this into—"

"Twist WHAT?" she cries. "Oh my god, Florence, did you know? Did you know the whole time that you were screwing your boss's ex? Were you waiting to make some sick announcement at roll call? Was this your plan?"

"No!" My voice cracks. "Lilly, no, I swear to you, I didn't know. I had no idea."

Her expression curdles with betrayal and disbelief.

"You expect me to buy that?" she chokes. "You didn't know he was my father, you didn't know he was your coworker's ex, you didn't know anything?"

I swallow hard, pulse roaring.

"I knew he had a daughter," I whisper. "But I didn't know it was you. He never said your name. And you never said his."

Her eyes go wide, hurt colliding with something darker.

"My mom is going to lose her mind," she whispers. Then louder and accusatory, "And you, you're just..." Lilly trails off.

"Lilly," August warns, voice sharp.

For a heartbeat, Lilly just stares at me.

And then her face crumples.

"I thought you were my friend," she whispers. It's the softest she's spoken. She's not screaming, and it's not a jab. It's something so much worse.

Something true.

"I meant it," I breathe. "I STILL mean it."

"Friends don't do this," she says. "Friends don't blow up my life."

August flinches like she slapped him.

I feel something tear open inside me.

Because I didn't just lose my boyfriend in this moment.

I didn't just lose my roommate.

I lost the closest thing to a sister I've had in a decade.

And the realization shreds something deep in my chest.

A waitress appears beside our table, trying to mask the tremor in her voice. "Evening, Chief. Whenever you folks are ready."

August barely glances at her. "Thanks, Jenna. Give us a minute."

She leaves, but not before giving me a look that says she knows exactly what's happening.

Everyone does.

I can feel the eyes.

The prickle of gossip starting.

The edges of the town closing in.

Lilly grabs her bag.

"This is disgusting," she says. She's not yelling now, she's just disappointed. "I can't look at either of you."

August reaches for her arm. "Lilly, please. Just come outside, let's talk."

She jerks away. "Don't follow me."

"Lilly."

"Don't."

Her voice breaks completely on that last word.

Then she's gone.

August hesitates, one fractured heartbeat, then runs after her. He looks back once. Just once. Torn. Apologetic. And then he's out the door.

The restaurant exhales as one.

I stand there, frozen, vibrating with shock and humiliation and heartbreak.

Someone clears their throat gently.

The waitress again. "Hon... can I bring you some water?"

I manage a weak shake of my head.

She nods sympathetically and backs away.

I force myself to breathe.

Then I walk out, because staying here feels like drowning.

I walk because I can't breathe, because my legs are moving before my brain catches up, because the night air feels sharper than the fluorescent lights and curious eyes.

I walk because I don't know what else to do.

Townsend Harbor glows with warm streetlamps and storefront lights, but it all feels wrong.

I wrap my arms around myself, shoulders shaking.

Lilly's voice echoes in my head.

You said I was your friend.

The words crack something open inside me.

I don't cry.

Not at first.

But as I turn down my street, alone, small, cold, and on foot, the ache hits harder.

I think about my mom.

About how she would've known what to say.

About how she would've held my face in her hands and told me I wasn't a bad person for wanting someone, for letting myself be wanted.

But she's not here.

She hasn't been here for years.

And right now, the silence of her absence feels so loud it could break me.

By the time I reach the house, tears are sliding down my cheeks without permission.

I wipe them away with the back of my hand.

Unlock the door.

Step inside to the too-quiet living room. Lilly didn't come home.

And the truth hits me with brutal clarity, I have no friend to talk to.

No boyfriend to lean on.

No certainty, no anchor, no one waiting for me on the other side of this hurt.

Just me.

Just the cavern of my own heartbeat.

RESTRAINT

Just the echo of Lilly calling me sick.
Just the look on August's face when she said it.
I close the door behind me slowly.
Lean my forehead against the wood.
And let myself break.

TWENTY-TWO
AUGUST

MONDAYS ALWAYS SUCK.

This one feels personal.

The ache in my chest wakes me before the alarm, a low, nasty throb that starts in the bone and radiates outward like slow poison. I lie in the dark, staring at the ceiling, listening to the house creak and the distant roll of waves, and tell myself it's just fallout.

Just fallout.

Right.

I roll to sit up. The motion is automatic, but it pulls at something deeper than muscle. Regret, maybe? Shame. I bite back a curse, plant my feet on the cold floor. My body feels seventy. My brain feels older.

My phone sits on the nightstand. Screen dark. Silent.

No new messages.

No Florence.

No Lilly.

My chest squeezes a slow, relentless Harboring. A punch is clean. This is just... weight. Increasing by degrees until breathing hurts.

I check my phone anyway. Because apparently I enjoy self-inflicted wounds.

Nothing.

The last text from Florence was before dinner.

> Florence: See you soon. I'm nervous. But...
> excited.

The last from Lilly was the day before. A meme of a raccoon in a hoodie holding a knife, captioned *me going into Monday.*

I stare at Lilly's contact photo. Her face is lit by neon, grin wide, eyes too bright. Then I set the phone facedown.

Shower. Clothes. Movements automatic, rehearsed. If I stop moving, I'll think. If I think, I won't get out the door.

In the mirror, I meet my own eyes. There are lines deeper than yesterday, shadows under them like bruises that won't fade. I've looked worse. After splitting with Ruth the first time and the second time. After holding the living while their loved ones die. Or calling them after no one walked away. Like that woman who kissed me seven years ago. Her mom died and she broke in my arms. She had a head lac. Her eyes.

Her eyes...

I shake away the thoughts. It's all a blur.

Coffee. Strong. Black. Coffee. No cinnamon, no pumpkin, no softness. The mug warms my hands but doesn't touch the cold knot in my chest.

I don't let myself replay the restaurant.

I fail.

Lilly's voice, sharp and shaking: *You replaced Mom with someone your daughter's age.* If Lilly only knew the truth of it. Ruth replaced me long before I gave up on her.

Florence's face. Not just shock. Betrayal at the universe, at me, at herself.

Florence's scar.

The girl from the wreck, the one I held in the rain while her world ended. Florence. How did I not see it sooner? The eyes. The strength. The way she looked at me like I was the only solid thing left.

Last night, when followed Lilly into the parking lot, I called out for her. *"Lil—"*

She spun so fast it was like she'd been waiting. Cheeks wet, eyes wild, hurt so raw I almost stopped cold.

"Don't," she snapped. "Don't come out here and do the dad voice."

I held my hands up, palms empty. "I'm not here as your chief."

"Good," she fired back. "Because my father sleeping with my roommate would be gross. Oh wait."

I flinched and then anchored my feet. I deserved that.

"Listen," I started.

"No," she held up a hand. "I've been listening to you my whole life. About Mom. About why you left. About your job. About everything. And I've been trying to understand. To be okay with it. To accept you did your best." Her laugh was brittle. "But this? This is not your best, Dad."

"Lilly, I didn't know she was your—"

"That's the problem!" she cut in. "You didn't know. You're not as involved in my life as you pretend to be. Dinner once a month doesn't build a relationship. Maybe that's it. You didn't know because you didn't ask. You just... went for it."

"It was one night," I said. "A year ago. Before she moved here. Before I knew she worked at the center."

"But then you did know," she said, each word a needle. "And you still kept seeing her. You still didn't tell me. You want me to talk to you about guys and roommates and Mom's job and never once thought, hey, maybe I should do the same? Maybe I should mention I'm fucking my daughter's mom's coworker who happens to also be my daughter's roommate."

"Watch your language," I said automatically.

She laughed in my face. "That's what you care about? Whether or not I say fuck?"

"No. It's not." I scrubbed a hand over my jaw, feeling every scar under my fingers.

"I was trying to protect you," I said. "Protect work. Protect her. I thought if we took it slow, if we were sure, then we'd figure out how to tell you and everyone else. I didn't want it to blow up anyone's life if it turned into nothing."

"Did you even think about Mom?" she asked.

I stopped.

The question hung between us, sharp as a blade. I'd carried that secret for years, buried it deep to shield her from the ugliness. But here, in the middle of the street, with my daughter looking at me like I was the villain in her story, the words clawed their way out.

"That's not fair," I said quietly. "Your mother and I have been over for a long time. You know that."

Lilly's eyes flashed, her face twisting with fresh hurt. "Yeah, because you left her. Because you—"

"She cheated on me, Lil."

The confession dropped like a stone into still water. I hadn't planned it. Hadn't wanted to drag that old poison into the light. But seeing her pain, feeling the weight of her accusation, it spilled out. Raw. Unfiltered.

Lilly froze, her mouth half-open, the anger draining from her expression like color from a fading photograph. "What?"

I swallowed hard, the memory surging up unbidden. Ruth's tear-streaked face, the confession in our kitchen, the way the world had tilted under my feet. "Your mother cheated on me. I didn't just fall out of love and leave her. She left me first. She broke my heart."

Her eyes widened, searching my face for a lie, for some crack in the armor. "No. No, that's... why wouldn't you tell me that?"

I stepped closer, voice dropping to a rough whisper. "Because every girl needs her mom. And I never wanted to take that from you. I didn't want you looking at her differently, hating her for something that was between us. You were just a kid, Lil. You deserved to love her without the mess we made."

Tears welled in her eyes again, but this time they spilled over softer, slower. Her shoulders sagged, the fight leaking out of her as she processed it.

For the first time that night, she looked at me not with rage, but with something closer to understanding. Pity, maybe, or the quiet ache of seeing a parent as human. She reached out, hesitated, then let her hand rest lightly on my arm, a small gesture that cracked something open in my chest.

"Yeah, but she doesn't just stop being my mom," Lilly said. Her voice cracked. "She still has to walk into that center and know you're screwing the woman she supervises. Do you know what that

looks like? Do you know what people are going to say about her? About Florence? About me?"

I did.

Of course I did.

I've been in this job long enough to know how people talk when the chief's name gets attached to anything messy.

"It's not just about you," she whispered. "You always say that about your cases, remember? 'It's never just about the one punch, Lil, it's about the pattern.'"

"That is not what I did with you," I said, sharper than I meant.

She went still.

"Isn't it?" she whispered.

The knife turned.

"Lil..." My voice was rough. "I did not walk away from you. I left a relationship that was breaking both of us, yes, but I have been in your life the whole time."

"On your weekends," she snapped. "On your terms. And now you want to waltz into my adulthood like you're some... romantic hero? 'Here's this woman who's almost your age, hope you don't mind if I make out with her in front of you.'"

"That is not what this is," I said, gutted. "I care about her."

"Yeah," she said, eyes blazing. "I could see that. Kinda hard to miss her walking in with that just-fucked glow, Dad."

I winced.

"She looked happy," Lilly said, voice breaking on the last word. "And I was happy for her. Because I thought she was meeting someone good. Someone her age. Someone who wasn't my father."

The parking lot lights haloed around her, making every tear glint like glass.

"You both lied to me," she said.

"We didn't lie," I protested. "We kept our relationship private from everyone in our lives. She didn't know. I believe her and that makes this different."

She stared at me like she didn't recognize the man in front of her. "Is it?"

We stood there, the space between us full of things I wasn't saying. That I'm terrified I'm my father. That I've spent my whole damn life trying not to be the man who wrecks the people around him. That I stupidly thought if I loved carefully enough, it would hurt less when life did what life does.

"Please come with me," I said. "We'll go somewhere else. Talk. Just us. No audience."

"No," she said. "I'm done talking tonight."

"Lilly—"

"Don't follow me," she said. "I mean it."

Her voice cracked on the last word. She turned and walked away, shoulders stiff, head high, like she's holding herself together by sheer force of will.

I stood and watched my kid walk away from me. Again.

I didn't follow.

Because I'm a coward.

The memory sits in my chest now, heavy and immovable, as I finish my coffee and head for the door.

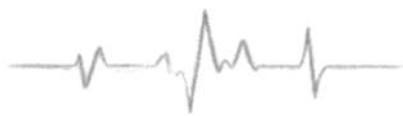

THE STATION FEELS different the second I walk in.

It's subtle. A shift in how conversations pause. A glance that slides off too fast. The way one officer's laugh cuts off mid-sound.

I've been the new guy.

The hero.

The asshole who made an unpopular call.

I've never been the scandal everyone pretends not to be talking about.

"Morning, Chief," someone calls. I don't see who.

"Morning," I answer automatically.

I move through the hallway toward my office, badge heavy, every step deliberate to hide the exhaustion.

Turner appears at his desk as I pass the squad room. He gives me a nod, eyes sharp, reading me the way only someone who's done time in your blind spots can.

I don't slow down. If I stop, someone's going to say something friendly, and I don't have the muscle for friendly right now.

My office is its usual mess. A mountain of files, coffee cups, one plant someone brought as a joke that I keep forgetting to water. I set my mug down, sink into my chair with a sigh my father would've made, and open my email.

Three official memos about follow-up procedures after a call on the weekend.

One calendar reminder about my meeting with HR. Subject line: Brief Check-In.

Small-town HR doesn't have a poker face.

I check my phone again. Nothing from Florence. Nothing from Lilly.

I type a text. Delete it. Type another.

How are you holding up?

Backspace.

Can we talk?

Backspace.

I'm sorry.

Backspace until the bubble is empty.

My thumb hovers over her name; then I lock the phone and shove it into my desk drawer like that will shut off the ache.

Voices drift from the hallway.

I don't mean to listen.

But they're not exactly quiet.

"Dude, I'm telling you, he's banging some young hot piece," Alvarez says.

My jaw tightens.

Another voice, Jenkins this time. "She's a person, you jackass."

"What? She's not a kid," Alvarez says. "She's what, mid-twenties? It's not illegal."

"It's messy," Jenkins says. "She works here. He's the chief. And her boss is his ex. That's like... nuclear."

I step into the doorway. "Morning, gentlemen."

Alvarez almost drops his donut. "Chief. Hey. We were just —uh—talking about the Maple Street case."

"Were you?" I ask mildly.

Jenkins stares at the coffee machine like it's the most fascinating object on Earth.

My patience is frayed. My better judgment should kick in and remind me not to make this worse.

It doesn't.

I walk to the counter, pour coffee I don't need. The room is too quiet.

"If you have questions about my personal life," I say finally, not looking at them, "you can ask me. Directly. Like grown men."

The silence gets sharper.

They don't take me up on it.

"Since no one's stepping up," I continue, "let me save you the trouble. People are blowing this whole thing out of proportion. Nothing is happening with me and the dispatcher. So stop the fucking rumors and do your jobs."

It comes out harsher than I intend.

Defensive.

Punitive.

Half true.

Something in my chest twists as soon as I say it, because the second the words leave my mouth, I know exactly how they sound.

Not like protection.

Like denial.

Like shame.

I close my eyes briefly, jaw tight.

Alvarez stammers, "Yes, sir."

Jenkins nods, cheeks red. "Got it, Chief."

I take a sip of coffee I don't taste and turn to leave.

That's when I see her.

Florence is in the doorway.

Headset around her neck, dispatch polo on, ID badge clipped to her belt. Hair pulled back in a loose knot, a few curls falling around her face. Her eyes are on me.

Flat.

Hurt carved in like someone took a chisel to something soft.

I don't know how long she's been standing there. Long enough, apparently.

Our eyes lock.

For a second, the room falls away.

It's just her and me and the echo of my own voice, still hanging in the air.

Nothing is happening with me and the dispatcher.

I see it land in her, in real time. The way her shoulders draw back. The way her mouth settles into something that isn't quite a line, isn't quite a tremor.

"Florence," I say, stepping forward before I think.

She doesn't speak.

Doesn't yell.

Doesn't cry.

She just looks at me like I've confirmed something she was afraid to believe.

Then she turns.

Walks away.

Doesn't look back.

The doorframe holds my handprint as I grip it, knuckles white.

"Chief?" Jenkins says carefully behind me.

I don't answer.

Because for the first time in years, I'm not sure I know how to be the man this job needs.

Or the father my kid deserves.

Let alone the man she saw as something good.

All I know is this, I open my mouth to protect the people I care about. And somehow, I end up hurting them instead.

TWENTY-THREE
FLORENCE

I DON'T RUN.

I want to.

Every cell in my body wants to bolt down the hallway like I'm eighteen again, lockers slamming behind me, everyone staring at the red in my face and the wet in my eyes and the way my dignity is a fragile thing held together by breath and spite.

But I don't run.

I walk fast enough that my shoes squeak once, sharp against the tile, and I hate myself for making any sound at all.

Nothing is happening with me and the dispatcher.

The words are still in the air behind me, still sticky on my skin, like I walked through a web and now it's clinging to my lashes, my throat, my insides. Like I can't blink it off. Like I can't swallow without tasting it.

People are blowing this whole thing out of proportion.

Nothing is happening.

I keep walking.

My badge bounces against my hip. The radio chatter in the distance sounds muffled, like I've shoved cotton into my ears. Someone laughs somewhere down the hall and it hits me wrong, like a slap, because how can anyone laugh when the ground is doing this?

The bathroom door is at the end of the corridor, past the bulletin board with the laminated "WORKPLACE RESPECT" flyer and the chipped paint at the corner where someone's chair always bangs. I grab the handle and shove it open too hard.

The fluorescent light inside is bright and merciless.

I lock myself into the first stall and press my forehead to the cool metal divider.

Breathe.

Breathe.

I've talked people through panic attacks with nothing but my voice and a script taped to the desk. I've counted breaths for strangers over a phone line while sirens screamed in the background. I've kept my tone calm while someone bled out on the other end of the call.

This should be easy.

It isn't.

My chest is tight, like there's a fist inside it closing harder each time I try to inhale. My hands are shaking, subtle but there. A tremor. A small betrayal.

Nothing is happening.

I close my eyes and August's voice is right there again, low and firm, the way he sounds when he's trying to control a room. Not yelling. Not pleading.

Dismissing.

And I can picture the men in there with him, their faces, their smirks, their curiosity. I can hear the edges of their joke, the way women turn into punchlines so fast you don't even feel the shift until you're already the thing being passed around.

Young hot piece.

Dispatcher girlfriend.

Is it legal?

I swallow, hard.

The first tear slips down my cheek before I even realize I'm crying. It's warm, humiliating, silent. I wipe it away with the back of my hand and stare at the smear it leaves on my skin like I can't believe my own body would do that to me here, in a police station bathroom, like I'm some cliché.

I don't cry at work.

I don't cry in uniform.

I don't cry where people can hear it.

I press my lips together until they ache.

You're not running, I tell myself.

You're not falling apart in a stall because a man said something stupid.

Except it isn't just a man.

It's him.

And that's the part that cuts. Not the rumor. Not the crude mouths in the break room. Not even the shame that crawls up my spine when I imagine Ruth's face tomorrow morning, when she realizes the story doesn't stop with her daughter walking into the restaurant.

It's that he knew what those words would do.

Or he didn't care.

Or he cared more about himself than the fact that I was standing three feet away, breathing the same air, and he still said it like I'm nothing.

I put my fingers to my throat, just above my collarbone, like I can steady my pulse that way.

The image that surfaces is not his face in the break room.

It's his hand on my wrist in the truck. The warm sweep of his thumb over the inside of my skin, so gentle it felt like he was learning me. The way he said, *I'm falling for you,* like it was a truth he couldn't keep behind his lips.

The way his eyes looked in the parking lot, dark and undone.

And then, that door.

The restaurant door closing behind him as he ran after Lilly.

Leaving me sitting at the table alone with the waitress and the stare of the town.

That was the first cut.

This is the second.

I sit back on the toilet lid without sitting, really. My body is braced like I'm expecting impact. Like at any second someone is going to pound on the stall door and tell me to get it together.

My phone vibrates in my pocket.

For one wild second my heart leaps, stupid and hopeful, and I hate myself for it before I even look.

It's not him.

It's a text from an unknown number that just says:

Unknown: You okay? Heard about the restaurant.

I stare at it until the letters blur.

Heard about the restaurant.

Of course they did.

In a town like Townsend Harbor, news travels faster than weather. Faster than sirens. Faster than truth.

I don't answer.

My phone vibrates again, a second message from the same number:

Unknown: If you need to talk, I'm here.

I swallow. Harder.

I can't even tell if the kindness is real or if it's just another set of eyes leaning close to see the wreck.

I shove the phone back into my pocket and force my breathing into a pattern.

In for four. Hold. Out for six.

In. Hold. Out.

The stall smells faintly of bleach and old tile. The fluorescent hums overhead like a bad memory. I press my palms to my thighs, grounding myself the way I tell callers to do when they're spiraling.

I've survived worse.

I survived the crash.

I survived my mother's death.

I survived my sisters too.

I survived moving here for a man I never thought I'd see again, telling myself it was fate when I knew it was obsession.

This is just another call I have to handle.

Except this time, the voice on the other end is mine.

And the person bleeding out is me.

I let out one slow, controlled breath.

My mind keeps trying to run backward, like if I replay the last forty-eight hours enough, I'll find the moment I could've stopped this. The moment I could've chosen a different road.

Sunday morning, waking up alone, my pillow cold, the ache in my chest fresh. Coming home from the restaurant with my face burning and my body Harbor. Unlocking the door and stepping into the living room and realizing Lilly wasn't there.

She hadn't come home while I was gone. No light under her bedroom door. No music. No rustle of her being awake.

I had sat on the couch for a long time with my shoes still on, staring at the blank TV screen like it could give me answers.

At some point I had gotten up to drink water, because my mouth tasted like metal and humiliation, and that's when I saw it.

A note on the fridge.

Small. Plain. No raccoon doodle. No flourish.

I need time. I'll be back for more stuff later.

No love, no signature. Like she had to keep it clinical or she'd break.

I remember my hand shaking as I touched the paper, like the words were alive. Like they could burn me.

I need time.

Time from me.

Time from this house.

Time from the fact that I'm not just her roommate anymore. I'm the woman who walked into a restaurant with her father.

My throat tightens again at the memory.

I had stood there in the kitchen, barefoot, staring at the note while the fridge hummed and the house felt too big and too empty, and the only person I wanted to call was gone.

Mom.

I could see my mother's hands in my mind, the way she would cup my face when I got overwhelmed. The way she'd say, *Hey. Breathe. You're not bad. You're not broken. You're just in pain.*

But there's no one to say it now.

Just me, trying to talk myself down like I'm my own dispatcher.

I blink hard, trying to keep tears from falling again.

In the stall, I pull my phone out and scroll to Nora's name.

My thumb hovers.

I shouldn't. She'll worry. She'll want to fix it. She'll remind me I'm stronger than this.

But the ache in me is so big it feels like I need a voice. Any voice. Even one that sees right through me.

I hit call.

It rings once.

Twice.

"Florence." Nora answers on the second ring, her voice warm and steady, like a hand on my shoulder. "What's going on, honey? You okay?"

No preamble. No stories about her day. Just quiet concern, honed from years of knowing when to listen first.

I press my forehead harder against the metal divider. The cold helps.

"Hi grandma. I'm... at work," I whisper.

A soft pause. "In the bathroom?"

"Yeah." My voice cracks. I hate that it does. "I'm trying not to cry."

She doesn't rush in with questions. Just lets the silence hold space for a beat.

"Take a breath," she says gently. "I'm right here."

I swallow. My mouth tastes like copper.

"I had a really bad night," I manage. "Something happened and... I don't have anyone right now."

There. That's the truth. Bare and humiliating.

Nora doesn't flinch. "You've got me," she says softly. "Always have. Now tell me what you can."

I close my eyes. Tears slip free anyway. "Lilly left," I whisper. "A note on the fridge. She needs time. She didn't come home last night."

Nora's breath catches. "Oh, Florence. I'm sorry."

"And August..." My voice breaks on his name. "He said something in the break room. To the officers. Like I don't exist. Like I'm... nothing."

A longer silence. Not empty. Heavy with understanding.

"That hurts," she says simply. "Deep, I bet."

"Yeah," I breathe. "It hurts."

She doesn't try to explain it away. Doesn't defend him or blame me. She just lets the hurt exist.

"I'm so sorry, honey," she says quietly. "You didn't deserve that. Not from him. Not from anyone."

My throat burns. "I thought... I thought he saw me. Really saw me."

"I know," she says. "And maybe he does, in his way. But sometimes people choose their own safety over yours when things get hard. Doesn't make it right. Doesn't make the pain any less real."

I press my palm to my eyes. "I feel so stupid. For hoping. For believing."

"You're not stupid," Nora says firmly. "You're brave. You let yourself love. You let yourself be loved. That takes guts, especially after everything you've lost."

A choked sob escapes me. I clamp my hand over my mouth.

Nora waits. Doesn't shush me. Doesn't tell me to pull it together.

When I can breathe again, she says, "You're not alone in this, Florence. You've never been. Even when it feels that way."

I nod, even though she can't see me.

"I miss her," I whisper. "Mom. I miss her so much."

"I know," Nora says. Her voice cracks. "I miss her too. Every damn day."

We sit with that for a moment. Two women carrying the same ghost.

Then Nora exhales, steady again. "Do you need me to come?"

I almost say yes.

But something in me straightens.

"No," I say quietly. "I'm... I'm okay. I just needed to hear your voice."

"You always can," she says. "Anytime. Day or night."

I nod again. "Thank you."

"Florence," she says, softer. "You're going to be okay. Not today. Maybe not tomorrow. But you will. You're stronger than you feel right now. And you don't have to carry this by yourself."

I wipe my face with the back of my hand. "I know."

"Good girl," she says gentle and with pride, the way she used to when I was small and scared. "Now go finish your shift. One breath at a time. One call at a time. You know how."

I manage a small, broken laugh. "Yeah. I know how."

"I love you," she says.

"I love you too."

She doesn't hang up first. She waits until I do.

When the line goes dead, I sit there for another minute, letting the silence settle.

Then I stand.

My knees are steadier now.

I stare at the black screen of my phone until my reflection ghosts back at me. Of course the only voice I have left is one that understands loss as well as I do.

My hand shakes as I shove the phone into my pocket.

I take one breath.

Then another.

And in the thin space between them, I make myself a promise.

Fine.

If no one is going to show up for me, I will.

Even if it hurts.

Even if it's lonely.

Even if the only person I can rely on is me.

I take a deep breath and wipe my face again, more carefully this time. I pull a tissue from the dispenser and dab under my eyes, check for mascara smudges in the tiny mirror above the sink when I step out of the stall.

My reflection looks... wrong.

Like someone wearing my skin.

A little pale. Eyes too bright. Jaw clenched.

I lean closer and whisper to myself, "You are not going to let him do this to you."

It comes out like a vow.

I rinse my hands under cold water and let it run too long, grounding myself in sensation. Cold. Wet. Real.

When I turn off the faucet, the silence roars.

I don't want to go back out there.

Not because of the officers. Not because of the gossip.

Because of August.

Because I can't decide if I want to slap him or fall into him or scream until my throat tears.

Because I can't decide if I'm more angry at him or at myself for ever believing his tenderness meant safety.

He knows how words work.

He knows how rumors work.

And he still said it.

Maybe he was trying to protect me.

Maybe he was trying to protect himself.

Either way, he didn't protect my dignity.

He didn't protect my heart.

And I'm done being collateral damage in someone else's life.

I take one last breath and head for the door.

My hand is on the handle when the hallway movement catches me and before I can think, I pull the door open. And collide with a body.

My shoulder bumps into a chest. A hand catches my elbow automatically, steadying me.

For half a second my brain doesn't register anything but the scent.

Cedar and coffee and him.

Then I look up.

August is right there.

Close enough that I can see the tiny crease between his brows. Close enough that I can see the fatigue sitting in his eyes like bruises. Close enough that my body remembers him on reflex, the way it wants to lean into him even now.

His hand is still on my arm.

His gaze flicks over my face, too fast, too practiced, like he's checking for damage.

"Florence," he says, and my name in his voice is almost an apology all by itself.

My stomach twists.

I step back, gently but firmly, breaking the contact.

"Chief," I say, because if I say August right now, it will soften me. And I don't trust softness.

His jaw tightens at the title. "Don't."

I lift my brows. "Don't what?"

He exhales through his nose, controlled. "Don't do that. Not right now."

I can hear the muffled sound of voices down the hall. A radio crackle. Someone laughing again. The station is alive around us, indifferent to the way my heart is hammering.

"Are you okay?" he asks, voice low.

I almost laugh. "No," I say. "But I'm upright. So I guess I'm functioning."

He flinches like I've thrown something at him.

"Florence," he starts. "About what you heard—"

"What I heard?" I cut in, too calm. Too careful. The cool in my voice feels like ice forming. "You mean the part where you told a room full of officers that nothing is happening with me?"

His throat moves as he swallows. "That's not what I meant."

"It's what you said," I reply, and my voice doesn't shake. That's the only victory I have right now.

His eyes darken. He takes a step closer, then stops himself, like he's remembering where we are.

"I was trying to stop the rumors," he says. "I was trying to protect you."

I tilt my head slightly. "Protect me."

"Yes," he says, as if it's obvious. "They were being disgusting. Talking about you like you're—"

"Like I'm what?" I ask, softly. "A piece? A rumor? A hot young dispatcher? Because I heard that part too, by the way. I heard enough."

His mouth tightens. His hands flex at his sides like he wants to reach for me and knows he can't.

"I should've shut it down differently," he admits. "I should've—"

"You should've told the truth," I say. "Or you should've said nothing. But you didn't."

His gaze flicks to my mouth, to my eyes, and there's something like regret, panic, and a desperate kind of wanting.

"I was trying to keep it from getting worse," he says.

I let out a quiet breath. "August... do you think I haven't lived under people's judgment my entire life?"

His brow furrows.

I don't wait for him to answer.

"I can take strangers talking," I say. "I can take a town staring. I can take people making up stories about me, because they always have. People have been deciding who I am since I was a kid."

His eyes soften, but I don't let myself fall into that softness.

"What I can't stomach," I continue, "is the way you left that restaurant."

His face changes.

I see the moment it lands. The memory flickering behind his eyes. Lilly storming out. His feet moving. The door closing behind him.

"I went after my daughter," he says, voice rough.

"And you didn't call me," I say, equally rough. "You didn't message me. You didn't even check if I got home. You left me sitting there with people watching me like I was trash."

His jaw clenches. "I assumed you'd go home. I assumed you needed space."

"Space," I repeat, and my laugh is small and sharp. "Yeah. Space. In a restaurant full of people who can't wait to tell everyone what happened."

He looks like he wants to argue. Like he wants to defend himself. Instead he exhales and says, "You didn't message me either."

The words hit.

Not because they're cruel.

Because they're true.

And because he says them like a counterpoint, like a score to keep, and something in me goes cold.

I nod once. "Yep."

His eyes narrow. "So—"

"But I wasn't the one who ran," I say. "I wasn't the one who left first."

His mouth opens, then closes.

"I was going after Lilly," he says again, quieter.

"And that's why I gave you space," I say. "Because I understood. I understood you had a kid. I understood she needed you. I understood that your life is complicated and I walked into it anyway because you asked me to."

His face softens at that, like gratitude tries to surface. I don't let it.

"I gave you space so you could sort your situation," I say. "So you could show up for your daughter. So you could figure out what the hell you were going to do."

He flinches.

"But I will not," I say, each word clean, "be someone's secret. I will not be the thing you deny in front of your men because you're scared of what it looks like."

His eyes flash. "That is not what—"

"It is what it looks like," I say. "And I'm done living my life by what it looks like for someone else."

His breathing changes. Deeper. He takes a step closer again, then stops. His hands curl, like he's gripping air.

"I'm sorry," he says, and there's a rawness in it that might have gutted me yesterday. "Florence, I don't know what to say to make this right."

I stare at him.

He looks wrecked. Tired. The kind of tired that doesn't come from a bad night.

Good, a bitter part of me thinks.

Good. Now you know what it feels like.

But then the bitterness shifts, because I'm not cruel. I don't want him suffering. I just want him honest.

"You can't take back the things you say," I tell him quietly.

His throat tightens.

"And I can't survive being reduced to a mistake or a rumor," I add. "Not again."

His eyes widen slightly.

I watch him try to say something, anything, and fail.

The hallway feels too narrow. The air feels thick. The station hums around us like a machine that doesn't care that I'm cutting myself free.

August's voice comes out hoarse. "I meant what I said in the truck."

My chest tightens at the memory, and I hate that it still affects me.

"I know," I say softly.

"Then don't do this," he says, and the plea in his voice is almost worse than denial. "Don't end it like this."

I hold his gaze.

I think about Lilly's note on the fridge.

I need time.

I think about Ruth's face when this hits her fully. When she realizes the gossip won't just be about him dating someone younger, it'll be about her, too. About her professionalism. About her authority. About whether she "knew." About whether she's "cool with it." About whether she's "jealous."

I think about the way I walked home alone that night, feeling like the only person who ever really knew how to hold me is buried in the ground.

I think about Nora's voice on the phone, steady and unwavering.

I think about how it felt to be wanted by August, how it felt to be seen, how it felt to believe for one bright, stupid moment that maybe I could have something that didn't turn into pain.

Maybe.

But maybe isn't a life raft.

Maybe is how you drown slowly.

"I'm not ending it because I don't care," I say, and my voice stays even, which is a miracle. "I'm ending it because I do."

His face shifts, like that's the last thing he expected.

"If you care," he says, low, "then let me fix it."

I shake my head. "You can't fix what you did with your mouth in that break room."

His eyes close briefly.

"And I can't," I continue, "be the woman you have to explain away when the room gets uncomfortable."

"I didn't—"

"You did," I say, not loud. Not dramatic. Just factual.

The quiet in my voice seems to hit him harder than yelling would have.

He opens his eyes again and they're wet, not with tears, but with something close. With the weight of wanting to reach and not being allowed.

"I don't want to lose you," he says.

My chest aches. It's a physical thing, like a bruise pressed.

"I don't want to be lost," I reply.

He swallows. "Florence—"

"I need you to hear me," I say. I step back one inch, putting just enough space between us that my body stops reacting to his heat. "I'm not going to beg to be chosen. I'm not going to wait in a parking lot of your life until you decide I'm safe to admit out loud."

His jaw tightens.

"And I'm not going to be punished," I add, "for your daughter's pain or your ex's anger or the town's hunger. I've spent too much of my life shrinking so people don't point at me. I'm done shrinking."

His eyes flicker, like he wants to argue, like he wants to promise, like he wants to swear he'll do better.

But promises don't erase what's already been said.

"You're right," he whispers, and it sounds like it costs him something.

That almost breaks me.

Almost.

I hold myself steady. "I need clean."

His brow furrows. "Clean?"

"Clean," I repeat. "No maybe later. No secret texts. No late-night phone calls that make me feel like I'm a sin you can only touch in the dark."

His face tightens like he's been hit.

"I'm not ashamed of you," he says fiercely.

I let that sit for half a second, then I tilt my head. "Then why did you say nothing is happening?"

He has no answer that matters.

Because whatever his intent was, the impact is already inside me, already carved.

His hand lifts slightly, hovering like he wants to touch my arm again. He stops himself.

I can see his restraint. His respect.

It would be beautiful in another moment.

Right now it's just painful.

"I'm sorry," he says again, quieter. "I was scared."

I nod once, because I believe him.

But belief doesn't mean I stay.

"I know," I say.

"And?" he asks, voice breaking just slightly.

"And I need to get to work," I reply.

The words feel like stepping off a ledge.

August's breath catches. His face goes still, like he's forcing himself not to crumble in public.

His voice is barely above a whisper. "Please."

I shake my head.

I don't give him a speech. I don't soften it with a hug. I don't promise we can be friends, because that would be a lie and we both deserve better than lies.

I just turn.

And walk away.

I don't look back.

The hallway stretches too long, the fluorescent lights too bright. My legs feel numb. My hands stop shaking only because I curl them into fists inside my pockets.

I pass the break room and feel eyes on me, like the story is already being written in people's heads. Like they're deciding what my face means.

Let them.

Let them talk.

They don't get my truth.

Only I do.

Dispatch is on the other side of a secure door with a keypad. I punch in my code with fingers that don't feel like mine.

The room smells like coffee and printer ink and the faint metallic tang of electronics. Screens glow in rows. Headsets hang like black necklaces from hooks. The familiar hum of voices and static and the soft murmur of operators talking people through emergencies wraps around me like a blanket made of sound.

It's the only place that still feels real.

Ruth isn't at her desk. Not yet. Or maybe she's in the back office. Maybe she's already heard. Maybe she's already piecing it together.

I don't let myself think about her face.

I go to my station. The chair creaks as I sit.

My hands move on muscle memory. Log in. Check the queue. Adjust the volume.

My heart is still pounding, but my face is calm. My posture straight. My mouth neutral.

I pick up my headset and slip it over my ears.

The moment the foam touches my skin, something in me switches.

Not heals.

Not forgives.

Just... compartmentalizes.

Because the calls don't care that my life just imploded.

The calls don't care that my best friend wants time.

The calls don't care that the man I want hurt me today.

People are bleeding. People are scared. People are alone.

And I know what to do with that.

The next call comes through.

The light blinks.

I click in.

"9-1-1, where is your emergency?" I say, and my voice is steady—professional, calm, controlled.

It sounds like it belongs to someone else.

TWENTY-FOUR
AUGUST

THE STATION FEELS TOO bright when she walks away.

Not fluorescent-bright. Not the normal, irritating hum of overhead lights that makes everyone look a little sick if you stare too long. This is like someone has turned up the exposure on my life until every edge is sharp and every shadow is an accusation.

I'm standing in the squad room with my mouth half open, my hand still slightly out like I could grab the air she left behind and pull her back into the shape of a conversation I don't ruin.

Florence doesn't even slam a door.

That's the part that guts me.

No scene. No dramatic goodbye. No tears she makes me witness to soothe my ego.

Just her turning her shoulder and walking away like she's practiced leaving people who don't choose her.

Like she's had to.

I see it in the line of her spine. In the set of her jaw. In the way she doesn't look back because she knows looking back is how you get hooked.

And my chest tightens, then drops, like my heart is trying to crawl out of my ribs to follow her.

"Chief?"

Someone says it like they're calling me from underwater.

I don't answer.

I don't trust my voice right now.

Because if I open my mouth in this moment, I'll either say her name or I'll say something that makes it worse. Something clumsy or defensive that turns her into a problem I have to manage instead of a person I already lost.

So I do what I always do.

I lock my face into stone.

I turn my body like nothing is happening.

The job is a uniform, and it fits me well because it has to. The job is the only thing I've ever been able to put on that makes the world stop asking questions.

I move through the hallway, nodding at people, returning greetings. I pretend the air isn't full of the last sentence I said about her.

But I can still hear it.

The exact cadence of my own voice plays over, hard and clipped and public, like I was slamming a door.

And she heard it.

Of course she did.

If she'd been anywhere else, if she'd walked in five minutes later, if I'd kept my mouth shut, if I'd chosen a different set of words—

If.

If.

If.

The word is a bullet. Clipping me again and again, and it never stops.

When I get to my office, I close the door and stand there for a moment with my hand still on the knob.

As if the door can keep the world out.

As if the door can keep the truth from bleeding through the cracks.

My computer monitor is dark. My desk is too neat. There's a file folder sitting exactly where I left it. A pen lined up parallel to the edge like I'm auditioning for a life where order means safety.

I stare at it until my eyes burn.

Then I collapse into my chair like someone cut the strings holding me up.

My phone sits on the desk untouched.

I'd like to think that I'm strong enough to ignore it. Alas, I'm not.

My thumb hovers over her name like it's a trigger.

Florence.

Her contact photo is the same. Of course it is. She doesn't vanish from my phone just because she walked away.

I stare at her face until the ache in my chest becomes physical, until it feels like I swallowed glass.

I open the message thread.

There are drafts in my head that form before my fingers move.

I'm sorry.

Too small. Too easy.

I didn't mean it like that.

Too pathetic. Too late.

Please talk to me.

A demand disguised as a request.

I was trying to protect you.

A justification. Not an apology.

My thumb sits there, motionless.

Because every sentence I can write feels like I'm asking her to carry my guilt for me.

And she has already carried enough.

I lock the phone.

Set it down.

Then pick it up again.

It's a sickness. A loop. A compulsion.

I look at the time.

I look at my calendar.

I look at the meaningless weight of the day still ahead of me, like the world didn't just split open.

I force myself to stand, to move, to do something that looks like leadership. I walk into the hallway. I speak to

Turner. I sign a report. I handle two problems that would have used to feel big but now feel like gnats.

At some point someone cracks a joke and the room laughs.

I don't.

My laugh is somewhere at the bottom of a well, and I'm not sure it's coming back.

By the time my shift ends, the sky outside has turned the color of bruised steel. The town is settling into evening, the same way it always does, with quiet streets, porch lights flicking on, the smell of someone's dinner drifting through the parking lot as I limp to my truck.

I catch myself scanning the lot for her.

For her car.

For some sign that she's still within reach.

There is nothing.

Of course there's nothing.

I get in the truck and sit there with my hands on the wheel.

The cab smells like old coffee and clean leather and the faint trace of her perfume, because she was in this seat, in this space, in my life.

And now she isn't.

The engine is off.

The radio is silent.

The only sound is my own breathing and the faint tick of the cooling metal.

I stare through the windshield as if the world might offer me instructions.

It doesn't.

So I drive home.

The roads are familiar, but tonight everything feels slightly wrong. Too empty, too wide, like the town has moved a few inches away from itself.

I pass the diner. I pass the little row of shops. I pass the turnoff that leads toward Florence's place, and the urge to swing the wheel is so strong my fingers tighten.

I imagine her inside. I imagine her sitting on her bed with

her knees pulled up, staring at her phone, deciding whether I deserve a chance to explain.

Then I imagine her not staring at her phone at all.

I imagine her choosing herself.

I imagine her walking away the way she did today, and my chest clamps down.

I keep driving.

Because showing up at her door would not be love.

It would be panic.

And panic has hurt enough people.

When I pull into my driveway, the house looks like a photograph of a life that used to mean something.

The porch light is off. The windows are dark. There's no car in the driveway besides mine.

No Lilly.

No Florence.

Just the empty stretch of gravel and the sound of my tires crunching on it.

I get out and my footsteps sound too loud as I move through the entryway, through the living room, past the couch where I've sat a thousand times and thought I was fine.

I drop my keys into the bowl on the table.

The clatter is sharp.

Then nothing.

I stand there, staring at the empty couch.

There's a pillow on one end that Florence stole and tucked behind her back. There's a throw blanket folded too neatly because I'm the kind of man who folds things when he doesn't know what to do with his hands.

Tonight, I don't fold anything.

Tonight, I don't know what to do with my entire body.

I move into the kitchen because that's what I do when I'm falling apart. I make coffee. I clean. I perform competence.

My hands go to the cabinet automatically. Mug. Filter. Grounds.

Then I stop.

It's evening.

Coffee is a terrible idea.

I make it anyway.

The machine gurgles and sputters, loud in the quiet. The smell fills the space and for a second it's comforting until my brain connects it to her.

She was in my kitchen.

She was here.

Not physically, but in the way she lodged herself into my days. In the way I started to imagine her laughing in this room, barefoot on my tile, stealing a sip and wrinkling her nose at how strong I take it.

The coffee finishes.

I don't pour it.

I just stand there staring at the pot like it's a question.

My phone is on the cushion beside me.

It lights up with a notification that isn't from her.

Just a weather alert. A work email. Something useless.

I pick it up anyway and scroll like motion will save me from thinking.

My eyes land on a photo from last week. A picture of Lilly on my porch with a takeout bag, rolling her eyes like she's too old for sentimental dads, but still showing up anyway.

My chest tightens.

I set the phone down.

I pick it up again.

I type something longer this time, careful, measured, the way I write reports:

Florence, what I said today was about the rumors. I was trying to shut them down. I wasn't denying you. I wasn't ashamed of you. I was trying...

I stop.

The sentence is a lie in its own way.

I was ashamed.

Not of her.

Of myself.

Of what the town is saying. Of the story they're building. Of the way my daughter looked at me like I was disgusting. Of the way my past came roaring back and told me: See? This is what happens when you love someone. You ruin them.

I delete the whole thing.

The blank screen stares back like it's judging me.

Good.

It should.

I set the phone down on my chest and lean back on the couch, staring at the ceiling.

The ceiling fan is off.

The shadows in the corners are still.

My breathing is shallow.

I listen to the house settle—tiny creaks, the faint hum of the fridge, the distant bark of someone's dog.

Normal life sounds.

My life sounds like a stranger.

My eyes burn.

I close them for a second and the closet comes back—dark, crowded, my knees to my chest, my heart hammering.

The vow I made in there wasn't noble.

It was fear.

And I've lived by it for so long I mistook it for morality.

If I never love anyone, they can't get hurt because of me.

But love isn't the thing that hurts people.

Fear is.

Control is.

Silence is.

I open my eyes again.

The tarot card on the laptop is still there, bright on the screen.

Strength.

Without armor.

And I realize something that makes my throat tighten so hard it feels like choking.

The fear isn't loving someone younger than me or what the town will say.

The fear isn't even losing my job.

It's being the reason someone cries in a bathroom stall.

The fear is watching my daughter's face fracture and hearing the echo of my father in my own choices. It might be different words, different fists, but it's the same damage.

I swallow hard.

My phone is heavy in my hand.

I hold it like it's a weapon.

Like it's a lifeline.

Like it's both.

I don't text.

I don't call.

I just... sit.

Because tonight, the only thing I can do without hurting someone more is nothing.

My eyelids start to droop, exhaustion pulling at me like gravity. I fight it at first, because sleeping feels like giving up.

But my body is done.

My shoulders slump.

The phone slips slightly in my hand, screen dimming.

I glance at the laptop.

Florence's tarot card photo fills the glow of the room.

Her detail. Her care. Her art.

A piece of her that she gave me without knowing how much it would matter.

I stare at it until my eyes blur.

Then my head tips back against the couch.

My breathing slows.

The phone is still in my hand.

My last clear thought is not a sentence.

It's a heavy and aching feeling. Frighteningly pure.

A want.

A need.

A truth I'm not brave enough to name yet.

And in the quiet of my empty house, with the past in my bones, I fall asleep holding my silence like it's the only thing keeping me from becoming my father.

TWENTY-FIVE
FLORENCE

"…MA'AM, I need you to stay with me."

My voice sounds calm. Professional. Like it belongs to someone who slept last night. Like it doesn't still taste like copper and humiliation.

"I'm here," the woman says, breathless but lucid. "I'm here, I'm just— I tripped, I think. I don't know. Everything hurts."

"Okay," I say gently, fingers flying across the keyboard. "Let's slow this down. Can you tell me where you are right now?"

There's a pause. A shuffle. The faint sound of a dog barking somewhere in the background.

"I'm in my kitchen. I was carrying groceries. I think my foot caught on the rug."

That'll do it. Rugs are treacherous. So are kitchens. So are men you think won't disappear on you.

"Are you bleeding anywhere you can see?" I ask.

"No, just…god, I feel stupid."

I almost laugh. It bubbles up in my chest, uninvited but real.

"You're not stupid," I say. "You fell. It happens to everyone eventually."

She snorts, a little surprised. "You sound like you've done this before."

I have. In public. Emotionally.

"I've seen a lot of falls," I say instead. "You're doing great. Let's check your pain level."

As she answers, I follow the protocol. Ask the right questions. Type the right codes. Let the muscle memory take over while my brain stays carefully partitioned off from the parts of my life that are currently on fire.

I am not thinking about Lilly's face when she said *friends don't do this.*

I am not thinking about August's voice, clipped and controlled, telling his officers nothing is happening.

I am not thinking about the empty apartment. The note on the fridge.

I just need some time.

Short. Careful. Polite. Like she was afraid of hurting me even while she fled.

"Florence?" the caller says.

"Yes," I answer automatically.

"I think... I think I can stand. I just needed a minute."

Relief loosens something in my chest.

"Okay," I say. "I'm still going to send medics to check you out. Falling can shock your system."

"Thank you," she says, softer now. "You're really nice."

I swallow.

"You don't have to be alone right now," I tell her. "Help is on the way."

When the call ends and the line disconnects, I sit there for half a second longer than protocol allows, staring at the blank screen.

I did my job.

That's the only thing holding me together right now.

I log the call, adjust my headset, and stare at the board. Another line flashes. Another voice. Another emergency that has nothing to do with my life imploding.

Good.

Let the world burn later.

Right now, I work.

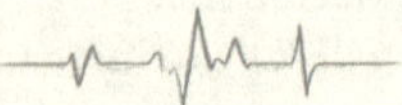

It's only during a rare lull, a fragile pocket of quiet, that my body remembers it's allowed to feel things.

My shoulders ache. My jaw is tight. My chest feels like it's been Harbored out and replaced with static.

I glance at the empty console next to mine.

Ruth's station.

She's not here today. She never misses mornings.

The thought lands heavier than it should.

I reach for my phone without fully deciding to. Just... reaching. Like muscle memory. Like my hand knows something my heart hasn't admitted yet.

I open my contacts.

Scroll.

Stop.

Ruth, Supervisor.

I've never saved Ruth's number. Never needed to my contacts. We talk across consoles, through headsets, in passing. She's always been *there* in the way steady people are. Present. Observant. Kind without being intrusive.

I tap the contact. And copy the number into my phone and save it with her name.

Switch to text messages, and that's when I see it.

Earlier today I got a message from an Unknown Number.

> Ruth Heart: Can we talk when you have a moment?

My stomach drops.

The blood drains from my face so fast I feel lightheaded.

Oh.

Oh, she knows.

Of course she knows.

The Unknown Number has been replaced with Ruth Heart.

The timing. The absence. The fact that I'm suddenly the subject of whispered conversations and averted gazes.

She knows.

My fingers go cold around the phone.

I scroll back. Check the timestamp.

Early this morning.

Before I even clocked in.

Before I had the chance to pretend this could be compartmentalized.

My brain starts to spin.

Did Lilly tell her everything?

Did August?

Is this about professionalism? Boundaries?

Is she angry? Hurt? Protective?

In a wild moment, I wonder if Ruth knows about everything. Does she believe Lilly? I imagine Ruth's face hardening. Her voice going cool. Her saying my name the way people do when they're disappointed.

I imagine her telling me I should have known better.

That I crossed a line.

That this will have consequences.

My chest tightens.

I type anyway.

> Florence: Hi Ruth. I'm so sorry I didn't see this earlier. I'm on shift today. Would it be okay to talk after I'm off?

I hit send and hold my breath.

The seconds stretch.

Then three little dots appear.

> Ruth: Of course. I'm not in today, obviously. I took the morning with Lilly. But I can meet later if you're free?

There it is.

Confirmation.

My throat closes.

Florence: Okay, sure.

Three dots appear.

Disappear.

Ruth: We can grab dinner if that's easier. No pressure. Just let me know.

Dinner.

My pulse stutters.

Dinner is... intentional. Personal. Not a disciplinary hallway chat.

Which somehow makes it worse.

I picture myself sitting across from her, confessing everything, watching her face change.

I almost type *never mind.*

Florence: Dinner is fine. Thank you.

I put the phone face-down on the desk like it might explode.

Okay.

That's happening.

I force my attention back to the console just as another call lights up. Another voice. Another small crisis that needs triage.

Good.

Give me structure.

The rest of the shift blurs.

I answer calls. I log incidents. I coordinate units. I smile when appropriate. I nod at coworkers who look at me like I might shatter if they speak too loudly.

No one says anything outright.

Which somehow makes it worse.

When my shift finally ends, my body feels like it's been wrung out and left to dry.

I clock out.

Grab my bag.

Pause at the door.

For half a second, my traitorous heart wonders if August will be there.

He's not.

Of course he's not.

I exhale, slow and careful, and head out into the evening.

The restaurant Ruth chose is quiet. Warm. The kind of place where conversations stay low and no one rushes you.

I arrive ten minutes early and immediately regret it.

I sit at the table and stare at the menu without reading a word.

The menu lies before me untouched. I don't order because I can't imagine eating before I say this out loud. Before I give Ruth the chance to hate me.

My knee bounces under the table.

I replay the words in my head.

I'm sorry.

I didn't mean for this to happen.

I understand if you're angry.

None of them sound like enough.

The door opens.

I look up.

Ruth walks in wearing jeans and a soft sweater, her hair loose, her expression unreadable.

She spots me immediately.

Smiles.

And something in my chest loosens just a fraction.

"Florence," she says, approaching. "Hi."

"Hi," I manage, standing too quickly.

Ruth pulls out the chair across from me. "I'm glad you reached out." She says it like she means it.

Which almost undoes me on the spot.

Ruth sits across from me like she's done this before.

Not this exact situation, obviously, no one rehearses their

life detonating in public because your roommate is your boyfriend's daughter and your boyfriend is your coworker's ex. But the steadiness in her posture says she's been in rooms where emotions run hot and words matter.

She sets her purse on the chair beside her and looks at me across the table with a calm that makes my throat tighten.

"You didn't order yet?" she asks, glancing at the untouched menu.

I shake my head too quickly. "I—I wanted to talk first."

Her eyes soften. "Okay."

Just that.

No *what's wrong*, no *are you okay*, no *do I need to brace myself.*

She gives me permission to start wherever I need to start, and it feels like my chest has been holding its breath since last night.

A server comes by, cheerful and oblivious.

"Hi there! Can I start you ladies with something to drink?"

Ruth smiles like she's done this a thousand times. "Water for me, please."

The server turns to me.

My mouth opens and nothing comes out.

I clear my throat. "Water is fine."

The server nods and leaves.

The silence that follows isn't awkward. It's... waiting.

Ruth folds her hands on the table, posture relaxed. Not defensive. Not closed off. Her nails are short and clean. Practical. Everything about her says: *I can handle whatever you're about to hand me.*

And I hate that I might need that right now.

I stare at the wood grain between us because looking at her feels like stepping too close to a ledge.

"I got your text this morning," I say, because it's the easiest entry point. The safest.

"I know," she says gently.

I clear my throat.

My fingers twist in my lap. "I didn't realize the number was yours. I... only realized today."

"I figured," Ruth says. "It's okay."

I swallow. My pulse is loud in my ears.

"I don't know what you know," I manage.

Ruth's gaze stays steady. "I know my daughter came to me last night with a look on her face utter betrayal."

My stomach tightens.

"And I know," she continues, "that you left a restaurant alone, and you showed up to work today looking like someone tried to put you through a paper shredder emotionally."

A laugh tries to escape me and turns into something dangerously close to a sob.

Ruth doesn't flinch.

She just... waits.

My hands come up to my glass of water when the server returns, like I can anchor myself by holding something cold. I take a sip that does nothing for the heat building behind my eyes.

"I'm sorry," I blurt. The words come out too fast, too raw. "I'm so sorry, Ruth. I didn't... I didn't know. I didn't know any of it. I didn't know you were his—"

I stop. The pronoun sticks in my throat like a fishbone.

Ruth tips her head slightly. "August."

Hearing his name in her voice does something strange to me. The sudden reality that he exists in a web of history I stepped into blindfolded is dizzying.

I nod once, hard.

"I didn't know you were—I mean, I knew you had a daughter. Lilly told me you were her mother," I say, voice cracking, "but I didn't know that you and August..."

My stomach turns.

Ruth's expression stays neutral, but there's something in the set of her mouth that suggests she's been biting back opinions for decades.

"You didn't know," she repeats, like she's offering me a rope.

"No," I whisper. "I didn't. I swear. And I know that doesn't change what it feels like. But I need you to believe me."

Ruth nods once. "I do."

The simplicity of it knocks the air out of me.

"You—" My voice wobbles. "You do?"

"I do," she says again. "Florence, I've worked with you long enough to know what your panic looks like. You don't fake that. You don't perform guilt."

I blink hard.

There's a bruise forming in my throat.

"I don't even know how to... explain it," I say. "None of it was—" I swallow. "And I don't want you to think I moved here and targeted your family. That sounds insane even saying out loud." My stomach churns.

Ruth's mouth twitches, almost a smile.

"I don't think you orchestrated a small-town romance scandal like a Bond villain," she says dryly.

A laugh cracks out of me, real and startled, and it hurts because it's the first time my body's done anything that isn't bracing for impact.

Ruth's gaze softens further at the sound.

I inhale, shakily. "Okay. So. The truth."

I push the words out like I'm forcing myself to step into cold water.

"I met August last year," I say. "In Seattle. It was... one night. It wasn't supposed to be anything other than that. I never asked what he did for a living—honestly I didn't care too much at that moment. My sister had just died and I was looking to get out of my head for a night." I spill the words and suck in a breath.

I keep my voice controlled, because if I let it crack too far open I'm going to fall apart in public and I can't do that again. Not tonight. Not with her watching.

Ruth listens like she's taking notes, but her face doesn't harden.

"I'm sorry about your sister," she says quietly. "I lost my mom a few years ago. I know that's hard."

I try to smile but I know it doesn't reach my eyes. "We ran into each other during Harbor Days," I add. "And then... it wasn't one night anymore. Not really."

Ruth's eyebrows lift a fraction. Then Ruth says, carefully, "Lilly told me you two..."

I nod.

The water glass trembles faintly in my grip.

"After what happened," I say, because the words are slippery and I need to name the thing that started the spiral. "After the shooting. After he got hurt, it wasn't just a hookup anymore." My breath catches. "I couldn't stop thinking about him. We both decided there was something deeper and we wanted to explore that. August asked me to dinner... to meet his daughter."

Ruth's eyes flicker.

Not surprise. Not anger. More like that quiet, motherly calculation of consequences.

"And you said yes," she says.

"Yes," I whisper. "I thought it meant... something. I thought it was him letting me into his real life."

Ruth's gaze stays on me. "And then you walked in and saw Lilly."

My stomach clenches like a fist.

"Yes."

I stare at the table because if I look at Ruth right now, I might start crying. I refuse to be that woman.

Even if I am exactly that kind of woman.

"I didn't know," I repeat, like a prayer. "He told me he had a daughter, but he didn't—" I stop myself. I won't say it like an accusation. It's not fair. Not when his attempt at discretion is part of what created the collision. "He didn't tell me details. She didn't either."

Ruth's fingers tap lightly against the table once. Twice. Not impatient. Just thinking.

"I can see how that happened," she says finally.

My head snaps up. "You can?"

She gives a small shrug. "Townsend Harbor is one of those places where people forget other people have full lives outside of town lines. We treat 'Dad' like it's a private title. Like no one else knows he exists."

My throat tightens again.

"And August," Ruth continues, choosing her words with

care, "has always been... protective about Lilly. Private. Especially after the separation."

Hearing *separation* in Ruth's voice makes something settle in my chest. This isn't a love triangle. It's a family. A history. A life already built long before I arrived.

"I didn't want to be a problem," I say, and the words come out small. "I didn't want to be—" I can't say *a mistake*. I won't reduce myself to that. "I didn't want to be something that hurt her."

Ruth's gaze softens, and when she speaks, her voice drops into something quieter. More personal.

"Florence," she says, "Lilly is hurt because of Lilly."

I blink.

Ruth leans back slightly, still watching me. "She's young. She's smart. She's capable. But she's also... my daughter. She has a very strong sense of what things are supposed to look like, and when they don't match that picture, she panics."

"She was disgusted," I whisper, the memory of Lilly's face sharp and immediate. "She looked at me like I was—like we were—"

"I know," Ruth says, and there's something like regret under the words. "I'm not excusing it. But I know my kid."

My hands curl tighter around the glass. "She thinks I betrayed her."

Ruth's mouth tightens. "She does."

The honesty stings.

Then Ruth adds, "She also thinks her father betrayed her."

That part lands differently. Heavier.

I swallow. "He didn't..."

Ruth's eyes flicker, something complicated passing through. "He rarely means to. That doesn't stop him."

I hold still.

Ruth looks away for a second, her gaze catching on the window, on the passing headlights outside, on the life moving beyond this table.

When she looks back at me, she seems... older. Not in years, but in the way you get older from being the person who has to keep things steady.

"Can I tell you something without you taking it as an attack?" she asks.

My pulse stutters. "Okay."

Ruth's voice is calm. "August is... a good man. He's also a man who sometimes believes doing something quietly is the same as doing it well."

My throat goes tight.

"He doesn't like mess," Ruth continues. "He doesn't like conflict. So he tries to prevent it by controlling information."

The words ring with a truth that makes my stomach twist. August and are are a lot a like in that way. Didn't I do the same thing. Left out information to control the potential mess.

"And then," Ruth says, "he's shocked when the controlled information explodes."

I exhale shakily.

"That doesn't make him bad," she adds, softer. "It makes him human. And stubborn. And sometimes a little stupid."

A laugh slips out of me, small and unwilling.

Ruth's mouth quirks, just briefly. "There it is. Your smile."

The comment hits me in the ribs like a nudge.

I blink fast. "I didn't realize."

"You don't do it often," Ruth says. Not judgment. Just observation. "But when you do, it looks like you're surprised it belongs to you."

My chest aches. My eyes burn.

I swallow, hard. "I didn't have anyone to talk to," I admit, and the truth spills out before I can package it. "After last night. I went home and Lilly was gone. She left a note. I—" My voice cracks. "I didn't know if she was safe. I didn't know if she was—"

Ruth's expression shifts instantly, alert. "She's safe."

The relief is so immediate it almost makes me dizzy.

"She's with you," I whisper.

Ruth nods. "She came by my house late last night. She didn't want to talk at first. She just wanted to be somewhere she didn't have to look at her ceiling and replay the scene."

My throat tightens. "I worried she went to a friend's and..."

"She came to me," Ruth says. "She's sleeping. She's eating. She's alive. She's just... furious."

My shoulders sag, the tension easing for the first time since the restaurant.

"I didn't want to blow up her phone," I admit. "Because she said she needed space. And I... I didn't want to cross that."

Ruth's eyes narrow slightly, curious. "She left you a note?"

"Yes." The image flashes in my head, the small square of paper stuck to the fridge with a magnet shaped like a smiling ghost. Lilly's handwriting, fast and slanted.

I just need some time.

My throat closes around the memory.

Ruth studies me. "She didn't tell me that."

My stomach twists. "I didn't tell her anything either. I didn't—" I swallow.

Ruth nods slowly. "Sometimes saying nothing is the kindest thing you can do when someone's not ready to hear you."

I look down at my hands. "I still feel like I'm failing."

Ruth's voice softens again. "You're not failing. You're navigating."

My throat aches with the effort of not crying.

The server returns, smiling, pen poised. "Hi again! Ready to order?"

Ruth glances at me, checking in without words.

I inhale. "Yes." My voice is steadier than I feel. "Can I get... a burger? Fries."

The words surprise me. The fact that I'm ordering at all surprises me.

Ruth orders something simple too, and when the server leaves again, the air between us shifts. Not lighter—nothing about this is light—but it feels less sharp.

Ruth reaches for her water and takes a sip. "Lilly told me what she said to you."

My stomach drops again.

"What did she?" I start, then stop. I can't ask for the replay. I lived it.

"She told me she accused you of being coerced," Ruth says, bluntly.

Heat rises in my cheeks. Shame. Anger. Something bitter.

Ruth continues before I can speak. "She was trying to make sense of the stuff that didn't fit neatly in her head. She went to the closest explanation that let her be protective."

I swallow. "It didn't feel protective."

"I know," Ruth says. "It felt insulting. And it was."

I blink at her, stunned.

Ruth doesn't soften it. "You're a grown woman. You get to choose who you sleep with."

My throat tightens.

"And," she adds, eyes steady, "Lilly doesn't get to interrogate your past like you're applying to date her. You live with her. You pay rent. You clean your dishes. That's the contract."

A laugh slips out of me, shaky and relieved, because hearing someone say the plain truth like that feels like oxygen.

"Thank you," I whisper.

Ruth nods once, like she accepts it as fact, not praise.

Then she says, quieter, "August... texted me today."

My heart stutters.

"He did?"

Ruth's mouth tightens. "He asked if Lilly was okay."

I swallow. "Did you tell him?"

"I told him she's alive," Ruth says. "And that he should stop trying to fix everything with one conversation."

My mouth parts, startled.

Ruth shrugs. "He's going to try anyway."

A silence settles between us, and in it I feel the shape of August's absence. The way he didn't text me last night. The way he ran after Lilly and left me under a thousand curious eyes.

The way my phone stayed silent.

Ruth watches my face as if she can see the thoughts there.

"Did he contact you?" she asks gently.

My throat tightens. "No."

Ruth doesn't look surprised. She looks... disappointed. Not in me. In him.

"I'm sorry," she says, and it's so simple, so human, that it makes my eyes sting.

"I didn't text him either," I admit. "I... I didn't know what to say."

Ruth nods. "You gave space."

"I didn't want to be in the middle," I whisper. "I thought he needed to handle his situation with Lilly. I thought... if I stepped back, it would help."

Ruth's gaze is steady. "That was reasonable."

I inhale. My breath trembles.

"It didn't feel reasonable today," I say softly, the words tasting like ash. "When I heard him."

Ruth's eyes sharpen. "You heard him say something?"

My stomach twists again.

I nod once. "He—" My throat closes, but I push through. "He told people... that nothing is happening with him. With me."

Ruth goes very still.

For a heartbeat, I see something flash behind her eyes. It's not anger exactly, but a sharp, familiar frustration. Like she's seen August do that kind of damage before.

"He was trying to stop rumors," Ruth says slowly, like she's testing the shape of the explanation.

"It didn't sound like that," I whisper. "It sounded like denial. Like I was... an embarrassment."

Ruth's mouth tightens. "Florence."

Just my name. Just a steady anchor.

"I'm not going to excuse him," she says. "But I will say this: August has a bad habit of thinking he can protect people by making them invisible."

The words land deep in my chest, because that's exactly what it felt like.

Invisible.

Erased.

A thing to be hidden so the town doesn't chatter too loudly.

My fingers curl under the table.

"I can't do that," I say quietly.

Ruth nods once. "Good."

The firmness surprises me.

Ruth leans forward slightly, elbows near the edge of the table. Her voice lowers. "Listen. You don't owe me the details of your relationship. You don't owe me a play-by-play. You're not dating *me*."

My cheeks heat.

"But," she continues, "you do work under my supervision. And I need to make sure you know this: your job is not in jeopardy because you made a personal decision."

My lungs loosen like someone cut a cord.

"You—you're not—" I can't even finish the sentence.

Ruth shakes her head. "No. And if anyone tries to make it your problem, I will handle it."

My throat tightens so hard it hurts.

It feels like standing under a roof after being out in the storm too long.

"Thank you," I whisper again, because it's all I have.

Ruth's eyes soften. "You're a good dispatcher, Florence. And you're a good person. I don't need to know the messy details to know that."

The food arrives then, a small mercy, something tangible in the middle of all this emotional wreckage.

Ruth eats like someone who's not afraid of silence. Like she doesn't need to fill it with chatter to prove she's okay. She takes a bite, chews, nods approvingly at something about the seasoning.

I take a bite too.

And for the first time all day, my stomach doesn't reject it.

We eat in fragments. Conversation comes in small, careful pieces.

Ruth asks how I'm sleeping. I almost laugh, because the answer is a joke and a tragedy.

"Not great," I admit.

Ruth nods like she expected it. "It'll come back. It always does."

I push a fry around my plate, then blurt, "Does it ever stop hurting? The... whole losing people thing?"

Ruth goes still.

I immediately regret it.

"I'm sorry," I say quickly. "You don't have to answer that. I—"

Ruth lifts a hand, gentle. "You don't have to apologize."

She looks down at her plate for a second, like she's choosing the truth she can give me.

"It changes," she says finally. "It doesn't stop. It changes shape. Some days it's loud. Some days it's background noise. Some days you'll laugh and then feel guilty for laughing, and then eventually you'll stop feeling guilty."

My throat tightens.

"And some days," she adds, eyes meeting mine, "you'll feel like you're drowning and you'll forget you've ever been able to breathe. Those days are lies. They feel real, but they're lies."

My eyes sting.

Ruth's voice stays steady. "You lost your mother and then a year ago you lost your sister. That is not enough time for your body to learn the new shape of the world."

My throat burns.

I nod, because if I speak I'm going to cry.

Ruth doesn't push. She just lets the truth sit.

A few minutes later, she says, lighter, "August *is* easy on the eyes."

I choke on a laugh.

Ruth's mouth quirks. "I'm not blind. We can be mature adults about reality."

Heat rises in my cheeks. "He—" I shake my head, trying to regain control. "He has a very unfair mouth."

Ruth's eyebrows lift.

I freeze.

"Oh my god," I say, mortified. "I did not mean to say that out loud."

Ruth stares at me for half a second, then snorts a real, genuine sound that makes her seem less like my supervisor and more like... someone I could actually talk to.

"Noted," she says dryly. "I will not put that on your performance review."

I cover my face with one hand, laughing through the humiliation, and it's ridiculous how much the laughter helps. Like it shakes loose some of the tightness.

When my hand drops, Ruth is watching me with something like... fondness.

Not motherly. Not invasive. Just warm.

"You can laugh," she says simply. "Even right now."

My throat tightens again.

I nod once.

Ruth glances out the window, then back at me. "Lilly is going to be angry for a while."

My stomach twists.

"I know," I whisper. "I don't blame her."

Ruth's gaze is steady. "You can empathize with her without accepting cruelty."

I swallow. "I don't want to lose her."

Ruth's expression softens. "I know."

I exhale shakily. "Is she... okay?"

Ruth nods. "She's okay. She's sleeping in my guest room. She ate half a pizza and watched some terrible reality show and pretended she wasn't crying until she was."

My chest tightens.

"I didn't want to bombard her," I admit. "I saw her note. I... I just didn't want her to feel cornered."

Ruth nods slowly. "That was wise."

My voice turns small. "Will she come back?"

Ruth's gaze doesn't flinch from the truth. "She will. Eventually. She has a lease and a life. She'll come back when she's ready to look at you without wanting to throw a chair."

A weak laugh slips out.

Ruth's mouth quirked, but her eyes stay serious. "But Florence... you can't ask me to be the bridge."

I stiffen. "I wouldn't."

Ruth's voice softens, but it's firm. "I need you to hear me. I love my daughter. I will always choose my daughter. That's the line I won't cross."

Something in me loosens. Not because it feels good, but because it feels honest.

"I understand," I whisper. "I would never ask you to choose."

Ruth nods once. "Good."

Then she adds, more gently, "What I *can* do is tell you she's safe. And I can tell you that she will come back to her apartment when she's ready."

Relief pushes air into my lungs again.

"Thank you," I say.

Ruth eats another bite, then looks at me over her glass. "As for August..."

My pulse spikes.

Ruth continues carefully, "That's between you and him."

I nod. My throat is tight.

"But," Ruth says, and her eyes sharpen slightly, "if you let him make you smaller to fit his fear, I will be disappointed in you."

Ruth's words are a slap and a hug at the same time.

I blink. "You'd be disappointed in me?"

"Yes," Ruth says matter-of-factly. "Because I've seen you hold it together on the worst calls. I've seen you stay kind when people are screaming at you. I've seen you keep your voice steady when your hands were shaking."

My throat burns.

"You don't do that for a man," she says quietly. "Not for any man."

I look away and swallow around the lump in my throat.

"I don't think I can do it," I whisper. "Be small. Be hidden. I don't think I can survive that."

Ruth nods once, satisfied. "Good."

My eyes sting again.

Something in me that's been alone for too long reaches for her steadiness like it's sunlight.

"I thought you'd hate me," I admit, voice cracking. "I thought you agreed to dinner to... to tell me off."

Ruth's expression softens. "I'm not going to tell you off for being human."

My throat tightens.

"I'm going to tell you to be smart," she continues. "To protect your job. To protect your heart. To protect yourself."

I nod, shaky.

"And," Ruth adds, "to stop assuming you deserve punishment for wanting something."

I blink fast. "I don't know how to stop doing that."

Ruth's voice is gentle. "You practice."

The check comes. Ruth reaches for it automatically, and I jerk forward.

"No," I say quickly. "Let me—"

Ruth lifts a hand. "Florence."

I freeze.

Her eyes soften. "Let me."

It's not a power play. It's not superiority. It's something else.

Care.

I swallow nod, letting her do it, letting myself accept something without paying for it.

Outside, the night air is cool and clean. The streetlamps throw soft pools of light onto the sidewalk.

We stand for a moment near the entrance.

Ruth adjusts her sweater. "Do you need a ride?"

I shake my head. "No. I can walk."

Ruth studies me. "You sure?"

"Yes," I say, and I mean it. Walking feels like clearing my head. Like proof I'm still here.

Ruth nods. "Okay."

Then she hesitates, just a fraction, and her expression softens in a way that feels almost maternal.

"I'm glad you told me," she says quietly.

My throat tightens again. "I'm glad you didn't... hate me."

Ruth's mouth quirks. "You're not that powerful."

A laugh escapes me, shaky but real.

Ruth's eyes soften. "Text me if you need anything work-related."

I nod. "Okay."

She starts to turn, then pauses. Looks back. "And Florence?"

"Yeah?"

Ruth's voice is steady. "Whatever happens with August... don't let this town convince you you're a story."

My breath catches.

"You're a person," she says. "Don't forget that."

I nod, because if I speak I'll cry again.

Ruth gives me one last small, warm look.

Then she walks to her car and drives away, leaving me standing under the streetlight with my chest aching but not Harbor.

Not entirely.

Because for the first time since last night, I don't feel like I'm floating untethered in space.

I start walking home.

The streets are quiet. The town is still itself, charming and smug and full of secrets.

But something in me feels... steadier.

Not healed.

Not fixed.

Just... held.

And when I reach my house, the living room is still too quiet. Lilly still isn't home.

But the note is still on the fridge.

I just need some time.

I stare at it for a long beat.

Then, slowly, I grab a pen.

I write beneath it, careful and small so it fits:

I'm here when you're ready. I'm sorry. I miss you.

I leave the pen on the counter.

I go to my room.

And when I crawl into bed, I don't reach for my phone.

Not for August.

Not tonight.

Tonight, I let myself breathe without waiting for someone else to decide whether I'm worth choosing.

Outside, the world keeps turning.

Inside, I keep turning with it.

TWENTY-SIX
FLORENCE

THE FIRST CALL of my shift comes in hot, like the line is already on fire before I even pick up.

"9-1-1, where's your emergency?"

A man's voice answers, panicked and loud in my headset. Wind. The slap of something flapping. A dog barking like it's narrating the apocalypse.

"My neighbor's goat is on my roof!"

I blink.

Once.

Twice.

My fingers hover over the keyboard because my brain wants to file this under prank, but his breathing is ragged, earnest, and outraged in a way no one fakes at six fifty-eight in the morning.

"Sir," I say carefully, because my voice is still capable of being professional even when reality isn't, "did you say... a goat?"

"Yes!" he shouts. "A whole-ass goat. On my roof. It's eating my Christmas lights. I don't even have them plugged in, I put them up early because my wife—listen, it's not the point. It's up there and it keeps stomping and I swear to God if it falls through—"

"Okay." I click into the call screen, pull up the address, and my hands do what they're trained to do even while my heart feels like it's made of wet paper. "I need you to take a breath for me. Are you inside the house?"

"Yes."

"Are you safe?"

"I mean—" He pauses, like safety is a complicated philosophical question when you live next to livestock. "I'm inside. The goat is outside. So yes."

"Good." My mouth twitches. It almost becomes a smile, but it doesn't get that far. "Is the goat aggressive?"

"It's a goat. It's... rude."

I cover the mic for half a second, not because I'm laughing but because I need the smallest private moment to let the absurdity tap the glass of my brain like a coin. Rude goat. Roof goat. Townsend Harbor, where the universe never runs out of ways to remind you you're not in control.

"I'm dispatching the fire department to your location," I tell him. "Please do not go outside to confront the goat."

"I wasn't gonna."

His tone says yes, he was.

"Sir."

He sighs like a man surrendering to the fact that his morning is now a story his coworkers will dine on for the next decade. "Okay. I won't."

"Do you know who the goat belongs to?"

"Yeah," he mutters. "The Haskells. They got goats because they 'read it's good for weed control.' Control. My ass."

I type as I talk, dispatching. The console glows. The room hums. The other dispatchers are settling in—coffee lids clicking, chairs squeaking, headset wires being untangled like the cords are resentful we keep needing them.

"Someone will be there shortly," I say. "If the goat falls through the roof, call back immediately."

"It's not gonna fall," he says. "It's just... standing there. Looking at me like I'm the one who's wrong."

"Goats do that," I say, and the line between me and the world almost feels normal. Almost.

"Thank you," he says, a little calmer now. "Sorry. I know this is stupid."

"It's not stupid," I tell him, because in this room we hear every kind of emergency, and sometimes the ones that sound stupid are the only ones that don't leave blood in your ears. "We'll take care of it."

I disconnect, log the call, and my hand lingers a second on the keyboard like it's a grounding stone.

Rude goat. Roof goat. Christmas lights.

For half a heartbeat an involuntary human response tries to rise in me.

Then my eyes catch the reflection of myself in the darkened strip of monitor edge. Pale. Tight. Eyes too flat. The kind of face that looks like it's been listening to the world drown for too long.

I blink hard, sit up straighter, and adjust my headset. The work is waiting. It always is.

That's the problem. It always is.

The gossip wave hits before nine.

It doesn't crash in like a dramatic confrontation. It slithers.

A pause that stretches too long when I walk into the room. A voice lowering mid-sentence. A shared look that flicks away the second I catch it. Someone's laugh turning sharp, then choking into a cough.

It lives in the corners. It hides in kindness.

"Morning, Florence," Toni says, too bright, like she's trying to prove she's not thinking about anything.

"Morning," I answer, sliding into my chair.

Toni's eyes dart to me, then to her screen, like the computers might explode if she looks at me too long. She gives me a tight little smile that doesn't reach her eyes.

I log in. The system pings. The line lights blink.

Breathe in.

Breathe out.

Do your job.

It should be as simple as that. It's not.

The thing about small towns isn't that they gossip.

It's that they gossip like it's air. Like it's weather. Like it's something they can't help, something that just happens to them.

And I'm not new to judgment. I've lived under it so long it's practically a childhood home. I know how to keep my face neutral while people decide what I am.

But this is different.

Because it's wearing a uniform.

Because it's happening at the place that is supposed to be the backbone of trust. The place where we tell people help is coming even when we can't promise anything else.

I hear it first as a whisper behind me, just on the edge of my hearing, like my brain is catching it before my ears fully do.

"...she thinks she can just—"

"...Chief—"

"...dispatch girl—"

I keep my eyes on my screen, fingers moving through routine tasks. My chest tries to cave in anyway.

Another voice, closer, harsher, from the far side of the room.

"Well," someone says, and the word is weighted, "some people have shortcuts."

I don't turn. I don't give them the satisfaction. The call log updates. The clock ticks. The fluorescent lights buzz like insects.

My pulse doesn't care what I do. It starts climbing anyway.

Ruth's voice cuts through the room like a door slamming.

"We don't talk about each other that way in this room."

Silence drops. The radio murmurs, the occasional phone ring, keyboards clicking, but the human sound stops. That particular kind of cruel camaraderie shuts its mouth.

I look up before I can stop myself.

Ruth is standing near the central console, coffee in one hand, her gaze sweeping the room like she's taking names without writing them down. Her hair is pulled back tight. Her expression is calm in the way a storm is calm right before it breaks something.

"Say it again," she adds, voice even. "So we can address it like adults."

No one speaks.

Someone clears their throat and pretends it was a cough.

Ruth's eyes land on me for half a second. Not pity. Not performance. Just a steady look that says: I'm here. I hear it. I won't let it metastasize unchecked.

Then she turns away and walks back to her station like the room didn't just collectively swallow its own teeth.

The damage is done anyway.

Because I heard it.

Because they said it out loud, even if it wasn't my name on their lips.

Shortcuts. Shortcuts. Shortcuts.

Like my entire life has been a series of doors opening for me.

Like the only reason I can sit in this chair, with a headset crushing my temples and a thousand strangers' emergencies pressing against my ribs, is because I'm someone's rumor.

My mouth tastes like metal.

I take a call. A routine one, noise complaint. I dispatch it. My voice is steady, my hands are fast, my screen fills with details.

No one would know I'm splintering from the inside unless they were watching the small things.

The way my knee won't stop bouncing under the desk.

The way I swallow too often.

The way my fingers keep missing the same key like my hands have decided to rebel.

A patrol officer steps into dispatch to drop off paperwork. He's not one of the ones I'm close with, not Turner, not someone whose jokes feel safe. Just a guy. Brown hair. Pink cheeks from the cold. The kind of man who thinks his expression is neutral when it's absolutely not.

He pauses at the counter, glances at me, and something like amusement crosses his face.

"Well, well," he says under his breath, but not under it enough. "Guess it pays to be... friendly."

The words slip into the room like oil.

My body goes still.

Not because I'm shocked. Because I'm tired.

Tired in a way that makes rage feel like a distant planet I don't have the energy to visit.

Ruth's chair scrapes as she stands again.

"Officer," she says, tone mild, which is somehow scarier than yelling, "what did you just say?"

He smiles like he didn't. Like he can play dumb and walk away untouched.

"Nothing," he says. "Just—"

"Just what?" Ruth asks.

His eyes flick around the room. He sees the attention. He sees the risk. His smile tightens.

"Just making conversation."

"This isn't a bar," Ruth says. "This is dispatch. We're here to do a job. If you can't speak respectfully to the people who are literally sending you to your calls, you can turn around and file your paperwork somewhere else."

His ears go red. His pride flares. He glances at me like I'm the problem standing in the way of his entitlement.

"Didn't mean anything by it," he mutters.

"That's the issue," Ruth says, still calm. "You didn't mean anything by it."

He opens his mouth, then closes it. He turns and leaves with his paperwork still in his hands like he's forgotten why he came in.

Ruth sits back down. The room exhales like it's been holding its breath.

I stare at my screen, but the letters blur for a second.

I want to say thank you.

I also want to vomit.

Because she shouldn't have to do that. Not for me. Not because grown adults can't control their mouths.

And because every time she defends me, I feel the invisible story getting thicker. The story they'll tell later. Ruth covering for Florence. Ruth taking her side. Ruth doesn't know what Florence's really like.

Ruth does know. She knows more than anyone in this building.

And she's still standing between me and the knives.

That should make me feel safe.

Instead it makes me feel like I'm a liability.

The hours drag.

Not because the calls stop. They don't. They never do.

A woman locked out of her car with a baby inside, voice shaking, sunlight flashing off windshields while she tries not to panic and I talk her through finding someone with a Slim Jim tool without breaking the window.

An older man who fell in his driveway, too proud to say he's scared, insisting he doesn't need me on the line while I listen to the tremor in his breath and dispatch medics.

A teenager calling about her mom's boyfriend yelling, the kind of call that makes my skin crawl because you can hear the carefulness in her voice, the way she's trying not to make it worse.

I do the job. I do it well. I give them my calm voice. I give them my training. I give them the part of me that can stay steady even when my heart is shredded.

And in the spaces between calls, the room keeps doing what it does.

People glance at me.

People glance away.

People whisper like the words taste better when they're hidden.

The worst part is the kindness.

The sudden "You doing okay?" from someone who has never asked me that before.

The too-soft smile.

The way someone offers me half a donut like sugar can patch a public humiliation.

It's all a performance. It's all a way to be near the story without getting cut by it.

By noon my jaw aches from holding itself in place.

By two my shoulders are a single knot.

By the time my break hits, I'm so tired I feel like my bones have been replaced with glass.

I grab my water bottle and stand up. The chair wheels squeak. I keep my face neutral. I walk like I'm not a person being dissected by the people I share oxygen with.

The break room is down the hall. The door sticks sometimes because the building is old and everything in Townsend Harbor has a personality problem.

I push it open and step inside.

Ruth is already there.

She's sitting at the little table with a paper cup of coffee and a sandwich wrapper. Her radio is clipped to her belt even on break, like she doesn't trust the world to behave without her on duty.

She looks up when I enter, and her expression changes. Softens. Not in pity. In recognition.

"Hey," she says.

I hover in the doorway like I'm not sure I'm allowed.

"Hey," I answer.

She gestures to the chair across from her. "Sit."

I do.

The room is quiet except for the hum of the vending machine and the faint echo of dispatch noise bleeding through the walls. Phones ringing. Voices. The world refusing to pause.

Ruth takes a sip of coffee, then sets the cup down carefully. Like she's choosing her movements on purpose.

"You don't have to pretend with me," she says.

My throat tightens. I stare at the table because if I look at her face, I might break in a way I can't put back together before my break ends.

"I'm not pretending," I lie.

Ruth's mouth twists slightly. "Okay."

A beat passes.

My hands are in my lap, twisted together. I can feel my nails pressing into my palm.

"I heard it," I say finally, voice low. "What they said."

"I know," Ruth replies. "I shut it down."

"I know."

Another beat.

I hate this part. I hate being the person who needs something. I hate feeling like a burden. I hate that my chest feels tight, like my ribs are trying to protect my heart from getting hit again.

"I don't know if I can keep doing this," I say.

Ruth doesn't react like it's dramatic. She doesn't scoff. She doesn't tell me to toughen up.

She just waits. Lets the words breathe.

"Doing what?" she asks.

I swallow. My eyes sting, but I refuse to let tears win in this building.

"This," I say, lifting a hand slightly, like the whole station is contained in my fingers. "The room. The whispers. The way people look at me like I'm not a person. Like I'm... entertainment."

Ruth's gaze stays steady.

"And the calls," I add, because it's the truth I've been avoiding. Because the calls are the part that doesn't just hurt me today. They hurt me always. "Not just the people. The calls too."

Ruth's eyebrows lift just slightly, like she's acknowledging something she already suspected.

"I'm good at it," I say quickly, because I need her to know that before anything else. "I'm good at this job."

"I know," she says.

"And I know it matters," I continue, voice tightening. "I know the work matters. I know what we do matters. But sometimes it feels like I'm... like I'm swallowing everyone else's worst day and it never comes back up."

Ruth leans back in her chair, folds her arms, thinking.

"This job isn't a test you pass or fail," she says after a moment. "It's a choice."

I blink. The word hits me in the chest like a small stone. Choice.

Ruth keeps going, voice calm, matter-of-fact, like she's stating something as simple as the sky being blue.

"And you've already given it more than most."

Something in me loosens. Not enough to cry. Enough to breathe.

I stare at her, and for a second I see what she is in a way I haven't let myself fully see yet.

A woman who has survived. Who has been through enough that she doesn't treat other people's pain like it's a nuisance. Who can sit here with her coffee and her sandwich wrapper and hold space like it's a weapon.

My voice comes out smaller than I mean it to.

"If I wasn't doing this," I say, "what would I want?"

The question hangs in the air.

It's not rhetorical.

It's not a fantasy.

It's the first honest thing I've asked myself in so long I barely recognize the sound of it.

Ruth's gaze stays on me, but she doesn't answer for me. She doesn't tell me what I should want. She doesn't steer me.

She just nods once, like yes, that's the question. Finally.

I exhale, shaky.

My bag is on the chair beside me. I didn't bring it in on purpose. I didn't think. It just came with me like my body doesn't know how to go anywhere without carrying something.

I unzip it with fingers that feel too stiff and pull out my tarot deck.

The box is scuffed from use. The corners are worn. The cards inside are soft around the edges from being handled, shuffled, loved.

The sight of it in my hands makes my chest go tight and warm at the same time.

Ruth watches, her expression unreadable but not judgmental.

"I keep it with me," I admit, like it's a confession.

"Why?" she asks.

Because it's mine, I want to say. Because it's a part of me that doesn't belong to this building. Because it doesn't demand I be made of steel.

But what comes out is simpler.

"Because it makes me feel like... me."

Ruth nods slowly.

I run my thumb along the edge of the box. The simple physical motion anchors me.

Smith Summer's shop flashes in my mind without permission.

The bell above the door. The smell of incense and old books and something citrusy welcomes me. The way the shelves are crowded with crystals and candles and dusty decks in plastic wrap. The way the light falls through the front window, making the floating dust look like glitter.

The way my heart lights up when I talk about cards.

The way I can feel my voice become more animated when someone asks me what a card means and I get to tell a story instead of logging a complaint.

In dispatch, my body is braced all the time. Even when I'm sitting still. My shoulders are always up around my ears. My jaw is always clenched.

In Smith Summer's shop, I breathe.

Ruth's voice pulls me back.

"You want to do readings," she says.

It's not a question. It's not accusatory. It's the kind of statement that lands gently, like she's naming something I've been circling.

My cheeks heat. I don't know why. Like wanting joy is embarrassing.

"I don't know," I say, because fear is always my first language. "I mean. Maybe. I've done them for friends. For myself." I glance down at the deck. "It's different than doing it for... strangers."

"It is," Ruth agrees.

I look up, surprised.

"I've gotten readings," she adds, like it's nothing. "Not a lot. But enough to know it can help."

That makes my throat tighten again.

"People think it's stupid," I say, quieter.

Ruth's mouth curves, not quite a smile, more like a familiar understanding.

"People think a lot of things," she replies. "Half of them are wrong. Besides, do you want to be around or take advice from people who think something you clearly love, is stupid? They're not your people."

I let out a breath that almost becomes a laugh.

Then the nasty comment from earlier returns like a slap, and the warmth drains away.

Shortcuts.

Friendly.

Earn our positions the old-fashioned way.

My stomach turns.

"I hate that this is happening here," I say. "In this room. These people. I thought—" I stop. Because I don't know what I thought. That professionalism would protect me? That a headset and a badge number would make me safe?

Ruth's gaze sharpens.

"This room isn't supposed to be like that," she says. "And I'll handle what I can handle."

"What about the things you can't?" I ask before I can stop myself.

Ruth holds my gaze for a long moment.

"What I can't," she says, voice steady, "is make you stay in a job that is killing you slowly."

My breath catches. Because once someone says the truth out loud, you can't unknow it.

The door opens. Someone steps in, grabs something from the fridge, avoids looking at us, and leaves again. The break room swallows the interruption and returns to quiet.

I stare at my deck, then at my hands.

My hands are shaking slightly.

Not from fear.

From possibility.

I hate possibility. It's always felt like a trick. Like something that shows up just long enough to make you want it before it disappears again.

But the idea of not being tethered to other people's emergencies every minute of every day feels like taking a breath after being underwater.

I don't say it out loud because I'm afraid it will shatter.

Ruth's radio crackles at her hip. She glances at it, then at me.

"Break's almost over," she says.

I nod, throat tight.

Ruth stands, picks up her cup, tosses it. She pauses by the door, looking back at me.

"You don't owe anybody here your whole life," she says. "And you don't owe this job forever."

No one has ever said that to me like it's allowed. Like leaving doesn't make you weak. Like you're permitted to choose yourself.

Ruth opens the door and steps out.

I sit there for another second, tarot deck in my hands, and let myself imagine something that doesn't make my chest hurt.

Not a perfect life.

Not an easy life.

Just a life where I'm not shrinking to fit other people's expectations.

I stand, tuck the deck back into my bag, and head back to dispatch.

The room is the same.

The screens glow. The phones ring. The air hums with tension and caffeine.

But I'm different.

A call comes in. I take it. I do the job. My voice is steady.

And between calls, I feel the weight of my bag against my leg, the tarot deck inside it like a secret heartbeat.

By the end of my shift, my head is full of noise.

Not just the calls. The looks. The whispers. The constant sense of being watched.

When I finally log off, my body feels like it's been holding itself together with tape.

I walk out into the evening air and let it hit my face, cold and clean.

My phone buzzes in my pocket.

Nothing important.

Just the usual.

And yet my thumb hovers like something is about to change.

Smith's name isn't in my contacts.

Not really. Not yet. We've talked at the shop. We've laughed. He's offered opinions on decks like it's a sacred duty. He's made me feel seen without trying to own me.

He's safe.

At least, he feels safe.

And right now, safe is what I need.

I stand on the sidewalk outside the station, streetlights flickering on one by one, the sky bruising purple over Townsend Harbor. My shoulders ache like I've been holding myself upright with sheer will.

For a second, I consider going home.

Letting the quiet swallow me. Letting the hurt have its turn.

But my feet don't move in that direction.

They carry me the other way instead.

Smith Summer's shop is still lit when I reach it, warm amber spilling out onto the sidewalk like an invitation. The bell above the door jingles softly when I step inside, the familiar scent of incense and old paper wrapping around me like a held breath finally released.

Smith looks up from behind the counter.

His expression shifts when he sees me. It's not surprise, exactly. More like recognition.

"Well," he says, leaning his elbows on the wood, a small smile tugging at his mouth. "Did you change your mind?"

Something in my chest loosens.

I don't answer right away. I just smile, a real one, tentative but honest and for the first time all day, it doesn't feel like I'm forcing myself to exist inside my own skin.

Maybe I don't know what comes next.

Maybe I don't have answers about August, or Lilly, or my job, or the shape my life is going to take from here.

But standing in this quiet little shop, with the hum of

possibility around me instead of the crackle of crisis, I feel it. The smallest, strangest thing.

Not relief.

Not happiness.

Not peace exactly.

Just the sense that I'm allowed to step toward what doesn't hurt.

And for now, that's enough.

TWENTY-SEVEN
FLORENCE

IT'S BEEN A WEEK.

Seven days since everything split open.

I feel it in the way my body still flinches when my phone buzzes. In the way my chest tightens every time I walk through the front door. In the way time has started to feel thick, like I'm moving through syrup instead of air.

August hasn't texted.

I haven't texted him.

Which is fair. I'm the one who said the words. I'm the one who drew the line and walked away from it without looking back. I don't get to be shocked that he's respecting that.

It doesn't make it hurt less.

Two nights ago, I came home from a late shift and almost tripped over Lilly's shoes by the door.

They were kicked off in a careless, familiar, way. Her keys were back in the bowl. The hallway light was on. And under her bedroom door, a thin stripe of yellow glowed against the dark.

Her presence was palpable.

I stood there longer than I meant to, staring at the shoes like they might move on their own. Hoping she might come out and say something that would fix everything. Forgive me for a transgression I didn't realize I'd made.

She didn't.

The next morning, I hear the coffee grinder before I even open my eyes.

That sound used to signal comfort. It meant Lilly was up. It meant life was happening in the kitchen. It meant I wasn't alone in this house.

Now it just makes my stomach knot.

I lie there for a minute, staring at the ceiling, working up the nerve to exist in the same space as her.

When I finally step into the kitchen, she's standing at the counter in one of her old college sweatshirts, hair in a messy bun, bare feet on the tile.

She looks... normal.

She's just Lilly.

For a moment, I could almost believe that nothing shattered between us.

"Hey," I say quietly, leaning against the doorframe to avoid making her think I'm cornering her.

Lilly stills.

"Hey," she says without turning around. Lilly's voice is flat. There's a carefulness to her tone.

The coffee machine hisses between us, loud in the silence.

I step a little closer. My voice cracked as I whispered the words, my palms slick with sweat. "I know you said you needed space. I'm giving you that. I just..." My throat tightens. "I care if you're okay."

Her shoulders rise and fall once.

"I'm alive," she says. "Which seems to be everyone's favorite bar."

The words aren't screamed. They're not even sharp.

They're tired.

She pours her coffee, grabs her mug, and walks past me so close I can feel the heat of her body.

Her eyes never wavered to mine. Not even a fleeting glance. She doesn't slow down.

It's like I'm furniture she's learned to move around.

I stand there long after she's gone, the smell of coffee thick in the air and my chest aching with the hole her friendship left behind.

That's where we find ourselves.

We don't fight.

We don't talk.

We orbit each other like strangers who happen to know each other's toothbrush colors.

We pass in the hallway and pretend the walls are more interesting than each other. We take turns in the kitchen like it's a shared resource, not a shared life. She doesn't slam doors. She doesn't glare.

She just... doesn't see me.

Yesterday, I tried again.

She was sitting on the couch with her laptop open, legs tucked under her, headphones on. She looked up when I said her name.

Just once.

"Lilly," I said, waving a little to grab her attention.

She slid one earcup off.

"Can we talk for a minute?"

"About what?"

About everything. About nothing. About how I miss you and don't know how to fix this.

Instead I said, "About us."

Her mouth tightened. "I'm busy."

"I won't take long."

She stared at me, deciding whether I was worth the energy.

Then she slid the earcup back on and looked away.

I exist only as a ghost beside her.

I don't know if this place is still my home. It feels as warm and inviting as any hostile territory can feel.

Work is unbearable. Home is worse.

I don't know if leaving would hurt her less, or if it would just make everything final.

Everything feels like choosing between two kinds of wrong.

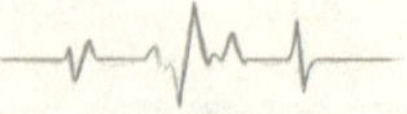

I WAKE UP LATE, tangled between sweat-slick sheets and a dream.

Or maybe not a dream. Not entirely.

That space between sleep and morning is still soft around the edges. Blurry. Blinding.

If I keep my eyes closed, I can still pretend I'm not in my bed.

I can pretend I'm back in his.

Pretend the sheets smell like cedar and soap instead of lavender and loneliness. Pretend the warm breath against the back of my neck belongs to someone who once begged me to choose him. Someone who didn't stay.

Someone who still haunts my fucking skin.

For a moment, I let it happen.

His hand slides down my stomach, palms between my thighs and I open for him, reflexive and already wet.

Because even if it's a dream, my body knows him.

Remembers how to beg.

"Fuck, sweetheart..."

That voice. That gods damned voice.

Sleep-rough and low and wrecked.

The way he used to sound when he woke up hard and needy and didn't bother with good morning, just dragged me to the edge of the bed and took me.

I arch into his touch and I swear I feel his fingers slipping between my folds, dragging through the slick he put there, teasing me until I whimper.

"That's it," August murmurs, nosing against my jaw, kissing up behind my ear. "Still so greedy for me. Still so fucking sweet."

My hips move on instinct, chasing pressure, breath catching as he slides two thick fingers inside me—curling slow, filling me just enough to make my legs tremble.

I clutch the sheets, thighs parting wider, breath breaking apart at the seams.

His mouth finds my throat.

He bites.

Not gentle. Not fairytale. Just mine.

The possessive kind of bite that leaves marks. The kind that told the world whose girl I was, even if he never said it out loud.

I moan into my pillow, helpless and half-asleep, my body cresting on a memory I don't want to miss.

But I do.

Gods, I do.

"Come for me, baby," he growls. "I know that's what you want. I will ruin you for everyone else. You will never be able to fuck another person without thinking of this moment."

And fuck him because he does.

Even in a dream.

Even now.

The orgasm rolls through me like a sin I've already confessed. It's hot and sudden, curling through my spine until I'm trembling, gasping, clenching around nothing.

Nothing.

Because when I open my eyes, I'm alone.

My sheets are damp.

My hand is still between my legs.

My chest aches with the memory and eyes prick hot tears.

I roll onto my back and stare at the ceiling, hating how easy it is to want him.

Hating that I still do.

Wanting him is easy.

Being angry is easier.

And pretending I didn't just come with his name in my mouth?

That's the part I haven't figured out yet. Anger doesn't beg. Anger doesn't remember the way his mouth softened when he said my name. Anger doesn't ache in the quiet.

So I choose anger.

I shove the image of him out of my head, hard and deliberate, like slamming a door.

I don't get to miss someone who made me feel like a rumor.

I don't get to want someone who let me disappear.

I breathe in.

I breathe out.

And when I finally get out of bed, I leave him there, imaginary and fading. Because holding onto the memory hurts more than letting it die.

After the hottest shower I could bear, I dress in something soft and make a pot of coffee.

Lilly's door is closed.

I don't knock, but I leave a note on the counter anyway.

Gone out for a bit.

Be back later.

—F

I don't know if she'll read it.

But it feels worse not to try.

Smith Summer's shop is a few blocks away, tucked between a bakery that always smells like sugar and a closed-down travel agency with sun-faded posters of places people stopped dreaming about years ago.

The bell over the door sings a little jingle when I walk in, and the smell of incense and old books and something faintly sweet wraps around me like a memory that doesn't hurt.

Smith looks up from behind the counter.

"There she is," he says, a smile radiating from his eyes. "You look like you've had a week."

I laugh before I can stop myself. It comes out a little broken. "That's one way to put it."

He nods like that explains everything. "Good chair or judgmental chair?"

"Good chair," I say solemnly.

He pours me tea without asking. He doesn't bombard me with questions either. Just lets me sit, breathe, exist.

The shop is quiet in that gentle, living way. Wind chimes

by the door. Soft music playing low. Dust motes floating with nowhere urgent to be.

Eventually I pull my deck from my bag.

Not the one I've been drawing. The one that taught me how to listen.

I shuffle slowly, letting my hands remember what my head keeps trying to forget: that this is a language too. That meaning doesn't only live in sirens and trauma and emergency codes.

A woman wanders over, curious. Mid-fifties. Soft eyes. Wears too many rings.

"Do you read?" she asks, nodding toward the deck.

"Sometimes," I say. "If you're open to it."

She hesitates, then slides into the chair across from me. The wood scrapes softly. Her hands tremble just enough to give her away as she folds them in her lap.

"I don't really believe in this stuff," she says quickly. "I just...Smith said you were kind."

I smile a little. "You don't have to believe anything. Just breathe."

She does. It takes her a couple tries.

"I won't ask what you want to know," I tell her. "Just think about what feels heavy. The cards are better at talking sideways anyway."

She nods, eyes closing.

I shuffle slowly, listening to the soft whisper of cardstock. When it feels right, I cut the deck and turn the first card.

Two of Wands.

A figure standing between worlds. One foot in what's known, one in what's possible.

The second card is the Eight of Cups.

A person walking away under a dark sky, leaving something behind that once mattered.

The third is The Star.

Naked hope. Wounds exposed to starlight. Healing that doesn't pretend it didn't hurt.

Her breath catches. Just a sound, barely there.

"Tell me what you see," I say.

She stares at the cards like they might blink back.

"The first one looks... stuck," she murmurs. "Like they can see something better but they're scared to leave."

I nod. "And the second?"

She swallows. "That looks like giving up. But not in a bad way. Like... choosing to stop pretending something still fits."

Her eyes lift to the third card and soften.

"That one looks like someone who survived."

Her voice cracks on the word.

I don't rush in. I let the quiet hold her.

Finally she speaks again. "I left my husband six months ago," she says. "We didn't fight. We just... disappeared from each other. Now I'm in this house that still smells like him and I don't know who I am without the shape of him next to me."

Something in my chest shifts in recognition.

"The cards don't say you failed," I tell her. "They say you stood at a door, you walked through it, and now you're standing in the dark long enough for your eyes to adjust."

She wipes at her cheek, embarrassed. "I thought leaving would make it stop hurting."

"Sometimes leaving is what starts the real healing," I say softly. "The Star doesn't show up when everything's fine. It shows up when you're brave enough to be broken in the open."

She nods, slow and shaky.

"I don't know if I can be alone," she whispers.

I glance at the Eight of Cups. At the way the figure walks not toward joy, but toward honesty.

"Being alone isn't the same as being empty," I say. "It's just... quiet enough to hear yourself again."

She sits with that.

So do I.

Because I think of Lilly, moving through our apartment like I'm a piece of furniture. I think of how sometimes space isn't punishment, it's grief trying to breathe. I think of how walking away doesn't always mean abandoning someone. Sometimes it means not breaking each other further.

When she stands to leave, she looks different. Not healed. But... lighter. Like someone who believes she might be.

"Thank you," she says.

I smile. "The stars don't light the whole road. Just the next step."

After she goes, I sit there for a moment, staring at the cards.

Two of Wands. Eight of Cups. The Star.

I think about choices. About walking away. About hoping anyway. The reading feels like it wasn't just for her.

When she leaves, she looks lighter than she came in.

So do I.

Another person sits. Then another. A college kid worried about switching majors. A man who just lost his brother and doesn't know how to exist in a world that kept spinning anyway.

By mid-afternoon, my chest feels different.

Not healed but no longer clenched.

Smith leans against the counter beside me, arms folded, watching the last customer drift out the door.

"You've been giving readings all day," he says. "When's the last time you had one for yourself?"

I blink at him. "I don't really—"

"Sit," he says, already pulling out a chair. "Humor me."

There's something gentle but unmovable in his voice. The kind of tone that doesn't argue.

I sit.

He takes the deck from me, hands sure but respectful. He knows these cards matter. Smith shuffles slowly, eyes on me instead of the deck.

"Don't tell me what you're worried about," he says. "Just think it."

I snort softly. "That's... a lot of material."

He smiles. "Good."

He cuts the deck and lays three cards.

He studies them longer than I expect.

Then he looks up at me. "Why are you stressing about money?"

I laugh once, startled. "I'm not. I mean, I am, because everyone is, but—"

"You're worried about using it," he says. "Not about having it."

My mouth opens. Then closes.

"That's... weirdly specific," I say.

He taps the table. "You don't think you deserve it."

My chest tightens.

"I think you're afraid that if you use what your mom left you, you're somehow... spending her."

The words land exactly where it hurts.

I swallow. "It feels like turning her into groceries. Or rent. Or a mistake."

Smith nods like this is a language he understands.

"Your mom didn't leave you money," he says quietly. "She left you time. Options. Safety. She left you room to breathe."

My eyes burn.

He gestures at the cards. "These say you're standing at the edge of something wide open. You could stay where you are. You could leave. You could go back to school. You could read cards. You could do something you haven't even imagined yet."

He shrugs lightly. "The world is obnoxiously available to you."

I let out a shaky laugh. "That sounds exhausting."

"It is," he agrees. "Because no one gets to tell you what you're supposed to want. You have to figure that out yourself."

I stare at the cards. At possibility sitting there like it's patient.

"I don't know what I want yet," I admit. "I just know dispatch... it isn't the whole answer anymore."

"That doesn't mean it was wrong," Smith says. "It just means it was a chapter. Not the whole book."

Silence stretches between us, soft and thinking.

He gathers the cards, sliding them back into the deck. "Life's short," he says simply. "If you're not happy, change something. It doesn't have to be everything. Just... something."

I nod.

The house is quiet when I get home.

Lilly's shoes are by the door but her light is off.

I set my bag down and sit on the couch, letting the silence settle.

I don't know if I'll stay in this house.

I don't know if I'll stay in this job.

I don't know if August will ever stop feeling like a bruise that looks like a memory.

But I know this: I'm allowed to want a life that doesn't hurt all the time.

I'm allowed to take up space without apologizing for it.

I'm allowed to leave someday, when I'm ready. On my own terms.

For now, I stay.

I breathe.

And I let myself imagine, just a little, that someday my life might feel less like survival and more like choosing.

TWENTY-EIGHT
FLORENCE

THE LINE OPENS in my ear like a door that never fully latched.

No voice.

No greeting.

Just sound. Thin, muffled, wrong.

A low scrape, like fabric dragging across tile. A breath that isn't quite a breath. Something metallic tapping once, twice then stopping.

I straighten in my chair so fast the wheels squeak.

"9-1-1," I say, calm on instinct. "This line is recorded. What is the address of your emergency?"

Silence.

But not empty silence.

It's a held hush. The kind that means someone is alive on the other end and trying very hard not to be.

I glance at my screen. Incoming location pings in near Route Seven, Miller's Creek Gas & Mart.

There's not a lot out there. Just a dark stretch of road and that one bright rectangle of fluorescent lights people mistake for safety. Pumps. A convenience store. Always open too late. Always staffed by one exhausted clerk who knows everyone's cigarette brand by heart.

My pulse tightens.

"Okay," I say, dropping my voice without meaning to, because the line is telling me how to speak. "If you can hear me, you don't have to talk. Just listen."

A faint sound of a shaky inhale.

"Can you hear me?" I ask. "If yes, press any button on your phone one time."

I wait, counting in my head.

One... two... three...

A soft beep.

One press.

My lungs unlock a fraction.

"Okay," I murmur, and my voice stays even like I'm not suddenly aware of my heartbeat in my fingertips. "You're doing great. Stay quiet. Don't hang up unless you have to."

I type fast with one hand while my voice stays steady.

OPEN LINE 911. POSSIBLE ROBBERY IN PROGRESS. CALLER INSIDE. USING BUTTON PRESS YES/NO.

"Now," I continue, "I'm going to ask you questions you can answer with button presses."

I swallow, already feeling that familiar burn behind my sternum of adrenaline that wants to become panic.

"One press for YES," I say. "Two presses for NO. Okay?"

A beat.

Beep—yes.

Good.

"Are you in danger right now?" I ask.

The pause stretches. I can hear a faint rustle, like a phone being repositioned in a shaking hand.

Beep—yes.

The hairs on my arms rise.

"Okay," I whisper, and my voice stays calm like I'm not picturing worst-case scenarios in high definition. "Are you inside the gas station on Route Seven?"

Beep—yes.

"Are there other people inside with you?" I ask.

Beep—yes.

"Is someone threatening people?" I ask.

Beep—yes.

My stomach turns cold.

"Is there a weapon?" I ask, already typing WEAPON before the answer comes.

Beep—yes.

I pivot into tone-out mode, fingers moving like muscle memory.

"Units respond. Armed robbery in progress, Miller's Creek Gas & Mart, Route Seven. Open line 9-1-1. Caller inside, unable to speak. Weapon reported. Use caution."

The radio crackles back immediately.

"Unit Two responding."

"Unit thirteen en route."

A half-second later, "Unit One responding."

The voice hits the air like a blade.

August.

My throat tightens so fast it almost closes.

I don't let it touch my voice.

I don't let it touch my hands.

I don't let it touch anything except the part of me that is quietly, violently aware that the man I ended things with, who I have not heard from in a week, is about to walk into my nightmare.

And the caller...

The caller is already inside it.

"Okay," I say softly into the headset. "Listen to me. You are not alone. Help is coming. I need more information to keep you safe."

I keep my words simple. One idea at a time. No panic syllables.

"Are you able to hide?" I ask. "One press for yes, two for no."

Beep—yes.

"Good," I whisper. "Stay hidden. Stay low. Don't move unless you have to."

I take a breath and aim for what I need most: identity. Not because it matters for paperwork. Because it changes how I talk. Because it changes how I fight.

"Okay," I say. "I'm going to ask a different kind of question. Answer with button presses."

I wet my lips.

"Do you know me?" I ask quietly. "One press yes, two presses no."

The line goes so still I can hear my own blood.

Then—*beep*—yes.

My stomach drops in a slow, sick roll.

Okay. Okay.

"Are you calling from Townsend Harbor?" I ask, voice careful. "One yes, two no."

Beep.

Yes.

My fingers go colder on the keyboard.

"Are you someone who comes to my house on Monday nights?" I ask before I can stop myself, because that's where my brain goes when panic tries to turn into grief.

A pause.

Then a tiny beep.

Yes.

My chest compresses. The air feels too thin.

"Okay," I whisper. "I'm going to narrow it down. Stay with me."

I swallow hard.

"Are you Lilly?"

One press for yes.

I wait.

The silence holds for a heartbeat too long.

Then, finally, a *beep*.

Yes.

For a second I can't feel my hands.

For a second the room around me goes distant like I'm underwater. My console, the fluorescent lights, the other dispatchers, the coffee that tastes like burned patience all fade to nothing.

I force myself back into my body.

Back into my job.

Back into now.

"Okay," I say softly, like my voice can become a shield if I keep it gentle enough. "Lilly. I hear you."

I do not say her name again. Not yet. Not where someone could hear it on the other end.

I type with precision so sharp it aches.

CALLER IDENTIFIED: LILLY. FRIEND/ROOMMATE. KEEP ID CONFIDENTIAL ON AIR.

"Lilly," I say, keeping my tone flat and controlled because I know what fear does to sound. "You are doing exactly what you should. Don't make noise. I'm going to ask questions. You answer with button presses."

A shaky exhale flutters across the line like she's trying not to become a sound.

"Can you see the person with the weapon from where you are?" I ask.

Beep.

Yes.

"Is the weapon a gun?" I ask.

Beep.

Yes.

"Handgun?" I ask. "One press yes, two no."

Beep.

Yes.

My mouth goes dry.

"Is the person with the gun inside the store with you?" I ask.

Beep.

Yes.

"Is it a man? One press for man, two for woman."

Beep.

Man.

"Is he alone?" I ask.

Beep beep.

No.

My blood goes ice.

"How many suspects?" I ask. "One beep for one. Two beeps for two. Three beeps for three or more."

Beep beep.

Two.

I key my radio without letting any emotion rise into my throat.

"Units responding to Miller's Creek: handgun confirmed. Two suspects. Caller is hiding inside. Use caution."

"Copy," Unit Two says.

A half-second later: "Unit One, ETA two minutes."

August's voice is crisp, controlled, carved from something hard.

It hurts, because my body remembers him soft.

It hurts, because my mouth remembers his.

It hurts, because I remember his arm heavy over my waist, breath against my hair like the world couldn't touch me while he was there.

And it hurts because none of that matters.

Not like this.

Beside me, Ruth shifts.

She's on nights tonight, same as me, because she says she likes the quiet. Except there are Shakespearian rules about saying the word quiet in a dispatch center.

Ruth's head tilts toward my screen.

And then she goes still.

Not startled. Not loud.

Just... locked in. Like she's just seen a ghost. "Flo," she says under her breath.

I keep my eyes on the call.

"Yeah?" I say, clipped, professional. Like my ribs aren't tightening around my lungs.

Ruth leans closer, reading the phone number on the screen like it's an obituary.

"That's..." Her voice catches, barely there. "That's Lilly's number."

The room tilts.

No.

No no no—

My brain rejects it so hard it sparks.

Lilly is supposed to be at home. Or at least somewhere

safe. Somewhere with lights and people. Somewhere that isn't Route Seven in the dark.

Ruth's fingers curl around the edge of her desk like she needs something solid to hold her upright.

"I know that number," she whispers. "I know it."

My mouth goes numb.

I don't get to panic.

Not here.

Not now.

I lean into procedure like it's a railing.

I turn my voice back into the headset, softer now, slower, like I'm speaking to an animal in the road so it doesn't bolt.

"Okay," I say. "Listen carefully. You're doing great. If your name is Lilly... press one time for yes."

The line holds its breath.

Then—*beep.*

Ruth makes a sound beside me, small and involuntary, like grief trying to claw out of her throat.

My fingers move like they belong to someone else.

RP: LILLY HART.

I don't let my face change. I don't let the room see me crack.

"Okay," I whisper into the phone, and my voice is steady only because it has to be. "Lilly. Stay hidden. Keep the phone close."

Her breathing trembles across the line, thin and fast, like she's trying to make herself smaller by breathing less.

I can hear muffled voices now. A man's voice, low and aggressive, words slurred or swallowed by distance. Another voice whimpering.

Then a sharp impact.

Flesh on something hard.

A yelp cut off too fast.

My stomach flips.

I key the radio, tone flat.

"Advise: sounds of possible assault heard in background."

"Copy," August says instantly.

I dip my voice lower, closer to the mic, like I can shrink sound into safety.

"Lilly," I whisper. The line catches a tiny scrape.

Like fabric shifting across a floor.

My nails bite into my palm.

"Where's the rest of the damn money?" a man snarls.

The clerk makes a sound that turns my blood cold—half plea, half sob.

Lilly's breath comes sharp in my ear.

"I shouldn't have—" she whispers, so faint I almost miss it. "I just wanted..."

"Stop," I say gently. "You did nothing wrong."

The words land and I feel them for what they are.

Uncomplicated truth.

Ruth is crying silently beside me, hand over her mouth, eyes fixed on my screen like if she stares hard enough she can pull her daughter out through the pixels.

I can't look at her.

If I look at her, I'll fall apart.

"Lilly," I say, "police are outside. They're coming in soon. You stay hidden until an officer physically reaches you and tells you it's safe."

A shaky exhalation.

"Then you do what you have to do to live," I say. "But we're going to try very hard to make sure you're safe. They're almost there Lilly."

A sound escapes her but she crushes it down.

Heavy, aimless, angry footsteps can be heard.

A man mutters, irritated.

"Where the hell did she go?"

My vision narrows.

I taste fear.

I taste old fear.

My sister's last call, the silence afterward.

My mother's last whisper, the sound that split my life in two.

I force it down.

This is not then.

This is now.

Now means I can do something.

Now means I keep the line.

The man's voice is suddenly closer, sharper.

"Hey," he snaps. "Who's back there?"

Lilly's breathing turns to ice.

I go so still my spine aches.

The footsteps come closer, each one thudding through the phone like a countdown.

"Come out," he says. "I saw you go back there."

A pause.

"You think you're smart?"

I press my radio mic, voice controlled.

"Unit One, suspect actively searching rear aisles near shelving. RP in immediate danger."

"Copy," August answers instantly.

Over the phone line, shelving rattles. Something metal clinks.

Lilly makes a tiny involuntary sound.

"Stay still," I breathe. "Stay still."

The man's voice rises, impatient.

"Come on," he says. "Don't make this harder."

Closer.

Closer.

"There you are."

My blood goes ice in an instant.

Lilly's breath snaps into a broken gasp.

"No," she whispers.

He laughs once, low.

"You calling somebody?" he says.

Lilly tries to speak, tries to deny, but fear makes her voice thin and useless.

"I didn't— I didn't—"

"Give me that."

The words crack like a whip.

There's scuffling. Fabric. The phone jostling as his hand grabs for it. Her whisper breaks into a plea.

"Stop!"

I lunge forward in my chair like I can physically reach her.

The man's voice slams into the microphone, close enough that my skin crawls.

"What the hell is this?" he growls.

My mouth goes dry.

I press my radio mic, fingers that do not get to shake.

"Unit One, suspect has located RP. Repeat, suspect has located RP."

The line explodes with noise. Lilly's crying, the man swearing, the clerk sobbing somewhere distant.

A hard thud, like her shoulder hits shelving.

Then a sharp crack of plastic.

The phone hits the floor.

For one sick heartbeat, I can still hear her thin, animalistic whimpering.

Then the call cuts out.

Dead air.

No breath.

No muffled sound.

No Lilly.

Just the cold, blank hiss of an ended connection.

For a heartbeat, I can't move.

I stare at the screen like if I will it hard enough, the line will reopen.

Like if I sit perfectly still, the universe will undo what it just did.

Ruth makes a sound beside me, raw, strangled before she swallows it whole, because she's still on shift. Because she's still a dispatcher. Because the world doesn't care that her daughter might be dying.

I slam the callback button.

It rings.

Once.

Twice.

No answer.

My throat tightens until it hurts.

My fingers fly to the keyboard.

CALL DISCONNECTED. CALLBACK NO ANSWER.

I press the radio mic, voice razor-steady only because it has to be.

"Emergency traffic only. All units responding Miller's Creek— line went dead. Suspect had physical contact with RP."

The channel crackles instantly.

"Unit One, copy. Moving."

My heart splits open.

Because the last sound I heard from Lilly was fear.

Because the line went dead.

Because I am sitting safe in a chair while the man I ended things with runs into a building to save the woman who binds us all.

I stare at the blank screen, listening to the radio, listening to my own breath, listening to the awful silence where Lilly's voice used to be.

And I don't let myself cry.

Not yet.

Not while there's still a chance she's alive.

Not while the story is still moving.

Not while Unit One is going in.

TWENTY-NINE
AUGUST

THE RADIO CRACKS to life while I'm stopped at a light, hip aching. I'm supposed to be on desk duty but I couldn't sit there listening to her over the radio.

"All units be advised, armed robbery in progress, Miller's Creek Gas & Go. Silent RP. Stand by for updates."

Silent RP.

My hand tightens on the wheel.

I hit the MDT screen, pulling up the call before the Florence even finishes the tone-out. The system lags for half a second, just long enough for my reflection to stare back at me —eyes too hard, jaw locked, a man who has no right to be afraid anymore.

The call populates.

Location: MILLER'S CREEK GAS & GO

Type: ROBBERY IN PROGRESS/ OPEN LINE

RP: LILLY HEARAT 23 YO F

My chest stops.

Not figuratively.

Literally.

Like someone reached inside and shut something inside of me off.

I stare at the name like it's a mistake. Like the system glitched. Like if I blink hard enough it'll resolve into something else.

Not my daughter.

Not Lilly.

Not...

I slam the accelerator.

The siren comes alive like a wounded animal, blue and red tearing the night open.

Mentally I pull up a map of the inside of Miller's Creek Gas & Go in my mind.

Candy and chips on the left. Drinks and toiletries on the right. Counter straight ahead. Hot case that always smells like burnt roller dogs. Bathrooms in the back corner. Storage room door near the rear aisle.

And somewhere inside it, a girl named Lilly is hiding.

I don't know who's running the call. I don't know whose hands are on the keyboard right now. I just know someone is trying to keep her alive.

CAD updates start appearing as I drive.

RP possibly hiding in rear aisle.

Suspect armed with handgun.

RP using button responses.

My hands go numb.

Button responses.

Someone is smart enough, calm enough, steady enough to get Lilly through this without a sound.

"Dispatch," I key up, voice already breaking through protocol. "Unit One—confirm RP is Lilly Hart."

A pause.

"Unit One, affirmative."

Not like this.

Not on a call sheet.

Not tied to the words armed robbery.

More notes populate.

RP confirmed inside store.

RP remaining hidden

I imagine her exactly where I used to picture monsters as a kid—behind something thin, praying it's enough. Shelves. Cardboard. Cheap metal.

I cut across an intersection without fully stopping. Horns scream. Someone yells. None of it registers.

Another update:

SUSPECT YELLING, AGITATED

WEAPONS

SUS W/ CONFIRMED HAND GUN

I say her name out loud like it can travel faster than the cruiser.

"Lilly."

Hold on.

Hold on.

The radio crackles.

"Units respond Miller's Creek Gas & Go, robbery in progress, silent RP, suspect armed."

Voices come back.

"Unit 12 en route."

"Unit 04 copy."

I'm already too close to care about backup.

Then the update that splits my spine open.

RP LINE DISCONNECTED

No.

No, no.

I brake hard enough to make the cruiser fishtail before I correct. My hip flares like fire. I don't care.

Line disconnected means one of two things: She hung up because she had to or she couldn't anymore.

I'm a block out.

I don't remember deciding to open the door. I don't remember thinking. I only remember motion.

I tear into the parking lot of Miller's Creek so fast gravel kicks up under my tires. The store is lit too bright, all fluorescent glare and fake normal. A pickup at pump two. A minivan idling at pump four like someone ran inside and never came back.

Blue and red lights cut across the gas station windows as I swing in hard and bail out of the car before it's even fully stopped.

Gun out.

Breath loud.

World narrow.

And somewhere inside, my daughter is either hiding or already found.

My entire body goes cold.

A flash hits me, wrong and bright.

A closet door.

Me at seven years old, knees pulled to my chest, listening to the house break apart one slammed cabinet at a time. Listening to my father's voice turn into thunder. Listening to my mother breathe like she's trying not to become a target.

I blink hard, dragging myself back to the present.

I am not that kid.

Lilly is not trapped the way my mother was trapped.

Protocol collides with panic.

Training says slow down. Set a perimeter. Wait for backup. Don't rush in alone.

My blood says get her out. Get her out. GET HER OUT.

That's the terror of it. When the line goes quiet, your brain fills the empty space with the worst ending.

The front doors of the convenience store are shut.

But the OPEN sign is still on.

That's wrong. That's wrong.

My breath is too loud inside my own head.

"Unit One on scene," I snap into the radio. "Set perimeter.

Approach from cover. Suspect armed, unknown. Possible hostage inside."

I don't say her name over the channel. I don't say my daughter is inside. I don't say that if anyone drags their feet I will go feral.

I move along the side of the building, staying low near the windows, trying to catch a glimpse inside without silhouetting myself.

Through the glass I see shelves.

Candy.

Chips.

A narrow line of aisle that disappears into the back.

No movement.

No people.

Just the hum of fluorescent lights like the world is pretending everything is fine.

My heart is hammering hard enough to rattle my ribs.

A sound from inside.

A thud.

A muffled curse.

I freeze.

My mind maps the store again. The rear aisle. The storage room door. The back corner.

Lilly.

Where would she hide?

She's smart. She's cautious. She's not a kid anymore, but she's still my kid. She knows to go small. She knows to go quiet. She knows where blind spots are because she grew up watching me walk rooms like it was instinct.

I hear my own voice in my head from years ago: If you can't get out, find cover. If you can't find cover, find concealment. Breathe through your nose. Don't move unless you have to.

The back door of the store is locked from the inside. Metal. Solid. I test it anyway but there's no give.

Front entry is glass.

Front entry is exposure.

Front entry is also the fastest way in.

I glance over the hood of my cruiser and see Unit Thirteen pulling in, lights washing the lot.

Good. Backup.

But not enough.

Not fast enough.

I make the call.

I come around the front, using the soda machine as cover, rifle up. I angle toward the entrance and look through the glass.

And there is movement.

A man near the counter. Hood up. Gloved hands. A gun angled downward like he's bored with the fact that he's holding someone's life.

The clerk is behind the counter, face pale, hands up.

The suspect barks something. The clerk flinches.

Then the suspect turns his head, like he heard something.

Like he sensed something.

His gaze flicks toward the rear aisle.

My blood freezes.

Because if he saw her.

"Unit One to Unit Thirteen," I say low into the mic, "I have visual on suspect. Counter area. Clerk present. Suspect attention drawn to rear aisle."

The response comes back, breathless. "Copy, One. We're stacking at front."

I take one more breath.

Then I shove the door open.

The bell above it jingles.

Of course it does.

Everything about this place is designed to announce you.

The suspect's head snaps up.

His gun rises.

Time stretches.

There are a thousand decisions in one second.

I step in, rifle trained, voice like a blade.

"Drop it."

He swings the gun toward me.

And in the corner of my vision, behind the shelf line, something shifts.

A dark braid.

A cardigan.

A flash of wide eyes.

Lilly.

She's crouched low.

The suspect sees it.

His attention splits.

And I know, in my bones, that if I don't end this right now, he will.

"Gun!" I shout, and the word is a command to the universe.

The suspect jerks, and his gun fires.

The sound is deafening inside the small store.

The shot punches into the cooler behind me, glass exploding, soda spraying like shrapnel.

I fire back.

Two rounds.

Clean. Controlled.

He goes down hard, collapsing near the endcap display of beef jerky as if the world just unplugged him.

For a fraction of a second, everything is still.

Then the clerk screams.

Lilly makes a sound that rips my chest open.

And I'm moving, rifle down, eyes scanning, training screaming at me to secure the weapon, confirm the threat, don't tunnel vision.

But I can't not see her.

I can't not go to her.

"Lilly!" I shout, already crossing the aisle.

She's shaking so hard her whole body trembles. She tries to stand and her ankle gives out. Pain flashes across her face, sharp and bright.

"Don't move," I tell her, dropping to a knee beside her. My hands are gentle even as my pulse is a siren. "It's okay. It's over. You're okay."

She stares at me without recognition.

I'm not Dad right now.

And she whispers, "Florence..."

The name hits me like a bullet.

My throat tightens.

My voice comes out rough. "Is she here?"

Lilly's eyes fill. She shakes her head. "She—" Her breath catches. "She was talking to me. And then, he—"

Her voice fractures.

I grip her shoulder, careful, grounding. "I know. I know. You did everything right."

Behind me, Unit Twelve bursts in, weapon up, shouting commands. "Hands! Show me your hands!"

"Suspect down," I bark, pointing. "Weapon on floor," I point to it.

They move fast, cuffing him even as he groans.

EMS is already being toned. I can hear it in the radio squawk. The world re-expands beyond my own fear.

I look back at my daughter.

She's alive.

She's breathing.

And my chest aches with the near-miss of it.

"Where are you hurt?" I ask her, scanning for blood? bruising? shock?

She swallows. "My ankle. I think I," Her voice wobbles. "I fell when I tried to move. He—he grabbed me—"

Rage detonates in my veins.

I force it down.

Not now. Not in front of her.

"You're okay," I repeat, like I can speak it into permanence. "You're okay."

Her mouth twists, and suddenly she's not just scared, she's furious, humiliated, shattered.

"I called 9-1-1," she whispers like it's an accusation against herself. "I couldn't..."

"You did exactly what you needed to do," I say. "You saved these people and yourself."

Her eyes flick up to mine.

And for the first time since the restaurant, I see something in her expression that isn't just disgust.

It's pain.

And underneath it is love, despite herself.

The ambulance siren wails outside.

The world floods back in.

I reach for my mic, throat still tight.

"Dispatch," I say, voice steady by force. "Unit One. RP is conscious and breathing. EMS taking over. One in custody. Suspect is Benjamin Marvel, DOB eleven-zero-two-eighty-nine."

There's a beat of silence on the channel. The whole room holds its breath.

Then Florence's voice comes through, a little thick, like she's holding herself together with her bare hands.

"Copy, One. Benjamin A. Marvel, DOB eleven-zero-two-nineteen-eighty-nine. Active warrant for robbery. EMS en route."

I close my eyes for half a second at the sound of her. At the way she says it with a thread underneath that I feel in my bones.

Florence listened to the line go dead.

She just had to sit there helpless while my daughter disappeared into silence.

And she still sounds like dispatch.

Still sounds like control.

Like strength without armor.

The paramedics push in with a stretcher, voices brisk. They assess Lilly, splint her ankle, ask her questions. She answers in a daze, eyes locked on me like I'm the only solid thing in the room.

I help lift her onto the gurney.

My hands shake as I smooth her hair back.

"Hey," I murmur, leaning close so only she can hear. "You're okay."

Her eyes shine.

"Florence..." she says again, quieter, like she's saying it to herself.

And I understand.

I understand in the most brutal way.

Because I am standing here in the aftermath, gun smoke in the air, my daughter alive.

And the reason she's alive is the woman I pushed away.

The stretcher rolls out.

The ambulance doors yawn open like a mouth.

Lilly grips my wrist before they load her in, fingers tight.

"Don't," she whispers, panicked. "Don't leave."

My chest caves.

"I'm right here," I promise. "I'm right here."

The doors start to swing shut.

And I know, deep and certain, this is going to change everything.

Because I almost lost my daughter.

And Florence is the reason I didn't.

The ambulance doors close with a final, Harbor clang, and the sound hits me like a judge's gavel.

Done.

Over.

She's inside. Strapped down. Alive.

Alive.

I stand in the wash of red and blue lights for a second too long, watching the rig rock slightly as the paramedic shifts weight. I can still feel Lilly's grip on my wrist, the panic in it, like her fingers were the only thing keeping her from floating away.

"Cheif."

Turner's voice cuts through the fog. He's stepping up beside me, eyes hard, scanning the lot, scanning me.

"You hit?" he asks.

I blink. It takes effort to remember he's talking about bullets and blood and not the fact that my entire life just tried to cave in on itself.

"No," I get out. "I'm good."

He gives me a look that says *you look like you're about to shatter into pieces*, but he doesn't push it. He glances through the open front doors of the store. Glass glitters on the floor, the hot case still spinning its sad little rollers like nothing happened.

"Suspect's breathing," he says, voice flat. "He's gonna wish he wasn't, but he is."

"Good," I say, and the word is ice.

Because it should've never gotten to this. Should've never been her. Should've never been the sound of a gunshot in a place where my daughter buys coffee and gas and little packs of gum.

I turn back toward the store and the reality of it slams down again.

The suspect is on the floor, cuffed, bleeding from the shoulder where one of my rounds caught him. One of my officers is holding pressure with a wad of gauze, face blank and professional. The clerk, only a kid really, barely old enough to legally sell cigarettes, sits behind the counter with his hands over his head, shaking so hard his whole body trembles.

And there's blood.

Not much. Not a pool. But enough to make the world feel different.

Enough to remind me that this is the part where the adrenaline starts to drain and the what-ifs get loud.

I step back inside. The bell jingles again like a goddamn joke.

"Chief," Officer Delaney says, eyes flicking to me. "We've got the weapon secured. Ruger. It looks like a nine. Magazine half full."

"Good," I say.

He nods. Someone else is already snapping photos, gloves on, movements deliberate.

I walk past the suspect and force myself not to look at his face too long. He's just a man. A man who made choices that put my daughter on the floor behind a shelf praying not to be seen. A man who turned a normal Tuesday into a nightmare.

I keep moving.

The rear aisle is narrow, shelves cramped, and I hate how ordinary everything looks back here—cheap shampoo, cleaning supplies, dusty boxes of candy bars, little travel-size bottles of aspirin. There's a broken display near the bottom shelf, chips spilled like someone dropped their hands and ran.

I see the space where Lilly must've been crouched.

The angle behind the shelf line.

The thin strip of shadow where she hid herself small.

I press two fingers to the bridge of my nose.

Get it together.

You can fall apart later.

Not here. Not now.

Turner follows me into the aisle, posture careful. "You want me to take command and you step out?"

"No," I say immediately.

He studies me. "August."

The way he says my name, without rank, tells me he's not asking as an officer right now. He's asking as the man who's watched me carry too much for too long without dropping it. He's stepping up when I should be with Lilly right now.

I swallow. "If I step out right now, I'm going to do something stupid."

Turner's jaw tightens. "Like what?"

"Like drive after the ambulance and tear the doors off," I admit, voice low. "Like go to the hospital and stand in the waiting room until they kick me out. Like... like try to fix this with my hands instead of letting the world do its job."

He nods once, like he understands. "Okay. Then do your job. Let it keep you upright."

I exhale through my nose. It's the closest thing to gratitude I can manage.

We return to the front.

The clerk's eyes lift as I approach, red-rimmed, terrified, trying to hold himself together.

He looks at my uniform, my badge, my face, and something shifts in him. Relief. Fear. Recognition.

"Sir?" he croaks.

"You're safe," I tell him, firm and clear. "You're safe. EMS is going to check you, and then we'll get your statement when you're ready."

He nods too fast. "I— I didn't."

"You handled that really well," I say without thinking.

His eyes flick up. "I didn't even see her at first," he whispers. "I thought it was just me and him."

My throat tightens. "You did what you could. You stayed alive. That matters."

His breath shudders out. He nods again, slower this time, like he's trying to believe me.

Outside, the ambulance pulls away, lights flashing, swallowing my kid into the dark.

My phone buzzes in my pocket. And on instinct, I flinch. For half a second my body believes it's going to be Florence. Like my brain is still stupid enough to hope.

It's not.

A text from the watch commander: *Media scanner picked up call. Keep scene tight.*

Of course they did.

Townsend Harbor doesn't let anything stay private. Not when the chief is involved. Not when there's blood and sirens and an ambulance.

Not when the rumor mill has already tasted this week.

I pocket the phone fast enough to make the case creak.

"Chief," Delaney calls. "We're ready to transport suspect."

"Good," I say. "Get him to the hospital first, then to holding. Make sure he's medically cleared. No one lays a hand on him unless he moves first."

Delaney gives me a look and nods.

They haul the suspect up. He groans, trying to play weak, trying to play victim. He looks at me as they drag him past the counter.

"You shot me," he slurs, like I'm supposed to feel something.

I step close enough for him to hear me over the noise and the officers and the crackle of radios.

"You were aiming at a girl," I say quietly. "You're lucky you can still talk."

His eyes flicker, fear, calculation, rage. He spits on the floor.

Delaney shoves him forward.

I watch the suspect get loaded into a cruiser. The door slams. Another neat, final sound.

Then I turn away before I do something I can't take back.

My radio crackles again, dispatch channel busy with units clearing, additional officers checking the surrounding blocks for any secondary suspect, any getaway vehicle, any accomplice.

I force myself to key up.

"Dispatch," I say.

A beat.

Then Florence's voice, still controlled, still professional, still that steady thing that makes people survive.

"Go ahead, 1."

Just hearing her say my call sign is enough to punch air out of my lungs.

Because she's not supposed to be in my ear anymore.

Not like this.

Not after the way I watched her walk away.

Not after my own stupid mouth made it sound like she was nothing.

And yet here she is.

Holding the channel like she's holding the world.

"Code Four," I report. "Suspect in custody. EMS transported RP. No further threat."

"Copy, One. Code Four. Units can clear."

A pause. Tiny. Almost nothing.

But I hear it.

The faint thickness in her voice she's fighting.

The seam in her control.

I swallow hard. My thumb presses too tight against the mic.

"Dispatch," I say again.

"Go ahead."

My heart is hammering. My brain is running a thousand directions. I choose the only thing I can say on an open channel without breaking rules or breaking myself.

"Good work," I manage.

There's another pause. Longer this time.

And when Florence answers, her voice is soft in a way that doesn't belong on a public frequency.

"Copy," she says. Professional word. Human tone.

But it's not just her job.

It was her being there. With Lilly. When I couldn't be.

The radio clicks off.

I stand in the middle of the lot, the store's fluorescent glow behind me, and the cold air hits my lungs like punishment.

My hands are starting to tremble as the adrenaline fades.

I've been trained not to show it, but my body doesn't care about training. My body remembers what it felt like to see Lilly's braid behind the shelf and know I was one second away from losing her.

I walk to my cruiser on autopilot. Pop the trunk. Pull out the first aid kit and the orange cones.

Busy work.

Keep moving.

Don't think.

But the thinking comes anyway.

I lean my forehead against the roof of the cruiser, eyes closed, breath slow.

A flash of the past hits me without permission. Me at ten years old, holding my mother's wrist after my father stormed out, feeling her pulse like I could anchor it, like I could keep the world from happening to us if I just held tight enough.

I promised myself then, I will never be the reason someone is afraid in their own home. I will never be the reason someone goes quiet and small.

And yet, I've done it.

Not with fists or shouting. Not with broken plates. But with silence. With fear. With the choices I made after the restaurant. With my cowardice in the station.

With my instinct to deny instead of protect.

I straighten up and open my door. The MDT glows. The call still sits there in the log, like the system is refusing to let it go.

RP: LILLY HART.

I stare at it until my eyes burn.

Then I click into the notes field and start typing because if I don't put something down, my hands will keep shaking.

Words. Facts. Timeline. Everything clean. Everything clinical.

Because if I make it clinical, it can't hurt as much.

It doesn't work.

My phone buzzes again.

This time it's a hospital number.

I answer on the first ring, voice tight. "Calder."

"Mr. Calder, this is Jefferson County ER. Your daughter—"

My breath catches so hard my vision flickers.

"She's here," the nurse continues quickly, calm. "She's doing well. We're evaluating her ankle and wrist for a possible fracture, likely a sprain, but we're doing imaging to be sure. She's asking for you."

I close my eyes.

"I'm on my way," I say, already moving.

I hang up and stare at my dash for one second longer.

Because my next step is going to matter.

The hospital means Ruth will be there. As will the messy reality of our shared past.

And it also means Lilly, hurt, scared, angry, but alive.

And somewhere in all of it is Florence, sitting behind the console, headset on, voice steady, doing her job while her heart breaks.

I want to call her.

I want to say her name like a prayer and tell her I'm sorry and thank you and I was wrong and I don't know how to live in a world where I lose you.

But I don't.

Because I don't get to use my fear as a reason to drag her back into my orbit.

Not like that.

Not when I already made her feel like a rumor.

I start the engine.

The siren is off now. The emergency is over.

But the aftermath is going to be worse.

As I pull out of the lot, the store shrinking behind me, I realize something with brutal clarity. Florence didn't just keep Lilly alive tonight.

She kept me alive too.

Because if my daughter had died in that store, I would have never forgiven myself.

And the worst part is, I would have deserved it.

I grip the wheel hard enough my knuckles ache.

The road to the hospital stretches ahead, dark and narrow.

And for the first time in a week, the question isn't whether I can fix what I broke.

It's whether I'm finally brave enough to face it.

To face Lilly.

To face Ruth.

I reach for my phone and dictate a text.

August: Can we talk?

The hospital lights appear in the distance like a promise.

Or a reckoning.

And I drive straight toward them.

THIRTY
FLORENCE

MY VOICE SOUNDS NORMAL. Which might be the scariest part of this, because inside, something inside of me is ripping itself loose.

I sit there for two more calls. I don't remember them. My hands move, my mouth speaks, my brain floats somewhere above my body watching me pretend to be alive.

When I clear the last one, my vision blurs so suddenly I think I'm going blind.

I hit unavailable.

I don't tell anyone where I'm going.

I just stand up.

My legs wobble like they forgot what they're for. I make it halfway down the hall before my face crumples and the tears start pouring out of me like someone turned a faucet.

Thank gods Ruth left already.

I shove into the bathroom and lock myself in the far stall like I'm fifteen again and hiding from a world that feels too big to survive.

My back hits the wall and I slide down until I'm on the floor.

And then I break.

Not pretty crying.

Not quiet crying.

This is the kind of crying that feels like something inside you is trying to claw its way out. Carnivores butterflies hatched in my stomach and they're hungry.

I press my fist into my mouth to keep from screaming.

Lilly's voice is still in my ears.

My mom's voice overlaps it in my head, soft and shaking from years ago, bleeding into now like time doesn't care what it ruins.

I can't do this, baby.

August's face flashes next, except I can see the blood on his shirt, eyes wide with shock when he got shot. The way my hands wouldn't stop shaking after. Begging the world to let him live.

My sister, oh gods, my sister—I bite down on my fist harder.

And now Lilly.

Now her.

The world starts to tilt.

Not like dizziness exactly, more like the floor is quietly sliding out from under reality.

My hands go numb.

Then my arms.

Then my lips start tingling because they're not mine anymore.

I try to breathe and my chest won't open.

It's like there's a belt around my ribs and someone is pulling it tighter, notch by notch.

"No," I whisper. "No, no, no—"

Air won't come in right.

It comes in sharp and wrong, shallow like I'm sipping it through a straw.

My heart slams so hard it hurts.

My vision tunnels. The edges of the world turn gray.

This is it, my brain says calmly.

This is how I die.

I clutch my shirt at my chest like I can hold my heart still.

"I'm okay," I whisper, even though no one is listening. "I'm okay. I'm okay."

I'm anything but, okay.

My hands curl into claws. My jaw locks so tight it aches.

I try to think of something solid. Something real.

The smell of August's coffee.

Lilly's stupid cereal box jokes.

My mom's hands on my hair when I was little.

None of it sticks.

Everything is slipping through me.

My breaths turn into little broken sounds. My throat closes like it's trying to protect me from air.

The room feels far away.

My body feels wrong.

My thoughts scatter like birds.

I slide sideways without meaning to.

My cheek hits the cold tile.

That feels important. Like I should care.

Then even that fades.

The world folds in on itself and goes dark.

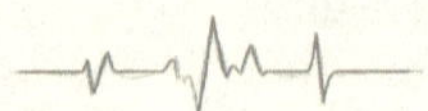

"Florence? Florence. Hey, hey, can you hear me?"

A voice swims into me from far away.

Hands on my shoulders.

My head lolls.

"Call EMS!" someone shouts. "She's not responding!"

"No," I croak, or try to. It comes out like air leaking from a tire.

My eyes flutter open. The ceiling swims.

Faces hover over me, warped by tears and panic that aren't even mine.

"I'm okay," I say, but my tongue feels too big for my mouth. "I'm okay, I just—"

"You passed out," someone says gently. "I found you on the floor."

Nothing feels real.

It must have been a panic attack. I haven't had one since... since Lacy.

I try to sit up and the world lurches sideways.

"Easy," a hand presses me back down. "Just breathe."

I am so tired.

So bone-tired I could cry just thinking about standing.

"I don't need EMS," I whisper. "Please. I'm fine."

They don't look convinced.

But eventually someone helps me up. Someone else brings water and tells me I'm being sent home for the day whether I like it or not. Someone suggests the hospital.

I nod at everything and mean none of it.

I collect my purse and phone like they belong to someone else.

When I sit in my car, my hands start shaking again.

I drop my keys twice before I get them in the ignition.

My phone lights up.

One new message.

August: Can we talk.

My stomach flips so hard it almost hurts.

The first text.

The first reach.

After everything...

I stare at it until the letters blur.

I don't answer.

Not yet.

I can't hold him and this at the same time.

I drive home on autopilot.

I make tea I don't remember making.

I curl up on the couch with a blanket and my knees to my chest like I'm trying to disappear inside myself.

I stare at August's message again.

Can we talk.

I don't know if I'm strong enough yet.

I don't know if I ever will be.

And then the door opens.

And Lilly walks in.

And everything spins again.

I lift my head from the couch and it takes more effort than it should.

Lilly stands in the doorway.

Her hair is tangled. Her hoodie is too big. There's a hospital bracelet still on her wrist and her ankle is in a boot.

She looks at me and for or one heartbeat, neither of us moves.

Then her face crumples.

Not loud or dramatically. More like, she turned off whatever was holding her together.

Lilly crosses the room in three wobbly steps and drops to her knees in front of me.

"I thought I was going to die," she says.

The words punch straight through me.

"I thought he was going to kill me. I thought I'd never get to say—" she chokes on her words.

I reach for her without thinking. My arms wrap around her shoulders and she clings to me like I'm the only solid thing left in the world.

We cry like that for a long time.

The kind that shakes out everything you were holding inside because you didn't have space to fall apart before.

"I'm sorry," she keeps saying. "I'm so sorry, I was so horrible to you, I said things, I—"

I press my face into her hair. "You were scared. You were hurting. That doesn't make you horrible."

"I hated you," she whispers. "I hated you for existing. I hated you for being young. But more than all of that, I hated you for making him happy."

I pull back enough to look at her.

Her eyes are red and swollen and honest.

"I never wanted to replace anyone," I say softly. "I never wanted to take anything from you."

"I know," she says. "I know that now. I just didn't want my dad to belong to anyone but me and Mom. Especially with someone my age."

The idea that love should stop where grief begins is a concept I know intimately.

"I was wrong," Lilly says. "I was so wrong. You didn't deserve the way I treated you."

"You felt betrayed," I tell her. "Even if it wasn't intentional, it still hurt. You're allowed to be angry."

She wipes her face with the sleeve of her hoodie. "But I didn't have the right to make you feel like trash. I didn't have the right to say you were sick. Or selfish. Or a mistake."

My throat tightens.

"I never stopped loving you," I admit. "Even when you wouldn't look at me."

She takes my hand, careful of her wrist. "You saved me."

I shake my head. "You stayed alive. You stayed on the line. That was all you."

"You didn't hang up," she says. "You promised."

My chest aches.

"I would never," I whisper. "Not on you."

She leans into me again, slower this time. Less desperate. More real.

"I thought I was going to die," she says quietly. "And I regretted the way I treated you. I was wrong and I'm sorry."

My eyes burn.

"I love you," I say before I can stop myself.

She goes very still.

Then she squeezes my hand. "I love you too."

It feels terrifying and healing at the same time.

We sit there like that until the shaking in both of us fades.

Then she pulls back, chewing her lip. "Are you in love with my dad?"

The question is small. Careful. But heavy.

I stare at my hands.

"Yes," I admit. "I didn't stop just because I walked away. I just... couldn't be someone's secret."

Lilly nods slowly. "He's wrecked."

I believe that.

"I don't know if I can fix that," I say. "I don't even know how to fix me."

"I don't need you to fix him," she says. "I just need you not to disappear."

I meet her eyes. "I didn't go anywhere. I promise, I won't disappear on you, if you promise you won't either."

Lilly smiles through tears. "Deal."

She squeezes my hand again, then stands carefully. "I'm going to shower and sleep for about a year."

"Fair," I say softly.

When she disappears down the hall, the house feels different.

Still fragile.

But not hollow.

I sit back on the couch, exhausted in a way that feels more earned.

There's still August.

There's still the panic attack.

There's still the part of me that doesn't trust my own lungs yet.

But tonight, one thing is mended.

And that's enough to let me breathe again.

THIRTY-ONE
AUGUST

I SIT in my truck outside Florence's place for thirty-five fucking minutes, engine off, jaw clenched so tight it aches.

The street is quiet. The porch light glows. And I can't move.

Every version of myself is in this cab with me—the man who wants to run up those steps and hold her like a lifeline, the man who knows he has no right, and the man terrified that even if she does answer, she'll look at me like a wound.

I grab the paper bag from the seat beside me. Soup. The place near the hospital that Florence once said it smells like comfort. Like healing.

I don't bring it to fix anything. I bring it because when everything's cold, you show up with something warm.

That's all I have left to give.

The air hits me sharp and clean as I step out. My boots echo louder than I mean them to. Every step up to her door feels like walking toward a verdict.

I knock once.

Silence. Then soft footsteps. A lock clicking. The door eases open a sliver.

Florence stands in the gap, her eyes shadowed, her lips drawn tight.

"August," she says.

Not with anger. Not with warmth. Just... my name. Like it hurts to say it.

"I—" My voice cracks betraying me.

She doesn't move.

I lift the bag. "I brought soup. From that place. The one you..."

She opens the door the rest of the way and steps aside.

Not an invitation. But not a wall.

It feels like a door propped open during a storm.

Inside, everything smells like her. Tea and clean linen and the faintly sweet smell of almond oil and honey. Her home wraps around me like a place I'm not sure I have permission to miss.

It hits me then, I haven't been here since Lilly moved in. Not since Lilly's shelves. Not since before everything cracked open.

She sets the bag on the counter without comment. We stand at opposite ends of the room like two planets caught in opposing gravity.

"Thank you for coming," she says quietly. "I think."

"I didn't come to make you uncomfortable." I force myself to hold her gaze. "I came because I owe you more than silence."

She nods once. No emotion. Just agreement.

I breathe out. My heart pounds in my ears.

"You gave me my daughter back."

Something flickers behind her eyes.

"I don't have words big enough for that," I go on. "You kept her alive. You kept her breathing. Long enough for us to get there."

My voice roughens, but I don't stop.

"I'll carry that with me for the rest of my life."

She swallows.

"I was just doing my job," she says softly.

"You were doing more than that," I say. "And it mattered."

I step closer. Slowly. Careful not to cross a line she hasn't drawn but I can feel anyway.

"I'm sorry," I say, the words tumbling from my lips.

Not rushed. Not rehearsed.

"I'm sorry for freezing at the restaurant. For choosing control over courage. For trying to manage a disaster instead of standing in it with you."

Her jaw tightens. Her arms fold across her chest like armor.

"I'm sorry for the hallway. For making you feel like something to be hidden. Or some kind of mistake to be managed."

She looks at the floor.

"I told myself I was protecting everyone. But the truth is, I was protecting myself from feeling like I break the people I love."

When she looks up, it nearly brings me to my knees.

"I didn't mean to make you a secret," I say. "But I did. And that's on me."

Silence.

"I believe you're sorry," she says. "I know you didn't mean to hurt me. I know you love Lilly. And maybe you even loved me."

My ribcage cracks open at her words, leaving my heart sliced open. Her words nearly destroy me.

"But I can't go back to being something you only defend when it's easy. Or something you clean up after you've made a mess."

I nod. My throat burns.

"I won't survive being made small again, August. I won't survive being explained away."

"You're not—"

She lifts a hand. Gentle. Firm.

"You don't get to define what I am to you. Not alone. Not anymore."

I lower my eyes. Swallow everything else.

"I hear you."

She moves to the couch. I follow but sit across from her, like we're in therapy instead of a battlefield of the heart.

"I'm taking time off," she says. "From dispatch."

My stomach twists.

"I had a panic attack," she adds. "I passed out. At work."

Guilt detonates in my chest. “Florence...”

“It wasn’t just you,” she says. “It was everything. My mom. My sister. You. Lilly. Holding everyone and being held by no one.”

She looks at me. It’s direct and unflinching.

“I can’t build a life bracing for the next collapse. I need to learn how to stand still without expecting the ground to disappear.”

She presses her palms to her thighs.

“I need to know who I am when I’m not someone’s girlfriend. Or someone’s secret. Or someone’s afterthought.”

She pauses.

“Then I’ll know if choosing you makes me whole... or smaller.”

The words don’t need to be cruel. They still ruin me.

“So this is goodbye?” I ask.

“No,” she says softly. “This is... not yet.”

The ache in my chest has nowhere to go.

I stand.

She stands too.

We hover in the space between us, just short of gravity.

“I want to kiss you,” I say. My voice shakes with how badly I mean it.

“I know.”

“I won’t. Unless you ask me to.”

Her lips part. Then close.

She steps in close enough that her breath hits my skin.

Our foreheads touch. Nothing else. Just skin, breath, restraint.

Her hands curl in my shirt.

Mine don’t move.

I want to fall apart. I want to worship her. I want to beg.

But this isn’t about taking.

It’s about honoring.

“This is hard,” she whispers.

“I know.”

Her lips brush mine with a question made of heat and hesitation.

I don't deepen it.

I don't claim.

I let it exist.

Then she pulls back.

"I need to mean what I say."

"So do I."

I step back first.

It feels like tearing out my own ribs.

"I love being with you," I say. "But I won't be the reason you don't become yourself."

Her eyes shine. No tears.

"Thank you for hearing me," Florence says.

"Thank you for not slamming the door."

At the threshold, I stop.

"I'm here," I say. "Whenever. If ever."

She nods.

I leave.

And for once, I don't try to fix it.

I let love be love, even when it means letting go.

THIRTY-TWO
FLORENCE

I GO BACK to dispatch because I need to be sure.

Not because I owe anyone anything. Not because I think it will suddenly feel right again. I go back because I don't want to quit out of fear. When I decide to quit, it's because quitting is my truth.

The building looks the same when I pull into the lot, it's too bright, too flat, too familiar. I sit in my car for a minute with my hands on the wheel, feeling my pulse thud in my throat.

You don't have to be brave anymore, a voice inside me says.

You can choose.

Inside, the air smells like coffee, recycled breath, and a hundred old emergencies haunting the corners. The hallway hums with voices, keyboards, radios. Normal. Ordinary.

It's the kind of normal that used to make me feel useful.

Now it makes my chest tighten.

I take my seat. Log in. Put on my headset.

The screen blinks alive.

And something inside me goes quiet, a room that used to be full and now just echoes.

The first call is anything but dramatic. A noise complaint. Mrs. Robertson's poodle won't stop barking after she leaves for work. Apparently Dutchess hasn't acclimated to a post-Covid world.

Me neither, pooch.

On paper, every call is fine.

But I'm watching myself do it.

Removed from the process.

Another call. This time a woman crying in a parking lot. After a lot of tears, I learn she's just been through a breakup that involved being left in that same parking lot. No violence. Just heartbreak so raw it feels like skin torn off.

I want to anchor her. Keep her talking. Give her space to exist without falling apart alone.

But that's not my job. And when the phone rings again, I move on.

My hands are shaking.

Not from adrenaline.

From bone-deep exhaustion.

It isn't the pain that breaks me.

It's the sameness of it.

The way every call asks me to hold someone else's worst moment while pretending my own doesn't exist.

My chest tightens before every ring with dread.

My body remembers the night Lilly called. It remembers the night my mother died. The night August was shot. The way trauma stacks itself inside me like furniture in a house with no rooms left.

By lunch, my head is pounding. My shoulders ache. My jaw is locked from clenching.

A dispatcher across the room says something too quiet to be professional and just loud enough to be cruel.

"Some of us actually earned our positions the old-fashioned way."

The words don't just hit my back.

They crawl under my skin.

I turn in my chair.

Slow.

Deliberate.

Every head within earshot goes still.

I meet his eyes. "Say that again."

He blinks. "What?"

"What you just said," I tell him. My voice is calm, which is somehow worse. "You said some of you earned your positions the old-fashioned way. I didn't quite catch the punchline."

He shifts in his seat. "I was just joking."

I stand.

My headset cord goes taut like it's trying to hold me back.

"I don't get it," I say. "Explain it to me. I love jokes."

A few people stare at their screens like they might combust if they look up.

He laughs awkwardly. "It's not that deep."

"Oh, it is," I say, stepping closer. "Because you said it about me. So let's get really clear about what you meant."

He opens his mouth.

Closes it.

I don't give him time to regroup.

"You've been doing this job what—six months?" I ask. "Maybe seven?"

He bristles. "So?"

"So I've been doing it six years," I say. "Six years of overdose calls, suicide, screaming parents, dead air, dead kids, dead mothers. Six years of not freezing when someone's whole life is falling apart in my ear."

His face goes red.

"You didn't 'earn' anything," I continue. "You were born into a system that already liked you. You're a cis white man with a cop for a father. You walked in with the door already half open."

"That's not—"

"Privilege isn't a personal insult," I snap. "It's a fact. And you don't get to use it like a weapon and then call it a joke when someone bleeds."

The room is so quiet I can hear someone's mouse clicking.

"If you've got a problem with me," I finish, "say it to my face, not to the air like a coward. Otherwise shut the fuck up and do your job instead of trying to make someone feel small because they don't fit your idea of what 'earned' looks like."

His mouth opens.

Nothing comes out.

Ruth's voice cuts in, low and lethal. "Back to work. All of you."

I turn back to my console.

Sit down.

Put my headset back on like nothing just happened.

My hands are shaking but my spine isn't.

I finish my shift.

Four more hours of calls. Of voices. Of breathing through other people's fear.

And when I log out, my hands don't hesitate this time.

I walk straight to the supervisor's office.

And I say it steady.

"I'm giving my notice."

Silence falls.

But silence doesn't erase what's already landed.

"I realize something simple and devastating, I don't feel proud anymore about doing this job. I don't feel strong. I feel small. And scared. And tired of pretending that being strong means staying somewhere that hurt me."

After, the room didn't collapse.

The world didn't end.

No one yelled. No one begged.

The supervisor just nodded slowly and said, "Okay. Let's talk about timelines."

When I walked out of their office, my body was trembling.

Not from fear, but from relief.

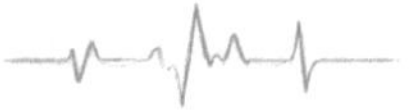

Smith Summer's shop smells like incense and old books and tea when I walk in that afternoon. It feels like receiving new lungs after after drowning.

He looks up from behind the counter and smiles.

"You look like you've had a day."

I laugh, weak and honest. "That's one way to put it."

I wander between the shelves, letting my fingers brush spines of books and linger on crystals. I pause at a velvet tarot cloth, picking one up, debating if I need it. My chest loosens with every step.

This place has a way of holding me when I forget how to be.

"Do not buy that," Smith calls from the counter without looking up. "You already own seventeen identical cloths. You're not a dragon. Stop hoarding textiles."

I huff a laugh and keep the cloth in my hands anyway, stroking the velvet like it might talk me out of making choices.

"I'm not hoarding," I say. "I'm curating."

"Curating," he repeats, finally looking at me over the top of his glasses. "You're one more 'curated' purchase away from me staging an intervention with a PowerPoint."

"I would attend your PowerPoint," I say.

"You would," he agrees, deadpan. "You love emotional suffering."

That lands a little too close to the bone, which is probably why he says it like a joke. Smith has a gift for putting truth in glitter and tossing it at your forehead.

I set the cloth back on the shelf like I'm being punished.

He slides a mug across the counter toward me, it's chipped ceramic, mismatched, and utterly familiar. Something herbal and warm and vaguely like cinnamon got hugged by honey.

"Drink," he orders.

"Bossy," I say, but my hands wrap around it like I'm starving.

"Someone has to be," he replies. "You're out here acting like you're fine, and you're doing it badly."

I take a sip. My throat tightens. My eyes burn.

Smith softens, just a fraction, and nods toward the little round table by the back window. The one that catches the late afternoon sun and makes the dust look romantic instead of depressing.

"Come sit," he says. "Before you start crying into the

amethyst display and I have to cleanse the entire front section."

I follow him back there because I always do. Because when your life is on fire, it helps to have a friend who hands you tea and mocks you gently while you burn.

We sit. The shop hums around us with soft music, the chime of the door, and someone murmuring at the incense shelf like they're negotiating with their demons.

Smith leans back in his chair and studies me like he's reading the part of me that keeps trying to hide.

"You look different today," he says.

"Different good or different bad?" I ask automatically.

He makes a face. "Different brave."

I snort. "Absolutely not. I feel like I jumped off a cliff and I'm still waiting to hit the ground."

"Okay," he says, nodding like that's valid. "So... you're in freefall. That's still movement."

I stare into my mug. The steam fogs my lashes.

"I quit," I say.

The words leave my mouth like a pebble dropping into deep water.

Smith's eyebrows shoot up so fast they nearly leave his forehead.

"You quit-quit?" he asks, like he doesn't trust reality and honestly? Same.

"I put in my notice," I say. My heart does this weird fluttering thing that's half proud, half terrified. "I didn't walk out. I didn't scream. I didn't do anything dramatic." Then I remember my small brow up. "Nothing more dramatic than telling this asshole where he could shove it. But that aside, it was really good."

Smith looks faintly disappointed. "Shocking," he says. "I had 'dramatic exit' in my 2026 bingo card."

"I know," I mutter. "I'm sorry to rob you of joy."

"Oh, I'll find joy," he promises. "But tell me."

I take a breath that catches halfway.

"I went back because I needed to be sure," I say. "Not

because I owe them anything. I just... I needed to know if I was leaving because I'm scared or because I'm done."

Smith nods slowly, all joking gone now. "And?"

"And I'm done." The truth of it spreads through my ribs like warmth. "The calls don't... fill me anymore. They just take. And every ring feels like my body bracing for the worst moment of someone's life."

His eyes sharpen. "Because you've had enough worst moments."

The words are gentle. Not pity. Just fact.

I swallow. "My mom. Lacy, August getting shot. Lilly calling me from a robbery like...like she was going leave this world the same way Lacy did."

Smith's mouth tightens. His jaw works like he's chewing on something he wants to spit into the universe's face.

"And then," I add, quieter, "going home and living with someone who won't look at me because she thinks I ruined her family."

Smith lifts his mug in a tiny toast. "Ah yes. The classic 'I am actively falling apart but also I make dinner and pay rent' experience."

That gets a laugh out of me. It's small but real.

He leans in. "How's Lilly now?"

"She's... better," I say. "We talked. Not fixed. But... real. She cried. I cried. We admitted things we were too stubborn to say."

Smith points at me like I've proven a theory. "Look at you. Communicating. Like an emotionally available person."

"Don't make it a thing," I warn.

"I'm making it a thing," he says, delighted. "It's a thing. I'm proud of you."

My eyes sting again, and I hate how much I need that. A friend. A witness. Someone outside the tornado who still sees me as... me.

"And August?" Smith asks, carefully.

My stomach flips, traitorously.

"He apologized," I say. "A real apology. Not... perfect. But honest. He didn't try to bulldoze me back into his life. He just..." I exhale. "He showed up. He listened. And then he left when I asked him to."

Smith's expression shifts to something akin to approval, but not softened. Smith doesn't romanticize men; he audits them.

"Good," he says. "A man respecting a boundary is the bare minimum, but in this economy, we celebrate minor miracles."

I laugh, despite myself. "God."

"No," he corrects. "Gay."

That makes me choke on my tea.

He grins. I know he secretly lives for these exact moments.

I wipe my mouth, still laughing, and then the laughter fades because the fear is still underneath everything.

"I don't know what I'm doing next," I admit. "That's the part that's making my skin buzz. I quit and I feel... free, but also like I just cut the only rope I had."

Smith's eyes soften again. "Baby. You didn't cut the rope. You climbed out of a cage."

I blink hard. "You can't call me baby like that."

"I can and I will," he says. "Because you're twenty-five and sad and you're trying to be made of steel when you're allowed to be human."

My throat closes.

Smith clears his throat, like he can feel emotion trying to get too close and he refuses to let it take over the room.

"So," he says lightly, "congratulations on quitting a job that was actively eating you alive. Very sexy of you. Love that for you."

I snort. "Thank you."

"And," he continues, tapping his mug against mine, "now that we've done your big dramatic character growth moment... I have my own."

I blink. "You're quitting too?"

He points at me like I stole his line. "See? You know me. We're bonded. Like lesbians."

"I'm not—"

"You're a lesbian spiritually," he says. "It's a vibe."

I roll my eyes, but I'm smiling.

"Yeah," he says, sobering. "I'm selling."

The words land wrong. Like he just said he's moving the sun.

My chest tightens. "Selling the shop?"

"Mm-hm."

"But you—" I gesture helplessly around us. The shelves. The cards. The little corner where people cry and laugh and buy candles like they're buying hope. "You *are* the shop."

Smith's face goes softer in a way that makes my stomach dip. "I know. And I love it. But loving something doesn't mean you're meant to stay in it forever."

I stare at him. "Why?"

He leans back, exhaling. "My mom's health is getting worse. She's doing that thing where she insists she's fine while actively disintegrating out of spite."

I wince. "Smith."

"It's true," he says. "And my son—" His voice changes on that word, all sarcasm drained. "He got accepted to this collage. In the city."

My heart stutters. "That's huge."

"It is," he says. "And he wants to go. And I want to support it. I want to be there for him. Not half here, half running back and forth, not constantly trying to split myself into pieces so everyone gets a version."

My chest aches because I understand that in my bones.

"And also," he adds, and his smile returns, "I'm single and fabulous, and I would like to stay that way without dying behind a counter surrounded by teenagers asking if rose quartz will fix their situationship."

I bark a laugh.

Smith lifts a finger. "It will not. Only therapy and self-respect will fix your situationship."

I shake my head, laughing, and then the laughter fades because the reality is too big.

"So you're really selling," I say.

"Yeah," he replies quietly. "I am."

My voice goes small. "What happens to this place?"

Smith makes a face like he's tasted something bitter.

"Someone buys it. And I pray they don't turn it into a novelty vape shop."

I groan. "Please don't speak that into existence."

"Or worse," he says, eyes widening dramatically, "a minimalist boutique that sells one candle for eighty-seven dollars and calls it 'intention.'"

"I would commit arson," I say, dead serious.

Smith points at me. "See? That's why I love you. You have ethics."

I swallow. My fingers tighten around my mug.

"Have you already—" I hesitate. "Have you already listed it?"

"Not yet." He watches me carefully. "I'm telling you first because you're here. Because you care. Because—" he shrugs. "Because you're part of this place now, whether or not you want to admit it."

My chest does something strange. A throb of belonging.

I force my voice steady. "How much?"

Smith's eyebrows lift. "You asking as a friend or as a woman who just quit her job and now looks like she's about to do something unhinged?"

"Both?" I squeak.

He gives me a look. "Gods, you're adorable."

"Smith."

He names the number.

And the world tilts.

Not in a panic way.

In a *holy shit* way.

Because it's... possible.

Not easy. Not casual. Not "throw money at it and hope."

But possible.

My brain does the math before I can stop it.

Half.

About half of what I have.

Half of the money I've been treating like a shrine. Like a haunted relic. Like if I touch it wrong I'll lose my mom all over again.

I just stare at him.

Smith's smile fades into something gentle and sharp. "Oh no."

"What?" I whisper.

"That face," he says. "That's your 'the universe is putting something directly in my lap and I'm about to either ascend or throw up' face."

"I don't—" My voice cracks. I clear my throat. "I could... I could afford it."

Smith points at me again. "No. You could *maybe* afford it. Those are different sentences. One is math. One is a life."

My throat burns.

"I know," I say quickly. "I'm not— I'm not saying I'm going to. I'm just—"

"Feeling the door open," he finishes, softer.

I nod, breath shallow. "I quit dispatch. I'm terrified. August is... August. Lilly and I are trying. My nervous system is basically a feral raccoon. And now you're telling me the one place I can breathe is," I swallow. "For sale."

Smith's eyes hold mine, steady.

"Okay," he says. "Here's what we're not going to do."

I blink.

"We're not going to do the thing where you talk yourself out of joy because you think you have to earn it through suffering," Smith says, voice firm. "You've suffered enough. You're allowed to build something that feels like *you*."

My eyes sting.

"And before you spiral," he adds, lifting a finger, "you don't have to decide today. I'm not a villain. I'm just gay."

A laugh bursts out of me, wet and shaky.

Smith leans in, elbows on the table, tone gentler. "Talk to me. What's the fear?"

I exhale. "That I'll waste it."

"The money," he says, confirming.

I nod. "My mom's inheritance. Every time I think about using it, it feels like I'm spending her. Like if I buy the wrong thing, I failed some test she never assigned."

Smith's mouth twists. "Oh, babe."

"I know."

He sits back, sighs, and then says, very matter-of-fact, "Your mom did not die so you could live in a museum of grief."

My breath catches.

"She left you that money because she loved you," he continues. "Not because she wanted you to sit on it like a dragon guarding a pile of sadness. She wanted you safe. She wanted you okay."

I swallow hard. "What if I'm not okay enough to do this?"

Smith smiles, it's soft but wicked. "No one is okay enough to do anything big. That's why it's big."

I laugh through my tears. "That's not comforting."

"It's practical," he says. "And I'm deeply practical. For example," he gestures at me. "You are not going to buy a business because you're emotionally fragile. You are going to *consider* buying a business because your life is changing and you are allowed to choose what it becomes."

My heart pounds.

"And," he adds, eyes narrowing, "if you're going to build a safe place for weird, grieving, heartbroken humans, you're already doing it. You do it every time you read for someone. Every time you hand them a card and say 'you're not crazy.'"

I blink. "I do that?"

He stares at me like I'm slow. "Florence. Yes."

The shop door chimes again up front. Someone laughs softly. Life keeps happening.

Smith taps the table once, grounding me.

"Listen," he says. "If you want this, *if* we do it right. We talk to someone boring. We look at paperwork. We don't let your trauma run the show. And we don't let your fear make the decision either."

My throat burns. "Okay."

He studies me for a beat, then smiles like a knife wrapped in velvet.

"And for the record," he adds, "if you buy this place and turn it into a soft, witchy sanctuary for sad people? I will haunt you if you don't name at least one shelf after me."

I laugh, real this time. "I'll name the entire building after you."

"Good," he says, satisfied. "Because I deserve it."

I stare at him, tea warm in my hands, sunlight spilling across the table like a blessing I don't know if I'm allowed to accept.

The idea doesn't feel like a fantasy.

It feels like... a doorway.

Like the universe is standing there, hand on the knob, looking at me like, *You sure?*

My pulse jumps.

The fear in me isn't just dread.

It's also something bright and electric.

Possibility.

THIRTY-THREE
FLORENCE

THE BELL over the door gives its soft little chime, and for half a second my body still does that old dispatch thing where my whole body is alert, ready, and bracing.

Then I remember where I am.

Not a room full of screams and headsets and fluorescent dread.

A shop that smells like incense, paper, and possibility. A place I own now. A place that's mine in a way I'm still getting used to.

I'm behind the counter with a clipboard and a highlighter, knee-deep in inventory hell. It's been four weeks since we signed contracts. Someone—me—thought it would be a great idea to reorganize the back stock by category and then, mid-task, discovered there are approximately nine thousand tiny jars of herbs that all look like someone ground up the same color of regret.

I've got the register open on the tablet, the spreadsheet open on my laptop, and a stack of invoices threatening to become sentient and unionize.

"Okay," I mutter to myself. "If you're labeled 'mugwort' but you're actually 'mullein,' I will personally set you on fire."

The bell chimes again.

This time it's followed by the unmistakable smell of coffee and sugar and something warm, like if cinnamon had a baby with a blackberry.

I glance up.

Lilly steps inside with a cardboard tray of drinks in one hand and a pink bakery box in the other. She's wearing a hoodie that looks like it's been through an emotional war and lost. Her hair is pulled into a messy bun.

She looks... normal.

Not normal like nothing happened.

Normal like she lived through it.

And she's trying.

My throat tightens so fast it almost hurts.

"Okay," I say, leaning forward over the counter. "Either you're here to rob me, or you're here to feed me."

Lilly's mouth quirks. "I brought coffee and donuts."

"Definitely robbing," I decide. "You're stealing my dignity by witnessing this spreadsheet situation."

She sets the box and drinks down on the counter like she owns the place. Like she belongs here.

Like we're a version of us that isn't made entirely out of landmines.

"I come bearing offerings," she says solemnly.

I lift a brow. "To which deity?"

"The deity of people who quit their jobs and become witches overnight," she says. "She's notoriously cranky."

I laugh, surprised by how easy it is. By how the sound doesn't catch on pain first.

"Bless," I tell her, and slide out from behind the counter. My legs pop like I've been standing in the same position for three hours, which, honestly, is possible.

Lilly nudges the donut box toward me. "Eat. You look like you've been subsisting on caffeine and spite."

"I have," I say. "It's very nutritious."

She gives me a look. It's so familiar it makes my chest ache.

I open the box. The scent of fresh glaze, fried dough, and sugar so soft it feels like a hug, wraps around me.

"Oh my gods," I whisper.

"I know," Lilly says, like she personally baked them. "Local bakery. Mom insists we keep them in business single-handedly."

"Your mom is a hero," I say around a sudden, stupid lump in my throat.

Lilly takes a coffee from the tray and hands it to me. It's warm through the cup. Real. Solid. Not something I have to earn.

"You want to sit?" I ask, gesturing toward the little round table by the window.

She nods and walks over like she knows the path by heart, like she's been doing it forever. Like she's not still learning how to exist in the aftermath.

I follow with my coffee and a blueberry donut, and we settle into the sunlight that slants through the front windows.

For a minute, we just... eat.

It's absurd how healing it is to chew something sweet while the world keeps turning.

Lilly bites into a chocolate frosted donut and immediately makes a face like she's having a religious experience.

"Okay," she says with her mouth full. "This is obscene."

I laugh. "Language."

"No," she says, swallowing. "It's literally pornographic. I'm calling the cops."

I point toward the front door. "You'll have to call someone else. I no longer answer emergency lines."

Her eyes flick up. Careful. Checking. That's still there sometimes, little moments where she forgets we can joke and then remembers, oh right, everything changed.

"Do you miss it?" she asks, quieter.

I take a sip of coffee and let myself answer honestly.

"I miss Ruth," I say. "I miss... some of the people. I miss feeling like I was good at something that mattered. Like I made a small difference in the world."

Lilly nods like she understands that specific kind of grief.

"But I don't miss dispatch," I continue. "Not the job. Not

the dread. Not the way it crawled into my bones until I couldn't tell if I was anxious because of a call or because I was alive."

Lilly's hand tightens around her coffee cup.

"Mom still fusses over me," she says, like she needs to change the subject before it gets too heavy. "It's honestly kind of embarrassing. She's like... constantly offering me soup."

"Soup is love," I say.

"She brought me soup and said, 'This is restorative.'" Lilly mimics her mother's voice with terrifying accuracy. "'It has bone broth.'"

I snort. "Bone broth is allegedly healing."

"It tastes like grief," she says.

"Maybe grief is healing," I offer.

Lilly glares. "Don't get poetic at me in the middle of a donut conversation."

I lift my hands. "Sorry. I've been around too many crystals lately. It's contagious."

She laughs. It's small but real, and then she looks out the window, staring at nothing for a moment like she's watching her thoughts drift by and deciding which ones are safe to speak.

"Dad's been... weird," Lilly says finally.

My stomach flips so hard I almost drop my donut.

I keep my face neutral by force. Keep my posture casual. Like August's name doesn't live under my skin.

"Define weird," I say, too carefully.

Lilly sighs and leans back in her chair.

"You know that heavy little cloud cartoon?" she asks. "Like the one that follows someone around and rains on them even when the sun's out?"

I swallow. "Yeah."

"That's him," she says simply.

My throat tightens. I take a slow sip of coffee to give myself time to breathe through the ache.

Four weeks.

It's been four weeks since the robbery. Since the line went dead. Since my body decided to malfunction in a bathroom stall and I learned what panic can do when it wants to kill you without actually killing you.

Four weeks since August stood in my kitchen and apologized like he was pulling glass out of his throat.

Four weeks since his lips brushed mine like a question before he left in an attempt to respect the answer.

And in that time, I have been so busy building a life that belongs to me that I've barely had time to fall apart about the life I still want.

I miss him with every fiber of my being.

I also refuse to go back to being someone's secret.

Both truths live in me like twin flames. Warming and burning me at the same time.

"I don't know what to say to that," I admit, because it's the only honest thing I've got.

Lilly's eyes flick to mine. Sharp. Young. But not naive anymore.

"I mean... he's trying," she says. "He's doing the dad thing. Making dinner. Asking about my day. Pretending he's fine."

Her mouth twists. "But he's not."

I nod slowly. My chest aches like it wants to open.

I hate how much I want to reach for August through this conversation. To ask a million questions.

I hate how I still feel like I'm holding my breath.

Because that's what it is.

Even now, with Lilly trying, with things gentler, I'm still living inside the rubble of what happened.

I can't see a clean future while I'm still sleeping under the same roof as his daughter.

Not because Lilly is the problem.

Because the three of us are tangled in something that needs space to breathe.

Lilly watches me carefully, like she can feel me pulling inward.

"Florence," she says, softer. "Are you okay?"

I let out a laugh that isn't funny.

"I'm... busy," I say. "Which is a very cute way of saying I'm avoiding thinking too hard."

Lilly's mouth quirks. "Relatable."

I glance toward the counter, toward the stacks of inventory sheets and the open laptop and the little mess of my new life.

"This place is... saving me," I admit. "In a way. It gives my brain something to do besides spiral."

Lilly nods. "It's good on you."

"Yeah?" I ask, and my voice cracks a little. "Does it look good on me?"

"It does," she says, immediate and sure. "You're like... less haunted."

I blink fast. "High praise."

She smiles, then her expression shifts again into something more serious.

"Are you going to... talk to him?" she asks.

My stomach drops.

"I don't know," I say honestly. "I want to."

Lilly's eyes soften. "But?"

"But I can't be in the middle of you and him," I say quietly. "Not while I'm still living with you. Not while everything is still... so close."

Lilly stares at her coffee cup for a second, jaw working.

"I've been... trying," she continues, voice wobbling. "Trying to be normal. Trying to be fine. Trying to pretend none of this is my fault."

I open my mouth, but she holds up a hand.

"Let me finish," she says, and her voice is sharper now, like she's holding herself together by force. "I know I've been awful. I know I treated you like you were poison and then I got mad when you didn't magically stop existing."

My eyes burn.

"I was angry," she says.

I swallow. "Lilly—"

"I know," she cuts in, and her eyes shine. "I know it's not fair. I know you didn't do anything wrong by being young. That's... my shit. That's me having to grow up."

She wipes her thumb under one eye like she's angry at the tears for showing up.

"And I'm trying," she repeats. "But I can't try while you're here looking like you're one bad day away from disappearing."

My throat closes so tight I can barely breathe.

I set my coffee down carefully.

"Okay," I say, voice shaking. "Okay. You're right."

Lilly exhales a breath she was holding.

I swallow once, then twice, and then I say the words that have been sitting in my chest like a stone.

"This is as good a time as any," I say softly. "I'm giving you notice."

Lilly goes still.

"I've been thinking about it for weeks," I continue. "I'm going to get my own place. Smith Summers has an apartment downtown I'm going to sublet when he moves out, but it won't be for three more weeks. So..." I lift a shoulder helplessly. "Five weeks. Might be sooner. But I want to make sure you have a proper thirty days like we agreed."

For a second, Lilly just stares at me.

Then her face does something I don't expect.

Relief.

"Oh," she breathes.

And then, like the dam breaks, she laughs through her tears and says, "Good."

I blink, stunned. "Good?"

"Good," she repeats, nodding hard. "Because I love you, and I'm going to miss living with you, and I hate that it's been weird, but you deserve to have a life that doesn't revolve around my emotional whiplash."

My eyes fill instantly.

"Lilly..." I whisper.

She reaches across the table and takes my hand.

"I want him happy," she says, voice small but steady. "I want you happy."

My throat tightens so hard it hurts.

"And if that means you're together," she continues, eyes locked on mine, "then... I'll figure my shit out."

Something in me cracks open.

The sound I make is embarrassing. Something between a half sob and half laugh-snort. I squeeze her hand.

"I didn't think you'd ever say that," I whisper.

Lilly's mouth wobbles. "Yeah, well. Almost dying makes you less interested in being an asshole."

I snort, crying. "That's one way to put it."

She squeezes my hand harder. "I'm serious."

"I know," I whisper.

We sit there in the sunlight with tears in our eyes and sugar on the table because grief and sweetness can exist together.

Lilly swallows hard.

"And for the record," she adds, suddenly defensive, "I still think he's an idiot."

I laugh, wet and shaking. "Fair."

"But," she says, voice quieter, "I also think he loves you."

My chest aches.

"And I think," she continues, cheeks flushing, "you love him. Which is... disgusting."

I bark a laugh, and she smiles through her tears like she can't help it.

"I do," I admit softly. Out loud. Without flinching. "I love him."

Lilly nods like she already knew, like she's been watching it in the way my eyes go distant when his name comes up.

"I'm sorry I made it worse."

My throat tightens again. "You were hurt."

"So were you," she says.

I squeeze her hand.

We sit for a moment longer, letting it settle. Letting the future inch into the room.

Then Lilly stands carefully, grabbing the bakery box and her coffee like she's trying not to make this feel too heavy.

She pauses at the table and looks at me with a glint of mischief in her eyes.

"Okay," she says, pointing at me. "But like..."

I lift a brow. "Like what?"

She gives me a wink. A full, dramatic, daughter-who-thinks-she's-a-genius wink.

"Maybe don't make him grovel forever," she says. "Just like... a little while."

I laugh so hard it turns into a sob at the end.

Lilly grins, satisfied, and heads toward the door.

The bell chimes when she leaves.

This time the sound doesn't make me brace. It lets me breathe.

THIRTY-FOUR
AUGUST

THE RUMOR REACHES me the way most things reach me in Townsend Harbor, sideways, half-laughed, carried on coffee breath and bad acoustics.

I'm in the hallway outside briefing, when I hear Delaney and Ortiz talking near the vending machine like the vending machine is their therapist.

"—I'm telling you, it's not Smith's anymore," Delaney says, voice low but not low enough. "She bought it."

Ortiz snorts. "Florence? No way."

Delaney makes the sound men make when they know something and can't wait to be right about it. "Yeah. Florence. The one who quit. Apparently she straight-up purchased the whole shop. Like, signed papers, handed over money, 'congrats on your new life' kind of purchased."

My hand tightens around the paper cup of coffee I'm holding. The cheap lid squeaks under my grip.

As if she's not a person with a spine made of fire and a voice that saved countless lives through a line that constantly tries to die.

As if she's not the woman I can't stop thinking about.

Ortiz whistles. "That's... kinda badass."

"Right? Smith Summer's out," Delaney continues. "Selling because of his mom or something. But the shop? It's hers now.

I guess she's turned it into this whole thing—local artists, classes, all that witchy stuff. My girlfriend is obsessed."

Ortiz laughs. "Town's gonna eat that up."

Delaney leans closer, lowering his voice like he's about to confess a crime. "And I heard she renamed it."

Ortiz perks up. "What'd she call it?"

Delaney shrugs. "Something cute. Heart-something. Harbor-something. I can't remember. I saw the sign, driving by."

My chest goes tight in a way that has nothing to do with my hip.

Heart-something.

Harbor-something.

Of course she would take a place and put her whole soul into it. Florence doesn't know how to do anything halfway.

I can picture her behind a counter, sleeves pushed up, hair falling into her eyes because she's too busy building a future to remember to pin it back. I can picture her chewing the inside of her cheek while she does math in her head. I can picture the little crease between her brows when she's concentrating.

Her laughing.

It hits me like a shove that I haven't heard that laugh in weeks.

I set my coffee down on the ledge before I crush it. My fingers are stiff. My pulse is steady, but there's something restless under it. It's an itch in my bones that doesn't go away no matter how much I work.

Delaney catches sight of me then.

His face shifts. That micro-second where he realizes he's been talking about the chief's personal life like it's a community bulletin board.

"Chief," he says quickly, posture snapping into something more formal.

Ortiz straightens too, eyes flicking between my face and the floor like he's trying to decide if I'm about to make an example out of someone.

I don't.

I should, maybe, in some universe where I still care what

people say. But I've spent too many years policing everyone else's behavior while my own life falls apart quietly behind my badge.

"Morning," I say, voice flat.

Delaney nods like he's bracing. "Morning."

I look at him for a second longer than necessary. Not to intimidate. To make a decision.

Because I could walk away and let this be another thing I don't touch.

Or I could acknowledge it like a man who's tired of pretending everything important is optional.

"What's the name?" I ask.

Delaney blinks. "Sir?"

"The shop," I say, like it's obvious. Like my throat doesn't tighten on the words. "You said she renamed it."

Delaney looks relieved I'm not angry. Too relieved. He exhales and scratches the back of his neck.

"Hearth & Harbor," he says. "I think. Yeah. Hearth & Harbor. It's painted on the front window."

Hearth & Harbor.

The words settle into me like a brand.

Warmth and darkness.

Home and the unknown.

It's her, distilled into two words.

"Copy," I say, because I don't know what else to do with the feeling that hits me—pride, awe, grief, longing, all braided together until I can't tell which one hurts most.

Delaney nods fast. "Sir. Sorry. We were just, talking."

"I heard," I say. "Try talking more quietly in the hallway next time."

"Yes, sir."

Ortiz gives me a nervous little smile like I'm a storm he's hoping will pass.

I pick my coffee back up, careful now, and walk into briefing like my heart isn't doing something stupid inside my ribs.

Like a shop name didn't just knock the air out of me.

Like I haven't been living the last month with the sensation of holding myself back from the one place I want to go.

Briefing is normal. Crime stats. Staffing. The same three issues we always have: not enough bodies, too much territory, too many people with problems they refuse to solve until they become my problem.

I do my job. I ask the right questions. I assign the right shifts. I am competent. I am composed. I am the chief.

And the whole time, in the back of my head, I keep seeing those words on glass.

Hearth & Harbor.

When briefing ends, I stay behind, gathering papers I don't need to gather.

It's not that I'm avoiding leaving.

It's that leaving means facing my day.

And my day has started with the confirmation that Florence didn't just survive quitting dispatch.

She built something.

She took her grief and her fear and her mother's money and made a life that belongs to her.

A life I'm not part of.

Not yet.

My phone buzzes with a text from Lilly.

That's the other constant in all this.

Six weeks ago, I watched an ambulance swallow her.

Six weeks ago, I tasted the kind of fear that rewires your brain permanently.

Since then, I've been doing the work I should've been doing all along: showing up.

Not as the dad who hovers like a cop, monitoring, controlling, managing. But as the dad who sits on the couch and watches dumb reality shows because she likes them. As the dad who makes pasta and burns the garlic bread and laughs at himself instead of getting angry. As the dad who apologizes without excuses. And who listens to what's happening in my daughter's life.

Lilly is different now.

Not fragile by any means. More like she's... awake.

There's a seriousness in her eyes sometimes, like she saw the edge of the world and decided she's done wasting time pretending she doesn't care about people.

It's made her sharper.

It's made her kinder, in her own stubborn way.

It's made her look at me like she's measuring whether I'm going to keep being the man who hides behind duty and fear.

I've been trying not to.

Trying to be someone she can trust.

Trying to be someone Florence could trust.

I don't know if I'm too late.

A knock taps the open doorway of my office.

Ruth steps in without waiting, like she always has. She's holding a folder and a coffee that smells like the expensive kind, because Ruth has never been subtle about her standards.

"Morning," she says.

"Morning," I answer.

She sets the folder down. "Budget revisions. The county wants our overtime justification in writing."

I exhale. "Of course they do."

Ruth's mouth quirks. "They love paperwork. Paperwork means they're doing something."

"Paperwork means I'm not," I mutter.

Ruth sits in the chair across from my desk without being invited, crossing her legs like she's settling in for a conversation she's been waiting to have.

I don't miss the signal.

I know Ruth. I know when she's here for business, and I know when she's here because she's decided I'm not allowed to drown quietly.

Ruth's brow lifts.

I sigh and lean back in my chair.

Ruth's gaze sharpens, careful and calm. "How are you?"

I could lie.

I could do the thing where I smile, shrug, say I'm fine, and let the conversation die.

But Ruth is not easily dismissed.

"Tired," I say truthfully.

Ruth nods like she expected that answer. "Yeah."

I stare at the budget folder like it might save me from an uncomfortable conversation.

Ruth's voice softens. "You've been giving her space."

My head lifts before I can stop it.

Ruth doesn't say Florence's name. She doesn't have to.

The air in the room changes anyway.

"I have," I say, careful.

"You've done the right thing," Ruth says. "For once."

The jab is gentle.

"I'm trying," I mutter.

Ruth studies me. "You miss her."

It's not a question.

My jaw tightens. "That's not—"

Ruth holds up a hand. "August. Don't. Not with me."

I close my mouth.

Ruth leans forward a little, elbows on her knees, coffee cupped in both hands like it's something she's warming her palms on, not drinking.

"I'm going to tell you something," she says, "and I need you to hear it without turning it into a defensive speech."

I don't even pretend. I just exhale through my nose and nod once.

"Okay."

"Lilly is a grown-up," Ruth says. "Not fully. Not in the way she thinks she is. But she's old enough to understand that she doesn't get to be the steering wheel for your whole life."

My throat tightens anyway, because she's right and because it's my favorite kind of pain, truth.

Ruth continues, voice steady. "She can have feelings. She can be scared. She can be protective. But she can't be the reason you live small."

I swallow. The words land in the soft place under my ribs where guilt likes to nest.

"I'm not trying to live small," I say.

Ruth's mouth tilts. "August."

I go quiet.

She watches me for a beat, then softens just a fraction. "You've spent years acting like if you just keep everything controlled, nothing bad can happen."

I flinch. Because it's not a flinch at her, it's a flinch at myself.

"And I get it," she adds. "I do. You grew up with chaos. You built yourself into the opposite of that. But you can't keep shrinking your life down to 'safe' until there's nothing left in it but duty."

My jaw works. "I'm not—"

Ruth lifts a finger. "Don't. I said no defensive speech."

I shut my mouth.

She takes a sip of her coffee like she's letting the point settle.

Then she says, quieter, "Lilly isn't a little kid anymore. She's old enough to understand that love isn't a betrayal."

My eyes lift to hers.

"And she's old enough," Ruth adds, "to learn that her dad is allowed to be wanted. Allowed to be happy. Allowed to be seen."

The words hit hard. Not because they're dramatic. Because they're so plain.

I look down at my desk like it might save me from feeling this.

"You don't either," I say, because it's the only way I know how to breathe when I'm cornered by truth. "You can't live your whole life for her."

Ruth's eyes flicker with surprise at first, then something like amusement.

"Look at you," she says. "Throwing my own wisdom back at me."

"It's true," I say, quieter. "You deserve... someone. Something. Not just co-parenting and work and being the town's emotional janitor."

Ruth snorts, and it's real enough that I almost smile.

"Emotional janitor," she repeats. "That's exactly what it feels like."

I lean forward. "You should meet someone."

Her expression shifts. Not defensive. Not angry. Just complicated in that way people get when they're standing in front of an old door they're not sure they want to open again.

"I don't know if I want to," she admits.

"That's not what I said," I reply automatically. "I didn't say you had to want it right now. I said you deserve it."

Ruth's gaze holds mine, and there's the weight of history, regret, the kind of familiarity that doesn't need romance to be intimate.

"You don't get to fix me," she says.

"I'm not fixing you," I say. "I'm... seeing you."

For a second, Ruth looks like she doesn't know what to do with that. Like she's not used to being looked at without the lens of blame.

Then she exhales and sets her coffee down carefully.

"Okay," she says, soft. "Then I'm going to see you back."

I brace without meaning to.

Ruth's eyes don't flinch.

"You can't keep using me as your cautionary tale," she says. "You hear me?"

My mouth goes dry. "I don't know what you're talking about."

"Yes, you do," she cuts in, not cruelly. "You do this thing where you act like love is a liability because it didn't work out with me. Like the universe proved a point and now you're supposed to stay alone and responsible forever."

I stare at her.

Ruth swallows. Her voice drops.

"I cheated on you," she says simply.

The words are old. They don't explode anymore. They just... sit there. It's a scar I can touch without bleeding.

My jaw tightens anyway.

Reflex.

Ruth doesn't let me look away.

"I did," she repeats. "And I'm not bringing it up to punish myself. I'm bringing it up because I need you to stop carrying it like it's proof you should never risk anything again."

My throat works around the tightness. "Ruth..."

"I was wrong," she says, sharp and clear. "I was selfish and I was lonely and I did the thing people do when they don't know how to ask for what they need without burning everything down."

I stare at my hands for a second because I can't stop the image. It was years ago, the moment we cracked. The humiliation. The rage. The way I felt stupid for believing in a future.

Then I look back up. "I'm past it," I say, voice rough. "We've talked about this."

Ruth nods. "I know. And I'm grateful you're past it. It's let us love our daughter more fully. But you still flinch at the idea of loving someone. Like it's a trap you refuse to get caught in again. Like it's going to turn you into a man you can't recognize."

I swallow. My chest aches in that slow, deep way...

Ruth's eyes soften. "Don't let me be the reason you give up on love, August."

I blink hard once.

"You don't get to make my worst choice into your life sentence," she adds.

The words hit like a hand on my shoulder.

Steady.

Not forgiving me. Not fixing me. Just... anchoring me.

I exhale slowly.

"Okay," I manage.

Ruth's mouth quirks, barely. "And for the record?" she says. "If Florence makes you better, and she does. I don't know how but she's something special and you'd be lucky to keep her. You'd be an idiot to keep punishing yourself."

My throat tightens again.

"Go ask," she says. "Like an adult. No badge. No rescuer bullshit. Just you."

Ruth breaks it first.

"I heard Florence bought Smith Summer's shop," she says casually, like she's talking about the weather.

My chest tightens again. "Yeah."

Ruth watches my face. "You proud of her?"

"Yes," I answer without hesitation. The truth comes out too fast to hide. "I'm... proud. I'm happy for her."

"And are you going to tell her that?" Ruth asks.

My jaw works. "I don't know."

Ruth tilts her head. "Why not?"

Because I'm terrified she'll look at me like I'm a lesson she already learned.

Because I'm terrified she'll say no and I'll deserve it.

Because I'm terrified she'll say yes and I'll ruin it again.

Because I don't trust myself to want her without trying to control the outcome.

Because wanting her feels like stepping into a room that could burn down around me and choosing to stay anyway.

"I don't want to show up like..." I search for the right words. "Like I'm entitled. Like I'm assuming she'll take me back because I'm sorry and I'm the chief and I can offer things."

Ruth's expression softens.

"Then don't," she says simply.

I blink.

Ruth shrugs. "Show up as an equal."

My throat tightens.

"Also, for the record? Lilly's went by Florence's shop last weekend, I think."

My heart stutters.

"She did?" I ask, too fast.

Ruth gives me a look. "Yes. *She* did. And she came home with donuts and a weird little crystal and a face like she'd finally unclenched something."

I swallow.

She stands like she's decided the conversation is done before I can wriggle out of it.

Then she pauses at the door and looks back at me over her shoulder.

"August," she says.

"Yeah?"

Her eyes hold mine, serious now. "You can love someone in the open. You can do that. It won't kill you."

It might, I think.

But I don't say it.

Ruth leaves.

And I sit there with the budget folder and the ache in my chest and the reality that the town knows things before I do.

By the time my shift ends, the decision has been stalking me all day like a shadow.

I tried to ignore it.

I tried to bury it under paperwork and patrol maps and overtime spreadsheets.

It didn't work. Because love doesn't go away just because you give it space. It just becomes quieter. It becomes the thing you think about when you're stopped at a red light.

The thing you almost text at midnight and then delete because you don't trust yourself to want what you want without making it her responsibility.

The thing you carry into every empty room.

So when I leave the station, I don't go straight home.

I drive through town with my hands tight on the wheel, the late afternoon light painting everything gold and soft like the world is trying to pretend this is normal.

I pass the diner.

I pass the hardware store.

I pass the library and flip around and go back to the hardware store briefly. When I'm done, I keep driving until I see it.

The storefront that used to belong to Smith Summer.

Only it doesn't look like it did.

The windows are different.

There are framed prints hanging in the front display. The art is bright and bold and manages to catch the eye from the street. A small chalkboard sign sits on the sidewalk, handwritten with neat, confident lettering:

TAROT READINGS TODAY
CLASSES COMING SOON
LOCAL ART INSIDE

And across the glass, painted in warm white letters, a name that makes my chest hurt: Hearth & Harbor.

I park down the street because my instincts are still stupid. Still worried about being seen like I'm committing a crime by wanting her.

Then I force myself to get out anyway.

I walk toward the shop with my heart in my throat and my pulse steady like I'm approaching a scene call.

Only this is a different kind of danger.

This is the kind that can change your life.

The bell chimes when I step inside.

The smell hits me first. It's a mix of incense, old paper, tea, something sweet like cinnamon and clove.

Warm.

Safe.

I take a breath I didn't realize I was holding.

The shop is brighter than I remember, not in a fluorescent way, but in a curated way. Soft lighting. Lamps tucked in corners. String lights draped along the top of a bookshelf like someone decided the world deserves a little magic even on an ordinary Tuesday.

The shelves are still there, but they're reorganized. Cleaner. Intuitive. Labels on little handwritten tags. A section for local artists. A section for decks. A display table near the front that didn't exist before, showing off prints and books and small handmade candles.

There's a wall to the right that used to be bare.

Now it's a gallery.

Framed prints. Some of them are tarot-inspired with bold linework, rich color, and it's the kind of art that feels like it has teeth. Some are landscapes of the coast, stormy and gorgeous. Some are abstract. All of them are labeled with small tags: ARTIST NAME, PRICE, LOCAL.

It's brilliant.

It's her.

It's not just a shop anymore.

It's a community.

It's a home for the weird.

A voice carries from deeper in the store. It's quiet, focused, talking to someone I can't see.

I freeze, listening.

It's not Florence's voice.

A customer, maybe.

Or an employee.

Then the voice fades, and I realize I don't see Florence right away.

My shoulders loosen a fraction.

Good.

I didn't come here to ambush her.

I didn't come here to corner her behind a counter and force a conversation she didn't consent to.

I came here to ask.

To show up as an equal.

To let her say no without punishing her for it.

I move slowly through the aisles, letting myself take it in.

It's not just candles and crystals anymore. There are notebooks and pens and art supplies. Small jars of herbs labeled with actual names and uses. A shelf called "Grief & Healing" with books that look worn, like they've been held by hands that needed them.

There's a bulletin board near the back:

COMMUNITY EVENTS, THERAPISTS ACCEPTING NEW CLIENTS, SUPPORT GROUPS, CLASSES.

Someone has pinned up a flyer:

WITCHES WHO PAY RENT MEETUP.

I huff a laugh before I can stop it.

Florence would die before she admitted she wrote that.

I can see her handwriting in the flourish of the letters.

My fingers brush the edge of a display table.

And then I see it.

A small wooden stand near the center of the shop, lit by a single warm lamp like it's sacred.

On it sits a tarot deck box.

Not one of the mass-produced ones.

One with art on it that looks familiar.

Because I've seen it on her tablet.

I've seen it in her hands, unfinished, late at night when she thought she was just tinkering with a dream she didn't deserve.

Now it's printed.

Finished.

Real.

A small sign sits next to it:

THE TOWNSEND HARBOR DECK
Exclusive to Hearth & Harbor

My throat tightens.

Pride blooms in my chest so suddenly it surprises me.

Not the kind of pride that's possessive.

Not the kind that says I did this.

The kind that says she did it.

She made something out of pain.

She built something with her own hands.

I reach out before I think too hard about it, and my fingers lightly touch the box.

It's solid.

The edges are crisp.

The art is hers. It's sharp and beautiful and a little haunted.

A sound comes from behind me.

"Careful," a voice says, amused. "That deck bites."

I turn.

Florence stands a few feet away, half-hidden behind a shelf line. She's holding a clipboard and a pen, hair pulled into a messy knot, sleeves rolled up. There's a smudge of ink on her thumb like she's been labeling something.

Her eyes land on me.

Time shifts.

The air around us changes density.

She doesn't smile right away.

She doesn't frown either.

She looks at me like she's deciding what I am in this moment.

A memory.

A risk.

A possibility.

"August," she says my name with a breath..

My name from her mouth still hits the same place it always did.

Low.

Direct.

"Florence," I answer.

She glances at my hand on the deck box, then back to my face. "You touching merchandise without buying it, Chief?"

I exhale a laugh and it feels like a small bit of relief. "You're charging me with a crime?"

"Don't tempt me," she says. Then she shifts her weight, and I notice how tired she looks and how alive she looks at the same time.

Like she's been working too much.

Like she's been sleeping better anyway.

My throat tightens.

"I heard," I say carefully, "that you bought the shop."

Her eyes narrow slightly. "You heard."

"Town talks," I admit.

"Town gossips," she corrects, but there's no real bite in it. More like resignation.

I nod once, letting my gaze drift around the store again. "They were right. You... changed everything."

Something flickers in her expression.

Pride?

Or fear?

Or both.

"It needed changing," she says quietly.

"And you did it," I say. I look back at her. "It's... incredible."

She swallows.

"Thank you," she says, softer.

We stand there for a beat too long.

The space between us feels full.

Not tense like a fight.

Full like a storm cloud. It's heavy with everything it's carrying, undecided about whether it's going to rain or pass.

Florence doesn't move from behind the counter. She's close enough that I can see the tiny crease between her brows like she's trying to read me without using words. Maybe it's a learned skill from dispatch, maybe it's from grief. People tell the truth in everything except their mouths.

I don't rush.

I let my eyes keep traveling the room because if I look at her too directly, I might forget how to breathe.

The shop looks like her now.

Not in the way a place "belongs" to someone because their name is on paperwork.

In the way a place belongs to someone because it's shaped around their heartbeat.

Florence clears her throat softly.

This is the part where I stop hiding behind admiring the room and actually say what I came to say.

My hand slides into my jacket.

The box is in there, tucked into the inside pocket like I was afraid if it sat anywhere else it would shake itself apart.

It's small.

It shouldn't feel like much.

But it does.

It's suddenly heavy, like it's filled with everything I'm risking.

My fingers close around it, and my pulse jumps like it thinks I'm about to make a mistake.

Florence's eyes flick to the movement.

Then back to my face.

"Are you..." she starts, and the word catches, unfinished, like she doesn't want to accuse me of something that big but she also can't help bracing for it.

My stomach drops.

I shake my head quickly. "No. Not what...I'm not..." I trail off not sure how to finish the thought.

Not a ring.

Not a claim.

Not that kind of pressure.

Not ever, if she doesn't want it.

I swallow, forcing my body to slow down. This isn't a call-out. This isn't an emergency. I don't get to bulldoze my way into her life like I'm responding code three.

I take my hand out of my pocket but I don't pull the box out yet.

I just let my fingers rest on it through the fabric like I need to feel it there to remember why I'm here.

"Do you have a minute?" I ask.

It comes out steadier than I feel.

Florence studies me for a second, like she's measuring the weight behind the question.

Then she nods once. "I have a minute."

That single sentence does something to my chest.

I shift my weight. I'm terrified.

And yet.

This is the thing that actually terrifies me.

Not a gun.

Not a suspect.

Not blood.

Her.

The chance that she'll look at me with that calm dispatch voice in her eyes and decide I'm not safe enough to keep.

"I saw the sign," I say, nodding toward the chalkboard like it's easier to start with the shop than with what's underneath my ribs. "You've... you've changed a lot in here."

Her mouth twitches like she's trying not to smile. "Yeah. Well. It needed it."

"No," I say, and my voice roughens. "It needed you."

Florence stills. Just slightly. She didn't expect it to hit the center of her.

We stand in that for a second.

The storm cloud shifts.

I keep my hand in my pocket because taking the box out feels like stepping onto a ledge.

I didn't buy it thinking I'd give it to her like a grand gesture.

I bought it because when I walked into the hardware store and saw it hanging there and my brain did what it does, it created a plan for safety. A plan for solutions. A plan for what comes next.

But this isn't a solution.

It's a question.

And questions are terrifying when you don't get to control the answer.

Florence's gaze dips again, just for a flicker, to my jacket pocket.

"You're making me nervous," she says quietly, and there's humor in it, but there's also honesty.

I let out a breath that almost becomes a laugh.

"Yeah," I admit. "Me too."

I finally pull the box out.

It's plain.

Nothing fancy.

My thumb rubs the edge of it, grounding myself.

"I didn't come here to—" I stop, because the truth is I did come here to do something. I just didn't come here to push. "I didn't come here assuming anything."

Florence's eyes stay on the box, then lift back to me. "Okay."

I nod once, throat tight.

"I went to the hardware store," I say, and that sounds ridiculous out loud until I add, "and I kept thinking about how you said you needed to stand on your own two feet."

Her expression shifts.

Softens.

Warms, in that careful way she does when she doesn't want to hand over too much too fast.

"I still do," she says.

"I know." I swallow. "This isn't me trying to undo that." I hold the box between us. "I bought something," I say. "And I need you to know you can tell me no."

Her brow lifts. "August..."

"I'm serious," I say, voice low. "No consequences. No guilt. No wounded pride. Just... the truth."

The storm cloud swells.

Florence's breath catches. "Okay," she says. "Show me."

"Not a ring," I say quickly. "I swear."

She blinks, then her mouth tightens like she's fighting a laugh and a panic at the same time. "Okay, because I was about to throw you out of your own embarrassment."

That earns a breathy laugh from me. "Fair."

I flip the box open.

Inside is a key.

A simple house key on a small, plain key ring.

Florence stares at it.

Then she looks at me like I've lost my mind anyway.

"That's... also fast," she says.

I nod, because she's right.

"It is," I admit. "And you can say no."

Her gaze holds mine, sharp. "Why?"

I swallow. My throat burns.

"Because I'm done living like love is something I only get to have in private," I say. "Because I'm done making choices based on fear."

I keep going before my courage dissolves.

"I grew up thinking love meant chaos," I say, voice low. "Breaking things. Shouting. Silence. Doors slamming. People walking on eggshells and calling it normal."

Florence's expression softens, ever so slightly.

"You showed me something else," I continue. "You showed me love can be choosing people. Even when it's hard. Even when you're terrified."

My chest tightens.

"I'm still learning," I admit. "How not to run. How not to hide behind my badge. How not to think control is the same thing as safety."

Florence's eyes shine.

"And I know this," I say, voice rough. "I want you. In the open. No more secrets."

I gesture to the key, sitting there like a dare.

"This isn't me trying to trap you," I say quickly. "It's the opposite. It's me saying... you get to decide what access I have. What place I have in your life."

Florence's jaw works. She looks down at the key again like it's radioactive.

"If you say yes," I say, "everyone in this town is going to know I love you."

Her breath catches.

"If you say no," I continue, forcing myself to say it because it matters, "I'll still be the one sitting in the front row of everything you do, cheering you on. I'll still show up for you the way I should have. Without asking you to pay for it with your pride or your forgiveness."

Silence stretches.

In the front of the shop, the bell chimes again as someone enters.

A murmur of conversation drifts.

The world keeps going.

But here, in this small nook, it feels like everything is balanced on one breath.

Florence's voice comes out quiet. "You've been giving me space."

"I have," I say.

"And you've been... okay?" she asks, like she doesn't believe it's possible.

I let out a humorless laugh. "No."

Florence's mouth twitches.

I shake my head. "I've been functioning. I've been working. I've been doing the dad thing. Lilly and I... we're better. We're talking. We're trying."

Her eyes flicker at the mention of Lilly.

"And I miss you," I say, because lying would be insulting at this point. "All the time. In every stupid way."

Florence's throat moves like she swallows something sharp.

"I'll be at the station and I'll hear a dispatcher laugh and my brain will look for you," I admit. "I'll drive past the diner and think about that night you told me you like your fries extra crispy. I'll open my fridge and see your stupid oat milk and feel angry at myself for not throwing it away."

Florence lets out a small laugh, then it breaks into something softer.

"I miss you in my house," I add, voice dropping. "In my bed. In my life. And it's... humiliating how empty everything feels without you."

Her eyes are wet now.

"I've had love in my life," I say, raw. "I've taken the adventures. I've done the things people think are supposed to make you whole."

I swallow hard.

"None of it matters if you're not with me," I finish.

Florence looks down at her hands, then back at me, like she's trying to decide if she trusts the version of me that's sitting here asking instead of grabbing.

"You're scared," she says quietly.

"Yes," I admit.

Florence's eyes sharpen. "Of what?"

I breathe out slowly.

"Of ruining you," I say. "Of being too late. Of you looking at me and seeing the worst part of your life instead of something you can build with."

Florence's lashes flutter. Her voice is barely audible. "August..."

I lean forward slightly, careful not to crowd her. Careful not to make my longing her problem.

"This is me asking," I say, steady. "Not assuming. Not pushing. Not trying to sweep you back into my orbit because I'm lonely."

I nod toward the key again.

"If you want it," I say. "Take it. Not as a promise you owe me anything. As a symbol that I'm not hiding you anymore."

Florence's breath shakes.

"If you don't want it," I add, "I'll close the box and walk out and I will not punish you for choosing yourself."

Her eyes lift to mine. In them I see hurt, hope, stubbornness, desire.

"And if you want something else entirely," I say, voice softer, "tell me. I'll listen."

Florence sits very still for a moment.

Then she reaches out. Not to the key, but to the edge of the box.

Her fingertip touches the velvet like she's testing reality.

She looks up again, and her mouth trembles.

"You don't get to be dramatic with ring boxes," she whispers. "It should be illegal."

A laugh punches out of me, shaky and relieved. "I'm sorry."

"No, you're not," she says, and it's almost a smile.

I swallow. "I'm sorry for a lot of things. Not that."

Florence's eyes shine.

"Six weeks ago," she says softly, "I passed out on a bathroom floor because I couldn't breathe."

My chest tightens.

"I know," I say. "Ruth told me."

Florence rolls her eyes faintly. "Of course she did."

I exhale. "I wanted to come to you then. I wanted to show up. But," I look glance away, "I didn't."

"You gave me space," she says, like she's repeating the phrase to convince herself it was real.

"I did," I say. "Because you asked for it. Because for once I wanted to love you the way you deserve. That even though I wanted to be by your side, I also knew it wouldn't be fair. Not to you, not to us." I find her eyes again. "I had to know you were okay though, and I did ask about you."

Florence's gaze drops to the key again.

"I'm moving out," she says quietly.

I already know. But hearing it from her makes something in me unclench.

"I know," I say. "Lilly told Ruth. Ruth told me."

Florence's mouth quirks. "Town."

"Town," I agree.

Florence's fingers curl around the key ring, lifting it slightly, then setting it back down like she's still deciding and feeling the physical weight of that choice.

"I'm not ready," she says, voice shaking, "to be someone's secret again. I can't do it."

"I know," I say. "Never again."

Her eyes lift to mine. Steady. Open. Raw.

"And I need to know I'm choosing you because I *want* you," she says. "Not because I'm lonely. Not because I'm trying to rebuild something I lost."

My heart thunders, slow and wrecked.

"Yes," I say, barely more than breath. "That's what I want too."

Her bottom lip trembles slightly. She bites it. Holds it.

Then she says, softer this time, like it's something dangerous, something sacred, "I want you."

And it knocks the air right out of me.

My whole body stills. Heat rises in my chest like a flare.

She looks at the ring box sitting between us. Then back at me. And something shifts in her expression becomes braver.

Choice.

She reaches out, closes the box gently, and slides it across the table.

My stomach drops like I've been punched.

But then she says, with a voice made of steady hands and burning coals, "Not yet."

I nod. "Okay."

Then she stands.

And I do too. My body *knows* it has to meet hers.

She steps around the table and closes the distance between us, one heartbeat at a time. Her hand finds the front of my shirt, fisting the fabric, needing something solid, something *real*.

Her eyes lock on mine.

"Come here," she whispers.

And then she *kisses* me.

Not sweet.

Not tentative.

Not gentle.

This kiss is a goddamn homecoming.

It's heat and hunger and forgiveness and every word we haven't dared say burning through our skin.

Her mouth opens against mine and I fall into her like gravity finally figured out where I belong. My hands lift, hovering just shy of her waist. Still asking, still waiting.

She breaks the kiss just enough to breathe, our foreheads pressed together, breath mingling.

"Equal," she whispers.

"Yes," I rasp, barely holding it together.

"Ask me."

My voice shakes with it. "I want to touch you. Can I?"

She kisses me again, slower this time.

"Yes," she breathes against my lips.

My hands find her waist and pull her to me, reverent and aching. She melts into my chest like she's been holding herself up too long.

Her hands slide up my chest, over my shoulders, until she's cradling the back of my neck like she owns me.

And maybe she does.

We kiss like we're learning each other again. Like we *want* to relearn. Like we can't breathe without this.

When we finally pull back, we're panting.

She rests her forehead to my chest, eyes closed, heart racing.

"I'm not saying yes to everything," she murmurs.

"I know."

"I'm saying yes to *you.* Right now. In this moment."

God, she wrecks me.

"I'll take it," I whisper. "And I'll keep earning tomorrow."

She looks up at me, eyes sparkling like she might cry or cuss me out or climb me like a tree.

Maybe all three.

"Good," she says. "Because I'm going to make you grovel a little."

I huff a breathless laugh. "Fair."

She leans up, one last kiss, soft and brutal.

"Welcome to Hearth & Harbor," she whispers.

FLORENCE
3 YEARS LATER

I WAKE to August's mouth between my thighs.

His tongue moves with long, flat strokes that drag over my clit before dipping lower to tease the entrance he already knows by heart. He's not rushing. He's savoring. Like this is the only place he wants to be for the rest of his life.

My hips jerk off the mattress before my brain catches up. A gasp tears out of me, raw and unguarded.

"August—fuck—"

He hums against me, the vibration ripping straight up my spine. His big hands clamp down on my hips, pinning me exactly where he wants me while he works me open with that reverent, filthy focus that still undoes me after two years of marriage.

Two years of waking up to this man and I still come apart like it's the first time.

He groans when I grind against his face, like he's the one being wrecked. His stubble scrapes the tender skin of my inner thighs. Rough enough to mark, soft enough to promise more.

"God, I missed this," he rasps, voice sleep-rough and thick with want. He pulls back just long enough to let me feel the loss of his mouth, then dives back in, sucking my clit between his lips with slow, pulsing pressure.

"We did it yesterday," I pant, already breathless, fingers knotting in his hair.

August lifts his head just enough to flash that dangerous, lopsided smirk. His lips are glossy with me. His eyes are dark, pupils blown.

"Exactly."

And then he buries his face again.

I feel his tongue circling, lips sucking, the flat of his tongue pressing hard against me before flicking fast and light in that rhythm he discovered months ago and never lets me forget. My thighs tremble. My breath fractures. My toes curl into the sheets.

My hands fist tighter in his hair, tugging hard enough to make him growl against me.

He adds two thick fingers and slowly curls them deep inside me until I nearly sob.

"Aug—"

"Shhh," he murmurs, dragging his mouth up my body in a hot, open-mouthed path. "Don't wake the baby."

My laugh turns into a moan when he sucks a bruise into the soft skin of my inner thigh, high enough that I'll feel it every time I move today.

I don't even care.

Let me walk around Hearth & Harbor branded like this. Claimed. Kept. His.

He slides up my body, settling between my legs. His cock presses hot and heavy against my thigh, already leaking at the tip. I reach between us, wrapping my fingers around him, stroking slow and firm until he swears low in his throat.

"You wanna test how quiet I can keep you?" I whisper, brushing my thumb over the slit, spreading the slick there.

His breath catches. "You're playing a dangerous game, Mrs. Calder."

I smile, wicked and slow. "Then fuck me like you're winning."

He thrusts into me in one long, deep stroke.

We both groan.

My body opens for him like it was made for this. It was.

He still takes his time, hips rolling in that devastating rhythm that hits every spot at once. Each thrust is deliberate, controlled, filthy in its tenderness. He's fucking me to feel.

I meet him thrust for thrust, nails raking down his back hard enough to leave marks of my own. He buries his face in my neck, whispering my name like a prayer between bites and kisses.

"Florence... fuck... you feel so good..."

When the pleasure coils tight and frantic inside me, I start to shake. My breath turns sharp, desperate. He covers my mouth with his, swallowing the cry as I come clenching around him, shuddering through wave after wave.

He follows right after, hips stuttering, a choked groan against my lips as he spills deep inside me.

We stay locked together for a long moment, skin slick, hearts slamming in sync, breathing ragged.

A soft crash from the other room thumps.

We freeze.

August lifts his head slowly. "Was that?"

Our son lets out a gleeful squeal, followed by the unmistakable sound of something expensive hitting the floor.

"Yup," I say, still breathless and wrecked. "Jacob's awake."

August groans and flops onto his back beside me, one arm flung over his eyes. "He's got your timing."

I laugh, still panting. "He's got your appetite."

We throw on robes barely tied, and stumble into the nursery half-naked.

Jacob is standing in his crib, curls wild, cheeks flushed, stuffed dragon dangling from one chubby fist like he just conquered a kingdom. His grin is pure sunshine when he sees us.

"Hi, baby," I say, scooping him up.

He immediately grabs my necklace and tries to gnaw on the pendant.

August comes up behind us and kisses the top of Jacob's head. "Morning, little monster. Did you knock your books off the shelf again?"

Jacob responds with a full-body wiggle and a delighted "Da!" that's definitely not a word, but we both pretend it is.

"We've got brunch with Auntie Lilly and Auntie Ruth today," I tell him, bouncing him gently. "And you're going to be nice. Which means no food in Ruth's hair."

Jacob giggles like he already knows he's going to do exactly that.

August raises a brow at me over Jacob's head. "He's definitely putting food in her hair."

I grin. "Yeah. I'm just trying to manifest a miracle."

Jacob rests his head on my shoulder, thumb in his mouth, eyes soft and sleepy again.

This.

This is the life we built.

We don't live in a magazine spread. There's no white picket fence. The laundry is piled on the stairs. There's glitter in the grout from Ruth's last craft day with Jacob. The kitchen sink has a permanent ring from coffee mugs we never quite finish washing.

But there's warmth.

There's forgiveness.

There's holy hell, heat.

August's hand finds my waist, thumb brushing the curve of my hip under the robe. His eyes meet mine over Jacob's head still hungry.

Later, I think.

Later we'll lock the bedroom door.

Later I'll ride him slow and deep until he's begging.

Later we'll remember why we fought so hard to get here.

For now, Jacob pats my cheek with a sticky hand and babbles something that sounds suspiciously like "more."

August laughs, low and warm. "Yeah, buddy. More."

He leans in and lingers kisses on me that taste like promises.

And in that moment, with our son between us and the morning light spilling across the floor, everything feels exactly right.

Messy. Loud. Chaotic. Beautiful.

Ours.

Hearth & Harbor opens in two hours.

But right now?

Right now is home.

And every second of it—every gasp, every giggle, every quiet promise whispered against skin—feels like the only place I've ever belonged.

ACKNOWLEDGMENTS

First, thank you to you, the reader.

If you hadn't shown up, if you hadn't cared, if you hadn't kept reading and reaching back with your encouragement, I might have stopped after my very first book. Your support is not background noise, it is the reason I keep going. Every message, every review, every quiet reader somewhere turning pages at midnight matters more than you know.

I want to say a quick thank you to some early readers, the attention to detail and feedback is always so valuable. Thank you to Jackson, Angie, Jen, Janet, Jada, Heidi B, Sara G, and anyone else who took the time to read Flo & August's story.

To my husband, Peter, thank you for loving a woman who writes at 4 a.m., who "watches" TV while typing furiously, who pulls out her phone in the middle of dinner to jot down a line before it disappears. Thank you for never making me feel like my stories are too much, too loud, too time-consuming. You are my favorite place to land, and I love you more than I could ever fit into a book.

To every dispatcher out there, I see you. I was you. It was one of the most emotional, adrenaline-filled, heartbreaking, and important jobs I've ever done. You carry voices, fear, courage, and endings that most people never have to hold. Whether you stayed for decades or only a short while, your work mattered. You mattered.

To Jackson and Kaytie, two dispatchers, two true heroes, and two people I am lucky enough to love in real life. Thank you for standing in the storm and still choosing kindness. You remind me why this story needed to exist.

And to Angie, who has been an eager beta reader and fierce

supporter from day one. Thank you for reading early drafts, loving messy pages, and believing in my stories before they were finished. Every writer needs someone like you. I'm endlessly grateful that I get to have you.

ABOUT THE AUTHOR

Miranda Levi, author of *A Tear In Time*, *The Fountain of* Youth series, and *Mother Nature.* She lives in the Pacific Northwest with her husband, Peter, their demon fur baby, Hamilton, and their angel fur baby, Eggs Benedict. A former high school English teacher with a love for raccoons and rainbows, Miranda also writes middle-grade fiction under the pen name Isla Watts with her best friend. You can visit her at https://mirandalevi.com.

ALSO BY MIRANDA LEVI

Restraint

The Fountain of Youth Trilogy:

From A Youth A Fountain Did Flow

The Sea Withdrew

What I've Tasted of Desire

Stand Alones:

A Tear In Time

Mother Nature

Poetry

In Orion's Hands: a collection of poetry

Mythiverse Series

Co-written with Justin Jackson as Isla Watts

A Fairy Bad Day

Surprise! You're a Vampire

Mork The Handsome Orc

Adopted by Werewolves

Gorgeous, Gorgeous, Gorgons

That's the Spirit

Bite Me if You Can

www.ingramcontent.com/pod-product-compliance
Lightning Source LLC
LaVergne TN
LVHW041054080826
845145LV00007B/1569

9781961714816